YOU KNOW HOW SOMETIMES
YOU DREAM ABOUT SOMEONE ELSE,

but you know it's really you? Like you see a girl going into the wrong door and you shout at her, "No, there are monsters there!" But she doesn't listen, and you are the one who gets eaten by the monsters. In your dreams, of course. Or else you dream about yourself, but it's really someone else?

Just so, I dreamed I couldn't move my legs. I started to panic, but I told my sleeping self that I was simply re-visualizing the paralyzed heroine of my current work in progress, the young girl in a wheelchair, Hetty. She was desperate to get out of whatever room she was in. Even knowing that she was a figment of my imagination, that I'd written her into that small, cold room, I felt trapped. Doubly trapped, because I couldn't get out of the dream, either. I started to panic.

No, stay calm, I told myself mid-dream. *Look around. Find the door.*

There was no door. No windows, either, just rough wood plank walls with a bare lightbulb shining overhead. Where the hell was my wheelchair? I pulled myself over to the wall so I could lean against it, panting with the effort. I could feel my sides heaving, dampness on my skin. Why couldn't I get out?

A noise. The monster was coming!

Wake up, Hetty, I tried to scream. As if I could warn my sleeping self or my character or my alter ego. *There are no monsters!*

Oh, yes, there are, she/I shrieked back.

"Readers will love the first Willow Tate book, Willow is funny, brave and open to possibilities most people would not have even considered." —*RT Book Reviews*

Night Mares
IN THE
HAMPTONS

A Willow Tate Novel

CELIA JEROME

DAW BOOKS, INC.

DONALD A. WOLLHEIM, FOUNDER

375 Hudson Street, New York, NY 10014

ELIZABETH R. WOLLHEIM
SHEILA E. GILBERT
PUBLISHERS

www.dawbooks.com

First Printing, May 2011
1 2 3 4 5 6 7 8 9

To Sheila Gilbert, for taking a chance

PROLOGUE

THE GATES BETWEEN THE WORLDS WERE closed forever. Except for the time a desperate troll broke the rules, and when a megalomaniac tried to conquer both universes, and when a half-breed boy was returned to his rightful place.

Who knew what else crossed the lines while the barriers were down. . . .

CHAPTER I

A WAITER ON HIS WAY HOME FROM WORK
flipped his Nissan on Montauk Highway to avoid a
deer. Only it wasn't a deer, he swore after he passed the
alcohol test, but a white horse that disappeared in front
of his car. Shock, the EMTs said when he went delirious
on the way to the hospital, and bad driving.

A bunch of kids at a beach party in Amagansett
trampled each other when three white horses trampled
their driftwood campfire and vanished into the surf.
Mass hysteria, the police said, and bad weed.

Three fishermen driving out to Montauk before
dawn saw three white shapes flickering in and out of
sight. They pulled over to argue about what they'd seen
and beat each other bloody. Beer for breakfast, everyone said, and bad blood.

The trouble did not end there. Tempers flared all over
Long Island's East End and the fabled Hamptons, especially in little Paumanok Harbor, the site of the recent weirdness. Nestled on the northern, bay side of the
South Fork, east of East Hampton, Paumanok Harbor
was mostly ignored by the press and the police, more so
since the recent weirdness.

No one nearby could sleep at night, troubled by horrible, sweat-inducing, throat-closing, ripping-the-sheets
dreams, and not just because the economy was in the
toilet and summer rentals were way down. The Season

had arrived; the rich tourists had not. Which meant restaurants stayed empty, boats stayed at their moorings, farm stands and art galleries stayed full of unsold merchandise, and the locals stayed cranky. Fistfights broke out all over town, plus divorces, lawsuits, road rage, spite fences, and nasty letters to the editor. Meanness clung to the little village like a cold, damp fog.

I couldn't sleep either, so I was just as bitchy as everyone else in the Harbor. Maybe more so, because I didn't want to be here in the first place. I should be back in Manhattan, writing and illustrating my latest Willy Tate graphic novel in my cozy East Side apartment. I should be going to free concerts in Central Park, gallery openings, sample sales, and art movies. Instead, I was in a backwoods fishing village that didn't even have a movie theater of its own. It did have a bowling alley, though. Oh, boy.

Someone had to look after the dogs, my mother said. She rescued abandoned animals from shelters, then kept the ones she couldn't find homes for. Right now she was in Florida, not trying to reconcile with my father the way I hoped she would after his heart surgery, but crusading against greyhound racing. So I was elected to watch over a pack of ancient mutts no one wanted, the snippy three-legged Pomeranian I'd kind of adopted, and Grandma Eve, whom no one wanted either, but that was another story.

According to my doting mother, I could scribble and doodle just as easily in the country as in the city. Scribble and doodle? I'd been supporting myself for years with my books, and was damned proud of them. I got great reviews, even awards. I had long lines at my book signings, and almost more fan email than I had time to answer. I wanted to tell my mother I was saving kids from video games and illiteracy while she was out saving canines, but I'm a grown woman, just turned thirty-five, and I didn't need my mother's respect. Sure.

Besides, I liked dogs better than kids, too, which was half the problem. Mom didn't want a shelf full of books; she wanted grandkids.

On the other hand, my mother and her nagging were

in Florida, and New York City wasn't at its best in the heat of summer. The air was unbreathable, the park was crowded, the galleries were elitist, the movies pretentious, the sale prices still exorbitant, and everyone who could leave for long weekends did. So I wasn't altogether unhappy to be spending a month or so minutes from a secluded beach, in a comfortable old house down a private farm road, but don't tell my mother.

Even the little village had its own kind of charm, once you got over the fact that the librarian knew what book you wanted to read before you asked, the harbormaster predicted the weather better than NOAA, the town clerk was ninety-five percent accurate about the sex of an unborn baby, and the police chief always found your lost keys. Oh, and a bunch of the natives could tell truth from lies, and another bunch spoke to friends around the world, living or dead, without telephones or knowing the language. And my grandmother was a witch.

You get used to it.

You don't get used to the bad dreams.

My cousin Susan did not seem to be affected. "You're not grouchy because you're sleep deprived," she announced over lunch of lobster-corn salad. "You're sex deprived, that's what you are. And you look like shit."

Eight years younger than me, Susan was a pain in the ass as a kid and still had a bratty streak about her that everyone tolerated because she'd had cancer. She also had a promiscuous streak that her parents could not tolerate, so she spent a lot of time at my house. Not that she spent the time with me. She brought home a steady stream of surfer dudes and haul-seiners and laid-off stockbrokers when she got off work as the chef at Uncle Bernie's restaurant. I put up with it because she was my cousin. And her cooking was spectacular.

"I've been having nightmares, that's all. Some of us can go a month without a man, you know." That's how long it had been, not that it was any of Susan's business. "You ought to try it."

"Why? I'm having a hell of a lot more fun than you are."

Judging from her radiant good looks, with a hint of freckles across her nose and not a shadow under her eyes, I couldn't disagree. I kept my mouth shut, except for another mouthful of the herb-seasoned salad.

Susan licked mayonnaise off her fingers and grinned. That was another thing about Susan: she never got fat, no matter what she ate. Sometimes I hated her. "Don't the bad dreams bother you?"

"After having cancer, surgery, chemo, and radiation, to say nothing of having my hair fall out, you think a little anxiety is going to keep me awake?"

"I guess not."

"Damn right. Besides, I don't sleep much at night, you know."

She got off work about eleven, then went drinking or dancing until the bars closed, and spent the rest of the night with whatever lucky guy she'd found. Sometimes the same one for a whole week. "I know. You make more noise than a rhinoceros stamping out a fire."

She grinned again. "That's the loose headboard in the guest room. I've been meaning to tighten the screws before the whole thing collapses."

I didn't want to think about Susan's guests or screws or how she was daring me to loosen up. I guess being so close to her own mortality gave her the right to be reckless. Kind of like self-affirmation. I had nothing to prove. And I wasn't her keeper, no matter how my mother, my aunt, and my grandmother always expected me to look after her just because I was older.

"Have you ever seen the horses?" By now, everyone agreed that three white horses, mares, someone said, had taken to flickering in and out of sight around Paumanok Harbor in the dark. The nightmares started at the same time.

"No, but a lot of the locals have seen them. None of the tourists or summer people do, which is even freakier."

Not really, if you accept that anyone born in Paumanok Harbor, or related to someone who was, or who'd attended a certain college in England, had eccentricity in their genes. An odd kick to the gallop, in equine terms. Talented, sensitive, gifted with extrasensory perceptions in pseudo-scientific lingo. Nut jobs, in other words. I hadn't decided what I thought. Or where I fit in.

Susan had it all figured out. "So what are you going to do about it?"

"Me?"

"Of course you, dummy. Who else can save the town?"

"Me?" I choked on a piece of celery in the salad. Susan hit me on the back, far harder than needed. "You've been watching too much TV," I told her. "This isn't save the cheerleader, save the world crap. I'm no hero."

Susan took away the plates and brought out a piece of the molten chocolate cake that was on every restaurant's menu these days. And on my hips, thighs, and butt. I groaned.

Susan mistook my whimper. "I didn't think so either, but you're all we have."

"I can't even sleep at night. What do you think I can do about some phantom horses?"

She shrugged. "It's not me. The whole town thinks you'll fix things. They're just wishing you'd get on with it already."

"Get on with what? I don't know anything about wild horses and mind games."

"You got rid of the troll, didn't you? Of course you brought the troll here, so it was only right."

"I didn't bring—"

"And you rescued the missing kid and got that bastard Borsack fried before he could hurt anyone else. That was cool. And brave."

Someone with an eyebrow ring thought I was cool? I sat up straighter. But brave? "I was so scared I almost peed my pants. Just thinking about that night still gives me chills. We could all have been killed then. The storm, the lightning, the guns and bombs."

I shook off the tremors before Susan ate the whole cake. I waved my fork at her before stabbing a big chunk. "You're as crazy as the rest of the kooks in this town. I'm not brave, and I can't do anything about some wild horses except pull the covers over my head."

"Mm." She licked her fork. "So why do you think you're here?"

I looked around my mother's kitchen, at the old dogs sprawled on the terra cotta tiles to keep cool, at Little Red back to sleep in my lap after I told him chocolate wasn't good for Pomeranians. Then I looked out the window to my grandmother's herb farm, where the old bat was watering some new sprouts in pots, likely with eye of newt and dragon's tears.

"I'm here to take care of the dogs and make sure Grandma Eve doesn't poison anyone."

Susan took the last piece of cake before I could get my fork on it. "You're dumber than I thought if you believe that."

"Yeah, I know Grandma Eve's a world renowned herbalist, but the woman still scares me." A lot of things scared me, to be absolutely truthful. This whole conversation was turning my stomach.

"Not Grandma. The crap about staying here to watch the dogs. Do they look like they're going to run away or attack the mailman?"

They were snoring, all of them.

Susan went on: "Anyone could come in to feed them and put them out in their pens. I offered. So did my mother, now that school is out. Un-uh. It had to be you. You're here to save the town and the horses, Willy. And you need to start soon before more trouble breaks out. I hear Mrs. Terwilliger bought herself a pistol."

"The librarian?"

"Don't be late bringing those books back."

"But I don't— I can't—"

She got up and took the plate to the sink. "You will. You're the hero."

Me?

CHAPTER 2

I AM NOT BRAVE. EVERYONE KNOWS THAT. My mother thinks it's because my father spoiled me, not making me face my fears. My father thinks I can walk on water; my mother thinks I'll sink like a lead weight every time. I know I can swim. If the surf isn't too rough and there are no jellyfish in the water.

Snakes, thunder, dark alleys, driving in snow, Grandma Eve, taxi drivers with eye patches, choking on a chicken bone when no one is around, doing something stupid when everyone is around, loving the wrong man, not being loved by the right man, plane rides—I could go on and on, with what I'm afraid of. Most times I rise above it. I've been on planes, thanks to modern pharmaceuticals. I'm not afraid to leave my house, or my apartment, though I have to admit I'm happiest there. Spiders are okay as long as they are not big and hairy and in my bathtub. Superstitions, black cats, ladders, and stuff don't bother me at all. Not after spending most summers of my life in Paumanok Harbor. I might not be as comfortable among strangers or crowds as Susan—hell, she'd talk to anyone, then bring him home for drinks or more. I spoke in public at the last graphic books convention, even if I did puke afterward.

I do what I have to do, like it or not. Like now, I had to call Agent Thaddeus Grant of the Department of Unexplained Events, and I really, really did not want to.

Not that I had a choice. Save the town? How about if I spun straw into gold? But let people, my friends and neighbors and relatives, start using each other for target practice?

If they all believed I was what they needed, it sure as hell wasn't because of my books or because I had some magnificent talent for manipulating the forces of another dimension, the ether world, magic. Call it what you will, I didn't have it. What I had was connections. Important connections to the Royce-Harmon Institute for Psionic Research, the geniuses who understood paranormal woo-woo. Cripes, they might have invented it, they went so far back in time. DUE was their international investigation and action arm; Grant was one of their agents. Think 007 with ESP.

Grant was also my lover, my almost fiancé. He was a hero and a TD&H stud and a master of so many talents—normal and para—that he kept my head spinning. Even though he swore he wasn't a telepath, sometimes I thought he was in my mind, he was so good at knowing what I wanted and when. He was gorgeous and rich and smart and kind, and I was afraid to call him.

I wasn't afraid *of* him. Hell, no. He was kind and caring, a real gentleman. Little Red, who snarled at everyone, including me, liked him. So did Grandma Eve. I am positive Grant would never hurt anyone who didn't threaten the universe. I worried about that for a minute, but no, he was in England after all, far away. And he loved me. Even if I . . .

I wouldn't think about that.

I'd make the call. Right after I had a snack.

Little Red and I went into the kitchen and filled a dish with coffee ice cream. Red got to lick the spoon. I poured a tiny bit of Kahlua over the ice cream, just for the taste. And the courage.

I told myself I wasn't really afraid of Grant, except for the damage he could do to my heart and my head. I loved him, unless that was just infatuation because he was nearly a god and a great lover. That was over a month ago, and you know what they say about absence.

It makes the heart grow fonder. They also say out of sight, out of mind.

Thaddeus Grant was out of sight, but he'd taken up permanent residence in my thoughts. My heart, though, shook in its boots. He'd kind of proposed, and I'd kind of accepted in the heat of the moment. Now I felt a definite cold shiver down my spine at the thought of marrying a man I'd known for less than a month. Especially a man already bigger than life.

We spoke less often than we did when he first left America, but now we email every day. Somehow the distance seemed longer, and he's more impatient for me to come to England, to meet his family, to see how he lives.

I kept putting it off. I was writing. My mother needed me here. I couldn't find anyone to leave Little Red with. I actually admitted how much I hated the idea of flying. Mostly, truthfully, I did not want to meet his parents. His father was a frigging earl! They knew the Queen! They lived in an ancient palace! Anyone who's ever read a Regency romance knows what that means. Pride and prejudice, pomp and privilege, along with vast fortunes, hordes of servants, and a hundred pieces of silverware on the table. Yeah, I'd fit right in.

Grant said we didn't have to spend all our time in England. They were setting up a branch of the Royce Institute here in Paumanok Harbor, so he could use Long Island as an alternate base. He flew all over the world and I could go with him, he promised. As if constant air trips were a selling point. Or as if I could write in a plane, a hotel, or a palace.

No matter what he did now, where he lived, how far he traveled, he'd be the Earl of Grantham some day. I'd be a countess, taking tea with royalty.

I could talk about my writing. What my own family called comic books. Or how I put myself through college working at my grandmother's farm stand. Maybe they needed tips on picking a melon. And I could wear my denim cutoffs and flip-flops under the ermine—or was that for dukes?—and tiara.

Grant said they'd love me, because he did. Besides,

we were meant for each other. He was the only one who could translate the tender inscription on my pendant, wasn't he, the one made from my mother's heirloom wedding band? What he meant was that the matchmakers at Royce decided we were genetically compatible, which I resented. Oh, boy, did I resent that. No one was going to pick a husband for me, no matter how brilliant and talented our children might turn out. Look what such a preordained coupling did for my parents, not that I am complaining about being born, but they've been divorced for almost as long as they were married. Besides, what if he only loved me because someone said he should? How could I know?

It wasn't going to work, Grant and me. The distance, the life-styles, the way *I'd* be doing most of the compromising. I touched the pendant. I and thou, one forever. That's what it said in an ancient mind-speaking language I could not imagine or comprehend. Like I could never imagine a happily ever after for the two of us. I had a great imagination, but I'm only human. I wasn't sure about Grant.

That's why I was afraid to make the call. I had to ask the most wonderful man I'd ever met to come help this poor, plague-ridden little village. And tell him I couldn't marry him.

I poured a little more Kahlua over my melting ice cream.

I got his voice mail. What I had to say couldn't be left on a machine, so I just asked him to call me back as soon as he could.

Reprieved for now, thank goodness. I could wring my hands, go for a walk, or get some work done. I chose to lose myself in the book I was writing, usually the perfect escape from reality for me. I hadn't done much on the story since the nightmares began, so I had to reread it from the beginning.

I'd decided to write about a teenaged girl this time. Girls read more than boys, and they deserved the kind of heroic adventure I tried to write and illustrate. There'd be a boy later, but as a partner, not any knight in shining armor come to rescue the helpless maiden. No, my heroine was going to be a kick-ass kid, doing battle with evil. The problem was, according to my outline, she was in a wheelchair and she needed a magical flying steed. A white magical flying steed. Holy shit.

I went back to the kitchen. Instead of a little Kahlua with my ice cream, I served up a little ice cream with my Kahlua. I didn't usually drink, but desperate times called for dire measures. And this was medicinal. Heaven knew, I needed a shot of something. I looked at the drawings I'd done. I looked at the ringing phone. I didn't usually pray either, but this seemed like a good time to start.

"Hello, sweetheart," he said. I could hear the smile in his voice.

"I didn't do it!"

"You didn't make the plane reservation yet?"

I had reservations, all right, but I had bigger problems now.

"My mother would like to throw us an engagement party. I'd like you to pick out rings with me, too."

I chickened out on the ideal opportunity. "I can't come right now. We have a problem here in the Harbor."

He didn't say anything, but I heard the frustration in his silence. I quickly launched into an explanation about the horses, and the bad dreams, the mayhem and Susan's expectations, without mentioning my link, however tenuous, to any fantastical white horses.

"Yes, we've been getting reports about them and their effect. Some of our research associates are quite excited."

"And you didn't call me?"

"I've been a tad busy here, darling. A few other, um, oddities have been spotted here and there. We've managed to convince the gremlins to find their way back, but the yeti appears too stupid to find the portal."

"Can you come help?"

"Sorry, Willy. I'm needed here. I've acquired a bit more of the Unity language, so I cannot be spared. Further, since I was involved in at least one of the events that permitted the, uh, aberrations to get through, I feel responsible to get them gone."

"But what are we going to do here?" I hoped he didn't hear the desperation in my voice. Or the disappointment. What kind of hero refuses to ride to the rescue?

"You needn't do anything. Now that the horses are in Paumanok Harbor, with all its ambient power, they'll be able to find their way back. Horses do that, you know, return to their barns whenever they can."

I didn't know anything about horses. I was doing research online. Lord knew I wasn't going near Mrs. Terwilliger at the library. "What about the nightmares?"

"They'll end as soon as the horses are gone."

"How the devil can you know?" I realized I snapped at him, which was better than whining, I guess, but he was so calm, when I was the one with no sleep and a guilty conscience. Besides, he was supposed to handle these Unexplained Events, not me. I never claimed to be a kick-ass heroine. I could hardly get my leg higher than a kneecap.

He explained how the Institute's archives had copies of every ancient reference to eldritch lore they could locate, from when magic and men lived in harmony. Some were in cuneiform, some hieroglyphs, petroglyphs, or cave paintings. They had scraps of every ancient or dead language, some translated by Grant's own father, a master linguistics expert before he had to retire to be earl. One told a fable, as far as anyone could determine, of magnificent creatures that gleamed with moonlight and brought great happiness to the spirits of men.

"They are bringing mayhem. Chaos and violence and bitter anger."

"We think the horses are mood projectors. The source of our word 'nightmares.' If they are troubled, as yours must be, lost and far from home and their herd, then they will project distress. People react badly to terror and the unknown."

Yeah, they ate ice cream and drank. "How come people can see them if they're from another world? No one but me could see the troll. They saw trolleys and trains and troopers. By the ancient rules, you said."

"People see them because we have horses of our own. Our minds have to put labels on things. Horses are easy. They'll be gone soon." Grant sounded so certain, I started to relax, until he added that until then we should add more patrols to the police force and extra operators on the suicide hotlines.

"Suicide?" God, I hadn't thought of that. Not for me, of course, but for some poor soul who didn't realize the frigging horses were causing such despair.

"We really need you here, Grant. You can talk to them."

"People contemplating suicide? That's not my field."

"No, the horses. You can help them find a way back to their home world."

"I'm sorry, Willy. I just can't get away now. You know I would if I could. I miss you."

"And I you." I figured I'd sleep a lot better with some therapeutic sex, like Susan did.

"Don't worry. It'll be over soon and things will be back to normal."

Or as normal as they got in Paumanok Harbor. "I hope so."

"And when everything is settled here too I'll come visit, shall I? I need to confer again with Martha about Royce's plans for purchasing the Rosehill property."

"That would be wonderful." So did not having to tell him by phone that the would-be engagement wouldn't happen.

"And when I leave, I'll drag you back with me so Mother can introduce you around and you two can start planning the wedding."

Did suicide hurt?

CHAPTER 3

DUMBASS CHICKENSHIT. THAT'S WHAT I called myself. Stupid, mean, and immoral, too. Not just because I hadn't confessed to Grant that I was not going to marry him. I hadn't lied. I did miss him. I did love him, sort of. I just couldn't live my life living his life.

That wasn't the dumb part. What really pissed me off was expecting him to come rescue me and then being disappointed when he wouldn't. What was I, some wimpy Wanda who needed a man to change the tires and carry out the garbage? A spineless Sadie whose security blanket had a hairy chest? A nervous Nelly who—

I was not. I am not. I helped a troll. I saved a lost kid. Not by myself, of course, but I got it done. I am Willow Tate. Hear me roar.

If the town thought I could handle the spectral horses and their side effects, and Susan and Grant thought so, too, then handle them I would. Especially now that I knew the whole mishmash would end soon.

So I went into town and spread the word at Jane's Beauty Salon, the post office, the deli, the garage, and the one-room police station at Town Hall. Which meant the entire village would hear the news within the hour. The horses were lost but on their way home, I told everyone. They were broadcasting their own emotional distress, that was all. Nothing to worry about, nothing to stay up nights over. We needed to take a few extra precautions for a couple of days; maybe some sleeping pills—but not too many!

Some people looked relieved. Some appeared skeptical.

"How do you know, Willy?" Walter at the drugstore asked when I picked up *The Times.*

Because I was smart and clever and the town's resident rescuer? No, damn it. "Because Grant told me. They researched it at the Institute."

"Oh, that's okay, then."

By the time I picked up pizza for dinner, people were smiling again. I even saw a Mercedes yield to a pedestrian at an intersection.

All was right with the world. I walked the dogs before sunset when we had the beach to ourselves as far as the eye could see: my favorite time, my favorite place. The old boys kind of ambled along while Red hopped around in circles until he exhausted himself and had to be carried home. On the way I stopped in at Grandma Eve's like the perfect granddaughter I was, and because I knew she'd been making strawberry jam that afternoon.

She handed me two jars and a jab. "What are you going to do about this horror?" Talk about sweet and sour.

"I told you, Grant thinks the horses will disappear in a few days."

"Of course they will. And then we will all forget about them as if they never existed, until next time. I am referring to your cousin."

"Susan? What, did she steal some of your herbs for the restaurant's special tonight?"

"Do not be flippant, missy."

I didn't have long enough hair to be flippant.

Grandma Eve pursed her thin lips. You wouldn't know her age so well without the lines around her mouth. She was trim and fit, and dressed in denim and beads like an old hippie with a tan from working in the fields of her herb, vegetable, and flower farm. "I mean the men. She is getting a bad reputation in town. If she is not getting some disgusting disease."

"I haven't been her babysitter since I was seventeen. We both hated it then. I cannot tell Susan what to do now."

"Of course you can. That's what families are for."

To be nags and tyrants? Grandma seemed to think so. I juggled the jam jars in my arms, so I could pick up Little Red again.

Grandma wasn't finished. "Furthermore, you just told half the town to take sleeping pills. I do not believe in them, you know."

Or doctors or vitamins or shrinks. Which was maybe why my whole family was so messed up. I hoped Grandma Eve wasn't feeding Susan some witches' brew as a contraceptive. My grandmother knew every herbal cure known to man, and more she'd invented herself. She hadn't cured anything yet, not that I'd heard. Oh, but she did read tea leaves.

"I don't see why Susan stopped seeing that lovely boy she met during her treatments."

"Toby was an investment banker. He lost his job and moved in with his brother in North Carolina."

"Then she should find a nice young man like you did and settle down."

I couldn't tell her about unsettling the nice young man, not until I told him. "Come on, Red, it's time to go."

"You'll talk to her." That wasn't a question, but a demand.

I nodded. Soothe the town, shape up the cousin, screw up my future. Oh, yeah. Hear me whimper.

I made myself another ice cream with Kahlua. This time I left out the ice cream.

I went to bed early, with a headache. That's why I don't drink. I vowed not to do it again. I also vowed to call Grant in the morning, so he could cancel his mother's engagement party for us before she ordered the champagne and hors d'oeuvres. Waiting until he got to New York, whenever that might be, was cruel and rude. He deserved better than that. I'd sleep better at night, once the horses left, knowing I'd done The Right Thing.

Susan wasn't home yet, but I decided to speak to her as soon as I threw out her latest bar friend when they came in and woke me up with the bouncing headboard. If she didn't show a little moderation, I'd throw her out next. I'd say it was on Grandma's orders. I needed my z's, damn it.

All resolved in my aching head, I fell asleep surprisingly easy. Then I started to dream.

You know how sometimes you dream about someone else, but you know it's really you? Like you see a girl going into the wrong door and you shout at her "No, there are monsters there!" but she doesn't listen, and you are the one who gets eaten by the monsters. In your dreams, of course. Or else you dream about yourself, but it's really someone else? Like if I dreamed I slept with a different man every week, when I knew that was Susan flitting like a honeybee.

Just so, I dreamed I couldn't move my legs. I started to panic, but I told my sleeping self that I was simply re-visualizing the paralyzed heroine of my current work in progress, the young girl in a wheelchair, Hetty. She was desperate to get out of whatever room she was in. Even knowing that she was a figment of my imagination, that I'd written her into that small, cold room, I felt trapped. Doubly trapped, because I couldn't get out of the dream either. I started to panic.

No, stay calm, I told myself mid-dream. *Look around. Find the door.*

There was no door. No windows either, just rough wood plank walls with a bare light bulb shining overhead. Where the hell was my wheelchair? My pretty room with the ruffled bedspread and curtains? My computer and iPad, so I could call for help? I pulled myself over to the wall so I could lean against it, panting with the effort. I could feel my sides heaving, dampness on my skin. Why couldn't I get out?

A noise. The monster was coming!

Wake up, Hetty, I tried to scream. As if I could warn my sleeping self or my character or my alter ego. *There are no monsters!*

Oh, yes, there are, she/I shrieked back. Somehow I knew it was a man, bearded, smelly, in dirty clothes. He'd come a couple of times, tossing me food that I didn't like, that made me ill. I don't know how I knew about the man or the food, because the other part of me, the one looking on, realized I hadn't written this scene.

No matter, I could overpower him, surprise him with my strength.

I had no strength. I could not stand.

Then I could trip him, hit him over the head with my two fists. Gouge at his eyes, bite his nose. Kick him in the balls. I took a self-defense course once.

You only went three times.

So what? I took a year of karate in college. This is my dream. Fight!

I can't! I can't!

You have to. Everyone depends on you.

Mama!

I was calling for my mother in my dream? Wow, speak about nightmares, that was the worst.

Bad enough to wake me up. Or else Little Red's barking had done it. Susan must have come in, or maybe I'd shouted out loud, frightening the dog. I'd rather that, than having my cousin hear me yawp like a baby. What kind of village heroine calls for her mother in the night?

I untangled myself from the stranglehold of the sheets, turned on the bedside lamp, blew my nose, and petted Little Red until he was convinced we weren't under attack. I could still feel the adrenaline rush through my body, speeding my pulse rate, until the noise was so loud I couldn't tell if that was my heartbeat or Susan's headboard. I got up, went into the bathroom to pee and get a drink of water. I couldn't face Susan and her guest, not tonight.

I went back to bed, pulling Little Red closer for comfort. His and mine. "I'll get her out of the box," I reassured both of us. "Without her mother."

I made some notes on the pad that was always by my bed, then turned off the light again. I figured I was safe from more nightmares, so I turned on my side and pulled the sheet and the one light blanket up to my ear.

"Good night, Red."

The clock dial said 2:15. The dog was snoring.

3:26. Susan was taking a shower.

4:01. I was going to kill someone. Maybe the clock. I threw an extra pillow at it, knocking it to the floor. One of the old dogs downstairs growled in a halfhearted, sleepy way, as if the second floor wasn't really his territory to guard. The steps were too rough on his arthritic joints. I was being protected by a six-pound Pomeranian with three legs, all of them in the air now as he slept.

I fell asleep, too, finally. And fell right back into that cold narrow room without furniture. I was terrified.

The monster is coming.

It's only a man. If I talk to him, maybe he'll let us go. I figured he'd send a ransom note. Hetty's parents were rich. They hadn't been in my preliminary notes, but they sure as hell were going to be. My books were supposed to entertain kids, not terrorize them.

Then I heard footsteps. And singing. "On the Road Again." Don't let it be Willie Nelson, I begged. That would be too weird, even for a nightmare.

Hetty whimpered.

I looked around for a weapon, for anything I could use on the kidnapper. The bare bulb showed every corner of the wooden room. It must be a closet, I thought. No, the ground beneath me was cold, like packed dirt. Maybe I was in a tool shed that had electricity.

But no tools were in sight, nothing but some straw on the ground. That made no sense, but dreams didn't have to follow any kind of logic, not like a book. So I decided I'd gather handfuls of straw, throw it at his eyes when he came in. I'd be able to see where the door was and make a dash for it.

With no wheelchair and no feeling in my legs.

Okay, I'd throw the straw in his eyes, grab him at the knees, topple him over, and stuff straw down his throat until he went unconscious. Hey, I was a writer. I could come up with a hundred ways to foil a villain.

Monster's too big.

Come on, Hetty, work with me. I felt stupid arguing

with one of my characters, who might or might not be myself working through a Freudian-based Electra complex. I did not like this dream any more than poor Hetty did. The longer we played Poor Pitiful Pearl, though, the longer we'd be stuck here, cold and waiting. Waiting.

". . . Can't wait to get on the road again."

The door creaked. Now I could see that the seam for the opening looked like just another plank. Of course the hinge would be on the outside, if this was a tool shed. Or a cell.

"Makin' music with my friends."

Now I could feel the ice-cold terror seep through Hetty, through me. We were the same in our fear, and I could not divorce my rational mind from the small cowering figure on the ground, couldn't get myself in bed to wake up, or myself in the shed to move, to stand, to fight. What for? The monster would get me in the end. I was too young, too cold, too frightened to save myself. No one else was coming to help. My mother couldn't hear my cries. My father couldn't get here in time. I'd never get home, never see them again. Never. I'd die here, all alone.

I raised my head to wail out my despair. I opened my mouth . . . and whinnied.

Holy hell, I was a horse.

CHAPTER 4

I COULDN'T BREATHE. I WAS AWAKE, but I couldn't get enough air in my lungs. Either I was hyperventilating, or Red was standing on my chest.

My nightshirt was soaked with fear sweat, my hair was plastered against my head in damp Medusa curls, and every muscle in my body ached, as if I'd run from that shed, wherever it was, all the way back to the safety of my bedroom.

As soon as my throat opened enough for me to breathe and talk, and my fingers unclenched from the blanket, I picked up the phone and pushed Grant's speed dial number. I didn't care what time it was in England, or how busy he was, or that I was still in the dark, panting.

"Pick up, damn it."

He did. There were voices in the background. I didn't care about that either.

"They won't go away! It's a baby! Hurry!"

"Willy? You're pregnant? Are you in pain? I thought we were careful. We'll get married as soon as I get—"

"Not my baby, you ass. The horses'. That's why they're so distressed. And we're not getting married either way. And the baby's terrified and in a cell and you have to get it free." That wasn't at all what I meant to say, or how I wanted to say it, but he caught enough.

"Someone's captured one of the night mares' babies?"

"Yes, damn it! That's what I said. It's a small white horse with really, really vivid emotions that carry into my dreams."

"Shite," he said. Which was British stiff upper lip for we're going down the toilet. Sometimes he said "fook" which I used to think added to his charm. Charm wasn't going to help me now.

Nor was his doubting my word. "Are you sure?"

"Listen to me, Grant. I don't lie." Except when I said I was coming to England. "I am as sure as a nightmare can be. I dreamed it, but the baby was there, crying for its mother. And I did not do it! I never put a baby horse into my book. Never drew it, never wrote it, only the mares."

"Bloody hell! You visualized the mares, and that's why they came?"

"They came because there was an opening between our worlds. You said it yourself." I did not want to discuss any further connection between me and the mares' appearance, no more than I took credit for the troll showing up in Paumanok Harbor. Coincidence, only. "I never mentioned a baby!"

"They're called foals. Boys are colts, girls are fillies. Which is it?"

"I don't know! I saw it in a dream, in a lighted cell. Maybe it was a stall, now that I think about it. The poor thing is terrified."

"How big is it?"

"Are you listening to me? I was dreaming, not taking measurements! I was as frightened as the baby—and as helpless! I was here, in my bed. Do you even know what that is like, for crying out loud? I doubt you've ever felt weak and vulnerable with no way to change anything." I know I was sobbing, making my words run together, but he had to understand the horror for the baby, for me, for anyone else who'd shared the nightmare.

"I'm feeling helpless right now. Willy, you have to get a hold of yourself, darling. I'm trying to understand."

I could hear voices in the background, laughter. That made me madder. I'd bet they were all neatly dressed, cool and collected and smelling as sweet as his mother's frigging rose garden she was so proud of. Maybe he was in the frigging rose garden, drinking cocktails. Damn them all.

I took a deep breath, trying for rational composure. It didn't work. I was still crying. "I cannot get hold of myself, Grant. You said they project their emotions. Well, let me tell you, the baby did a fine job of nearly killing me. I don't know how anyone in Paumanok Harbor could survive that!"

"I doubt anyone but you is sensitive enough to pick up a foal's emotions, not if the mares haven't. They'd be at its side, otherwise. They'd find the young one in a second by following its outpourings. Maybe it's too young to project, but you fixed on it in your dream, so the emotions came through."

"Maybe." I *was* dreaming about Hetty from my book at first.

"The mother and the others will find a way to get the foal out of whatever enclosure it's in, then they'll race home and not bother anyone."

"Unless the baby is injured. They might take revenge. Or if it dies. Their grief alone could send everyone on the East End into terminal depression."

"That won't happen."

"How do you know? The mares are frantic enough just looking for the lost baby, and their frenzy is driving people crazy. If the baby is hurt . . ."

"Let me think."

I breathed deeply into the silence. Then I fumbled for the light switch to find the box of tissues and the clock on the floor. 5:14. I calculated five hours later for England, making their time perfect for 10:00 coffee break. I heard the clink of dishes, and more laughter. My world was falling apart, and Grant's world had their pinky fingers in the air. You'd think he would take the phone out of the room. You'd think he'd be booking a seat on the next flight if he had half an inkling of my anguish. You'd think—

"What did you mean, we aren't going to get married either way?"

Now? He wanted to have this conversation now? "I don't know. I'm just upset. The whole marriage thing is beginning to be another nightmare. It's not like being inside a poor infant horse's head, but it's tearing at me."

"The wedding or the marriage? Be honest, Willy. Just say it."

"The marriage."

"I guess I'm sorry I asked."

There was another silence. This one was too fraught for my jangled nerves. "I just . . . I can't. . . Can we talk about this after we find the baby?"

"The foal, Willy. It's not a baby. It's not our baby."

The sadness in his voice was like a knife to my heart. He wanted our child. He'd thought for a minute that we were starting the family he always wanted. He'd thought that if I was pregnant, we'd rush the wedding, foiling his mother's plans but starting our life together soon.

"No, it is not our baby."

Now he sighed.

I guess he finally realized there'd never be a baby. He was a para-linguist, after all, equally as good at interpreting what was said as what wasn't. I always believed he was a mind reader, too, even though he never admitted it. I knew he did have some of the original Royce-Harmon truth-sensing talent. "I'm sorry."

"Me, too."

"I know. And it hurts me, too. Truly. But right now, you're my only hope. You know more about these crazy things and the magic stuff from Unity than anyone in Paumanok Harbor. Maybe anyone in the world. You are the Department of Unexplained Events, and you're supposed to keep us all safe from things that go bump in the night." I was crying again, half because the dreams, the sweet dreams, were gone, and I'd done so badly at love; half because I was hurting the person who loved me, who deserved so much more from me.

"Don't cry, sweetheart. Please don't. You're killing me already."

"And me. And I am so afraid I can't handle this without you, and now you won't come."

"I'd come for you, whenever, wherever, if I could, forever, no matter what. You know that, Willy. I never lie."

I gulped back more tears for the guilt, for the loss. "I know."

"We don't have to decide anything today. You're upset and exhausted. You've got a lot on your shoulders right now. Things will look different tomorrow."

"They won't. They'll get worse if the baby dies, and you know it as well as I do. We have an expression: if Mama ain't happy, no one's happy. Those mares give new meaning to the old saying."

"I understand. And I will come as soon as I can. We'll talk about us then, all right?"

I did not know what more there was to say, but I murmured something he took for assent.

"Meanwhile, is the foal sick or only frightened?"

"It's weak. And cold. And doesn't like the food."

"How big, compared to a dog, say?"

"Bigger than a greyhound, but nowhere near as tall as me."

"Let's hope it's weaned, or its captor is giving it mare's milk. Otherwise, we have even less time to get to it."

"Why can't it just disappear like the mares? The troll popped in and out of view whenever he wanted. The white horses seem to also."

"You said the foal was in a lighted room?"

"A bare bulb hanging from the ceiling."

"That's it, then. From everything I've heard or read, the mares only come out at night. That's when they can vanish at will. The light might be what's keeping it in the enclosure, which means the horsenapper is smarter than I'd like. Or maybe the youngster is simply too immature to know the trick. No one on this side of Earth is going to be able to teach it, even if you could reach it in another dream."

"I am never going to sleep again. I can't bear the baby's anguish."

"You have to, Willy. You have to reassure it that help is coming. It will listen, now that you've made the connection."

"I can't!"

"Then draw it pictures if you have to, pretty pictures, with flowers and streams. No, paint it against a dark sky, with stars, so it knows you'll get it free. You're the Visualizer, Willy. Show the foal there's hope."

I sniffed. "I can do that."

"And you have to communicate with the mares somehow, too, so they know we're looking. Tell them we are on their side."

"I've never seen them. How am I going to talk to them? I don't know their language. You do. You're the one who can mindspeak, not me."

"I don't know if horses understand the little I've been able to translate. We got lucky with the troll, is all, because we had his brother with us. You can draw them pictures, too. Put them up where the mares have been spotted. Or dream about your paintings, of the horses all together again, on their way home."

"That might help until you get here."

I was really beginning to hate that silence at the other end of the line. "You're not coming, are you?"

"Ah, not right now. I have other commitments."

"Yeah, I heard the gremlins laughing. What did you do, invite them to brunch?"

"The gremlins are all gone, as far as we can figure. We gave them a box of cell phones, for all the good the electronics will do them. They gave us some feathers we've never seen before."

"Your scientists must be thrilled."

"We haven't let anyone examine the feathers yet. They might explode or something. They came from the gremlins, after all."

"Surely you are not involved in researching booby-trapped birds."

"No, but I am promised to another operation. Half the department is here now, trying to get an expedition together to go to the Himalayas. The yetis have come through the barriers, the same as your mares."

"Abominable snowmen? They're real and not just legends?"

"Now they are. And you cannot imagine what damage they can wreak. Already, whole villages have been buried in avalanches, not to mention how many mountain sheep of endangered species have been eaten. Yetis are huge, hungry beasts that can live through the most frigid temperatures."

I walked to the window to see the sun rise. "You're going?"

"We're just waiting to clear it with the Asian divisions now. Not step on anyone's toes, you understand."

Diplomacy and abominable snowmen in one breath. Who would have imagined two such rarities together? "If so many agents are there, why do you have to go?"

"People here think my experience with the troll might help me talk to the intruders, get them to go home."

"Or get eaten."

"That's not in the agency's guidebook."

The sun was barely visible over the treetops. It looked like another nice day coming to Long Island, for all Sir Edmund Hillary of DUE cared. "The mares aren't as important? Paumanok Harbor doesn't matter?"

Maybe the ice in my voice prepared him for what he was facing. Maybe not. "Paumanok Harbor has withstood centuries of Unexplained Events. And we both saw what the residents there can do if they work together. There's more psychic talent concentrated in your handful of native-born residents and their kin than anywhere else in the world beyond the Institute itself. Get them organized, get them looking for the foal."

"Just like looking for beach glass on the shore, hmm?"

"Paumanok Harbor isn't anywhere as big as the Himalayas, with fewer places to hide a stolen horse. You ought to be able to find your lost lamb in the few square miles with no trouble. Then the mares will come get it and everything will be fine. Meanwhile a horse whisperer might help. Read their body language, make the right moves, anything that might keep the mares calm. Are you familiar with horses at all?"

"I rode a pony at a friend's birthday party. And I took

a trail ride on the beach at Montauk once. The horse tripped. I walked home."

"Right. You draw pictures. I'll see if we have anyone on our rosters who can come."

That was the best I was going to do. I couldn't burden Grant with my worries and selfish demands anymore. "All right. I'll try."

"That's my girl. Or not."

I started crying again. "I do love you."

"Just not enough?"

"Maybe I need you more, and I don't want to need you. Can you understand that?"

I blew my nose, inelegantly, I suppose, but I didn't care.

"I'm trying to understand the whole thing. I wish I could hold you."

"And I wish I could feel your strength around me."

"You'll be strong enough, sweetheart. You really do have the courage of a lioness when you need it."

"Let's hope so."

I think he must have blown his nose, too. "I'll try to change your mind when I get there. Maybe I'll have a picture of a yeti to show you. We're not supposed to do anything of the kind, but I'll make an exception."

He sounded excited by the thought. If anything proved how unsuited to each other we were, that was it. Grant was actually looking forward to facing horrible conditions, dangerous creatures, mountains of snow that could collapse at any minute, life-and-death situations. I'd cut off my foot first.

"Wear warm clothes," was all I could say. "Be careful. Call when you can or send emails."

"You, too."

"It's summer here."

"So wear cool clothes, those short shirts that show your belly— No, don't wear them for anybody to see. But be careful. I miss you already."

Me, too.

CHAPTER 5

I SLAMMED A FEW DOORS. MAYBE EVERY single one I could. The bathroom, my bedroom, the back door when I let the dogs out, the screen door when I let them in, every cupboard I opened to make breakfast, every filing cabinet drawer that held my art supplies.

It worked.

Susan staggered down the steps in a football jersey and not much else. I hoped the football player wasn't still sleeping upstairs.

She poured a glass of orange juice while I put another English muffin in the toaster oven. "What's going on? It's barely light out."

"I've been up for hours working." I gestured toward the dining room table that I'd made into my studio. I already had stacks of posters printed out from my scanned drawings. The printer was churning out a second batch.

"Oh, are we having a yard sale? I have a bunch of old tapes and some shoes that hurt my feet and—"

"We're not having a yard sale. This is a whole lot more important."

"Ohmygod, you haven't lost one of your mother's dogs, have you? Tell me they're not Lost Dog posters. She'll kill both of us."

If Susan could count, or cared how many strays my mother fostered, she'd know the rescue dogs were all present, waiting for breakfast crumbs. "Why don't you read one of the posters and tell me what you think?"

Susan stuck a spoon into Grandma Eve's strawberry jam and licked it on her way toward the pile of flyers. "You've lost a pony?"

"It's not mine, and it's not a pony. If you'd read the damned thing instead of just looking at the picture, you'd see it's a baby horse. And don't you dare put your licked spoon back in the jam jar."

She brought the poster back to the kitchen table. "Cancer's not catching, you know."

"No, but venereal diseases might be."

She retaliated by informing me that baby horses were called foals, then fillies or colts.

I gnashed my teeth. "I know that, but I don't know this one's gender, and I'm not sure everyone else understands what a foal is. I need it to be as simple as possible for as many people as I can reach."

She read the rest: "Reward for information leading to the return of young missing white horse. With your cell phone number on those little tabs that people can tear off. So what's the reward?"

"A night with you."

"Very funny."

"Grandma doesn't think so either. You are embarrassing her. She told me to tell you to settle down with a nice young man."

"She's a fine one to speak, after she shacked up with that friend of Grant's that you thought was a molester at first."

"I was wrong about Lou, but I'm not sure Grandma is so wrong now. Aside from safety issues and ethics, I don't much like strangers coming through the house either. I have a lot of valuable equipment. And I don't like anyone seeing my work until it's finished."

Susan fetched the muffin from the toaster. "First off, they're not strangers. I don't bring any guys back here until we've hung out awhile. Second off, would you rather I went back to some man's motel room or bachelor pad where God knows what could happen? Third, I always insist on protection. Fourth, you are not my mother."

"Who's most likely embarrassed, too. The whole town thinks you're like a bitch in heat."

She slopped half the jar of jam onto her muffin and muttered, "Better than a plain old bitch," around a mouthful. "Besides, no one sees me drive down this private road, so no one knows how I spend my nights. You and I could be playing Monopoly."

"I won't play with you. You always cheat." I shoved a napkin toward her. "You think your partners don't talk? That's pretty naive of you."

She shrugged, then wiped jam off her chin. "It's nobody's business."

"Grandma thinks everything is her business."

"That's what's got you in a snit this morning, Grandma's moralizing about my love life? Or that you don't have one?"

I did not dignify that comment with a response. I did move the poster out of range of her sticky fingers. "Someone has stolen a young horse away from its family. Doesn't that mean anything to you?"

She shrugged. "Sure, but not on the scale of banks closing, icebergs melting, genocide, or—"

"I get the picture. But you're wrong. This particular crime has major repercussions, right here, right now. Not on a global scale, but not beyond our fixing either. We have to find the poor baby before it's too late."

"Willy, I know you are your mother's daughter, no matter how much you try to be different, but this is a horse you're talking about."

"No, it's a special animal, a rare, exotic breed. I think its mother—yes, I know she's called a dam—is the one causing everyone's nightmares. I know you haven't had any yet, but they are real and terrifying."

"Para horses, huh? Great, then Grant will be coming, and you'll be in a better mood."

Mumble mumble, while I drank my tea.

"Huh?"

I was never so glad to hear the phone ring, even if a call before eight usually meant trouble. This one did.

Uncle Henry Haversmith, who wasn't a real uncle but was really the police chief, sounded frazzled. He'd been up all night, too, with the nightmare Paumanok Harbor had turned into. A kid had pulled a Vincent. They Medivac-ed him to Stony Brook to reattach his ear. Another kid, a girl, tried to OD on her parents' prescription drugs. The Viagra hadn't done much harm, but no one was sure about the mother's arthritis meds. Mrs. Danvers ran over her husband, twice. The Patchen girl and her new husband fought over the wedding pictures, with scissors. And on and on. Uncle Henry wanted to know when the effing mares were leaving town or if he had to call in the county cops or the state troopers.

"Wait a minute. Tell Susan what you just told me. She doesn't think we have a problem."

I handed her the phone and watched as the color left her face, except for a dab of strawberry jam she'd missed. Without a word, she handed the phone back and stared at the poster of the white foal.

I explained about the baby—quickly inserting that I knew the difference between a colt and a filly before he could tell me. Then I had one of my better ideas.

"Hey, Uncle Henry, you can find keys and lost wallets. Maybe you can put your skill to use and find the foal for us. Then the mares will be happy and get on their way out of the Harbor."

He couldn't, to his regret. His talent only worked for inanimate objects, small ones at that, which still had an aura of the person who owned it. I should have realized his limitations, or he would have located the kidnapped boy we searched for last spring.

"But I'm making posters to ask for help finding the missing horse."

Uncle Henry didn't have a whole lot of confidence in my posters. He wanted to know when Grant was coming.

"Lord Grantham is not coming. I can handle this."

I turned off the phone while Uncle Henry was still

cursing. Susan was staring at me through narrowed eyes and lowered brow. I guess she finally noticed that my face was blotchy and my eyes were red and swollen from crying.

"Willow Tate, what have you done now?"

Damn Susan and her sensitivity to my sins. I took the offensive. "Me? Why is everything my fault, my responsibility? I didn't steal any supernatural horse. For your information—and the entire town's, I suppose—Agent Grant is rushing off to do battle with some other exotic creature, in a more exciting locale than Paumanok Harbor. I get to suffer nightmares until I can solve the horse rustling, or whatever you call it."

"I bet you two had a fight over that, and that's why you were banging around like a blind bear in an outhouse. You didn't want him to go."

"Of course I did not want him to fly into horrible danger, but there was nothing to fight about. He has his duties. I would respect him less if he did not honor them."

"You argued. I know you."

"I did not argue." I may have pleaded, but that was between me and Grant. I poured myself another cup of tea. "And I am going to tell my mother myself that the wedding is off, as soon as it's a decent hour to call. So you don't have to run for your cell phone to tell her or your mother, who'll call her the next minute. And if you tell Grandma Eve before I can, I'll throw your mattress out in the dog run. It most likely has bedbugs by now anyway."

"The wedding is off?"

"The wedding was never on, technically, but yes, our relationship is over, except as friends, I hope." I really did hope for that. I busied myself making more tea so she wouldn't see my eyes filling with tears again. I added too much sugar, but drank it anyway.

"He broke up with you?" She leaned forward, eager for details.

"He did not break up with me. We decided we, uh, we do not suit."

"That's straight out of one of those books you read.

He got tired of waiting, didn't he? I warned you no guy likes to be kept dangling. Or being celibate while his bride dithers. He didn't cheat on you, did he?"

"Grant would never go back on a promise. And he did not break the engagement. Not that we were formally engaged anyway."

"After you practically had sex in front of the whole town? I'd say that was as good as a notice in the paper."

"I never got a ring. We never made that announcement."

She stuck her spoon back in the jam jar.

"I bet he found someone else. Some gorgeous telepath or a clairvoyant heiress. Maybe someone with mixed blood so he can practice those ancient languages."

I shoved the lid on the jar. "Damn it, I broke up with him."

The spoon hung in the air inches away from Susan's open mouth. "You really are as crazy as everyone says. Even by Paumanok Harbor standards, and that's saying a lot. Maybe you should see a shrink."

I brushed at my damp cheeks with my napkin, leaving jam smears on my face. "I know."

Then, because she's Susan and because she loves me, my cousin said, "If you don't want him, can I have him?"

I cleaned the kitchen and went back to printing out flyers for every store window and bulletin board in town. Conversation over.

I set the computer to printing the posters to hang on trees. These pictured three white horses on a black background, with a small one prancing between them. It was as happy and hopeful as I could make it, with no words. I was going to get them laminated so they'd stay okay through any weather.

"You can help me put them up as soon as you get dressed. Then I'll need you to tell me where someone is most likely to stash a stolen horse. Backyard barns, abandoned cottages, that kind of thing. I'll check old maps at the library, and see if Uncle Henry has any ideas, but you might know better, from all your years sneaking around. Besides, I only spent summers here, but you grew up in Paumanok Harbor. You'll know every deer path and hiking trail where we can tack up a poster."

"It's really that important?"

"You heard Uncle Henry. It's going to get worse. A bunch of our upstanding citizens have illegal handguns, or legal hunting rifles. I hate to think what another week of nightmares will unleash."

"Yeah, I had two parties send their meals back last night at the restaurant. First time ever. Business is bad enough without that."

"Change the menu. Make happy meals."

"What, turn the Breakaway into Micky D's and churn out kiddy burgers and French fries?"

"No, you know what I mean. Don't think I don't know how you can affect people's moods, between your cooking and Grandma's ingredients."

"Maybe, but I never know how. It just happens."

"I don't care how. Do it. Or this place is going to explode."

"You're serious, aren't you?"

"Dead serious. Do you think I'd be calling my mother otherwise?"

"I'll find the number of that shrink."

CHAPTER 6

I ALMOST TOLD MY MOTHER THAT I—no, that Susan—had lost one of her rescue dogs. That way I'd get the screaming part over and she'd be relieved enough to listen when I explained what really happened. As long as her dogs were safe, she wouldn't care that I was breaking my almost-engagement and her chance of getting grandchildren. And that the town was under siege.

Or else I could chicken out and tell my father first, so he'd have to suffer her high-decibel dramatics. He'd just had open heart surgery, though, so I couldn't jeopardize his health that way. I wasn't even sure Mom was still staying with him in Florida since the reconciliation didn't seem to be working. When I spoke to my mother last week, she was going undercover at the greyhound track. If she found evidence of mistreatment, she could shut it down. Or get arrested.

Wherever she was, I needed to talk to her. I might be thirty-five years old, but I needed my mother. Not like the little horse, but badly enough. I wasn't proud of the fact either.

She was thrilled to hear from me. Before I could launch into my prepared speech, she said, "You are just the person I was thinking of, Willow. Maybe you are clairvoyant after all."

No, I only saw things other people didn't, and dreamed in the minds of magical beasts. That was plenty for me.

"Is Dad okay?"

"He won't take in any of the greyhounds, the toad. Condo rules, he says. Why anyone would choose to live in a place with no dogs is beyond me. It's not natural or healthy. I bet he wouldn't have had a heart attack if he had a pet. Research is starting to understand the health benefits to having a dog. Even a cat would be better than nothing. These retirees down here think they're adding years to their lives in their tidy town houses. Hah! Not without a dog, they aren't."

I'd heard it all before. Ad nauseam. "Mom, I called because—"

"Anyway, how many of your friends do you think can foster a couple of retired racers?"

"In the city? In an apartment? Not many."

"What about in the Harbor?"

"You've already placed dogs with everyone who ever wanted one. Or never wanted one, but couldn't say no."

"I was right about each one of them. Nobody would give up their beloved foundlings. No one but your father, that worthless piece of—"

I guess my parents wouldn't be retaking their vows any time soon. "Mom, I really need to tell you about what's going on here."

"Of course, dear. Then we can discuss holding a fundraiser to earn enough money to board the dogs until we find homes for them."

"Did you steal them?" I really didn't have time to hire lawyers or organize a charity raffle, pancake breakfast, or the fancy cocktail party she'd talk me into. I had to go hang posters.

Mother grew indignant that I'd suspect her of acting illegally, when we both recalled the time she broke into a house to rescue a mistreated husky, or climbed the fence at a research lab, and a hundred other scrapes with the law.

"Of course I did not steal the dogs. The racetrack people agreed to surrender a few, to better the conditions for the rest. That was all the concession I could get out of them, for now."

"How many is a few?"

"We'll work something out, I'm sure."

Which meant at least a dozen: a dozen very large dogs not raised as household pets, not housebroken if they've lived in cages their whole lives, maybe not in good health if the racetrack was ready to discard them. "Mom, someone else down there will have to deal with the greyhounds. We need you here."

Her voice got shrill again. "Are you okay? Your grandmother? Susan? What about the Pomeranian?"

"We're all as well as can be expected, under the circumstances. We're being plagued by—"

"Well, whatever it is, I cannot leave now. It's impossible."

"So are vanishing horses that cause nightmares. I need you to talk to them, to calm them down the way you do with stray dogs." There wasn't a dog alive that wouldn't eat out of my mother's hand in five minutes, snuggle up to her in ten. She'd have the mares dozing placidly in the sunshine—or moonlight—while the rest of us tracked down their missing offspring.

"I don't speak horse, dear. They're not half as trusting as dogs, or as genetically inclined to please people. Equines are a different specialty. You say they vanish? And cause nightmares?"

"All through town. The situation is getting nasty."

"Then they aren't normal horses. Get your Grant to come. This sounds like a job for that hush-hush group the dear man works for."

"He's off on a different mission, to Asia. Mom, I need you to come home."

"Why, are you getting married before he leaves next week?"

I took a deep breath and held the phone farther away from my ear. "I'm not getting married."

She didn't shatter any glasses, but Little Red ran under the sofa. "You're not getting married? Ever?"

"Maybe someday, but not to Grant."

I could hear her sniff. She did that a lot, either from dog hair allergies or aggravation. It was always hard to tell with my mother. This time I kind of had it figured out.

My mother loved me. Sometimes she even acted like it. This wasn't one of those times.

"How did I raise such a stupid, bubble-headed daughter?" Sniff. "The man is rich and smart and handsome and decent." Sniff. "He loves you, he's not gay, and did I mention he's rich? What are you waiting for? You already found Prince Charming. They don't grow on trees, you know."

"Mom."

She wasn't finished yelling. "Of course I am not surprised you've made a mess of this, too. You'd do anything to ruin my plans, wouldn't you? I had a lovely wedding all figured out. The Pom could have the ring tied to his collar. How cute is that?"

A three-legged furball lurching down the aisle? Not very. I knew better than to interrupt her mid-rant, so I just kept quiet.

"And you're not getting any younger, you know. I don't care what they say about fertility clinics. Between you and your father . . ."

When she went off on my father, I had to stop her or I'd be on the phone for another hour. "Mom, I did not make a mess of anything. Grant was not going to make me happy. You always told me I deserved happiness."

She sniffed again. "Every woman does. I suppose if he isn't there when you need him, you don't need him."

Damn, there were the tears again, not that I was a crybaby or anything. "Something like that." Now I had to sniff. "And I didn't want to commute between here and England or travel the globe looking for danger or have my husband gone half the time. I do not want to need him, or any man. All I need is for you to come talk to the horses."

"You need a psychiatrist."

Susan had said the same thing. "You, too?"

"No, I don't need one. I'm fine, no matter what your father says. I told you, I don't do horses. They're too big and unpredictable."

"You're not afraid of them, are you?" I didn't think there was anything on this earth or the next that frightened my mother. I felt a lot better knowing she was human after all.

She snorted this time. "I am not afraid of them simply because I don't relate to creatures who eat hay. It's just that your father's been muttering about horses. I thought he meant I should go to the racetrack instead of the dogs."

"Has Dad mentioned any other forebodings?"

"Your father couldn't predict an earthquake if the ground was shaking."

My father's precognition was admittedly a vague talent. He'd know if something bad was going to happen, or maybe could happen to people he loved, but he seldom knew any helpful details. Typical of my mother, she believed he could be a bigger help if only he tried harder. She must have inherited her attitude from her own mother, Grandma Eve, who believed Dad could have cured his heart condition with her herbs. Then again, my father's mother—I barely remembered her— heard voices that no one else heard. And spoke back to them.

Vague or not, my father's warnings were sometimes useful, if overprotective out of his affection for me. I needed whatever help I could get . . . and some of his ever-loyal support.

"Are you at his apartment?" I'd called on her cell. "Is he there? Can you put him on?"

"He'll be back from playing bridge at the clubhouse any minute. Bridge, when he could be out doing something important."

Like raiding puppy mills.

"I'll tell him to call you."

"I'll be out most of the day hanging posters and looking for hidden stables."

"What kind of posters?"

So I told her about the one with the missing horse. She, predictably, told me I was doing it wrong.

"You never mention a reward. You'll only get cranks

and fakes, and encourage other criminals to steal more dogs. Er, horses. Besides, if the horse thief is holding the animal for ransom, he'll name his own price. There's some cash in the bottom of my sock drawer, but if your horses are what I think they are, get the Royce Institute people to pay the ransom. They can afford it."

"Thanks, Mom. That'll be a help."

"And I'll ask around about someone good with horses."

"I'd appreciate that. Grant's looking, too, but we need someone quickly. Give my love to Dad."

"Oh, I forgot to tell you. He was going to call you tonight to warn you to look out for caves and alligators. Can you believe that? There aren't any caves in Paumanok Harbor, and I ought to know since I was born there. There sure as hell aren't any alligators on Long Island, unless someone has one in a fish tank. He's spent too much time on the golf course down here, where you have to be careful retrieving lost balls from the lagoons. How ridiculous is that, even if he was right about boats being dangerous last time? I told him not to bother you with that nonsense, but he'll want to tell you anyway, just to make you more anxious than you are now. You see how useless he is? All men are, I suppose. Maybe you're right about Grant. I wouldn't want my grandchildren living in Britain."

She obviously didn't give a rat's ass where I lived. I wrote down horses, caves, and alligators on the pad I always had nearby. "Okay, Mom, I better get to putting up my signs."

"You know, if you're out hanging posters, maybe you could make up one or two about adopting a greyhound?"

"Gotta go, Mom. Miles to cover."

"Think about the psychiatrist, dear. You can use one."

Didn't she know they always blamed a patient's problems on his or her mother? That worked for me.

Despite what I said about hurrying, I knew most of the businesses on Main Street wouldn't be open yet, so I went to see Grandma Eve at her house up the dirt road.

She was in the front yard, watering plants. She listened to me while she went from tub to tub of young greenery, with nasturtiums and marigolds mixed in to keep the insects away. I did not recognize half the herbs she was growing, despite backbreaking, boring summers of weeding and repotting and selling the plants from hell at the family's farm stand. Grandma kept adding more exotic species, with help from fellow herbalists and a blind eye from the FDA.

When I finished my story about horses, nightmares, and Grant—which I was getting sick of repeating—Grandma put down the hose. She pursed her lips, crossed her arms over her bony chest, then tucked a stray gray strand of hair back under her baseball cap. The Yankees. She stared at me for long enough to make my knees tremble while I tried not to think of Hansel and Gretel. Then she nodded, as if concluding that I was worth the interruption of her day. She said she'd fetch me something that might help and went inside the house.

I hoped for more strawberry jam, since I was feeding two now, but I figured she'd bring me a new concoction in a tea bag so I could sleep better. Instead, she came back out with a piece of paper with The Garland Farm logo on the top. Dr. Lassiter, it said, with a phone number.

"Let me guess. He's a shrink."

She nodded again. "A world-renowned therapist and an old friend. He retired after his wife died and he had a stroke. He's on Shelter Island. Call him."

I would, right after I started seeing alligators and caves.

CHAPTER 7

PAUMANOK HARBOR WAS NOT LIKE the other villages that made up East Hampton Township on Long Island's East End. In fact, none of the neighboring villages looked much like each other, or felt like each other either.

East Hampton Village was all glitz and glamour, Tiffany's and Ralph Lauren, with celebrity watching its tourists' favorite pastime. Old money, new money, big money, money-envy.

Montauk was a working man's two-week vacation: beach and bars, fishing and surfing. Downtown was full of T-shirt shops and souvenir stores, with rows of motels that sat right on the beach. Until the next hurricane.

Amagansett couldn't decide if it was chic or cozy, with galleries and gourmet farmers' markets and antique stores.

Springs had no central business district, just a strip mall and a scattering of necessities, like a liquor store and a pizza parlor.

Sag Harbor was almost a restoration village, with tiny shops and houses dating from its old whaling days.

Of course those are all short subjective opinions, without going into the natural beauty of each place or its cultural offerings or its family neighborhoods. I had friends in all of them and appreciated what they had to offer. None of them looked or felt like home. New York

City still had my heart—and my legal voting address, resident taxes, and rent-controlled apartment—but little Paumanok Harbor had grown on me. Like a jack-and-the-beanstalk vine, giants and all. Fee-fi-fo-fum.

Paumanok Harbor wasn't on the ocean, wasn't on the tourist route, didn't have a lot of motels or summer homes. Too much of the Harbor was unbuildable wetlands or town-owned preserves to be part of the Hamptons land rush and building boom of the last couple of decades. There were some new McMansions, but the monstrous eyesores were mostly scattered up wooded drives or on five-acre lots. The majority of houses and land and small farms like my grandmother's were still in the hands of the descendants of the early English settlers. Witches and warlocks all, it was rumored, fleeing oppression everywhere else.

They built up their new settlement like many New England towns, with a grassy commons in the middle, houses close together facing the center square, with a school at one end and a church at the other. Unlike other communities, the church was an afterthought, more for effect and public opinion than praying. These immigrants had way different beliefs, but they needed to conform to the neighboring towns.

Now stores and offices had replaced many of the old houses facing the square, and a much larger school had been built two blocks north. The library was in the old school building, refurbished, of course, and the handsome new community center and art building extended the central business district by another block east past the commons. The town offices, firehouse, and police station were on the next street, between the school's playing fields and the parking lots. The one gas station and the bowling alley popped up one block south of the village square.

Restaurants and bars and bait shops were strewn here and there throughout the village borders, but most of the necessities were right here on Main Street. The bare necessities, that was, for mail, groceries, coffee, house paint and Band-Aids. Some were located in the front rooms or lower levels of private houses, like Janie's Beauty Parlor and Martha's real estate office. Others were in a hodge-podge of styles, old wood, brick, stone, shingles, modern glass. Town planning hadn't been a big thing until it was too late, but at least the business area hadn't sprouted golden arches or luxury latte shops. Not yet, anyway.

Paumanok Harbor had incorporated decades ago, freeing it from East Hampton Township rules, but forcing it to keep its own police department and zoning board and bookkeepers. Taxes were high; independence was priceless, especially for the odd ducks in this particular pond.

When I had to spend summers here with my family, I thought the place was a boring backwater blight with ingrown, insular, ill-adjusted residents. The Harbor seemed stuck in the past, with no interest in improving or attracting more business or entertaining the people it already had. After the city, where we really lived, it was deader than a graveyard.

Now I appreciated how the pace wasn't as fast and the faces in the shops were familiar and usually friendly. Paumanok Harbor had Character, as well as characters.

I drove my mother's Outback into the school parking lot. She'd left the car at the airport, but one of her friends drove it back for me. Susan's mother was the vice principal and ran the summer school enrichment program there. She'd let us use the school's laminating machine on the posters meant for the mares. I didn't need to hear Aunt Jasmine lecture me about seeing the school's counselor, so I dropped Susan and a stack of posters off and drove to Town Hall. I wanted to tell Uncle Henry, Chief of Police Haversmith, what I was doing, but he was out on business. The cop at the desk was a guy named Barry who stank of fish, which was why I refused my uncle-by-affection's efforts to fix me up with him, and why I stayed as close to the door as possible. Barry said the chief had to go to Riverhead, the Suffolk County seat. The DA there wanted to know why the Harbor suddenly had so much crime, and if we needed a drug squad or a hate crimes unit.

Yeah, suddenly everyone hated everyone else. It had nothing to do with the Hispanic work crews or controlled substances. No one was controlling their tempers, because the mares were ruining their sleep. I'd love to hear Uncle Henry explain that to the DA.

"I'm working on it," I told Barry. I handed him one of the pictures of the young horse and asked him to post it, and think positive thoughts while he did.

I believe he mumbled something about how he'd like to think of me in my underwear, but I chose not to hear it. He might be the town's best surfcaster, always knowing which beach the blues or stripers would hit, but he still smelled.

I walked next door to the village office, where you could get a permit for the dump or complain about your neighbor's loud parties. Mrs. Ralston ran the place. I think her title was Village Clerk. Just looking at her in her beige pant suit and tidy bun, you knew she was efficient and perfect for the job. You could even forget she was one of the village loonies until she spoke.

First she stared at the poster, then at me and the Pomeranian in my arms, making both of us squirm.

"It's too hot to leave the dog in the car, even with the windows open," I explained, knowing damn well that no dogs except Seeing Eye guides were permitted in the office.

"It's a boy."

"Yes, his name is Little Red. My mother rescued him from a really bad situation, but he's learning to trust people again."

"Not the dog."

"Me? I'm not pregnant, Mrs. Ralston, I swear."

She tapped one perfectly manicured finger on the poster I'd put in front of her. "The horse, Willow. It's a colt."

"Are you sure?"

She gave me that hard stare again. She was never wrong about those things. If I ever wanted a clamming permit, I'd better apologize. "It's just that it's not a human baby, and it's already born. And . . . and it's not even here for you to look at."

"You dreamed it, didn't you? You drew it, didn't you? You put as much feeling into the picture as you could, didn't you?"

"Yes."

"It's a boy."

"Okay, that's a help. I can't change the posters, but I can tell people to concentrate on a colt. Maybe that'll reinforce the positive thoughts."

Mrs. Ralston said she'd tell the mayor, when he remembered to come in to work. Mayor Applebaum had been forgetting the office hours and board meetings as long as I remembered, but no one ever ran against him.

I shook my head when I was back outside. "This place gets weirder and weirder," I told Little Red. He growled at a squirrel across the street.

Paumanok Harbor had a volunteer fire department, so only one man was there, a young high-school kid, he looked like, washing the already gleaming fire trucks. I didn't know him, didn't know if he was one of the Paumanok paras or just a recent newcomer to the village.

He knew who I was, though, and knew about the mares. He looked as if he hadn't slept well for days. He said his name was Micky.

I explained about the missing colt. "At least, Mrs. Ralston at Town Hall says it's a male."

He nodded. "If my aunt says it's a male, it's a male."

Which answered that question.

"Can you . . . ?"

"Nah, but I can always tell if a guy is gay or not."

"That would come in handy in some Manhattan bars."

"East Hampton ones, too."

I left my car near the police station because I hoped to talk to Uncle Henry if he got back soon enough. I walked through a parking lot and an alley toward the commons, with Red anointing every fire hydrant and bush. I tried to discourage him from the neat flower beds my grandmother and the Garden Club tended. I also used a plastic pickup bag, good citizen that I am.

You could usually walk the square of the commons in less than fifteen minutes. Today it took me nearly two hours. I wanted to talk to everyone, to hear what they knew. I wanted them to look at the poster and think encouraging thoughts, just in case the kidnapped colt could pick up anyone's thoughts. Hey, in Paumanok Harbor anything was possible.

The bank was my first stop. Mr. Whitside barely glanced at the poster, but tapped his head and said, "I've got it here."

I wanted him to take a closer look, so I could judge his reaction, but then I recalled he had an instant eidetic memory. He'd remember. He never forgot a customer's name or an overdraft. He promised to help with a ransom, anything to get people spending money again instead of shouting at each other.

At the Seaview Real Estate office, Martha was crying at her desk. I let her pet Little Red for consolation. She was so tired from having her sleep so disturbed, she'd tossed her live-in boyfriend out this morning. They hadn't made love in five days, anyway.

Hell, I hadn't had sex in over a month, but I told her I was working on it—the nightmares, not the sex. She promised to fax me a list of every property she knew that had a barn or stable. And if I needed directions, she had a compass in her head, better than a GPS.

Joanne at the deli handed me an iced coffee before I could order. I thought I wanted iced tea, but Joanne said I needed the extra caffeine. She was right, as always. The coffee was delicious.

She'd seen the mares yesterday on her way to open the deli. Last night she'd thrown her current boyfriend's guitar out the second-story window. Then she'd tried to throw the boyfriend out after it.

"You want me to think happy thoughts so the colt will know we're working for him? Well, how's this? I won't have to listen to that freaking guitar anymore."

* * *

The hardware store had a customer I'd never seen before. He was wearing ironed jeans, loafers with no socks and a gold chain around his neck. He was asking Bill about keeping deer out of his ornamentals. Definitely a summer resident.

I was circumspect, showing the poster to Bill when the customer picked up some ant traps. I said I hoped the night mares would leave soon.

The customer glanced at the poster without really seeing it, then sneered at me and Bill. "Between the traffic and the taxes, this place is a nightmare, all right, but you locals forget where your money comes from. It's people like me who pay your rip-off prices, so you could show a little respect."

He stormed out, but somehow stepped on a tack that went through his fancy loafers and into his sockless foot.

Never mess with a cranky telekinetic in a hardware store.

Mrs. Findel at the grocery store was always unfriendly, so it was hard to tell if today's irascibility was caused by bad dreams or her usual bad temperament. She didn't want any stupid posters cluttering up her window. Besides, I'd been shopping out of town, so why should she do me any favors?

"For the young horse's sake?" I suggested, vowing not to shop here in the future, either. "Or for the townspeople?"

She cracked her chewing gum. I guess the rest of the locals shopped elsewhere when they could, too. I asked to speak to Mr. Findel, who was always nice to me, but she said he was gone. I wouldn't blame him if he never came back. I left one of the posters on the counter anyway.

I found myself at the eastern end of the commons, facing the library, Mrs. Terwilliger's domain. She of the new gun permit.

I looked at the stately library building. I looked at the posters in my hand. I looked across the square and decided to go to Janie's Beauty Parlor and the drugstore first.

CHAPTER 8

"AW, SWEETIE, I'M SORRY ABOUT YOUR boyfriend," Janie said, giving me an enthusiastic hug that slopped the coffee onto my jeans and set Little Red to barking in panic.

All the other ladies getting their perms and weekly sets nodded in sympathy. It wasn't that the town was telepathic; they were just terrible gossips. By now, they all knew my business and my mission. I didn't have to say a word about the horses or the kidnapped colt. Janie took the poster from me, said, "We'll find you, baby," and hung it in the shop window.

Then she walked around me, studying my hair. "Time for a new cut, sweetie. You know, out with the old, in with the new, just like last time. Or maybe a different color."

I'd let her cut and highlight my streaky blonde hair last spring, after I made a break from a loser named Arlen in the city. I hadn't done much with my hair since, and it showed, darker roots and all.

"I'm kind of busy right now." And I liked it longer, so I could clump it back with a scrunchie and be done. Then again, Janie always knew what made a woman look her best.

She returned to putting Mrs. Chemlecki's white hair onto big rollers. "I guess it's just as good you and the hunk split up. It never works out when the groom is prettier than the bride."

Mrs. Chemlecki quickly added, "Not that you're not an attractive woman, Willow dear."

Janie agreed, kind of. "But no one dumps on a gorgeous redhead."

"He didn't dump—"

"Of course not."

Red and I slunk out of Janie's and headed to the drugstore, feeling about as attractive as the pot of wilted geraniums out front that someone had forgotten to water.

Walter, the pharmacist, made me feel better. He took the poster and said, "You'll find the poor bugger if anyone can." Then he handed me a paper bag.

I looked inside to find a sample pack of condoms. "But I'm not—" I sputtered. "That is, Grant and I . . . He's not . . . I don't need . . ."

"You will," he assured me.

I smiled at him. "That's right. Blondes have more fun."

He winked and I held my head higher when I left, until he said, "Doc Lassiter doesn't usually prescribe drugs, but if he thinks they'll help, I'll make sure I have a bunch in stock."

Shit. Dumped, dumpy, and deranged, what a combination.

On that low note I dragged myself next door to the liquor store. I figured I better get my mother another bottle of Kahlua to replace the one I'd been sipping. Or slurping.

After discussing the horses and the hopes of reassuring the mares and the baby with Alan, the sales clerk, I paid for the bottle. And decided to buy a lottery ticket, one of the scratch-off kinds. Not that I felt lucky, but maybe my luck was due to change. I pointed to a one-dollar ticket that had fortune cookies on it.

"You don't want that one," Alan said.

"The one with the hearts?"

He shook his head.

"The penguins?"

He flashed his eyes toward the stack of horseshoes.
"That one?"

He winked again.

You learn not to question things in Paumanok Harbor, especially when they win you ten bucks.

One of the questions you don't ask is how come the postmaster has a Seeing Eye dog. The mail always got sorted properly and delivered on time. Outgoing letters and packages got the correct postage. Customers got the right change. Yet the old man in the bow tie couldn't see a thing.

I asked if I could hang my poster up on the bulletin board with the wanted flyers and the church schedule. Mr. Kendall took it from my hand.

"Handsome horse. About six months, I'd guess. He'd have to be, to be weaned."

Like I said, you learn not to ask questions.

By now I was at the far end of the square, nearing the church. I'd been here in the spring for the Patchen girl's wedding, but not since, which I did not want to discuss with Reverend Shankman. I hoped he was out visiting the sick or writing his sermon—not that many people listened, he was so long-winded and boring—so I could hang my poster on the bulletin board in the vestry and go.

Red was too tired to hop anymore, besides being exhausted from barking at everything bigger than he was. I juggled the Pom, the bottle of Kahlua, the condoms, and the rest of the posters to open the heavy wooden doors into the dark entry hall.

The church was empty, thank God, who might not be as grateful. The sanctuary was not well used in a place like Paumanok Harbor where the truth came in lots of colors, and the minister became tedious. Temple Yisroel used it on Friday nights, and two African-American Muslims prayed there to the east, or to Montauk, twice a day.

I started to lay my burdens down—the physical, not the soulful—starting with Red, when Reverend Shankman suddenly rose up from the last pew. Startled, I dropped the sack of condoms, which naturally spilled out across the marble floor. The bottle of liquor didn't break, but it did roll across the hall. And of course Little Red bit the reverend's ankle.

Proving his dedication, the man did not curse, just hopped once or twice while I stuffed everything back in their bags and grabbed Little Red's leash.

"Heaven knows you need our prayers." Silently, he took the top poster and tacked it to the bulletin board.

The gray-haired cleric had learned not to ask questions, either, it seemed. I know he always preached that, with God, all things were possible, but God would have to be a magician in this place. I thanked him and went back out to the bright sunshine.

I crossed the street to the next block, behind the stores on the square.

The bowling alley was closed, not surprisingly, since the owner, Joey Danvers, was the one whose wife ran him over.

Bud from the gas station next door saw me trying to juggle my packages and find the masking tape in my pocket so I could stick a poster to the bowling alley's front door. He came over and hung the notice for me.

"That should hold until someone comes to run the alley for Joey. The men's league plays tomorrow, so one of the guys'll get the keys until Joey's out of the hospital. Or Maureen's out of jail. It's not going to rain until the end of the week."

Bud was better at forecasting than the weather channel. Everyone knew that. "I'll tell Grandma Eve she'd better water extra."

"And Claire"—that was his wife—"says her nose is itchy, so tell your grandma to expect company."

Grandma hadn't mentioned anything to me, so I wondered if Lou was coming back. He worked with Grant at the Department of Unexplained Events, and I didn't much like him. Grandma did.

*   *   *

I doubled back to the square and bought a bottle of water and a corn muffin at the deli, sat on one of the benches, and shared with Little Red. I called Susan on her cell to see how she was doing and told her I just had the art center and the library left. Maybe she'd meet me at the library?

"When pigs fly," was her answer.

Which might be coming next for all I knew. I put everything I could into the deli bag and headed toward the arts and recreation center.

The center was only a few years old and the pride of Paumanok Harbor. Built with a huge legacy from one of the former residents on donated land, the place hadn't cost the taxpayers a lot, and benefited them all. On one side was a gym and a pool where they held youth nights and senior yoga and ballroom dance lessons. On the other was a gallery with much of the donor's private collection, classrooms for after school programs, and studios for visiting artists.

My friend Louisa Rivera used to run the whole thing. With two children and another on the way, she stuck to the arts side now. I was looking forward to seeing her if she had a rare two minutes to spare. We'd been friends forever, it seemed, since both of us were summer kids and not really part of the locals' groups.

Mostly I wanted to know what she was feeling. As far as I knew, neither she nor her parents were born in Paumanok Harbor, and I'd never seen a twinge of paranormal ability in her. Her husband came here as a young boy, a hellion, in fact. His only claim to extraordinary power, other than his amazing good looks, was in making money, first in the computer business, then in land speculation. Now I was curious if they or their children were affected at all by the nightmares.

"I'm pregnant," Louisa told me. "I barely sleep at night anyway. Who has time for nightmares between peeing every couple of hours?"

"What about mood shifts?"

"Willy, I'm pregnant. That's another name for bitchy.

And no, I don't know anything about white horses or the new missing one everyone's talking about this morning. Sorry."

"What about Dante?"

She smiled, the way she always did when someone mentioned his name. "Nope, he never mentioned anything about them, except to worry that our daughter wants pony lessons, too. We hardly get a chance to speak anyway. He falls into bed exhausted as soon as the kids are asleep and never moves once his head hits the pillow. The poor guy's been taking care of the children all day so I can get the summer programs up and running."

Which reminded both of us that I had agreed to teach a creative writing course for teenagers in a couple of weeks. It sounded like a good idea at the time. Now it sounded like another nightmare.

I looked at the flyers around Louisa's office while she hung one of mine and took several others to post in the classrooms and the rec center. Yup, my name was right there, with pictures of my latest book covers. No backing out now. I saw Louisa had talked Dante into doing two weeks on designing computer games. Someone else was teaching digital photography, and one of the summer interns had ongoing painting classes. I wish there'd been something like that when I spent summers here. All we had was the library.

Oh, boy.

Mrs. Terwilliger had been librarian when my mother was a girl, back when they used the old Shrade house on Main Street for a library. She had to be close to ninety, but no one ever even *thought* about her retiring. Hell, no. Everyone was afraid of the old bat. So maybe she never turned anyone into a toad when they talked out loud or gave them warts if they put a book back on the shelf out of alphabetical order, she was still scary. She'd give Dewey himself nightmares if he spilled juice on one of the books.

Put a gun in her age-spotted hand and you were asking for trouble.

Taking a dog into the library was putting your library privileges on the line—if not your life.

But this was Little Red, who did not take kindly to being left anywhere, anytime. Out in the sun, tied to a bench where seagulls and squirrels could insult him? My mother would kill me. So I left my bags and bottles near the bike rack and tucked the dog under my T-shirt. So what if I looked pregnant with a six-pound Pomeranian?

Mrs. Terwilliger reached down behind her desk when I opened the door. Uh-oh.

Instead of pulling out a pistol, she handed me a stack of books. You never knew what Mrs. Terwilliger was going to give you, but you could be sure it was something you ought to read.

The Horse Whisperer I was expecting. But three Louis L'Amour westerns?

"These are cowboy books, Mrs. T. I don't usually—"

"You do now."

"But the horses aren't like the Old West mustangs. Or cow ponies."

"Read them. And remember, the cowboy always rides off into the sunset."

"Yes, Mrs. T. Thank you."

Then she handed me another book, *Women Who Like Too Many Men Too Much*. I'd never heard of it. I looked down at the lump of Little Red. "I'm not . . ."

"For your cousin," Mrs. Terwilliger said with a curl in her lip. "If she remembers how to read."

"I'll tell her."

"This one is for Dr. Lassiter when you see him."

"I'm not going to—"

She reached back under the desk. I took the book, a pamphlet really, from the Royce Institute Press. *Transuniversal Metaphysics and the Human Mind.* An easy read, for sure. Before she could find more books for me to carry, I gave her a poster to hang, and to think about.

She looked at the colt's picture, then at me. "I'll read *National Velvet* tonight. Aloud. That should encourage him. In fact, I already put Secretariat's biography on various readers' lists."

"Thank you, ma'am."

"And the dog needs more air than that." She handed me a cloth book bag with the library logo on it.

"He doesn't like—"

"For the books, Willow. For the books."

"Yes, ma'am, thank you. I'll bring it back as soon as I can." And I'd put it in the book drop instead of coming inside the library. We left in a hurry, sweating, but alive.

CHAPTER 9

⚘

I MET SUSAN OUTSIDE THE POLICE STATION. She showed me the box full of laminated posters but decided to wait outside while I spoke to the chief. I didn't believe her when she said she wanted to sit in the sun. She'd always hated her freckles. What I believed was she wanted to check out the young cop walking a German shepherd that was wearing an orange vest with K9 on it. The officer was short and almost skinny, with a real honker of a nose, but he was Susan's type: male and breathing.

Red and I went in and found Uncle Henry at his desk in his shirtsleeves unwrapping a bologna and mustard sandwich. Red wagged his tail. Uncle Henry offered us a piece. I refused; Red whined.

"I didn't know you had a working dog here," I said, putting Red down so I could show Uncle Henry the posters. "What does it do?"

"The dog? He's our drug sniffer."

I looked out the window. Susan and the cop were sharing the bench. The dog was fast asleep on the grass at their feet. "The shepherd reminds me of one of my mother's rescue dogs. Hers had a chewed ear too."

"Yeah, she gave him to us. Want a soda? Root beer's the only kind we've got left."

"No, thanks." I kept watching out the window, more to see how close Susan was sitting to the young cop than to see what the dog was doing. "I didn't think Mom ever trained a dog to smell out drugs."

Uncle Henry took a bite of his sandwich and shrugged. "She didn't. She didn't teach Ranger to sniff out bombs or track felons either, but he does them, too."

"One dog can do all that?"

Uncle Henry shrugged again. "No, but Big Eddie can." He jerked a thumb toward where I was staring and took a long drink from his soda can.

I took a better look while the chief burped. There was nothing big about Eddie . . . except his unfortunate nose. "Oh."

"Yeah, but try to explain that to the big shots in Riverhead. It's easier to let them think we have a whole squad of trained dogs. The only problem with Big Eddie is you can't overload him with smells. Which means he can't take duty at the drunk tank, disinfected or not. He can't ride patrol with Baitfish Barry, can't be near Ranger after the old boy's been out in the rain."

He wouldn't be good near Little Red either, if Uncle Henry kept slipping the Pomeranian pieces of bologna.

"Then again," the chief went on, "we don't have a lot of drug runners, bomb scares, or escaped convicts."

"Do you think Big Eddie could find a horse?"

"Sure, but you'd be surprised how many horses are out here. Can't hurt to send him and Ranger out in a squad car except I need them in town at night. We've been getting hit hard these days. Every kind of violence, too. No murders yet, but the Danvers thing was a close call. I've got to tell you, Willy, I'm worried."

He looked it, his clothes more rumpled than usual, his deep-set brown eyes heavily shadowed.

"Me, too. But I'm working on it." I put two of the posters near the second half of his sandwich.

He studied the reward poster, then the plastic-coated one of the three mares and frolicking colt.

"You're good, Willy."

I started to thank him, until he said, "Maybe too good."

"What do you mean?"

He couldn't look me in the eye but took another swig of his soda. "People are beginning to worry that it's you, your drawings, that are calling this stuff to Paumanok Harbor. Like that troll we never saw except the damage the thing caused and now the horses and the nightmares. We all heard Agent Grant call you a Visualizer."

"But I never called anything to me! Nothing from my earlier books ever showed up. Not the sea dragon or the replicants or the feral child. And I never thought about having a young horse captured and kept from its family."

"Then how come you dreamed about it?"

"I wish I knew. And I swear I've been wondering about that a lot myself. The best I can come up with is that I'm more sensitive to the appearance of the, uh, aberrations. Maybe I feel them in my subconscious, so I think they're part of the creative process, so I incorporate them in my books. I refuse to believe that I write them into existence. That is just not possible."

"I sure as hell hope not, but cops hate coincidences, you know."

I needed a sip of something after all, my mouth was suddenly so dry. Not root beer, though, unless it had vanilla ice cream floating on top. I tried to shift any blame. "Grant says there are places of great psi power in the world: Tibet, Chichén Itzá, Jerusalem, a bunch more. And Paumanok Harbor. That's why the others come here when the walls are breached. For the ambient atmosphere. My pictures are incidental."

I didn't mention that Fafhrd the troll first appeared on the streets of Manhattan. On my block. On the day I wrote about him. "I might be the Visualizer who sees the beings; I'm not their creator."

He stared at the remnants of his sandwich. "Seems you can communicate with them, even if in your dreams."

"I don't know how. It's something about the drawings, I realize, but I wasn't drawing when I had the nightmare about the colt. All I can come up with is to put my feelings into the posters, to tell everyone else to try to reach the horses with their thoughts."

He didn't look convinced. Or full. I pulled two chocolate kisses out of my pocket and put them on the desk. A peace offering. "I don't even speak their language."

He unpeeled the candy and sucked on it for a while before saying: "We'd need Agent Grant for that, I guess."

And I guessed Uncle Henry—and the rest of the town—was blaming me for the special agent's absence. "He's trying to find us a horse whisperer, someone who can reach into a horse's mind without words. My mother said she'll ask her friends about someone like that, too."

"We need more help, sooner. A couple more nights of no sleep and bad dreams and this place will be the O.K. Corral. Or Saturday Night Smackdown. I don't have the manpower to control the whole town, can't even trust my own men not to go postal on me. And I hate to call in the county sheriff's office or the state troopers. No one wants a bunch of reporters coming to town either, sniffing out a hot story."

"Lord, no." Paumanok Harbor was a well-guarded secret. I hadn't known about its powers or inherited aptitudes until this year, even though I'd spent a lot of summers in the place. I used to figure the locals were just oddball quacks and charlatans, teasing kids with parlor tricks. Now I knew better. If anyone outside learned about it, the Harbor would be overrun with gawkers and paparazzi from the tabloids, or scientists wanting to study us like lab rats, or fanatics trying to wipe us out as spawn of the devil.

"I'll try harder, Uncle Henry. Susan and I will go out to hang the posters if you show me on a map where the mares have been spotted. Then tonight"—I shuddered at the thought—"I'll try to dream about the colt again, see if I can figure out where he's being kept."

"You need help."

"Maybe you could lend us Big Eddie for the afternoon. If you know of anyone else who wants to hang posters or go thinking happy thoughts in the woods I'll leave some posters here."

"I was thinking of Doc Lassiter."

That hurt. "You think I'm crazy, too? Everyone keeps telling me I need a shrink. Now you say people in town believe I'm nuts enough to bring this disaster into the neighborhood." I got up from my seat so fast I almost knocked the rickety wooden chair right over. "I am not crazy!"

"Don't go getting your knickers in a knot, missy. Everyone agrees you're the best thing we've got going. They all know you'll try your damnedest to save the colt and the town."

"You tell them that I am perfectly sane. As sane as old Ellen Grissom who talks to her husband, who's been dead since I can remember."

He held up one hand, with the last chocolate kiss in it. My peace offering, back. "Hold on, Willy. No one's saying you're insane, just that Doc can help if we can get him to come back. When he studied at Royce, they said he was the best empath anyone ever saw. He specialized in trauma because he's a miracle worker with distressed folks. They sent him to 9-11 and to New Orleans after the hurricane. Not for the victims, but for the rescuers, so they didn't lose hope."

"You mean he could keep the townsfolk from killing each other while we find the colt? Who knows? Maybe he can calm the mares, too. It's worth a try."

"That's what we've been trying to tell you. Go see him."

I had his number, somewhere. "He lives here?"

"He used to, except when he was sent out on emergencies. But he moved to Shelter Island after his wife died. His grief was tearing everyone apart, everyone who was sensitive to such things anyway. The tourists and outsiders never noticed a thing. One loner hung himself that winter. We didn't find him for weeks. That's when Doc left, to save the rest of us."

"You think it's wise to bring him in?"

"That was over fifteen years ago. Time cures a lot of hurts."

I was hoping to forget about Grant in time, so I understood. "I'll call and see what he has to say."

"Don't just call on the phone. You go see him in person. Then you'll understand why everyone wants you to work with him."

"Okay, okay. I'll call tomorrow."

"Call him today. We can't take too many more night-mares. Oh, and that pair of sunglasses you can't find? They're in the refrigerator. Throw out the milk you left on the counter."

But I wasn't crazy.

I didn't know how I was going to get through the night myself. Going to sleep trying to have a nightmare didn't sound like anything a sane person would try. Maybe Doctor Lassiter could give me a hint.

First we had to hang the second batch of posters. The chief lent us a staple gun, a map, and Big Eddie. I wasn't sure how much use Big Eddie'd be; with him so close to my cousin, all he'd smell was her perfume.

Ranger loped along with his head down. He could have been looking for truffles for all the good he did. Little Red nipped at his heels until I tucked the Pom into the papoose thing I'd made from an old shawl.

We hung posters everywhere off the main streets, along deer tracks and marked trails and even a few bri-dle paths Big Eddie said were recently ridden. I didn't need him or his nose for that, not after stepping in a pile of manure. None of us had any idea if the wayward horses pooped. Or ate. Or even smelled like our horses. Disappearing night creatures from another world did not follow the usual rules of nature.

They wouldn't be out in the daytime, we knew, but they might be somewhere they could hear us or pick up our thoughts. We kicked around every theory, and ended up singing every song or reciting every poem we could remember that had a horse in it.

". . . And called it macaroni."

"Ride a cocked horse to Danbury Cross . . ."

"Home, home on the range."

The Stones' "Wild Horses." "A Horse With No Name."

We couldn't remember all the words to the one where the girl and a horse named Wildfire die on a mountain, but we agreed that was a bad message to pass along.

U2's "Who's Gonna Ride your Wild Horses."

We made up the words when we couldn't remember them, or ad-libbed better choruses. Big Eddie knew most of the lyrics to "Beer for my Horses" and "Save a Horse, Ride a Cowboy," which had us all laughing, which might have done more to ease the mares' minds than my posters or whatever supportive, affirmative thoughts we tried to project onto them. I did my best to block out my own terror of falling into the abyss of a frightened colt's fears, filling my head instead with my hopes of finding him, of returning him to his mother and aunts.

The back trails seemed peaceful, with birdsong and wildflowers in bloom. How could we not be optimistic about finding the colt?

We finished down by Rick's boatyard and got servings of fried clams in cardboard buckets from the snack bar there, along with French fries and milk shakes, which were enough to give anyone nightmares later.

Then Susan had to go to work, and Big Eddie went on duty in town.

I went home and played with the big dogs, left a message on Doctor Lassiter's machine asking for an appointment, then called my parents.

Dad was still worried about alligators and caves. And lightning. Yeah, like I hadn't been afraid of electric storms my whole life, and more so now after a lightning bolt landed three feet away from me when we rescued the kidnapped boy, Nicky.

Mom thought she had a horse expert for me. Before I got his name and number, she hung up. Something about call waiting from a greyhound adoption agency.

I thought about calling Grant, but he'd be busy. And it was the middle of the night in England. Who knew what time zone he'd be in next? He wasn't going to be much help, wherever he was, so I decided it was better not to bother. More mature, more self-reliant. More scary.

My girlfriends in the city couldn't possibly understand what was going on here. How could I explain what I didn't understand? So I didn't call them either.

There was nothing worth watching on TV, so I could try to work, or try to catch up on sleep.

I flipped through the notes I'd made, but got no further than the handicapped kid looking for a magical flying horse.

I asked myself if I should try to stay awake and avoid the nightmare, or try to sleep, directing my dreams as much as possible? All the crap I'd eaten today was no help, the caffeine fighting with the grease and the sugar. Red was snoring. The big dogs downstairs click-clacking across the kitchen tiles. Crickets and frogs chirping outside my window. I'd never get to sleep any—

I woke up in a panic when the sun hit my eyes. I hadn't dreamed at all, not that I could remember. Did that mean the colt wasn't so scared now that he knew we were searching for him? Or his mama had found him?

Or did it mean he was dead?

CHAPTER 10

THE MARES HAD NOT GONE, nor had the nightmares, although Uncle Henry said there was less violence last night. The single bar fight with cue sticks might have happened anyway, since the Smith brothers were always going at it. There was also one nuisance call, from my grandmother. Not that Eve Garland could ever be a nuisance, of course.

I called her, knowing she was always up early. Every day except this morning.

Crankier than ever, she snapped at me when I asked if she'd seen the mares.

"Seen them? Heard them, dreamed them. They were right here, in my tomato plot, trampling whole rows of plants."

"That was the dream?"

"That was my summer crop!"

"But your fields are all fenced in." With high wires against the deer, and electrified against anyone who thought they could help themselves to Grandma's heirloom tomatoes.

"What does a fence matter to a creature who can appear out of the blue, then disappear only to show up miles away?"

"But you saw them, and they made noise?" I was envious, and eager to know more about the troublesome beasts. "Did they leave droppings? Eat the plants?"

"Get rid of them, damn it. And go fetch Doc Lassiter. He's expecting you. He'll need a place to stay, but between your sloppy housekeeping, the slobbery dogs, and your sex-crazed cousin, the poor man wouldn't have a moment's peace over there. I've made up a guest room for him. It's only right since I've known him forever. His wife and I were good friends."

Susan hadn't come home last night. I doubted she and Big Eddie were still singing horse songs out in the woods, but maybe that's why the mares were so close to our house, why only Grandma seemed affected. Not that I'd noticed much difference in her sour attitude.

Damn, they were so close, and I'd never known it. Despite everything, I wanted to catch a glimpse of the once-in-a-millennium myths. Maybe some of Grant's adventurous spirit had actually rubbed off on me. Or maybe I'd finally had a good night's sleep. Today, I was jealous of my grandmother and her squashed tomatoes. I got the headaches, not the high.

And now I was the chauffeur for a doddering old friend of my grandmother's, the guest Bud's wife Claire had told her to expect. If everyone knew he was coming, why didn't they just say so, instead of making me call him? This place could drive anyone nuts.

I had a great deal to accomplish today, but I stopped regretting the wasted time as soon as I left Paumanok Harbor. Just over the railroad bridge toward Amagansett, I felt the shadows in my mind start to melt away. Little Red relaxed enough next to me to curl up and go to sleep, once I assured him we were not on the way to the vet.

During the long drive, I let my new book spin around in my head until I knew where it was going at last. Then I considered the colt.

He couldn't be dead without the mares knowing. There was no logic to my certainty, but it felt right. They'd be more emotional, projecting more horror, not less. A few trampled tomatoes weren't revenge or a cry for assistance. I wondered if they were coming toward my house after they'd seen the posters and knew I was trying to help.

Not that I'd be much help today, on taxi duty. I'd be more effective fielding phone calls about the reward. Or I could be scouring the countryside for hidden barns. There were no caves in the whole East End; I'd checked. Or I could walk Big Eddie through Grandma's farm and see if he could pick up a scent if the mares left one.

Instead, Little Red and I were stuck behind a beat-up pickup filled with rakes and shovels and lawn mowers, on a two-lane road, in a no-passing zone. The whole drive should take about an hour and a half, one way, if there was no traffic and the ferry wasn't full. Landscapers and pool guys and garbage haulers added fifteen minutes at least.

Shelter Island was so close you could almost touch it on a clear day. And so far away you had to drive through three towns, a couple of dicey roundabouts where no one knew who had the right of way, and then take a ferry. It was a real island, with no bridges, only ten- to twenty-car ferries that ran on their own schedule. You drove and drove on a long stretch outside of Sag Harbor, then you found yourself on a line on a hill, watching one ferry leave and another come across the water to take its place. If too many big trucks were on the line ahead of you, you might have to wait for a couple of boats to dock and unload their cars and foot passengers.

Walt Whitman called Long Island by its Indian name, great fish-shaped Paumanok. The fish's split tail was made by the Island's north and south forks that divided in Riverhead. Poor Walt wouldn't recognize either one of them, though. Shelter Island sat right between the forked tail, separating Peconic Bay from Gardiner's Bay. If you drove across Shelter Island, you could take another small ferry to Greenport, at the end of the North Fork. From there, you could drive to Orient Point and catch a much bigger ferry that went to New London and the Indian casinos in Connecticut. You could gamble your life savings away without having to drive forty-some miles west from Paumanok Harbor to Riverhead, then thirty-some miles back out east on narrower North Fork roads through Mattituck, Southold, and Cutchogue. At least Route 25 took you through gorgeous farm country, vineyards, horse paddocks and potato fields, where nearly every house had a lush garden or a farm stand.

The long ride to the ferry made me wish for a convertible. It was one of those summer days that explained why so many tourists flocked to the Hamptons, away from the stifling cities. The weather was warm but not hot, with a lovely breeze of refreshingly clean air. T-shirt weather, with a hoodie in case.

I didn't have to wait long for a ferry today, maybe because it was early morning. The boat ride took less than fifteen minutes of sheer postcard heaven, with sailboats, egrets, blue waves in ripples. The saltwater scent and the slight rocking reminded you that you were on the water, a different world.

The ferry unloads onto Route 114, which sounds wide and important, but is wiggly and barely wide enough for a Hummer. I drove past old houses with gingerbread trim, huge mansions overlooking the bay, past the entrances to private beaches and private roads, then past a vast public nature preserve that had umpteen ticks per square inch. Deer carried the ticks; the ticks carried diseases. The whole region was inundated with both, contributing to vociferous arguments over hunting, spraying, deer contraceptives. So far, the deer and the ticks were winning.

I shoved Red over so I could find the directions to the doctor's house. No GPS in Mom's car. Right at the third Private Road sign, left at the second dirt driveway. The driveway seemed to go on for more miles than Shelter Island had, before I reached a gate with a speaker microphone on a cement post. I pushed the button.

"Yes?"

"This is Willow Tate, come to see Dr. Lassiter. Eve Garland said he was expecting me."

"Of course, and how wonderful to meet Eve's granddaughter at last. Thank you for coming so far, Miss Tate. Please drive through."

The gates swung open onto fields of wild daisies,

black-eyed Susans, and sunflowers. My grandma would approve.

The doctor's voice was deep, not all quavery like an old man's, and his welcome seemed genuine. "Maybe this won't be as bad as I thought," I told Little Red, who was trying to hop up to see out the window, not easy for a short dog with three legs.

Self-encouragement aside, my hands still felt clammy when I got out of the car, so I wiped them on my shorts, only to notice too late that the shrink was watching from his front porch.

The porch wrapped around a modest house that over-looked a pond. Tranquil was the word that entered my mind. No street noises, no traffic, no busybody neighbors. The doctor came down from the porch to meet me. He was about my grandmother's age, I guessed, late seventies, but seemed healthy except for the cane in his hand. He had silver hair, light blue eyes that twinkled behind gold-rimmed glasses, and a wide smile. He wore khakis and a tan polo shirt with an Izod alligator embroidered on the chest. Uh-oh. Not for the first time I wished my father's premonitions were a tad more specific.

I couldn't see the danger in this kindly seeming gentleman. Everyone trusted him. Everyone said he could help. It was my mother who always told me to judge a man by how he treated a dog, so I asked if it was okay for me to bring Red inside. Doctor Lassiter said, "Of course," and instantly went to fill a small bowl with water. He got extra points for asking Red if he'd like an ice cube in his drink.

I followed him farther into the window-filled house to a comfortable living area with leather sofas, and a tray of iced tea and ladyfingers waiting on a coffee table.

He waited for me to sit, then took the seat opposite. I couldn't help myself: He was a shrink, therefore I was nervous. My hand even trembled when I poured both of us glasses of the mint tea.

"It's sad, isn't it," he said, "how we cannot trust each other these days? Sometimes I wish we could see into each other's minds and know what we're thinking. We

can't, of course, although I suppose somewhere in Paumanok Harbor someone can."

I liked his voice, the reassuring way he smiled at me,
as if he were genuinely happy to be meeting me. As if
my nervousness was nothing out of the ordinary.

I ate a ladyfinger while he asked me about some of
his old friends. He kept in touch with a few, but had lost
track of others. Then we talked about my books, which
he thought was a great accomplishment. Three ladyfingers later, with a morsel to Little Red, we got to the
trouble in Paumanok Harbor. Doc—we were already on
familiar terms—had heard some of the problem, but he
wanted to hear my version, because I was closest to the
center. He nodded and made encouraging noises and
*tsk*ed when I told him about the Danvers incident and
the cue sticks.

He loved my idea about putting up the posters in-
fused with good intentions. "I bet it's working already."

"I think it might be, but it's a temporary Band-Aid at
best. We have to find the young horse."

"The one you dreamed about?"

"I dreamed I *was* him."

"The night horses are strong projectors."

"Especially of their distress." I confessed about
my fears and my worries that I couldn't help the colt,
couldn't help the town. "Somehow they made me responsible. I don't know if I am or not, but they all think
I can fix it."

"I know you can, or you wouldn't have come to me.
You need help with the people, so you can concentrate
on the horses."

"Exactly."

"It's a big burden."

"Huge."

"And getting lost in the colt's nightmare is terrifying,
while the people you count on for support aren't there
for you."

I sighed. "You are very understanding."

"And you are just what Paumanok Harbor needs."
He took my hand, and I could feel his approval and his

caring seep right through me. "You have the power and the strength, Willow Tate, and I am so pleased I got to meet you."

Damn, he was good. A touch and a smile, and I felt stronger and braver and not so alone. Hell, I was in love. I'd found what I hadn't known I was missing all these years: a godfather. Not a Don Corleone, ruthless mob boss, but a benevolent elder statesman with plenty of ruth. He was honest, and honestly pleased to be my friend. I felt like a kid whose grandfather handed out silver dollars for no reason other than affection and approval.

Doctor Lassiter was my own shiny silver dollar.

On the way back to the Harbor, he even taught me another horse song. An absurd ditty about a horse, of course, named Mr. Ed. I told him about Big Eddie and sang him "Wild Horses," off-key. We laughed and sang and pointed out pretty vistas, a special fish-shaped mailbox, a classic turquoise T-bird. Doc was happy to be going back to Paumanok Harbor; Red was happy on his lap so he could see out; I was happy I had someone on my side.

Doc explained that he used to visit his old friends until a stroke left his right leg weak, so he couldn't trust his driving. He was looking forward to seeing my grandmother again. "Is she still as good a cook?"

"Better, but wait until you taste my cousin Susan's cooking. She uses some of Grandma's recipes and a lot of her fresh ingredients."

"And a few incantations, too?"

We laughed again about Grandma's supposed sorcery, then I tried to bring him up to date on births and weddings and divorces, who moved away, whose children accepted the Royce Institute's free college tuition in England.

Doc knew Grant's father. All he said was that the earl was a true gentleman who handled his responsibilities well. His son, Doc heard, was just as fine a man. I didn't say anything.

When we reached Paumanok Harbor and drove

down Main Street, you'd think the circus had come to town. Everyone wanted to greet Doc, welcome him home, beg him to move back here, shake his hand. That was it, I realized. Not his caring, his sensitivity and understanding and good humor. His touch was the secret. That was why I couldn't just call him on the phone.

So many people filled the street, I had to pull over and park. Soon a whole crowd surrounded the Outback, everyone wanting a hug, a handshake, one of his big grins.

Which was fine for the town, but Doc looked weary. He wasn't a young man, and he wasn't used to the commotion. I made some excuse about having to get him to my grandmother's before she called out the cops. Someone asked if he could come back downtown later, and someone else suggested a block party on the commons. The volunteer firemen shouted that they'd make hot dogs. The deli had a freezer full of ice cream. Three high school kids offered to set up a sound system so that the school jazz band could play. Two people had fireworks left over from the Fourth of July, but don't tell the chief. Everyone else was to bring a six-pack, a salad, a batch of brownies.

Doc was touched. He took his glasses off to wipe his eyes. "Oh, it's so good to be here among friends, isn't it?"

It was. I smiled. My new godfather had a mob of his own.

CHAPTER 11

G RANDMA EVE GAVE DOC THE WARMEST
welcome of all, and he gave her the brightest
smile. I wondered how good friends they were, or could
be later. How about that, me matchmaking for the old
witch now? It seemed natural, since Doc had to be a
wizard to lift that pall of woe from everyone in town
with just a handshake.

I left them to check my phone messages at Mom's
house.

Dad left a new alert: a banker. Cave, alligator, banker.
Two were impossible, one unlikely knowing Mr. Whitside at the bank. Dad's message said nothing about
more horses unless you consider his comment about my
mother: "I wish the old nag would go home already."

The second message asked how much of a reward
was being offered. It was odd 'cause I'd left my cell
phone number on the posters, not my mother's, but I
guess the word was out about me. I didn't recognize the
male voice, and the return number was a cell phone, no
caller ID. I couldn't call back, but I could curse.

My editor wanted to know how soon before I had
cover art for my new book for him to work with. Someone else wanted to sell my mother a new cable TV plan.
A Police Benevolent Society I never heard of wanted a
donation, via credit card over the phone. Right.

Grant's message was garbled. He was at an airport,

found help, we'd talk soon. Yeah, if he didn't freeze to death on a mountain peak.

That was it. No miracle message saying someone found a pony trapped in their old outhouse, come and get him. No report of a neighbor suddenly getting a hay delivery. I tried to convince myself that it was early days yet, but I knew it was early for the posters, not for the colt.

I called Susan on her cell to let her know about the party. She'd already heard and was cooking up vats of clam chowder to bring. Her uncle decided to close the Breakaway Restaurant for the night because no one was going to pay for dinner when they could get it free on the commons. I congratulated myself on not asking Susan where she'd spent the night, or the morning, just said I'd see her later.

I took the big dogs for a walk, Little Red for a carry. He'd have to stay by himself at the house later. He'd be overwhelmed and underfoot at the block party, which was dangerous for him and everybody else's ankles.

Then I made some refrigerator slice-and-bake chocolate chip cookies to bring. I only ate five of them, testing for quality. They were so good I kept half a dozen before wrapping the rest for the party.

I showered, put on my favorite flowery sundress and strappy heeled sandals. I even blow-dried my hair. Funny to be dressing for a man old enough to be my grandfather, but I sure as hell didn't put on mascara for Baitfish Barry.

Grandma and Doc were going in her car so they could leave early. Even if the party was in Doc's honor, he wasn't strong enough for a long night's celebrating. From the militant look in Grandma's eyes, I figured she'd have him back in fighting shape before he left. I didn't think he'd mind some home cooking and coddling. I followed in Mom's Outback, and ate two more cookies.

The town square was already crowded when we got there. Plank tables lined one end, quickly filling with potluck offerings. The fire department had two big grills going, and Susan was ladling out chowder. People carried blankets and babies, and I set up the beach chairs I'd brought for Grandma and Doc. Pretty soon two lines formed, one for the food, the other to greet Doc, like excited children waiting to talk to Santa. Even people who'd seen him earlier wanted to shake his hand, introduce him to their kids, tell him how happy they were to see him.

They were happier when they went back to their blankets and beer.

I was too full of cookies to eat much.

Some of "them"—as in "us vs. them," Paumanok Harbor residents who didn't have the Paumanok Harbor propensities—looked a little confused at all the hubbub over a retired shrink. They enjoyed the music and the small town camaraderie anyway. Dante and Louisa Rivera waved to me as they herded their children back toward the parking lots, some of the first to leave. The grocery store owners were noticeably absent. They hadn't sent any food either. And they wondered why the locals shopped elsewhere whenever they could.

When the sun lowered, volunteers started to pack up the leftover food, fill the trash bags, and fold the tables. Despite the feeling of well-being, no one much wanted to be on the road after dark. No one wanted to chance seeing the mares. Besides, Uncle Henry had confiscated the fireworks before some idiot blew off his fingers or set the downtown on fire, so there was no reason to linger. Doc was yawning.

The noise level was still high for the cleanup and the good-byes, with a few latecomers still shaking his hand. The high school jazz band had been replaced by a loud rock trio that played for local weddings and cocktail parties. They'd go on as long as anyone was listening.

The music stopped mid-note. The chatter stopped. The cursing from the firemen's truck stopped. Even the whining from kids who didn't want to leave stopped. Everyone turned to stare up the street, where a man on a white horse rode toward the commons.

"It's one of them," a woman cried, turning her head into her husband's chest.

"Nah, the mares wouldn't let anyone put a saddle on them."

"Maybe he got lost on his way to the dude ranch at Montauk."

"Maybe it's the horse whisperer we need."

"Maybe I've died and gone to heaven," Susan said from beside me as we watched the horse and rider come closer.

Elegant white high-stepping horse, effortless straight-backed rider, orange-and-pink setting sun. Magnificent, and the horse and the sun were nice, too.

Another horse and rider came out of the shadows behind the first pair. This horse was brown and white. A pinto? A paint? I wasn't up on horse jargon. The second rider was smaller, hatless, with dark hair in a braid down his shoulder, tied with a rawhide thong and a feather. He kept his distance from the grass commons while the first man dismounted at the edge and led his horse forward.

The idiots from the party band swung into "Mamas, Don't Let Your Babies Grow Up to Be Cowboys" while the obvious head honcho strode forward. He took long steps, but with an almost bow-legged stride.

"Now that's a real cowboy," someone near me said. "You can tell he's spent his life on a horse."

A woman answered: "Either that or he's got more between his legs than you've got between your ears."

The laughter was a little subdued. We all knew this guy was special, and we all knew we needed him.

Then one of the local studs said he thought that walk looked gay.

"Trust me," Micky from the fire department said with a sigh of regret, "that dude's not gay."

With the cowboy's hat shielding his face and the dying light, it was hard to judge his age or his coloring or his looks, only his height—impressive—and his build—kind of lanky but solid. He wore a cream-colored Stetson, a faded blue chambray shirt and jeans tucked into high cowboy boots. Mostly what he wore was confidence, mixed, I thought, with a little arrogance. Or maybe that was my jealousy talking; I could never have sauntered

so calmly into a crowd of staring strangers, not even with
a prancing horse at my side.

When he got nearer, Susan started singing Big Eddie's song about saving a horse, riding a cowboy. "Hush,"
I snapped at her. "He's old enough to be your father."

"So?"

This close, I saw the weather and the years etched on
his face. He was about forty, I guessed. A crooked nose
kept him from being handsome, though he did have a
firm chin, high cheekbones, and not an ounce of extra
flesh that I could see.

"Your father never looked like that," Susan's mother
said.

Grandma murmured, "Oh, my," and Reverend
Shankman's wife added, "Amen to that."

The cowboy headed straight for me. I looked to either
side to be certain he wasn't looking for Uncle Henry, but
the police chief wasn't that close.

The crowd parted. They might have disappeared, for
all I knew. I didn't notice when the band stopped playing. I watched the man. He watched me, then stopped
and touched the brim of his hat.

"I reckon you're Miss Willow Tate, ma'am. I'm Tyler
Farraday. Folks call me Ty." He jerked a thumb back
toward the other rider. "That's Connor Redstone, the
Condor."

The Condor? The younger man nodded his head
from the pinto's back, still keeping his distance. I nodded back.

Mr. Farraday reclaimed my attention. "His lordship
sent us to y'all."

"Grant?"

"Brit with a poker up his—" He looked over my
shoulder to Grandma Eve. "Sorry, ma'am." He turned
his attention back to me. "With English reserve, I reckon
you call it."

"You know Grant? Lord Grantham, that is?"

"We shared some classes a few years back." He didn't
sound as if they shared a friendship. But I should have
known there was a Royce Institute connection. Or the

Department of Unexplained Events. I didn't think I should ask which or what classes he'd taken, not in front of half the village. "Well, thank you for coming, Mr., ah, Farraday."

"My pleasure, ma'am. His nibs said if I wanted to see some rare magic I had to haul my ass—sorry, ma'am—that is, hightail it north."

"The white night ma—" I started.

"Then he said that if I laid a hand on her, he'd have my guts for guitar strings."

Me? Rare magic? Thank goodness the light was fading so the stranger couldn't see me blush. He smiled as if he knew I was rattled, though. The smile started at one corner of his mouth and then widened, showing even white teeth. I heard Susan sigh.

Grandma, of all people, announced, "Agent Grant has no claim on my granddaughter. Not since yesterday, anyway."

"Oh, I wasn't worried, ma'am. The jackass's threats just added to the challenge. A cowboy never backs down from a dare."

Had I become invisible while Farraday planned my seduction and Grandma planned my wedding? I cleared my throat. "Mr. Farraday, I'd like to introduce you to my grandmother, Eve Garland."

He tipped his hat. "I've heard of your skills, ma'am."

"Our guest, Doctor Lassiter."

"Glad to meet you, sir. I've heard a great deal about you also. All good."

Doc and Grandma both looked pleased . . . because some dusty old cowboy had heard of them?

I quickly pointed to my aunt, uncle, cousin, and Chief Henry, who'd joined us. "You can meet everyone else tomorrow."

After nodding to acknowledge my introductions, Farraday turned to his horse, whose reins he held loosely in one hand. "This is Paloma Blanca, the White Dove. Bow to the lady, Pal."

The horse bent one foreleg and leaned forward, muscles gleaming and moving smoothly until her head nearly touched the grass, the long white mane flowing over her shoulder.

A little girl—Janie's niece Ronnie, I thought—clapped. The band's drummer played a fanfare.

"Where did you say you came from, Mr. Farraday?" Uncle Henry asked. "You got here awfully fast."

"We were performing in Atlantic City." He looked at me. "Trick riding."

My heart sank. A rhinestone cowboy, just what we needed.

"Can we see?" Ronnie begged.

"Not tonight, sweet pea. Pal's tired and we still have to find our bunks."

Before I could send him to one of the stables in Montauk—or back to Atlantic City—he said arrangements had been made for them to stay at a place called Rosehill. The Royce Institute, on Grant's recommendation, had bought the Paumanok Harbor estate as a conference center and outreach extension for the university. The renovations hadn't been done yet or any bureaucrats moved in, waiting on permits that Martha at the real estate office was working on, so there was plenty of space. My mother's widowed cousin Lily was housekeeper there and acting as caretaker. I could only imagine what care she'd take of the snake-oil salesman.

"There's no stable or paddock at Rosehill, or whatever you call a place to put a horse."

"There will be by morning, along with whatever supplies we need. His Highness runs an efficient organization, and I already spoke to Miss Lily about having Agway deliver. Paloma Blanca and Lady Sparrow can bed down in the horse trailer tonight. They're used to sleeping there. Con and I'll be happy for hot showers and cool sheets."

"I'll show you the way," Susan offered.

"No need, miss. Pal knows the way." He smiled at little Ronnie's awed expression. "And I have a GPS."

Susan wasn't giving up. "It's early still. Maybe I'll ask the Condor if he'd like to go out later, see the sights, such as they are."

I didn't know if Connor Redstone was partner, friend, or hired help, but his nickname sounded like he was part of the act. I could imagine Grandma's reaction to Susan's hooking up with a fly-by-night circus performer or rodeo clown.

"I'm certain Mr. Redstone must be tired, too," I tried.

Ty looked back at the other man, now half hidden by shadows. "Darlin'," he said to me, "Connor's twenty-three. Boys that age are never tired." Then he told Susan she could ask, but Con wasn't much for talking or for crowds.

She winked at him. "That just makes it more of a challenge. We Paumanok Harbor girls don't back down from a dare either."

She sidestepped the big white horse and headed toward where Connor Redstone sat slouched in his dappled horse's saddle, like a Remington painting of an early Native American.

"We need to talk, Mr. Farraday."

"Of course we do, darlin'. But I need to tend the horses first."

I appreciated that he gave his animals precedence. My mother would approve. My mother would *not* approve of my offering to go to Rosehill with the cowboy and his horses. Then again, maybe she would. "We need to make plans."

He gave me one of those smiles again, as slow as his drawl, which I suspected was as fake as his ability to read a horse's mind. "I already have plans, darlin'."

I didn't want my grandmother to hear me tell the pseudo cowpoke where to poke his plans, so I tried to show my annoyance with a set-down stare.

He took another step closer, took off his hat and stared right back. His eyes were green, and insolent and knowing all at once. He rudely looked me up and down, undressing me with those devil's eyes.

So I did a rude appraisal, too, up and down.

He had longish fair hair with sun streaks, and wasn't quite as old as I'd thought. His shirt had frayed edges at the collar. His belt buckle was as big as his ego, and his jeans were tight in all the right places. His cowboy boots were soft and well worn and . . . and made out of alligator skin.

Thanks for the warning, Dad. I already figured Ty Farraday was trouble.

CHAPTER 12

I'D NEVER MET A REAL COWBOY BEFORE. It's not like they were littering the sidewalks of Manhattan or riding the Jitney out to the Hamptons. This one was right out of one of those books Mrs. Terwilliger had given me. Larger than life, ready to stake his claim, lead the posse, round up dogies—or dance hall girls. I didn't think he was serious enough to be any help in our crisis. His horse might be well trained and perfectly disciplined. Tyler Farraday sure as hell wasn't.

"I don't know if you understand the gravity of our situation."

"I got an earful from London, then a pile of emails while we drove."

"Yes, but we mostly need help at night. This night."

He looked around at the people drifting away from the commons, calling out cheerful good-byes.

"Your townsfolk don't appear hostile or running loco, like I was expecting. I reckoned we'd have to pour some tranquilizer in the local water."

"Half the town drinks well water. But you wouldn't drug—" I realized he was laughing at me. I also realized he thought I'd pushed a panic button for no good reason. "The calm you see is thanks to Doc Lassiter, whatever he does. It can't last forever, not when the white mares are galloping through the town tonight. Or through my front yard."

He dropped the horse's reins—Paloma Blanca stood like a statue—and came closer still until we were almost toe to toe. "Darlin'," he whispered, "I wouldn't be much good to you tonight."

Oh, hell, he thought *I* was coming on to *him*, inviting him to spend the night. I stepped back and looked around to see if anyone had heard. Uncle Henry was saying good night to Grandma and Doc. Susan had flounced back from an obviously failed mission to capture the Condor, exchanged not so friendly words with her parents, then went to help load up the restaurant supplies. Everyone else was drifting away. "Stop that."

"Stop what?"

"You know, the flirting and the innuendoes. You weren't sent here to start an affair."

"I wasn't?" He stopped smiling. "Lady, no one sends me anywhere, not even your pretty boy Brit. I quit his organization years ago, and I don't take orders from anyone. Understand? I come and go when I want, or when I think I can help an animal or a person who needs it, or just for the hell of going somewhere new, seeing something different. Or when there's a big enough prize offered."

That bothered me even more than his independence. I knew he'd be hard to manage from the first "darlin'," not that someone had to bribe him to come. Money changed people's loyalties, made their motives suspect. "They're paying you, like a hired gunslinger?"

"What have you been doing, watching old John Wayne westerns? I came because a friend asked, and because I wanted to. Clear on that?"

"Clear. But that's no excuse for looking at me like I'm dessert. Or flirting."

He smiled again. "Honey, I'll stop flirting as soon as I stop breathing. And you are the prettiest sight I've seen in ages. Apple pie and whipped cream, with vanilla ice cream on the side."

"And Grant's girlfriend."

He grinned. "That, too."

"His former girlfriend."

"Even better."

"Well, I don't like being called darling, Mr. Farraday. Or honey or sweet pea. It's sexist."

He held his hat to his heart in mock chagrin. "It is? In my neck of the woods, it's called being friendly."

"Just where is your neck of the woods?"

"Anywhere I hang my hat, but I have a ranch in Texas."

"I should have known from the swagger."

"Yup, that's us all right. But I was born in London. My mother got her doctorate in animal behavior at Royce."

So did my mother, but that wasn't the point. "I knew that Southern drawl was false."

"No such thing. My folks moved back to the States when I was three. I only went back to study in England for a semester. I missed my horses. And the Southern belles. Now I see I should have come north years ago."

"You're doing it again!"

"Sorry, darlin'. It's like breathing, remember."

"Well, you can forget about it, Mr. Farraday, because I'm not like Susan."

He looked over at her, where she was giggling as Big Eddie, the band's drummer, and one of the waiters at the Breakaway tripped over each other to help load her soup cauldrons. "Hell, lady, I sure am glad of that."

I wanted to kick him out of loyalty to Susan, but I *was* a lady, most times anyway. "Do you think you could at least call me by my name? Willow or Willy."

"If you stop with the mister crap."

I agreed, and he held out his hand to shake on the deal. Not that he'd agreed to stop hitting on me. Or to get to work on the Harbor's problem, for that matter. But we had to work together, I supposed, so I put my hand in his.

Oh, boy.

His hand was big and strong, which I should have expected in someone who worked with horses. But I didn't expect my own reaction.

When I touched Doc's hand, I'd felt his warmth flowing through me, over me like a soft blanket of approval and encouragement. This wasn't like that. Not at all.

Instead of giving, Ty seemed to be taking. My thoughts, my will, my determination not to trust him, not to let him play with me. I didn't think he was actually controlling my mind. First, because I'd been told no one could without my permission. And second, because he seemed as surprised as I was at the spark that flared between us—a metaphorical spark, thank goodness, or I'd go up in flames. But his simple touch made the world narrow to just the two of us, a circle inside a circle, both of us wanting to give more, to take more, to share more.

No! I wasn't over Grant yet, or sure I'd made the right decision. I did not want anything from Tex and I'd be damned if I gave him another second's thought, much less a roll in the hay. I snatched my hand away and stepped back, right into Grandma, who'd come to say good night and invite Ty to breakfast at her house in the morning, where we could figure out what to do.

Ty thanked her for the invitation, set his hat back on his head, and whistled to Paloma Blanca, who trotted to his side.

I wished him a good night and pleasant dreams. Hah! If he had an iota of psi sensitivity, not just sex appeal, he'd be ragged by morning. If he didn't have the sensitivity we needed, I'd send him off in the morning. The man was too dangerous to keep around. Like having a bobcat in your backyard. Pretty and rare, but hell on house pets.

He got in the last word: "Oh, I intend to have real pleasant dreams, darlin', of a willow who bends but doesn't break."

In this day and age, when a woman meets a man she might want to know better, she doesn't invite him home for coffee or a beer. She goes on the Internet.

Tyler Farraday had a lot of links on a basic Google search. I went to his web page first. He looked younger in the picture, but who puts up an untouched shot? He also looked gorgeous in a fancy black Western shirt showing broad shoulders, with mountains in the background. Horses ran in a fenced-in area right behind him.

His bio was short, no age, place of birth, or hometown, but full of credits. This equestrian show, that breeders' award, a handful of civic citations for work with horse rescue groups, a man of the year award from a horseman's association, more charitable organizations he supported or served on the boards.

The second page showed his ranch from an overhead shot. The place was huge, so whatever he was doing must pay well. Or maybe such an expensive operation forced him to do the flashy stuff for income.

Beneath the ranch picture were thumbnails of several horses. Clicking on the first, a pretty mare not as pretty as Paloma Blanca, led to a page about the horses he raised and trained. The second horse led to modern, hotel-worthy stables where he boarded and conditioned other owners' animals. The horse names mentioned meant nothing to me, nor did the stables they belonged to. The fact that some were Olympic champions, rodeo winners, even racehorses meant Ty Farraday was no run-of-the-mill trainer. He handled unbroken horses, troubled horses, difficult horses, and made them right.

The next thumbnail was a spotted horse like Lady Sparrow. Its click led to a herd of wild mustangs on Ty's ranch. The text explained how the rescued horses were harbored there until they were fit for private use. Becoming a backyard pony mightn't be the ideal life for a free-ranging mustang, but it was better than the usual alternative for horses on overcrowded government lands: being rounded up and slaughtered for dog meat. A picture showed children riding rescued horses. Everyone looked happy.

Back at the home page, another button connected to a YouTube video of Ty and Paloma Blanca in an arena, performing dressage movements that appeared impossible for anyone but a centaur. Ty never moved, not a hand, not a leg, nothing, not even his lips, but the horse practically flew like the dove she was named for.

I followed the link to Paloma Blanca's own website. A calendar of bookings, a contact button for her agent, a page of fan mail, her pages-long Lipizzaner bloodline.

I never knew the famous Spanish Riding School ever let their rare horses be sold out of stable. I wondered how much Ty had to pay for such an animal, or who he had to screw. No, that was unworthy of me, and him. He was obviously good with horses, exceptionally good.

Maybe he could help the night mares after all, if he started using his talents instead of his libido.

I was getting blurry-eyed by now, but I followed one more link to the Condor's home page.

This one had even less personal information. Connor Redstone was one hundred percent Native American, but with no tribe named. He'd been raised on a reservation, but not which one. He held a two-year associate degree in veterinary technology, but not from what school. Scrolling down, I saw pictures of Connor on Lady Sparrow, who was described as a cutting horse, whatever that was. I followed the web path to see them chasing a bunch of sheep and, sure enough, cutting one with a dye mark on its back away from the others.

The only other link on Connor's page went right back to Ty's website.

I'd seen enough. They were professional horsemen, all right. That made me feel a little better. I worried what Connor was hiding, and I still didn't like Ty Farraday's attitude, his casual brush-off of Paumanok Harbor's horrors. It seemed the cowboy would rather score points against Grant than exert himself with the otherworld mares.

We'd discuss the horses, and his attitude, in the morning.

I brushed chocolate chip cookie crumbs off my lap and my laptop, then took the dogs out to the fenced-in yard for their last run. The night sky was clear, strewn with stars and a nearly full moon. The temperature had dropped some, but was still comfortable, with the usual dampish breeze from the bay to frizz my hair. I looked toward Grandma's place, thinking this was a good time to spot the mares, but what would I do if I saw them? Try to convince them to go home without their young one? They'd trample me for sure. I would, if I were a distraught horse mother or aunt. I didn't even know if I could communicate with them on any level. Or if Ty Farraday could.

I kept the dogs out longer than usual. I guess I didn't want to go to bed, even if my eyes felt scratchy and I couldn't help yawning. I didn't want to sleep, even though I knew I had to try to find the colt in my dreams. I wasn't getting any help from my posters. Or my new partner. I wasn't looking forward to another bad night.

With Little Red settled on the other pillow, I climbed into bed with Louis L'Amour. I skimmed to page seventy-five without finding one woman in the book except a boardinghouse landlady. There was no heroine, no tender feelings or soul-searching, no leavening of the testosterone level. Not my cup of tea either. I turned off the light, then got up again to pull the window shades down, to keep out the moonlight. The dogs were quiet, but I checked the yard once more, just in case, before getting back in bed. No horses in Grandma's herbs. No mares in the marigolds, no equines in the—

I fell asleep trying to come up with another alliteration.

I don't know how long I slept, but suddenly I could sense the bare little room with raw wood walls and a single light bulb. There was the young girl with useless legs, slumped against the wall, a figure of utter despondency. Her hair was tangled; her face was streaked with tears. I knew she was losing hope that her family would pay the ransom for her release.

Same as last time, I was an observer in this part of the dream, watching Hetty. Last time I shifted from watching to becoming, entering the mind of the colt, until I became him in my nightmare. I knew the handicapped child would be rescued soon—I knew because I'd written it that way—so I tried to skip past her, bracing my sleeping self to suffer the anguished emotions of the terrified young animal.

Instead, I was a redhead. Still asleep, I felt myself smile at Janie's influence on my dream. Except the me in my dream had red pubic hair. Red pubic hair? Holy hell,

I was wearing leather chaps, belted low on my hips, and nothing else. Not a stitch. I looked behind me, saw too many chocolate chip cookies on my ass. I looked down, saw my breasts, not quite as perky as they used to be or as lush as I wished, but still respectable. Then I noticed that my nipples were hard.

God damn, this was not me. This was not my dream! Wide awake and panting, I leaped out of bed. I was *not* going to be the star of that man's x-rated imaginings. I might be a horse. I sure as hell wasn't going to be a hooker!

CHAPTER 13

FURIOUS, I YANKED UP THE WINDOW SHADE. There he was, looking innocent as a lamb, waiting for magic by moonlight.

At least I assumed the man in my front yard, in my deck chair, was Ty Farraday. How many tall men wearing Stetson hats would be camped on my lawn, facing across the dirt road to Garland Farms?

I was outraged, but he'd come to my house. Despite his fatigue, he'd been here, instead of staying snug and comfortable at Rosehill. For that matter, he'd given up a vastly profitable engagement in Atlantic City to ride to the rescue. On a white horse, no less.

He was still an oversexed slut of a slime toad.

I gathered fortification. Black hoodie and gray sweatpants instead of my nightshirt. Blue Croc clogs. Yankee baseball cap to keep my hair from turning into a dandelion. Nothing sexy or suggestive, nothing of me showing for that matter. Little Red on a leash. That ought to be enough protection. A blanket to sit on. The rest of the chocolate chip cookies for comfort. And the posters to prove I was there on business.

He had to have heard me clomp across my porch and down the stairs, but he didn't turn around. Two empty bottles of beer lay on their sides beside his chair, so maybe he was drunk, or sleeping.

Then I heard his chant. I couldn't understand the

words, if there were words, just the cadence and the lilt, on and on, slow, low, and steady.

I suspected he was chanting in an Indian tongue, unless he'd studied linguistics with Grant during his semester at the Royce Institute. But Grant said the Others didn't have a true written or spoken language as we knew it, depending more on telepathy and imagery.

I tried to be quieter the closer I got to him, but Little Red started growling. Ty kept chanting until I was right behind his chair, then he said, "That's the song Connor's ancestors used to call the Great Horse Spirit, to lead them to good hunting, or carry them out of danger. I figured it was worth a try."

"No one called the mares here in the first place." I wanted to make sure he knew that, that I was not responsible for the chaos they'd caused. I spread my blanket next to his chair and fed Little Red a crumb of cookie—no chocolate—to shut him up. "Did they appear?"

"They might have, if you and the guard dog here hadn't scared them away."

"Bull. If Grandma couldn't scare the night mares out of her tomatoes, Little Red isn't going to keep them away. And I think they want to see me." I handed him the posters and explained why I'd drawn what I had, how I'd tried to imbue the pictures with my own wanting to help. He nodded, despite the posters' details being barely visible by the moonlight.

He still hadn't turned to look at me but went back to watching the road. I should have been glad. I'd dressed to be unappealing, hadn't I? Instead, I was pissed at being ignored.

"Do not dream about me anymore."

That got his attention. He turned to look at me, tipping up his hat. I could see his white teeth gleaming in a grin. "Yes, ma'am. I'll try."

"And it's elms."

He peered around my yard. "I might be wrong, but I thought those were white pines and oaks."

"Yes, but it's horses in the herbs, mares in the marigolds, equines in the elms. Alliteration, you know."

"Yes, ma'am. I do know what alliteration is." He laughed, a rumble of a sound from deep in his chest. "You really do have an odd kick to your gallop, don't you, darl—"

I cleared my throat.

"Willow."

"And I won't become a redhead."

"Won't much matter, you keep wearing a baseball hat."

So he did notice. "That's not the point. You twisted my dreams. I was trying to reach the colt again, to see if he was all right or if he could lead us to where he's being held. But I couldn't. You interfered."

"What did I do, sweet Willow—that's okay, isn't it? Bound to be better'n Weeping Willow or Pussy Willow."

I grimaced at the old high school taunts. "Plain Willow is fine."

"Nothing plain about you, lady, no matter how you tried to hide it. So what happened, you dream of me?"

"Hmph. Of course not."

"But your dream was my fault?"

I could tell he was laughing at me. I kept quiet.

"Don't suppose you'd tell me what you did dream about?"

"Never." God, just the image in my head made me blush.

"A redhead, hmm? In sheer pink silk?"

Because he was smiling, because my holding him responsible really was silly, and because it was the middle of a star struck night, I muttered: "In leather chaps."

"Oh, yeah. That would've been my dream for sure. I'm not apologizing."

To change the subject, I offered him a cookie.

He held up a half-filled bottle I hadn't noticed. "Sure. Cookies go good with warm beer."

"Sorry. I might have some pretzels inside. Should I go fetch them? Or see if there's a cold bottle in the fridge?"

"No, it's too pretty a night to miss any of it."

It really was a nice night. I couldn't remember the last time I just sat out, looking for shooting stars or fireflies.

The stars shone brighter here than in Manhattan, where all the building lights blurred the sky. I suppose the wide open spaces of Texas had even better night viewing, but I think they had more bugs and bigger ones, too. They definitely had snakes. Maybe scorpions. No sitting outside on a blanket for me there. Here you could hear the sound of the incoming tide against the pebbles at the shore. You could smell the scent of wild honeysuckle in the air. Other than a couple of mosquitoes carrying West Nile virus, the biggest threat was the two-footed one sipping his last beer. You couldn't ask for a much better night.

Except for a good night's sleep, of course.

Ty must be tired, too. "Maybe you should go back to Rosehill and get some rest. I can stay out awhile longer."

"I can go back to bed in the morning after building a corral for my horses and arranging for a car rental."

I started to tell him about the Escalade that belonged to Rosehill, but then I wondered how he'd gotten here. I doubted he'd have walked so far in the dark, or brought Paloma Blanca out again.

"I carry motorbikes in the back of the horse trailer. Most times it's easier, unless you want to go sightseeing with a pretty girl. I left the scooter out by the road so as not to wake anyone here."

I appreciated the courtesy for Grandma's sake and Doc's. So I told him about the SUV—Cousin Lily had her own car—and reminded him about breakfast at my grandmother's. "So you won't be getting back to bed"—I wasn't leaving that out there—"back to sleep in the morning."

"I'll take an afternoon nap, then. I don't expect the mares to be moving around in daylight."

"They never have yet, but I thought we'd start looking for hidden barns, abandoned stables, that kind of thing. I'm worried about the colt."

He took another swallow of beer. "I've been trying to figure why the mares can't sense him. At first I thought they knew where he was, just needed help getting him loose. They wouldn't be telegraphing fear and anger, though."

I'd been wondering about that, too. "All I can think of is the light bulb left burning so he can't disappear. Maybe they need the darkness to communicate. Or there's iron bars on his cage. If the mares care one way or the other about heavy metals, like eldritch beings are supposed to."

"We don't know enough about the critters. London wasn't much help. I kind of hoped they'd tell us," Ty said.

"London?"

"The mares."

It was one thing to talk to horses; another to expect answers. I'd stick to my plan. "Either way, we've got to start looking. Paumanok Harbor isn't all that big, and I've got maps from the planning department. They should show every outbuilding and shed."

"Who says the one we need is legal? Kidnappers don't usually follow the rules by applying for the right permits."

"No, but I doubt they planned this. No one could have known the mares would show up when they did."

"That's a point. On the other hand, the bastard might have the colt stashed in a garage or a pool house like the one at Rosehill. Perfectly legal, and perfectly illegal for us to search."

"But we have to start somewhere unless someone gives us a tip." I felt foolish saying it, but I was kind of hoping to feel some connection if we got close to the colt.

"It's worth a try, I guess. Connor can ride shotgun with you tomorrow. He's sacked out now."

Which gave me the perfect opportunity to admit that I looked both of them up on Google.

"Of course you did. Only sensible thing to do."

"There's not much information about Connor, or the Condor."

He took another sip of beer and a bite of cookie, then tilted his head, considering the combination. "He likes it that way."

"It didn't even give his hometown."

"He lived on a reservation. Not much of a town to speak of."

"But what tribe? You'd think he'd be proud of his heritage."

"Not much left to be proud of. Most of the tribe got assimilated years ago. He's trying to protect what's there by keeping them out of the spotlight."

I didn't understand, and said so. Without being specific or giving away confidences, Ty explained how Connor's people were like Paumanok Harbor's.

"Weird?"

"Special. Talented. Tribal legends say one brave could hear the buffalo three days away. Another chief was said to see a rattler blink. And they could ride like the wind, most of them. So other tribes stole their women, wanting strong sons with the spirit of the Great Horse. In later days, the young men left the res to ride the range, then the rodeo circuit. They didn't come back.

"They were healers, too, medicine men. A lot of their medicine was like your granny's herbal cures, but not all. Some had to be magic. That didn't sit well with physicians with medical degrees or the Bureau of Indian Affairs. They did their usual bit of sending kids to school off the res, away from the magic and the legends. A lot of them didn't come back either. Con's great-great-grandpa was famous for it, so he took off in a traveling sideshow wagon to make his fortune."

"Did he?"

"Got shot by a white man for letting his wife bleed to death after a stillbirth."

"That's horrible!"

"Yeah, but it convinced the others to play their cards close. So they said they were healing horses, not people. They became guardians of the last wild herds. Not owners, 'cause they didn't believe in that kind of thing, but brothers to the spirit of the Great Horse. They worked miracles with the mustangs. That's how I got involved. I spent two years with them, supposedly teaching, supposedly scouting for the Royce Institute, but it took that long for me to learn the chants."

"And you took Connor away from them?"

"He was lost before I got there. His father was a

medicine man, too, only for people. The problem was, he couldn't cure anything, just see what was wrong. He drank himself to death for not having the proper magic. Connor figured he'd find the way if he could open his mind. Shrooms and Pete. Mushrooms and peyote, all in ceremonial rituals, of course."

"Of course."

"And whatever else a kid can find on the res, which was anything. His mother begged me to get him away, so I did."

"But isn't that the same as destroying his tribe?"

"The money he sends back lets them live better than they ever have. The kids have good schools, scholarship money and, most important, counselors. Reasons to stay, reasons to come back and raise their kids there. And now the people from Royce watch over and protect them, the same as the tribe still guards the plains horses."

"If Royce is involved, Connor must be—"

"Special. Like you. Sometimes his gift hurts, like yours. Like his father's."

"He's a healer?"

"No, but with training he could be a brilliant diagnostician, according to the medical people at Royce. A Red Dr. House without the cane but with the chip on his shoulder. And a history of pharmaceutical excess. Can you imagine how people would be beating his door down, overrunning his town, if they knew?"

"But shouldn't he be serving the greater good? Helping people find out what's wrong with them?"

"Broken bones and brain tumors are easy. Anyone can see them with X-rays and MRI's. Con mostly sees what can't be fixed. Not everything is curable. It would destroy him to keep telling patients they're dying, without hope. Horses, he can diagnose and cure if a remedy exists. Or put them down if there's nothing but suffering ahead. You can't do that with people."

"Whew. That's a heavy burden for a kid."

"That's why he went to vet tech school, because he couldn't stand the suffering. He refused med school or a vet degree for the same reason, though he has the brains for either. Now he sticks to himself and the horses, and rarely touches a person." Ty chuckled. "We worked one rodeo where the manager wasn't treating his animals right. We quit. Connor took our paycheck, shook the bastard's hand, and said his heart was going to explode in two days."

"Did the man die?"

"Of course. We got the rodeo shut down and left in a hurry before anyone asked too many questions."

I thought about Susan, how she never knew if the cancer was coming back. "Would he . . . ?"

He seemed to read my mind. "Look at your cousin? Miss Lily told me about her and why she acts the way she does. I think Con would jump off a cliff before touching a female like that. Don't ask. The kid's got his head together now and a good thing going. In fact, forget this whole conversation. Except the redhead part."

"You can forget that."

He reached over and petted the Pomeranian, without getting his fingers bitten, which was a miracle in itself. "With apologies to Little Red, I really like blondes better."

That was good, right?

CHAPTER 14

W E WERE BOTH QUIET FOR AWHILE, not in
an awkward silence that itched to be filled, but
a comfortable pause filled with whispery night sounds.
Then something small moved in the row of junipers near
the road. Red started barking. Ty put one hand on his
nose and murmured something. Red sat back down, his
plumed tail curled around his feet.

I was impressed. "My mother would love you."

He laughed. "Most mothers don't."

"I can imagine, but my mother is different."

"I can imagine. You're different."

With the night as a cloak of invisibility, I felt comfortable asking more personal questions. "What's yours
like? Can she talk to animals?"

"I don't know. I know she had degrees in animal
behavior, but she died a year after we returned to the
States. I was too young to understand what she did. My
father never spoke of it."

"I'm sorry." As difficult as my mother was, I couldn't
imagine growing up without her.

"There's no need to feel sorry for me. My father re-
married to a nice woman who brought me up to say
please and thank you and yes, ma'am. Her family had a
quarter horse stud. I was in heaven."

I pictured Tyler Farraday as a cute little towhead
hanging over a corral fence or slipping out of his bed

to sleep in the stable. He must have been a devil. "Were you ever married? It didn't say on your bio page." (And I didn't say I was dying of curiosity.) "Divorced? Kids?"

"No, no, and no. Gun-shy, I guess. Besides, there are too many horses, too little time. Too good a time."

I leaned back on the blanket and stared up at the stars. The vastness above us made human foibles seen trifling. "Texas tumbleweed."

"Maybe."

The night also dismantled the social barriers, so I felt freer to say what I thought. "Do you miss it . . . home, family, children?"

"I've got it all anytime I visit my folks, my ranch, or Con's family. I love to visit, love to leave. Everywhere I go there are hordes of kids, all wanting a ride on Pal. There are hordes of aunties wanting babies to spoil."

"I get that, too."

"No inclination to play house?"

"I thought I did, but I guess I didn't like the architecture."

"Grant?"

"Yeah. We came close to a fairy-tale ending, but I got cold feet."

"His nibs seems warm-blooded enough, for a Brit."

Warm-blooded? Grant was a hottie. He was so hot I had burn marks on my sheets. He was so hot I had to carry a fire extinguisher when we went to parties to douse the women who panted after him. He was the sexiest man I'd ever met . . . until this afternoon. Lust is great for an affair, though not so good for a life-long commitment, especially if you have nothing else in common. In fact, I wondered if the attraction between us wasn't more physical than anything else.

"Heat was never the problem," I said, regretting it instantly. Damn, was I discussing my sex life with a man I'd just *met* this afternoon? "I realized I like my work, my home, my independence. I'm not ready to give it up, especially to a man I'd only known for a month."

"Paumanok Harbor petunia."

I know he was getting back at me for calling him a

Texas tumbleweed, but I wasn't a clinging vine, or a fledgling afraid to leave the nest. I wasn't. I had every intention of going back to my Manhattan apartment at the end of the summer. The apartment where I'd lived most of my life. Still . . .

"That's not it. I worried that he was set up by the Royce matchmakers. He was really into their philosophy. You're not, are you?"

"What, let some Brit researcher pick me a wife?" He laughed. "No chance."

"Good. Me, neither. Besides, I worried that I couldn't write my books if I was too busy living the life Grant led. I wouldn't be the same person. Does that make sense?"

"Yes, like I feel adrift if I'm not with my horses. Your cousin showed me your books. She keeps a special shelf of them in her apartment, said you put love and laughter into every one."

"She's my mother's cousin. She has to like my books."

"Nah. I saw some reviews, lists of awards. You're good."

So he'd checked me out online, too. I was okay with that, I guess. I wish I'd gone ego surfing to see if anyone wrote anything bad he might find. God, what if someone put an old college dorm party picture up somewhere?

"She said I could borrow one any time."

"I'll give you copies if you really want them. Your nieces and nephews might enjoy them, but you don't have to read them yourself."

"I want to. The excerpts I saw looked good." He tapped the poster on his chair's armrest. "And I know you're a fine artist. To do both, you must be some kind of creative genius."

I was embarrassed by the praise. And thrilled. "They're just graphic novels, not great literature."

"They get people's attention, get kids reading. I'd say that's worth a lot of dead Russians. In fact, maybe I can get you to help me write up a personal ad."

My mouth must have fallen open because a gnat flew in. When I stopped coughing, I asked, "Match.com? For you?"

Even in the dark I could see his grin. "Darlin', do you really think I need to advertise for a date?"

Well, no. A bodyguard, maybe, to beat the rodeo groupies away.

"It's time to breed Paloma Blanca. I don't want to send her back to Austria, and I didn't care for the one Lipizzan breeder in the States I met."

"Does she have to be bred to a Lipizzan? I mean, would she care?"

"The Spanish Riding School cares, and I signed a contract when I got her. In case you're wondering how I could afford a treasure like Pal, I did a favor for them in Austria, saved some horses they couldn't. I didn't charge them—hell, it was worth my time and trouble just to be near the horses—but she was my reward. The fools didn't think she was up to their standards."

"She seems perfect to me."

He rumbled a pleased thank you. The way to a man's heart—this man's heart, if anyone was looking for the path—was obviously through his horses. "But maybe she responds better to you than to the idiots who parted with her."

"Maybe. Anyway, there are enough stallions around and I could research who's at stud, for which arm and leg, but I haven't done it yet."

"I should think a picture of her on Facebook would have the stallions come running."

I could hear the smile in his voice. "She's a beauty, isn't she? I figure she deserves more than a vial of sperm."

I wanted to ask if horses cared and how he knew. I mean, mares didn't usually get to pick and choose their mates, did they? Breeders did it for them as far as I knew. Kind of like the Royce Institute playing match-maker with its young talent, breeding for whatever genetic traits they could invent or improve on, breeding to better the herd.

In the wild, in the past, the biggest, strongest stallion claimed his harem. He kept them together and guarded them against any other would-be stud. The females didn't get a vote. Like the Institute throwing big, strong prospects at recalcitrant mares, er, bachelor women. I was resisting.

Still, my ever fertile brain came up with an image of Ty fending off cowboys, cops, and bureaucrats to protect his leather-clad ladies. I bet that was how he got his broken nose. With the intimacy and the anonymity of the darkness, I asked.

"A jealous boyfriend or a horse that wouldn't listen?"

"Honey, they always listen. The horses don't always agree with me, is all. I've got a bunch of broken ribs and a cracked skull to prove it. But if a troublemaking guy doesn't listen, I talk a little louder, is all." He raised his right fist. "Real loud."

"The law of the jungle."

"Nah, just Texas. Don't tread on me."

"Someone did if it wasn't a horse."

He touched his nose. "The first one was from playing football."

"I would have thought you'd be too light for that."

"If you're in Texas and you want a girl, you play football. I quarterbacked. Mightn't have thrown bullets, but I could outrun those half-ton tacklers. Most of the time. The second break was a horse, or on account of a horse. Some bastard was using a chain whip on an old pinto. I took exception."

"What happened?"

"I got blood all over a cop car, the bastard went to jail for animal cruelty when he got out of the hospital, and the pinto lived an easy life on my farm until he died of old age."

"Nice. Like my mother's senior rescues. Not many people will take in an old, tired dog that's going to get expensive, then break your heart. They still deserve love and affection and the best care you can provide."

"Sure. I'd like your mother, too. Maybe I'll get to meet her someday."

"Not unless you're on a picket line protesting carriage horses in Central Park."

"I've been there. The horses don't seem to mind, now

that they don't have to be out in freezing cold or boiling heat. They kind of enjoy getting dressed up and having their pictures taken. It's better'n kids' birthday parties, anyway."

I couldn't tell if he was serious or not, but we were way off track, if our track was going to reach the colt. "Maybe I should go inside and try to dream about the missing horse."

"Can you order your dreams around like toy soldiers?"

Not if the redhead in chaps was any indication. "I can try. I was thinking about my new story the first time, about a paralyzed girl who needs a magic horse to help her fight evil. She's been kidnapped. But then she's the lost colt, in my dreams, of course. And I can feel his emotions."

"But you had nothing to do with the mares coming here?" I heard the suspicion in his voice.

"No! I would not steal anyone's baby just to make a better story. And I would never let the little guy be so scared. I need to get back to him, to let him know we're looking."

"I think that might require the both of us."

"Dreaming together? That would mean we were sleeping together!"

"All for the greater good, I reckon."

I reckoned, insofar as a New Yorker could reckon, that he was teasing for sure this time. Maybe. "I'll try it my way first."

He shrugged. "Stubborn as a mule. But I wouldn't be here elsewise. They could have sent an exorcist."

"To get rid of the magic horses? Is such a thing possible?"

He shrugged again. "The pied piper never talked to the rats, did he?"

I stood up and started to gather my stuff. "I can't tell if you're serious or not, Mr. Farraday, and this is too important to be making jokes about."

"It's no joke that I think we were meant to be partners. One way or another. Hell, it was all I could do to remember to chant, when I remembered you in that pretty dress you wore tonight. And the high-heeled sandals that made your legs look—"

I picked up Little Red.

"No, don't go yet. The mares might still come, and I need you to help me stay awake. Besides, you won't get to sleep while you're in a snit."

"I am not in a snit." But I set the dog back down. I doubted I'd get any helpful dreaming done while the cowboy was in my front yard. Dreaming together, my ass! I didn't even want to talk to him anymore, not if he was going to keep treating me like a cowgirl centerfold. But I did want to see the mares, and the stars were still out.

"Why don't you take a nap? I'll keep watch and wake you if I hear or see anything."

He yawned. "Can you chant?"

"No, but I can visualize the horses all reunited and home where they belong. I can try to do what Doc does, give them hope and confidence. Maybe they'll come to me for that."

"Chanting is good, too."

He started the low incantation, but I could tell by the hesitations that he was too tired to keep it up for long. I found the noise enchanting, but too distracting for me to concentrate on the mares. "Rest for awhile. I'll wake you if they come."

He pulled his chair over, so I could lean against his legs. "Your back'll ache otherwise."

Before I knew it, I was leaning back. Little Red had jumped up to curl asleep in his lap, which was about as much magic as I expected for one night.

I breathed in the smell of earth and salt water and honeysuckle and something else: horse. I peered into the darkness, ready to shake Ty awake.

Then I realized that was his scent, mixed with some spices and soap.

My new partner smelled like a horse.

And he snored.

I liked him better for it.

CHAPTER 15

I WOKE UP SCREAMING. NO, NOT MY SCREAM.
Not my nightmare.

"What?" Ty jumped up, dumping Red to the ground.
Luckily, the chair was a low one. "Willow?"

"Not me. I must have fallen asleep, but I didn't dream.
I didn't yell."

The scream came again.

"It's Grandma!"

Ty took off, hopping to shake an angry Red loose from
his ankle. I wasn't as fast, having to find my dropped
clog, my dropped dog.

Ty was chanting as he ran, as fast as a high school
quarterback racing for a goal line with truck-sized tacklers on his heels. His hat fell off halfway to Grandma's,
so I picked that up, too.

Grandma was cursing. "Get out of my garden, you
four-footed albino rat bitches! I mightn't be able to
keep you from my dreams, but I damned well will keep
you from my plants."

"No," Ty was yelling as he dashed across the road out
of my sight. "Don't frighten them!"

"Don't frighten them? They've terrorized me and
all my friends. Now they are destroying my seedlings,
my experiments. Tomorrow night I'll sit out here with a
shotgun, see if I don't!"

"No!" Ty shouted again. "Threatening them is the worst thing you can do!"

By now I was out of breath and almost to the front field. Lights were on at Grandma's house, the farm stand, and at Susan's parents' house down the road. I didn't see the mares, but I could feel a flood of panic wash over me. Ty cursed, Grandma wailed, sinking to her knees. Susan's mother was out on her own front porch, holding her arms across her chest, shrieking. Her husband, my uncle Roger, who managed the farm for Grandma, was next to her, shaking his fist in the air toward my grandmother.

"I told you the experimentals should be in the greenhouse, you old crone! I told you the seedlings were still too fragile to put out! I told you the imports were too valuable to chance out in the field. Did you listen to me? Do you ever? You ought to be locked up before you run the farm into the ground with your crazy ideas."

"Crazy?" Grandma shouted back across the dirt road. "I built this farm from a backward potato field. Now it's one of the most profitable stands on the east end. And it supports you and your family, you lazy good-for-nothing!"

Aunt Jasmine, who was known to never raise her voice, even on seventh-grade school bus trips, screamed at her mother. "Lazy? My husband works seven days a week and ten hours a day. Do you know where you'd be without his knack for growing things? You'd be picking potatoes, that's what! Roger almost died from some tick disease he caught on your fucking farm!"

"Don't you use that language at me, you ungrateful bitch. You wouldn't have a roof over your fucking head if it wasn't for me."

"You think I couldn't support my wife?" Uncle Roger yelled. "You think I couldn't get a better job? Anywhere, that's where! You fucking old bitch, I have a good mind to—"

Aunt Jasmine started hitting him on the head with a flyswatter from the deck. "Don't you talk to my mother that way, you—"

Uncle Roger grabbed at a cushion on the wicker rocker. "I'm not one of your damned students and I'll talk anyway I want!"

"Stop it!" I yelled, but no one listened except Little Red, who was so scared he peed on me.

Then Ty tried. "Can't you see it's the night mares causing you to say such foolish things? It's their fear and despair talking, not you. It's not worth arguing over a handful of plants."

Now both Grandma and Uncle Roger turned on him, saying that the plants weren't just high-priced organics for the tourist trade. Some of their experiments might eventually feed hungry people. Some of their seedlings were so exotic, they were on world endangered plants lists. Grandma had special permits for captive breeding, or whatever you call it for plants.

"And you'd kill the rarest creatures ever seen for some crappy seeds? Destroy your own village and all its precious resources in the process? Every sensitive and para in fifty miles would have a breakdown. What do you think would happen to Paumanok Harbor itself if you shot one of the horses? Do you have any idea of the powers behind the mares and the vengeance they could wreak?"

Doc limped out of Grandma's front door without his cane or his glasses. His silver hair stood up in peaks as if he'd dragged his hands through it. "Evie, stop yelling. Ty is right, this is the night mares' doing. Ty, shut up. And you, too, Jasmine, Roger. None of you mean what you're saying, none of you are helping."

He knelt beside my grandmother—he called her Evie?—and gathered her into his arms. His touch must have worked its usual magic because Grandma started weeping quietly onto his shoulder.

Aunt Jasmine and Uncle Roger were still going at it. I wanted to lead them over to Doc, but I was afraid to get close enough while flyswatters and flowered cushions were flailing. I knew they'd both turn on me or Little Red, who was shaking so hard I worried he'd break a bone.

Then, over the crying and yelling, and Ty stomping around, we all heard, "Hey, everyone, what'd I miss?"

Susan walked up the dirt road. Actually, Susan staggered up the road, carrying her shoes in one hand. Her hair was a mess, and her blouse was buttoned wrong and gaping open to show where her bra should have been but wasn't. Her parents took one look at their beloved daughter and started calling her a whore, a tramp, a humiliating embarrassment to them.

Susan took one look at me, Ty, Doc, and Grandma all listening to her parents' tirade. She started crying and stumbling back toward my house.

"Susan, it's the night mares. They don't mean it!" I called after her. "You should hear what they called Grandma!"

By now Doc had limped over to Aunt Jasmine and Uncle Roger, and his soft voice and gentle touch had them calmed down and remorseful.

"Maybe she won't remember in the morning," I told them, trying to offer consolation. "Or maybe she'll grow out of this phase and change her ways. You can look on the bright side: she wasn't driving."

Ty rejoined the group. Disgusted that he'd missed seeing the mares, he announced he was going back to Rosehill. There was nothing he could do here, and it was nearly dawn anyway.

Grandma had other ideas. "No, you are not leaving, young man. I said I would make breakfast, and that's what I am going to do. It's the least I can manage after causing such a scene. We could all use some good hot coffee or my special herbal tea."

"Coffee'd be good, but you didn't cause the ruckus, ma'am. You just reacted to it, like anyone would. But you can't go around threatening to hurt the mares. You've got to see that's not the way to solve this problem."

"But I cannot let them destroy my plantings, my income, my life's work. And Roger's," she added, sending her son-in-law a look of apology.

Roger nodded, accepting and holding out his own

olive branch. "I could really go for a cup of your tea and maybe a muffin."

Ty turned in a slow circle, trying to get a better feel for the layout of the three houses and the fields by the first glimmer of dawn. "Lights. That's what you need. They don't like the brightness. Maybe they are some kind of albinos and that's why they only come out at night. Sunshine might hurt their eyes. No one knows."

"But keeping the fields lit is worth a try," I seconded.

Ty looked at Grandma. "You could put floodlights on the fields, leave your porch lights on, and every lamp in the house. You can string Christmas lights as far as they'll reach, and get your hands on every solar lantern you can find. Maybe even those sacks you can fill with sand and put votive candles in."

"Luminarias, they're called." Aunt Jasmine was holding Uncle Roger's hand. "We have a box full of the ones left over from the Fourth of July, don't we, Roger? And two boxes of Christmas lights at least."

"Jas never lets me throw anything out," Uncle Roger told us. "I guess she's right."

Aunt Jasmine patted his hand. "I always am, dear. Maybe we can borrow the portable lights from the school's playing field. I'll get the coach and his football team to help move them."

"And those emergency floodlights the fire department carries. I'll call around in the morning. And we can hook up the generator for the far fields, to keep it lit."

"That's the ticket," Ty said. "The mares won't come into the light. Even if it doesn't bother their eyes, I think it ruins their ability to disappear."

"I bet my mother has Christmas lights in the basement," I said. "And those icicle drapes for the front yard."

Ty looked back, as if judging the distance we'd run. "That'll help, but not on your place, Willow. No, we keep your house dark. You and I will have to handle the emotions. It'll be easier because we won't be afraid."

We won't?

"And we won't frighten them. We'll try to befriend

them, not chase them away. I'll bring over some grain and hay when they deliver it to Rosehill for my horses. We don't know what the white ladies eat, but we can try apples and carrots, too, to show our good intentions. Calmer, they won't hurt anyone. It's our only hope. You've seen what they can do."

"There, Evie, we have a plan. We'll be fine and save your fields." Doc shook Ty's hand, then he asked Aunt Jasmine and Uncle Roger to help him back to Grandma's house. A muffin sounded fine. And maybe an omelet.

They'd be fine. I wasn't sure about Susan. And I had to change my wet sweatshirt anyway. I told them I'd be back in a few minutes.

Ty didn't notice my leaving. He was already on his cell phone, making who-knew-what arrangements for saving the planet and Grandma's plantings. At five-thirty in the freaking morning. The first rays of sun lightened his long hair almost to gold, which reminded me I still had his hat in my hand, with Little Red half in it. I went back and handed him the Stetson, without the Pomeranian.

He held the phone away. "Your dog bites."

"Only when he's nervous. He pees when he's really scared. I'd check the hat."

Right after I peeled off my wet sweatshirt, I poured a dose of my mother's special rescue remedy into a fresh bowl of water for Little Red. Then I poured a couple of drops into a Diet Coke for Susan, who was still crying on the sofa. So I gave her the last of my chocolate chip cookies, too.

She wiped her eyes, smearing mascara down her cheeks, took a drink, and ate half a cookie. "These are shit." She ate the other half anyway.

"Not everyone is a genius in the kitchen." I gave the big dogs biscuits for being woken up so early. They thought I was a Julia Child.

"Not everyone is a whore in their parents' eyes." Susan was weeping again, but she ate the second cookie and washed it down with the Coke.

Where was Doc when I needed him? For that matter, where was Ty? Maybe he could chant to her or something. Instead, I was on my own, in a minefield. "They love you. They just don't understand. It's a generational thing. Hooking up is no big deal to you—if you're careful. Casual sex is a crime to them. Hey, your mom is a schoolteacher, what do you expect her to think?"

"You don't approve either."

Well, I didn't, but mostly I was afraid she'd get hurt. Or ruin her chances of finding someone who really mattered. Instead of another lecture, I told her, "That's 'cause it wouldn't work for me. But I'm older. And wiser."

"Sure, you threw Prince Charming back in the frog pond."

I did not want to talk about me. Or Grant. "I bet Grandma understands. Didn't her generation invent free love? Besides, I think she's shacking up with Doc Lassiter. Or will be soon."

"You're kidding. Grandma Eve?"

"I thought she and Lou the Lout were getting it on, so why not Doc? He's handsome and pretty healthy, and he calls her Evie. He's just the sweet soul she needs to cure her sour personality. In fact, he's such a sweetie I'd be interested in him myself if he was a couple of decades younger."

"What, that steaming cowboy's not hot enough for you?"

"He's not my anything. We're just working partners."

"Yeah," she said, holding up the last cookie before taking a big bite out of it. "And you made these from scratch."

So I told her to scratch my ass.

At which she gave me the finger and told me I smelled like dog piss.

Isn't that what families are for, to love and support each other?

Chapter 16

D AWN AND I WERE NOT USUALLY on speaking terms. It was more like sending a Christmas card once a year. Not that I had anything against a pretty sunrise, but when you've seen one, you've got bags under your eyes.

It looked like another nice day, so I threw on a T-shirt and cutoffs, brushed my teeth, and did what I could with my hair, then fed the dogs.

While they ate—all two minutes of inhaling the kibbles—I thought about Ty and his intentions. Not toward me, which was obvious, but toward the mares. He was focused on talking with them, finding them, finding if he could communicate with them. He was like a Star Fleet ship commander excited to find intelligent life. The problem was, we needed to find the colt more.

Ty would be no help to me if he slept all day, which seemed likely. I'd had a few hours of rest before the raunchy dream, the one I'd never think of again, and was almost ready to go knocking on doors. If it weren't so early in the morning, I'd skip breakfast and get on the road with my maps, but I didn't want the hotshot horse whisperer making plans with the others without me.

I wanted Susan to come to Grandma Eve's. I used the raspberries I knew Grandma's crews had been picking as a bribe. And the hope for Grandma's crepes that she sometimes made in fresh berry season.

So Susan scrubbed the mascara off her face and put on a clean Hello, Kitty T-shirt, and her hair in pigtails. She looked about fifteen, and innocent.

When we got across the road, Susan hung back until Doc came forward from where he was scooping out melon balls and took her hand in both of his. "Just the person I was hoping to see. Evie says your omelets are inspired."

"They are," Grandma seconded, while she dipped bread for French toast. No crepes, but close enough.

Aunt Jasmine was whipping heavy cream for the berries. "Better than mine ever were."

Susan's father stopped feeding oranges to the juicer. "I've been missing my omelets since you moved in with Willow to keep her company."

Susan came to keep me company? That was news to me. She said she couldn't stand living by her parents' rules and their disapproval.

While everyone else was cooking, Ty was at the kitchen table making lists and phone calls. He did look up at me, then up and down. "Nice legs, blondie."

I wasn't really blonde, not without Janie's bottles and bleaches. Since I hadn't been back to the salon, my hair was more sandy-colored streaks, if not mousy. But Ty didn't even look at adorable Susan, who was laughing as she grabbed eggs, bowls, and whatever else she found in Grandma's extensive pantry. So I didn't say anything about this new nickname, just "Hiya, Tex."

He looked tired, and he wasn't wearing his hat, but he winked at me.

We were so many, we'd have to eat in the dining room instead of the kitchen, so I started to set the table the way Grandma liked: tablecloth, cloth napkins, pottery plates, fresh flowers in a vase. Just like breakfast at my house. Hey, a granola bar looks just as appetizing on a paper towel as it does on a porcelain plate.

Omelets, scones, fruit salad, French toast with raspberries and cream, fresh OJ. Maybe I ought to jog door-to-door instead of driving. But then I'd likely have a heart attack from clogged arteries. I was definitely going to have a salad for lunch.

I worried about Doc, who'd already had a stroke, until I saw Grandma refill his bowl with fruit.

I was amazed at how much food Ty consumed—to Grandma's delight and Susan's pride—and how much could be accomplished so early in the morning.

The police dispatcher reported they'd had no problems in the precinct last night and hoped Doc would hang around. The chief was thrilled the mares were out at the farm—but don't tell Eve—and he'd do anything to keep them away from Main Street. Ty wanted apples and carrots? A truck would be there by the afternoon. Lights? Uncle Henry'd put new batteries in the squad cars so they could stay on all night. A water trough? How about his niece's wading pool?

The school was cooperating; so was the fire department. The grapevine was warning everyone to keep the plan quiet. The last thing we needed was reporters or photographers from the East Hampton papers coming to stake out my backyard. Paumanok Harbor had enough trouble keeping out of the public eye without a hunt for wild horses . . . ones that disappeared in daylight.

The rest of the plan was for everyone to go back to bed when their assigned chores were completed.

Not me. My chore was covering as many Paumanok Harbor miles as I could. I went back home, showered, and changed to jeans and sneakers for trudging through high grasses. Then I designed, printed out, and cut quarter-page notices: A picture of the colt. "Have you seen this young white horse?" and my name and cell number for any information. I didn't offer a reward this time, but I intended to put one of these in every hand or mailbox I could.

Susan refused to come with me. She had to work that night and needed her sleep. I was kind of glad, because Ty wanted me to take Connor. I didn't think a day in the car together would be good for either of them.

When I got to Rosehill to pick up my passenger, I

punched in the combination at the estate's electric gate, that I knew from my stay here as Cousin Lily's replacement. Then I drove around to the back, past at least a dozen vans and pickups.

A huge horse trailer filled most of the rear gravel parking area. Paloma Blanca and Lady Sparrow might have traveled in comfort; now they were living in Hamptons luxury.

Rosehill's three-car garage had been converted to a stable, with hay and straw and brand-new feed bins and buckets. Outside, on the vast parklike lawns, the groundskeeper was directing an army of workers setting fence posts into holes in the grass. I'd have thought Emmanuel would be crying at the destruction of his green carpet handiwork, but he was smiling. Who wouldn't smile, watching Paloma Blanca prance across the yard? Emmanuel was talking to her in Spanish. I didn't have the heart to tell him she was born in Austria, then trained in obsolete Paiute with a Texas drawl.

Connor was walking every inch of the new enclosure inspecting the ground for wires, staples, poisonous plants, broken glass. As if Emmanuel would permit as much as a fallen branch.

An electrician's crew was starting to run wires to electrify the new corral, and a security specialist was up a spruce tree installing cameras and alarms. I wasn't sure about the pinto, but Ty's Lipizzan mare had to be worth more than me, my house, and my mother's Outback combined. I couldn't blame him for taking every precaution, especially with a horse thief already in the neighborhood.

Connor was ready as soon as the last wire was tied off and the gate secured. The horses had water, shade, a radio playing music and, if I wasn't mistaken, Emmanuel's nephew standing guard. I never saw Ty, which was aggravating since I'd put on a gauzy gypsy blouse. And I'd left Little Red home.

Connor was not a great conversationalist. Which was to say he didn't talk at all. I couldn't tell what he thought as I pointed out the local sights, not through his sunglasses and a wide-brimmed baseball cap from a rodeo association.

I started to explain about Susan, so he'd be prepared and could handle the situation in his own way. He grunted. He already knew.

I drove through Main Street and then out toward small pockets of residential neighborhoods between thick wooded preserved areas, interspersed with hidden drives. I decided to start on Osprey Street, where I knew some of the old-time residents.

Before we got out of the car, I had to ask Connor if he had any sense that could help us detect a hidden horse.

"Nope."

I was hoping I did. Meantime, I wished we had Big Eddie and his nose, but the young policeman was out on patrol. Even Vincent the Barber might have helped. He could see a nimbus around persons of psionic power. Today was his day off, and he'd gone fishing.

I asked Connor if he wanted to take one side of the street of modest homes while I took the other.

"Nope."

So he walked beside me up an impatiens-planted path to the Desmonds' house. Mrs. Desmond taught English at Aunt Jasmine's school, where I'd met her many times.

I handed her one of the flyers. "Do you know anything at all about a young white horse?"

"Dear me, no. I thought you'd found it by now, since things have settled down."

"Honestly, I don't even know if the colt is still alive."

"Oh, I can help you with that. I can make alphabet soup."

"Huh?"

She led us to the kitchen, set a small pot of water on to boil, then asked for the colt's name.

"I've been calling him Hetty, but that can't be right."

"We'll use the H for horse anyway." She sifted through a baby food jar filled with macaroni letters and found an H. "If it floats, the horse is alive."

We all held our breath. The tiny H bobbed right up to the surface.

Connor looked at me.

I shrugged. "They use Mrs. Desmond on ambulance runs sometimes."

The next house was larger, with a Jag in the circular driveway. I never knew what the Merriwethers did for a living, except that they traveled a lot. Mrs. Merriwether spent a lot of money at Grandma Eve's on plants and vegetables.

Mrs. Merriwether hadn't heard anything about the little pony. But she shut her eyes, opened them, and scrawled a nine on a scrap of paper. She handed it to me.

"Nine? Nine what?"

"I have no idea, dear. I can't be more help than that, but the number is certainly connected to what you are looking for."

"Do you ever play the lottery, Mrs. Merriwether?"

She grinned. "Every state that has one. We don't always win, but how do you think we bought this house and the ones in Maui and Vail, and the car and the boat and all those trips abroad?"

Margaret was a weaver who sold her work at the craft shows in Montauk and Amagansett. I had one of her scarves. We could barely find our way through the living room to her studio, for all the looms, baskets of yarn, dyestuffs, and finished goods. She hadn't seen or heard anything about the colt either.

"I don't suppose you have any of the horse's hair, do you?

"No, no one's seen him at all."

"Let me think . . ." She looked at Connor, leaned over, and pulled a long white hair from his dark western shirt.

"But that's from Paloma Blanca, Mr. Farraday's horse," I told her. Then said "Ouch" as she plucked one of my hairs.

"Yes, but I'll weave it, your hair, and your intense desire to find the colt all together with my favorite wool. I spun it from a shaggy dog your mother found for me. He could find a dog biscuit no matter where I hid it."

Connor shrugged, pulled a long black hair from his braid and handed it to her. When their hands touched, he didn't pull his back fast enough. "Ma'am, you don't have to keep worrying about that biopsy. It's just a cyst."

She looked startled, then looked at the bit of hairs and fibers her fingers were already braiding together and smiled. If her magic was possible, anything was. In five minutes she had a long enough chain to knot around my wrist.

"But won't it fall apart when I take a shower?"

"It will last until you find what you are looking for."

No one was home at the next two houses, but I left flyers under the doors. We peeked into the backyards to see if any sheds or playhouses were big enough for a small horse. They weren't.

At the last house, a man answered the door. He must have thought we were handing out bibles or selling something, because he slammed the door in our faces. I shoved a flyer in the mail slot and shouted, "Have a good day."

We looked over the fence into his backyard, too, but the whole width was filled with a swimming pool. He was breaking the building laws, but not harboring a stolen horse.

We crossed to the other side of the street.

They called her Leather Lips because her skin was so tanned and hardened from her years outdoors. She used to give trail rides along the beach until the town made her stop. Too many people complained about stepping in horseshit. My mother complained about how she left the horses out in the sun, saddled up and waiting for paying customers. I knew she still kept a couple of horses in her backyard, grandfathered into the zoning code, and gave pony lessons to kids.

"No, I haven't seen your weanling. And if any of my horses know anything about him, they're not talking. Of course, if that good-looking horse whisperer of yours wants to come chat, I'd be willing to let him try." She looked at Connor. "This one needs to age, like good wine."

She let us look over the three-sided stable. Connor stroked a pony and pulled a burr out of its ear.

In gratitude, Leather Lips gave us a couple of places to look, ones not on my list.

I knew the next few houses were summer rentals. I put the flyers in the mailboxes.

The last one we approached looked empty, no porch furniture, no curtains on the closed windows, no car out front. We looked around the side, saw no sheds or garage or lounge chairs, then headed back to the street.

We both heard the voice call out from the empty house. "Sorry I cannot answer your call, but if you leave your name and number, I'll get back to you as soon as possible. And no, Miss Tate, I have not seen your missing equine."

I ran for the car. Connor wasn't far behind me.

"Man, I love this town," he said as he jumped in and slammed his door. "It makes the res look normal."

CHAPTER 17

THE NEXT BLOCK WAS TERN STREET. The corner house had a sign outside: Jeweler, Clock and Watch Repairs, Custom Wedding Rings. Emil the jeweler had cut down my mother's wedding band to make the pendant I constantly wore, the one with the antique, archaic runes engraved on them that almost no one could read. *I and thou* is how Grant translated it, *one forever*.

We went in and waited while Emil served another customer. Connor looked at pocket watches while I, without intending to, looked at diamond rings.

Emil hurried over as soon as the customer left, setting the little bell on the door to ringing again. "Oh, no, Willow, not that one."

I hadn't picked out any ring in particular. "I'm just looking."

"No, not the ring, the young man." He tilted his head toward Connor and lowered his voice. "The diamonds always tell me if a match is going to succeed. This one won't. Of course young couples rarely take my warnings."

"I'll remember to check with you before making a selection. A man, before the ring. But Connor and I are simply searching for any information you might have about the horse we're all looking for. Have you seen the posters?"

"Yes, and I'm afraid I can't be much help. Now if you were looking for an emerald or a ruby, they sometimes talk to me. They don't have as much to say as the diamonds, of course."

Of course.

The rest of Tern Street was a newer neighborhood, with bigger lots, more space between the larger houses. Most of them had swimming pools—with the ocean fifteen minutes away, the bay beach less than ten—but no barns or stables.

Ty's horses were in a garage, and I worried my colt—I cared the most, didn't I?—could be somewhere we couldn't look into. In my dream, though, his walls were rough wood planks. Not a garage.

A few of these houses had For Rent signs out, an indication of the hurting economy. Usually every available house or cottage or upstairs apartment was rented out before June. I stuck my flyers behind the screen doors anyway, in case someone came to look at the rentals.

One house had five cars parked in the driveway and along the road. The cars all had overhead surfboard carriers. The porch railing had wetsuits and beach towels draped out to dry. We knocked on the door.

I could hear loud music. I could feel the bass vibrate through my sneakers, but no one answered. I knocked again, louder.

A blond guy with no shirt but a lot of tattoos finally opened the door partway. "What do you want?"

I handed him the notice. "That's cool," he said and stood aside so we could enter, showing an inked octopus crawling across his back shoulder. Yeck.

Eight or nine guys lounged in various states of undress and inebriation amid beer cans, pizza boxes, and a cloud of marijuana smoke.

Connor's look might have lingered on a water pipe; I drooled at the pizza.

The first surfer shouted to his buddies: "Hey, dudes, the broad and the Indian are looking for some horse."

"Shit, man, we don't do heroin."

"Maybe they're cops."

I shouted above the music: "No, we're just looking for a lost colt. Has anybody seen one? He's white."

"I saw a yellow squid on the way over here," one guy said. "Then it turned into a really big school bus, headed straight at me. Red eyes and all."

"You were driving? In this condition? And almost hit a school bus?"

"How else are we supposed to get to Ditch for the tournament?"

Ditch Plains was in Montauk and had some of the best surfing on the eastern seaboard, or so I understood. It had some of the nicest, classiest professional surfers. These stoned slobs weren't them. They were stupid rich boys having a good time and not caring whose house they trashed or whose kid they killed. I cared.

"I'm going to write down your license numbers when I leave. If I see any of you behind the wheel, I'll report you to the cops for DUI, to the code enforcer for having an illegal group rental, and to Miss Needlemeier for being shitheads."

"Who the hell is Miss Needlemeier?"

"She's the girls' phys ed instructor at the school, and she'll put warts on your winkies if you misbehave. We don't take kindly to reckless driving here in the Harbor."

Two guys clutched their privates. Another one puked. The octopus swore they'd call a cab next time. Or wait to party until they were home.

"Can she do that, your Miss Needlemeier?" Connor asked when we were outside in the fresh air.

"I don't know, but no boys ever tried peeking at the girls' locker room."

"My grandmother can shrink a guy's gonads to grapes with one touch."

"My grandmother can make a cheater's fall off with one cup of tea."

So we traded grandmother curses, or accursed grandmothers, for the rest of the block and had a great time exaggerating. At least I hoped we were exaggerating.

*   *   *

We spoke to everyone else on the street or left the flyers, then took a break for lunch down by the docks. On the way I asked Connor if he surfed.

"Sure, we have lots of big waves out on the res. Right between the mountains and the desert and the prairie."

"I bet you'd be good. A horseman like you must have incredible balance and"—grace sounded too effeminate for what I'd seen on the video of him and Lady Sparrow—"agility."

"Yeah, and if I broke an arm or dislocated my shoulder, I'd be unable to perform. No act, no money sent back home. People depend on me."

I thought of those college boys back on Tern Street, then my own life of relative comfort. I was bothered that people expected me to get rid of their nightmares? I couldn't imagine how Connor must feel.

The snack bar at Rick's didn't have salads, darn it. I had to make do with a cheeseburger. I offered Connor my fries. It was the least I could do.

Rick told us to check out a couple of backyards that were already on my list and the one Leather Lips had given us. He reminded me about the old Scowcroft ranch—which I was putting off for last, since the place was farthest from town. And since its caretaker terrified me.

Rick added a new stable near Amagansett that boarded polo ponies, and some summer people who used to have a pony for their kid. They kept a boat at his marina, that's how he knew, but only the father used the cabin cruiser now. When the kid got thrown, they shot the pony, but they must still have the facilities for a horse.

The Froelers sounded obnoxious; the Scowcroft ranch was scary. I drove toward the new polo field and stable.

The place looked like a miniature Epsom Downs, except the field was rectangular, not oval. It even had grandstands for spectators and a refreshments stand. Plenty of flowers in big concrete pots, plenty of room for exercising the gleaming horses, plenty of money on show.

While Connor entered the sleek-looking stables, a groom directed me to the man who owned most of the horses and captained the team when he wasn't in Palm Beach or South America. The captain was leaning on a rail, watching one of his teammates put a horse through its paces, or whatever polo ponies did. They weren't half as handsome as Paloma Blanca, nor as fast looking as Lady Sparrow.

The captain wasn't half as attractive as Grant or Ty, either, but he thought he was. He wore tight white knit pants tucked into shiny high boots, even a silk stock at the neck of his open-collared white shirt. The polo polish did not impress me, nor his slow appraisal of my body, as if he was looking for designer labels or availability. There was none of either. I'd been almost-engaged to a real aristocrat. This playboy did not make the grade.

I asked about a young white horse away from its mother.

The captain was paying more attention to another groom leading Connor into the crisp white stable complex. The man didn't like it, I could tell.

"He's a professional rider."

The polo guy curled his lip at the idea of a dark-skinned, long-haired person of unknown pedigree joining his team. "This is a private club, you know."

Which meant, I suppose, you had to put up a fortune and your Ivy League degree to join.

"It couldn't be anything less," I told him. He may have taken my words for a compliment, which it was not, because he gave me the benefit of his practiced smile. "We're just looking for a missing horse. We thought someone might have brought a stray to you, not knowing what else to do with him. It's like leaving a baby at a church or a hospital, somewhere you know it's going to be taken care of."

The smile disappeared. "Sorry, we don't take in strays. Our horses are all registered and documented. That one training"—he pointed a manicured finger at the enclosed field—"just came from Saudi Arabia. We would

have directed anyone with a lost horse to the police."
He looked at my flyer. "Now I'll send them on to you."

"Thanks. Please call me if you hear of any news."

"I've heard better come-on lines, honey."

"Have you ever heard of Eastern equine encephalitis?" I hadn't noticed Connor leaving the stables, but he
was right behind us.

The captain spun on his expensive heels. "Of course
I have."

"You better check it out."

Connor wasn't saying the horses were sick. He didn't
have to. Just his words could send any horseman, especially one looking for a trophy for his mantel, into a
panic. Mr. Cool took off at a run.

"Did you look in stall number nine?" I asked Connor
while we walked back to the car. "Or for a horse who
wears that number when they play?"

"There's a chestnut in stall nine. And the riders wear
the numbers, not the horses."

"Are the horses really sick?"

"Healthiest horses money can buy. But the vet bill
to come check might make a dent in that, or if rumors
get started and the team is quarantined and disqualified
from the coming match."

Gee, that would be too bad. I got us back on the road.

"We going to that Scowcroft ranch next?"

"Um, no. I thought we'd look at that house with the
stable." I checked my map. "It's got a permit for a horse.
Eight acres to keep it on. Pool, tennis courts, indoor
pool. The works. Summers only. And its house number
is nine."

"But they shot a pony 'cause their kid fell off?"

I had no answer. Connor hated the Froelers before
we got to the big white house. I could tell when he didn't
say a word the whole way there.

The gates had an intercom system, so I gave my name
and said we were looking for a missing horse. Maybe
someone knew about it?

The gates swung open. When we got there, the double
doors to the big colonial were flung wide. We parked in

the porte cochere and walked up the seven wide steps. I expected a maid, maybe, or the owners, not a young girl in a wheelchair. I almost tripped on the top step.

She was about twelve, I guessed, with long brown hair and thick eyebrows and brown eyes. She looked just like the girl in my book, the girl in my dream. "Hetty?"

She giggled. "Letty. Only my old nanny ever called me that. My mother insists on Letitia." She scooted the electric wheelchair back so we could enter. "I am not supposed to let strangers come in the house while the housekeeper is out, but I've heard of you. You're teaching a course at the arts center."

"Yes, and this is Connor Redstone."

She dropped her eyes, suddenly shy. "Pleased to meet you."

Connor nodded, which she couldn't see with her head down.

"Are you coming to my creative writing course? I think it'll be fun."

She looked up, but without the smile. "My mother won't let me."

I was sorry. She looked like a bright kid. "Maybe your mom will change her mind. You can tell her I don't bite. My dog does, but I don't."

She smiled at that, as I intended. "I wish I could. I'm writing a story right now about a magic horse."

"Wow, so am I! Can yours fly?"

"Oh, yes, and he has a magic healing touch."

"Mine doesn't, but that sounds like a great idea."

She turned shy again, hiding her face behind her hair. "Oh, I'm sorry. I should offer you something to drink. Would you like an iced tea or a soda?"

"That would be lovely. But would you mind if Connor takes a look at your old stable, just in case someone hid the missing colt there?"

"Why would they do that?"

"Because if it's as far from the house as it looks on the map, and no one uses it, it might be a good place to hide something you don't want found."

She did a wheelie in her electric chair and led us to

French doors that opened onto a terrace and the pool, and farther, to a gravel path that led out of sight. "There's a corral first, then the stable. I'd show you, but the gravel's tough to ride on. Besides, I'm not allowed outside by myself, or to go swimming. They're afraid I'll get stung by a bee—I'm allergic, you know—or drown or something. They won't let me go to the center because there'll be too many germs from the other kids there. I got pneumonia after the accident. I'm not as bad off as that Superman guy, though. I can breathe on my own and use my arms. My mother is just overprotective. And she likes me to keep to my schedule. Physical therapy in the morning, tutors in the afternoon, swim session before dinner."

I'd almost offered to accompany her and Connor to the stable until I realized there was no ramp from the French doors, and none at the front steps. The poor kid couldn't get down if she wanted.

She must have seen me staring because she said there was a ramp on the side door, with a paved path.

She wasn't in a cell or a closet, but Letitia was a prisoner nevertheless. She watched Connor stride away, and I watched her eyes fill with tears.

"I almost got stung by a bee. It wasn't Arabella's fault. We were practicing for the pony class of the Hampton's Classic Horse Show. We could have won. We already had a blue ribbon for the jumping event. I batted at the bee and frightened poor Arabella. She stumbled, and I went over her head."

"Your parents blamed her?"

"My mother said she never wanted to see her again. Never wanted another child to be paralyzed like me."

"But they didn't take down the stable."

"I made them promise I could get another horse when I walked again. We were hoping for stem cell research, but they say it's too late. My stepfather's company does medical research, and he says they're trying. So I write stories about flying horses."

I sighed. "Me, too."

"Really? I ordered your books on Amazon, but they haven't come yet. I didn't know they were about horses."

"They haven't been until now. I'll bring the first chapters for you to look at."

"You will?"

"Sure, and I'll ask your parents if you can come to my class. I'll be real careful no one has a cold or anything."

She almost dropped the frosted carrot cake she was cutting—refusing my help—in her excitement. I drank some lemonade while Connor walked back, shaking his head.

"I would have known if there was a pony out there," Letitia—damn, I'd call her Letty if she let me—said.

I thought I would have, too. "Have you ever been tested by the Royce Institute?"

"No, what's that?"

"Oh, just a research group that tests kids to see what they might be good at."

"Yeah, like a paraplegic has a lot of choices."

"Some."

She changed the subject. "He's awfully good-looking, isn't he?"

"The colt we're searching for?" I'd given her a flyer with my phone number on it.

She blushed. "Your friend."

I agreed he was very good-looking, then told her his website, so she could see him ride.

"He's a rider?"

She gave him a bigger slice of cake.

CHAPTER 18

ALWAYS GOT THE SMALL PIECE OF CAKE. I always resented it. Like now, I'd had two minutes of being a kid's idol before being replaced by a guy with more baggage than the boarding line at JFK. Connor'd said exactly two words to Letty: "Thank you," while I was adding her name to my list of things to rescue.

He hadn't said one word after putting his cake fork down either, not when I promised to email Letty about our search, nor when I drove the car around the circular driveway and back out the gate. I tried to remember if he'd talked since leaving the polo field. Ten minutes later, he still hadn't spoken a syllable.

I figured, after the surfers, the polo players, and now the Froelers' mansion, he was tabulating all the ridiculously conspicuous consumption of the Hamptons, and how different it was from how his family lived.

Mine, too.

"You know, Connor, no amount of money is ever going to get that girl what she wants most. She'll never ride a horse again."

Connor grunted.

Maybe I made my point. Maybe not. I kept driving. I thought we'd check out a couple more of the big estates while we were in the high-rent district. After the third long driveway, the fourth locked gate, and one sign saying Beware of the Dogs, with a silhouette of Doberman pinschers, Connor grunted again.

I looked over to the passenger seat. "You have something to say?"

"Yeah. Why don't you want to go to that abandoned ranch? You've been avoiding it all day."

Now he wanted to talk? "I thought we'd finish up here, then go back to see if Ty is awake and wants to come along."

"And?"

And I hated the idea of going to Bayview Ranch. I didn't think Connor needed to know all my reasons, but I gave him a good one. "Snakes."

He took off his sunglasses to see if I was serious. I was.

"But you don't have poisonous snakes here. I checked. Nothing that could hurt a horse. Or you."

"A person can die of fright, can't she?"

"I can't believe you're afraid of a couple of what? Garter snakes? Maybe a rat snake?"

I didn't know why he couldn't believe it. Everyone in Paumanok Harbor knew I was terrified of snakes. They'd heard me screaming from all the way up at the hill ranch, and never let me forget it, even seventeen years later.

Kids used to sneak up to the ranch on summer nights, even when it was in operation. The stable guys knew and didn't care as long as we didn't spook the horses or start fires. There was a lake and grass and no one in sight. I lost my virginity up there that summer to a boy named Tripp, John James Hennessy the Third. Or maybe it was James John. No matter, he was suntanned and cute and worked on some rich guy's boat.

The experience itself was not worth remembering. It was short, painful, messy, and entirely unrewarding. Then a snake slithered over my foot.

My screams spooked the horses, the grooms, the Scowcrofts and a whole cocktail party they were throwing for half the town, and Tripp's boss. Did I mention I was naked when I ran by the house?

I made my father take me back to our apartment in the city the next day. That deprived Grandma of an unpaid helper at the farm stand, which she never forgave me for either.

They closed the ranch soon after that. Not because I'd caused such a riot, and not because snakes always seemed to breed up there, big black rat snakes that ate the rodents inevitable around horse feed. They shut the ranch down because it finally lost more money than even Mr. Scowcroft was willing to waste on his pet hobby.

Thoroughbred racehorses were not pets, and throwing money down the toilet was a crazy hobby. The winters were too cold; the grass not rich enough; good trainers didn't want to be so far from the southern tracks; Mr. Scowcroft couldn't breed a winner if it already had a blanket of roses on its back. Then lightning struck the big house. No one was home at the time, but that was enough for the owner. Rather than rebuilding, he sold the horses, razed the ruins, and moved to Hawaii. His corporation put the ranch up for subdivision about the time land was multiplying in value and the rest of the Hamptons were getting filled.

The town was protesting. They'd given Scowcroft special variances to build a stable on the hill here in order to keep the land agricultural, like Grandma's farm. Bayview was supposed to stay that way, not be divided up into ten luxury lots, ten huge mansions with a view, ten behemoths filling the open vista.

While the court case was going on, for years now, Paumanok Harbor was dickering with the town and the county and the state and the Nature Conservancy to see about making the ranch public parkland, but the corporation wanted top dollar, and preservation funds were drying up.

Meanwhile, the old place deteriorated more. The fire department came and burned down the main stable after its roof collapsed. Everyone came to watch, including me. In high boots. Now almost all that was left was the old breeding barn, overgrown fields, and the bunkhouse where the staff used to sleep. And snakes, lots of snakes. And Snake.

Fred Sinese was the only one there, the only one who didn't mind the snakes, so everyone naturally called him Sinese the Snake. I didn't call him anything because I never spoke to him.

On my night of infamy, he'd been right there, near the lake. Maybe having a date of his own. Maybe watching summer kids doing the dirty. Maybe letting a snake out of a sack, for fun.

Without going into personal details, I told Connor about the ranch and its sneaky, slimy caretaker. "And he drinks, besides."

"Does he have a talent?"

"Other than frightening children? People used to whisper that he talked to the snakes. Like my mother and her dogs and Ty and the horses. Even Emil and the gemstones."

"Snakes are deaf."

"Harry Potter did it. What did they call him, a parselmouth?"

"That was a movie."

"And a book. But there are snakes up there. And Fred Sinese."

"And a lot of places to hide a horse. Especially if no one goes near the ranch."

Reluctantly, I turned the car and headed in the direction of Bayview. "I bet he won't let us search."

"Unless we say Ty is interested in buying it for his rescued horses. He's been talking about expanding to the east."

I had to admit that might work. Snake might let us look around. "Or he might lie and say we need to talk to the owners first."

I hit the brakes so hard Connor's head snapped back on the neck rest and his sunglasses went flying. When I made a quick u-turn on a narrow street, he said, "Never ask to ride my horse."

I sped through the village and skidded into Kelvin's Auto Body Repair.

"What the hell . . . ?"

"A lie detector."

Like a couple of other Paumanok Harbor residents who could trace their lines back to the Royce-Harmon-Stamfield English lines, Kelvin could distinguish truth from lies. Our local judge could do it, but they'd moved him to state court, he was so good at administering justice. The police chief could sometimes, besides finding lost objects, but he was too busy. Grant could, but he was several continents away.

That left Kelvin, who had the added advantage of being big and strong. You could never have enough muscle when facing down snakes.

Unfortunately, Kelvin couldn't come with us. He'd promised to have a Mercedes done by four. He volunteered his son, Kelvin Junior, instead.

I looked at Junior and was not encouraged. The kid was about nine or ten, but almost my height and overweight. I guess that's why they call him K2. He had chocolate smeared on his face and strawberry ice cream smeared on his NY Giants T-shirt.

"I'm not sure . . ."

Kelvin was. "You're dealing with Snake; you need to know when he's lying, even if you can assume it's every time he opens his mouth."

I knew Kelvin's big toe itched at a falsehood, so I asked about K2's telltale signal.

"His nose drips." Kelvin handed the boy a box of tissues, told him to mind his manners, and wear his seat belt.

"I guess he's seen your driving," Connor muttered.

K2 found the bag of potato chips we'd bought for later, but that didn't shut him up. "Are you a real Indian? Can Mr. Farraday really talk to the horses? Will he let me ride one? Can we get some ice cream? Do you think Mrs. Terwilliger will shoot me for losing my library card? Are we really going up to Bayview? Can I bring a snake back home with me?"

Heaven help us.

"And you can't lie to me, 'cause I'll drip snot all over your car."

Oh, God, he was worse than Little Red.

Connor went back to being a silent statue. I tried to answer the questions. At least that got my mind off the snakes.

When we drove up the hill, I warned K2 that we were going to speculate. All right, we were going to lie about our reasons for being here. He stuffed some tissues in his jeans pocket.

Snake met us at the top of the hill, before we could park the car. He was set to snarl at whoever was trespassing, until he saw me driving. He grinned. "Well, if it ain't Missy Tate. Ready to put on another show? How long's it been now?"

I didn't reply, but I put the car in park. Snake looked older than when I'd seen him last, but his denim coveralls looked—and smelled—the same. His complexion was still bad, only now it had age spots and maybe skin cancer on top of the acne scars, with an unhealthy yellowish cast. His grin showed a missing tooth, but his eyes were what I remembered most: small, black, darting from side to side.

Connor and K2 got out of the car. I had to force myself to unbuckle my seat belt.

Then I remembered something else: the voice on my answering machine asking about a reward. Snake's voice. I forgot about the script we'd planned. "Did you call about information on the missing colt?"

"Might have. Just to find what you were offering. See if it was worth my effort to go looking."

K2 sniffed.

"Do you know anything about it?"

"Just what I heard in town. Saw the posters."

K2 wiped his nose on his sleeve.

Now Connor took over. He walked toward Snake, held his hand out, and introduced himself. He so rarely offered to shake with anyone I wondered why. Then I decided he voluntarily offered to touch people he already didn't like. He didn't care what he found out.

"You really ought to cut out the booze, you know."

"Yeah, I heard that somewhere. So what do you want? You're wasting your time looking for a horse up here, and I'd lay odds you're wasting your time trying to get missy out of her drawers in the grass. Then again, you wouldn't have brought Porky over there along on a lovers' picnic."

"Hey, who're you calling Porky, snake-eyes?"

I quickly put my hand on K2's shoulder. This interview was not going the way we planned, not at all. Snake would be throwing us off the property in another minute. Or throwing snakes at us. "We're still looking for the colt, but Connor here is acting for Ty Farraday in inspecting real estate for sale."

"The sideshow cowboy?"

Connor's lips thinned. I hurried on: "He's a horseman, yes. He is thinking of establishing another sanctuary for rescued equines. There's more need now, with people tightening their belts and giving up their horses."

K2 wasn't blowing his nose, so maybe Ty really was considering buying a second ranch. "Is it okay if we look around?"

Snake spit into the overgrown grass. "No rhinestone cowboy's got enough cash to buy this place."

"Ty Farraday does." Connor had his arms crossed over his chest, as if daring Snake to contradict him.

I looked at K2. He was kicking at the tall weeds, most likely hoping to scare up a boa constrictor.

"Not much left standing. Place'd need a fortune to make it fit for keeping a herd of ponies here."

"He's got it," Connor said, starting to walk toward the remaining stable building.

Snake didn't try to stop him. Instead, he asked if I wanted to look at the bunkhouse, see if he was hiding a horse under his mattress.

I didn't want to see anything over, under, or near his mattress. I didn't want to walk through the grasses in Connor's wake. I didn't want to stay here chatting with Snake either. Talk about a rock and a hard place, with quicksand. I grabbed the back of K2's T-shirt before he could follow Connor. At least I wouldn't be alone with the viper.

His eyes darting from me to the stable to the road

leading up to the ranch, Snake asked, "So how much do you think a white colt is worth?"

The one I wanted was priceless. How could you put a value on magic, or on peace of mind for an entire herd, an entire village? "I have no way of knowing. A lot, I suppose."

Snake stroked his chin and spit again. "You sure there's any such animal? I've heard the females can disappear in thin air. Don't sound right to me."

I thought about my dream, the alphabet soup, the bracelet Margaret made for me. "I think they're all real. If you know anything about them, you ought to tell me. If we find out you withheld information, you'll be in big trouble."

"You threatening me, missy?"

Who, me? "No, not at all. Just offering a suggestion."

"Might be I can ask my little friends to look around. For a price. And maybe for a taste of what you're giving away free. That fancy-pants foreigner, and now the candy-ass cowboy. Why not me?"

Let me count the ways. I stepped back and pulled K2 with me toward the car, glad to see Connor come out of the stable, even if he was shaking his head. With my escorts around me, I felt braver. "You call if you have any information, then we can talk about a finder's fee. In money. But know this, Mr. Sinese, we will find the colt, with or without your help."

K2 didn't even sniffle.

Chapter 19

‟**W**HAT DID YOU SEE? Were there any snakes? Did you find the white horse?"

That was K2. I was more circumspect. "Well?"

Connor reported a lot of disappointment. He'd seen piles of stuff in the loose boxes. He explained those were big stalls for breeding mares, so they could lie down and give birth, and the vets and grooms had room to help. There were six of them, no number nine, and he couldn't see behind all the junk: furniture salvaged from the house, some extra lumber, moldy saddles. There was no light to see the back of the stalls, and I never gave him the flashlight from the car. Who thought he'd need it? There'd been a light bulb hanging from an overhead wire in my dream.

"There was no sign a horse had been there any time this decade. No spilled grain, no straw. I did a quick walk around the outside without spotting a manure pile."

"He could dump it in the lake. I bet Snake wouldn't care about polluting his own well water."

"Unless magic horses don't poop." That was from K2, and wasn't impossible.

"There was a lock on an equipment room door. I called out, but didn't get any response, not so much as a whicker."

Of course not. The colt thought all men were monsters. "I should have gone with you."

"Why? You had to keep Snake talking, find out what he knew."

We both turned to look at K2 in the back seat.

"He was lying, like my dad said. Most times. Or not telling the whole truth. That's harder to tell. You should have gone with him to the bunkhouse, Willow, when he invited you to look there."

Yeck. "Why?"

"Because he knew you wouldn't go. That's why he asked you. I bet the horse is there. He's got electric and everything."

That made sense, in a way. So the kid wasn't as dumb as he looked. But what if I had taken Snake up on the dare, with the intent of snooping? Snake couldn't take the chance, not if he was holding out for a ransom like it sounded. "I don't think our baby is in Snake's house, but you're right. It's worth a search."

"What'd he mean about you and the cowboy, Willow?"

"Nothing."

K2 wiped his nose with the back of his wrist. Which reminded me to ask Connor why he shook Snake's hand.

"There were signs. I wanted to be sure. His liver is shot from the alcohol. He'll be dead within six months, maybe less."

"Does he know he's dying, do you think?"

"His body does. There's no way of telling if his mind accepts it. He'll have to, soon."

"So what does he want with the money? A lot of money, by the sound of it, and only when he's good and ready. I think he's stringing us along, hoping we'll get desperate enough to pay some exorbitant price. But a dying man wouldn't need a fortune, and I never heard of any family for him to leave it to." I thought about that while K2 rattled off charities, a secret girlfriend, a last chance to see Disneyland.

Snake in Disneyland? I had a good imagination, but that one boggled my mind. "No, I bet he's hoping to pay for a liver transplant."

Connor shook his head. "No one would give an alky a donor liver. He'd kill it in a month. Except . . ."

"Except what?" K2 and I both demanded.

"Except no legitimate hospital would do the transplant. Some foreign countries aren't as scrupulous about who gets the organs. A lot of people in those places are so poor they'll do anything for the money, sell off one kidney or part of their liver. That's all you need, not the whole thing, for a transplant. There are even places where you can buy convicts' parts, or organs from kidnapped victims."

"Where? What countries?" K2 swore he'd never go to any of them.

I decided Snake had motive enough. All we needed was a more thorough investigation of the ranch. "I doubt the police will get us a search warrant without any hard evidence. And Snake will never let us go poking around again." Not that I'd done any poking.

"Ty can go look. Maybe bring a real estate agent so it looks good."

"Great. My friend Martha will come. With flashlights. And maybe a couple of engineers and surveyors."

Connor grunted. "It's a sweet prospect. Cool place for horses, once it's cleaned up."

"What about the snakes?"

"I didn't see any."

"I did." K2 reached into his pocket; I saw him in the rearview mirror.

I screamed, stopped the car, and jumped out.

He pulled out a tissue to blot his dripping nose. "I lied."

I got rid of the kid as fast as I could, then had one of the auto body guys vacuum out his cooties. After, I drove Connor to pick up some stuff he needed at the drugstore; I wondered if Walter was going to put condoms in his bag, too.

While Connor was shopping, I went to see Uncle Henry at the police station.

He couldn't send a search party up to Bayview Ranch, not without permission from the corporation that had its name on the deed. Tracking down their lawyers would take days, but the Preservation Fund people might have a phone number. They'd want to come, as an interested party. As I thought, Uncle Henry didn't have enough just cause to get a criminal warrant. And no one popped in on Snake out of friendship. The asp didn't have any friends.

But maybe the chief could drive up, neighborly like, saying he'd heard Snake was feeling poorly, asking if he needed a ride to a doctor or something. While he was away from the ranch . . .

"You could get arrested for trespassing, that's what."

Unsatisfied, I drove around the commons and fetched Connor, who had a grin on his face. Yup, I figured he got condoms and the word that he'd need them soon.

When we got to Rosehill, I drove around to the back to drop Con off. Ty was in the new paddock, with Paloma Blanca circling around him on a lunge line, Connor said they called it. I watched while the white horse changed direction, changed gait, changed how she carried her head or her tail—all without a word I could hear from Ty, or a movement of his hands on the line. Maybe he could talk to her. Or maybe the routine was so well memorized, the brilliant horse didn't need any direction. And maybe I was spending too much time staring at Ty's tight butt in his tight jeans.

I cleared my throat.

Ty unclipped the mare from the line and came over to the fence. "Any luck?"

Connor gave one of his rare smiles. "Maybe soon, according to the wacky pharmacist they've got here."

I frowned at the younger man and told Ty, "We think we have motive, and the place, but no, we didn't find the colt. We thought you could go up with a real estate agent and pretend to be interested in purchasing the property."

"I'll go tomorrow. We're all invited out to your cousin's uncle's restaurant tonight. Is everyone in this place related?"

"Not everyone, and not always by blood, only by familiarity. Who's invited to the Breakaway?"

"Mrs. Garland, Doc, Susan's parents, you, me, and Connor."

Connor opened the gate to the paddock and walked toward the horse. "I'm not going."

Ty raised his brow. "Folks mean well by us. And it's Miss Lily's night off. No one's cooking here."

I could understand Connor's reluctance to go out with the group. He'd be rubbing shoulders with an old man who'd had a stroke, another who had a rare tick-borne disease, Susan with her recent history, and a witch. Not easy for a kid who can sense illness or incipient death.

"Susan will be in the kitchen," I told him, "and Doc is the nicest man you'll ever meet."

He still looked mulish. "I'm not wearing a suit and tie."

"This is Paumanok Harbor. Half the men don't own a suit or a tie. Or they save them for funerals and court appearances. You'll love Susan's cooking. Everyone does."

Maybe out of a young man's pride, or just because he wanted to cut out early, Connor insisted he'd take the motorbike. He knew his way around the town and could find the restaurant easily.

Ty said he'd pick me up in Rosehill's SUV. No question, no suggestion. No argument from me.

Black shirt, black ironed jeans, black cowboy hat. Damn, I was driving with Johnny Cash. Only Ty was a lot younger and a lot better looking. And Johnny Cash never made my pulse rate increase with a smile and a "Looking good, blondie." I guess racing home to get Little Red, then begging Janie for a haircut and blonder highlights was worth it.

He left his hat in the car. I left my sense of self-preservation behind and took his hand to walk into the restaurant. Half the Breakaway's patrons must have thought he was a country music star or something, too, because they all stared as we looked around for our party. Or maybe they were just watching Willow Tate making a fool of herself again.

Connor came in right behind us. I'd bet he waited in

the parking lot for reinforcements. I would have. Then again, he performed in front of hundreds of strangers, thousands even. Sure he didn't have to touch any of the audience, and he had his horse under him, but no one was going to bother him here. Not with Ty and me on either side of him. I wanted to take his hand, but that was the last thing he'd want. I squeezed Ty's hand harder, instead.

None of us should have worried. Doc came forward to lead us to the far corner of the restaurant. I guess he'd been warned, or he just always knew what was right, because he had his cane in one hand and a glass of wine in the other. Doc wasn't going to shake Connor's hand, but he made sure to tell him how pleased he was to meet a man of his courage and caliber. Connor looked at Ty, as if Doc must be speaking of the head honcho, but no, Doc looked right at him and said the burden Connor carried would strangle a lesser man.

Connor stood a little taller. I wanted to hug Doc, but Ty held me back, scowling at my obvious affection for the older man. I wondered if he was jealous, and smiled more warmly at Doc, just to see. Yup, the crease between Ty's eyes deepened.

We took our places at the big table in the corner, with Connor and me vying for the seat farthest from my grandmother.

We weren't a hard drinking party, it seemed, when a waiter came to take our bar order. Doc couldn't have more than the one glass of wine; Grandma wouldn't have any. Aunt Jas and Uncle Roger said they'd have wine with dinner, whatever the man recommended to go with whatever Susan was cooking. Connor ordered a sparkling water with lemon, so I did, too. I expected Ty to ask for a studly drink, Maker's Mark or Dewars on the rocks, maybe. He settled on a draft beer from the microbrewery in Southampton, just because it was called Caballero.

How good could a beer from Southampton with a Spanish cowboy name be? Not very. Ty drank half, in a toast we all shared to good company and better times ahead. Then he asked the waiter for whatever I was drinking.

Both Ty and Connor looked around to see that other tables of diners were studying their menus. We didn't get any.

"Susan's showing off for you and Doc tonight. But don't worry, she's really talented." I didn't have to explain that while she was a talented cook, some other skill was involved in how she almost always pleased her customers and made them feel happier for eating her food. Kind of like Doc and his natural, contagious good cheer. He was beaming now, telling everyone how glad he was to be back with old friends and making new ones.

It worked . . . the food and the friendliness. Everyone chatted and I relaxed, until Ty put his hand on the back of my neck and whispered: "Did I tell you how good you look tonight, darlin'?" He inhaled deeply. "You smell good, too. Like summer in a field of flowers."

I didn't know what to say other than that he didn't smell of horse tonight, so I kept my mouth shut. I didn't want to tell him that his spicy, musky scent reminded me of sex and sensuality and getting naked and—

Thank goodness the wait staff placed a goat cheese salad in front of each of us. There were pecans, tiny oranges, and baby greens I knew came from Grandma's Garland Farm. Connor looked dubiously at the greens, but after a forkful he held his glass up to me in a toast of acknowledgment. Susan could cook.

The salad was just what I needed to get my mind away from Ty and his obvious efforts at seduction. It was all that I needed, I told myself, the way I'd been eating. But then huge platters of seafood bruschetta arrived on the table. Mussels, clams, shrimp, scallops, and chunks of lobster sat atop wedges of artisanal bread, all in garlic sauce. There was a large bowl of pasta, too, but I didn't even look at the additional carbs. Or the vegetable gratin or the ham-wrapped asparagus spears or the six or seven other dishes the waiter kept bringing.

While everyone else was talking about the news of the day, I was counting how many miles I'd have to jog to burn off this dinner. And that was without dessert. Thank goodness I had to put my fork down to give my news after Ty explained his intent to draw the mares to my yard. Connor then described what we'd seen at Bayview Ranch. He went back to figuring how to get a mussel out of its shell without dripping butter and garlic down his shirt.

Ty put his hand on my thigh under the table, almost causing brain lock. Definitely causing the temperature in the restaurant to go up a few degrees.

Grandma Eve had to repeat her question about the houses we'd visited before I remembered it was my turn to speak. The devil smiled and winked, but he didn't remove his hand.

I took a sip of my drink as if my throat were dry. It was. Then I recounted where we'd gone before visiting Snake. When I mentioned the Froeler girl, Doc offered to call the mother about getting Letty out of the house and into my course. They all laughed about K2 and his dripping nose, but Grandma Eve said the child wasn't eating properly. She'd send some vegetables over to the auto body shop. The boy would eat them, or else.

Connor choked. I just smiled and showed them Margaret's bracelet.

When Aunt Jasmine started a story about a baby blanket Margaret wove for Cousin Lily's daughter, who hadn't been able to get pregnant, Ty held a scallop up to my mouth.

"What are you doing?" I whispered, looking around to see if anyone noticed the intimacy.

"Just trying to fatten you up. You're too thin."

To hell with seduction. I think I could fall in love with this guy.

CHAPTER 20

PERMISSION TO EAT PROFITEROLES? Now that was a worthwhile whisper of sweet something in my ear.

Ty grinned at me. "I like a woman with some meat on her bones. I don't have to be afraid she'll break when I love her."

That was moving way too fast, profiteroles or not. They were light pastry shells, split and filled with ice cream, then draped with chocolate sauce and whipped cream and raspberry icing ribbons. They were a signature dish at the Breakaway, along with the freshest seafood you could find.

Ty would be worse for me than a whole plate of the things. He was a high-calorie, high-fat, high-carb luxury of no nutritional value. He was instant gratification in one gorgeous cream puff, with nothing left but crumbs when he was gone. So I had to resist him and his smile and his smell and his sex appeal.

With my nonexistent willpower? My "I'll jog tomorrow" rationalizations? I didn't dare start enjoying them, or I'd never stop. Pastries or playboys.

I took a tiny bite of the dessert. That's all I was going to allow myself of Ty Farraday, too. I swore it.

Susan came out of the kitchen and was congratulated by everyone. Uncle Bernie, Uncle Roger's brother and the owner of the restaurant, brought his second wife,

Ginnie, over to have coffee with us. Ty needed both hands to stir his coffee, so I relaxed and listened to my family and friends. Connor was flirting in Spanish with the Dominican busgirl; Doc was nodding his approval at everyone; Aunt Jasmine was trying to convince Ty to come talk to the kids in the summer school program while Ginnie thought he ought to put on a show to benefit the food pantry, her pet charity; the uncles were planning a fishing trip; even Grandma seemed to be enjoying herself talking cooking with Susan and a couple she knew at the next table.

I liked it. I felt at home, comfortable, confident. Hey, I hadn't spilled anything on my silk shirt yet and the primo dude in the place was playing footsie under the table with me, except his were in black alligator boots. I kept the alligator in my mind, not the shivers running up my leg. And I congratulated myself on the self-discipline I showed in having a paltry two bites of the decadent dessert. So what if the waiters took the plate away before I lost self-control?

Things were good . . . until I remembered the mares and the mayhem they could cause in Paumanok Harbor. And how people—the people I'd known my whole life—were depending on me to fix it. The colt was depending on me, too.

I announced that I better get going. The dogs needed to go out, I had to check in with my parents, I'd had a long day. Everyone knew I'd have a long night, one way or another. I ignored the smirks from Susan. The exodus from the restaurant began.

"I really like your family," Ty said when we got into his car. "And you were right about your cousin's cooking. Paloma Blanca'll be complaining if I keep on eating like that. Watching you enjoy your meal was the best part."

The glow of good food and good feeling lasted until we drove out of the parking lot.

Ty thought he'd drop me off, go back to Rosehill to change his clothes, then come back and camp out in my yard, with me. I thought he ought to watch from inside, downstairs, listening for me while I slept upstairs, so he could help if I got caught in a nightmare.

Once again, we argued over which was more important, finding the baby or comforting the mother.

I stared at the passing scenery without noticing if we were going in the right direction. "You just want to see the mares."

"And you don't. You're afraid of them, afraid of the bad vibes they give off."

Shouldn't everyone be? "I'm afraid something will happen to the colt while we're sitting around in the damp air communing with nature."

"You have no way of knowing you'll even dream about the colt."

"And you have no way of knowing if the mares will come, if they'll understand you, if they will listen to whatever you want to say to them."

His fingers got tighter on the steering wheel. I could see a muscle moving in his cheek, too, as he clenched his teeth. "I want to tell them where we think they should look. I want them to tell me how they got here, and why the colt couldn't follow them. They can get him out. Willow, they have magic. They can disappear and reappear. We cannot. But if we can't reach the mares, they can destroy your town, your family. All those nice people in the restaurant."

"But if we find the colt, if we bring him out, back to his family, we'll accomplish the same thing."

"How will we bring him to the mares if we don't know where they are? For that matter, how do we know what will hold him? Rope, and he vanishes so no one, us or the mares, ever finds him again? Cold metal, and he's stripped of his magic so he can't return to wherever he belongs?"

"He can tell me." I know I sounded uncertain, but how else could I refute Ty's logic?

He wasn't convinced, or finished. "What if we kill him trying to free him? Say we break the door down. Maybe he is some rare albino and we blind him or burn him with the sunlight. Worst case, what if he goes up in flames or a puff of smoke?"

I hadn't thought about that. "We'll bring blankets to wrap him in, and cover his eyes. We'll hold umbrellas over him. Or we could go in the dark." Visions of my long ago experience at Bayview at night made me shudder. "And avoid the snakes."

"The snakes are the least of our worries."

That was easy for him to say. "They are less active in the nighttime, aren't they, especially when the nights are so cool?"

"Forget about the frigging snakes already. We can't go invade someone's property in the middle of the night. Even if it was legal—and I'm not saying I wouldn't take on that Snake person on principles alone—we could get shot. A moke like Sinese is bound to have a shotgun, and he'd be within his rights. Besides, we'd never have enough light to search everywhere on all those acres. I bet there are supply shacks and hay silos and a cabin for the stable master. We'll go in the daylight tomorrow. With a real estate agent and a lawyer if we need to, and we'll bring in some more help, to cover every inch of the place. Tomorrow, I promise."

"Very well. You try to get more information from the mares tonight. I'll try to find more about the colt my own way, without your help. And I don't care if I miss seeing the sight of the century. I've seen a troll and that was enough."

We'd arrived at my house before I could rant about how we were supposed to be partners, how he thought it took both of us working together. I got out of the car and slammed the door. "Be quiet when you come back. I'll be asleep."

"I'll come kiss you good night."

"Not if you don't want your nose broken again."

My exit would have been more dignified and more impressive if I hadn't stepped in dog poop I forgot to pick up.

I understood what Ty was saying. I could see his logic. But I still felt the way I had when Grant was too busy to come help: deserted and betrayed.

I was on my own again. I never counted on Ty. I barely knew him, hardly knew what he was capable of, and distrusted half of that. Yet I'd felt the connection, the same as he had. I thought he wanted to have a relationship, not just a quick tumble. I know it was on short acquaintance and too soon after splitting with Grant. But I thought—I felt—there was something special between us.

I wasn't planning any long-term line dancing with the cowboy. Hell, he was like a gypsy, traveling from show to show in a horse van. He was worse than Grant as a permanent fixture. He'd never settle in Paumanok Harbor. Or New York City, away from his beloved horses. Me in Texas? Now that was laughable.

But there was definitely something between us. Maybe it was just sex that I'd been missing, but I didn't think so. Whatever it was, I'd lost it.

I didn't need a man in my bed, although I thought Ty just might be another once-in-a-lifetime lover.

I didn't need a man to support me. I did fine on my own. Maybe not enough to purchase Bayview Ranch or million-dollar ponies, but I had everything I needed.

I didn't need a man to agree with me all the time. Where was the fun in that?

What I needed, what I'd wanted, was for Ty to be my friend. I guess I was just disappointed. I'd expected too much, like finding a pretty feather and expecting the bluebird of happiness to sit on your shoulder. I wanted Ty to be there for me. He wasn't.

Doc wasn't. Uncle Henry wasn't. Even Susan wasn't. Grandma Eve never was. So I called my father.

And wished I'd eaten the whole profiterole.

According to Dad, my mother and a friend were off driving a truckload of greyhounds to a foster facility in Georgia. He was celebrating having his condo back to himself by having some of the "boys" in for pinochle. He couldn't talk long.

"Okay, Dad, but I need to know if you've been feeling anything new. I've got the alligator thing covered, and I won't be getting swallowed up anytime soon. I haven't figured out the cave or the banker yet."

"You will, baby girl. I know you will. Should I serve beer or hard stuff?"

"Ask the company what they want. And don't let them drive home."

"They all live in the complex. No need to move the cars."

"Good. But Dad, are you sure you can't give me any tips on finding the missing horse?"

"I wish I could, Willy, but you know that's not how it works. I only sense what can hurt you or people I care about."

"I'm not the one in danger."

"No, but now that you mention it, maybe you ought to worry about the snow man."

"A snowman in July?"

"You know I can't be more specific. I go with what I've got, vague as it is. Snow man."

"Maybe you mean show man. Ty does trick riding exhibits. I already mistrust him. I know he's trying to snow me, if that's what you mean."

"No, it's definitely a snow man, baby. Gotta go."

Oh, God; it was the yeti! Dad's premonition was not for me, it was for Grant, climbing mountains to find the Abominable Snowman. I bet there were caves there, too. I couldn't figure where the banker came in, but Grant was definitely in danger.

Then again, the man thrived on danger. Any agent worth his badge knew Things lurked in caves: bears, bats, and dragons. So what was I going to warn him about? My father's foggy precognitions?

I called anyway and left a message. And sent a text message and an email. Maybe they had satellite service for the net. They would if a banker was along.

All I said in all of my messages was that my father saw danger in snow men and caves. Grant should be careful.

I didn't know how to sign off.

Love, Willy? But not enough.

Yours? Until this week.

TTYL? That was cold and uncaring. And impossible if he didn't have a cell connection.

Wish you were here? No, I was going to do this myself.
Grant would be like Ty, wanting to see the mares and
trying to see if he could mindspeak with them.

Wish I was there? Hell, no.

I left no sig line. He'd know who I was.

CHAPTER 21

WHILE I WAS ON-LINE, I checked my email. And my website, and my Amazon ratings. I thought about a new blog, but I couldn't talk about anything that was going on. I was too amped up for sleep. The sugar, the caffeine, the lust, the adrenaline, the fear, the lust. Life was complicated. I couldn't write about that either.

So I walked the dogs. I checked that Grandma Eve's house and fields as far as I could see were lit brightly enough for Monday night football. Susan's parents' house was a berserker's Christmas, with every color of the rainbow blinking, twinkling, and fluttering in the slight evening breeze. Only a faint glow reached my place, and the backyard was in near total darkness except for the lights I'd left on in the kitchen and my bedroom.

I decided I could get some of my real work done before Ty returned and made me shut off even my bedside reading lamp.

On paper, I reassured my book's heroine that someone was paying the ransom and she'd be free soon. The kidnapper said so. Suddenly the markers in my hand had the villain wearing dirty overalls. He needed a name, but I couldn't call him what I wanted to—that could be slander—so I paused to check the translator site on the Internet and looked up snow, for my father's presentiment. *Schnee* in German, *Neige* in French, *Nieve* in Spanish. Scheve sounded right, even if I was the only one to get the reference. Okay, Scheve, you bastard, here's a yellowish complexion and small, beady, slitted eyes.

While I was there, I blacked out a tooth, no, two teeth.

Uh-oh, that was a bad sign. Hetty could identify him. Now he'd have to kill her.

Quickly sketching, I told her help was coming. The silver horseshoe charm she wore around her neck held wizard magic. The flying horse she'd been wishing for was on the way. He'd trample the snake—oops, the kidnapper—before Scheve could throw poor Hetty off a cliff when he retrieved the ransom money. The horse was going to pick her up and fly away in the next chapter. She'd walk through fields of flowers and learn how to cure nerve damage.

I wasn't finished, but the story was coming along. I'd ask Letty if she minded my using her healing horse. On second thought, flying was enough magic without adding miracle cures. And my handicapped kid didn't need to walk through flowers. She and her white horse could fly around solving mysteries, fighting crime, punishing evildoers. I liked that better. Hetty was strong in herself, rising above adversity. A role model had to have more steel in her backbone—her damaged spine—than a charm and a charmed horse could lend her. She'll eventually find out her stepfather'd put counterfeit money in the ransom bag. I never liked him anyway. I did like a sequel. Justice for all.

Finally, I thought I could sleep. I performed my evening rituals. Brushed my hair, brushed Little Red. Washed, put on the one sexy nightie I owned, from when Grant was in town. That was just in case Ty did come in to kiss me good night and wish me sweet dreams.

Unfearful for once about leaving the house unlocked—who was going to break in with Ty sitting in the yard?—I left the back kitchen door open. That way Ty could help himself to coffee or tea if he got cold, or soda or ice water if he got hot. But no, I was not going to think about him getting hot.

I put the Pomeranian on the bed, on the pillow next to mine. I put my drawings of the white colt on the night-stand, where I could see them, concentrate on them, force myself to dream about them. This time, I told my-self, I would not be afraid. I would not become the horse and absorb his fears, but I would be me, lending my strength to him. First I had to apologize. I felt I owed the colt that much for not calling out to him myself while we were at Bayview, if he was there. If he'd answered in any way, a whicker, a whinny, a picture in my mind, we could have forced Snake to release him.

I still thought he was at the ranch with Snake, simply because the man exuded evil along with his body odor. Poor little horse. Before I turned out the lamp by the bed I whispered aloud: "I'll find you, little one, I prom-ise. But in my dreams first."

I touched the bracelet Margaret had knotted at my wrist and made a wish. It couldn't hurt.

My head did. I couldn't sleep with the pounding in my ears. Too much concentration, I thought. I was trying too hard. Then I realized the sound wasn't in my brain at all. It was in my bedroom. Or right outside the window. Damn.

I opened the shade without switching on the lamp. A few stars shone through the clouds, and a little moon-light. I could barely make out the shape of the wicker sofa from my porch, and that only because it had a re-cent coat of fresh white paint. As my eyes adjusted, I spotted the cowboy hat and the seated figure who wore it. What I didn't recognize was the sound I heard, above the chant.

Hadn't some native tribes put dried beans in a gourd to use in ceremonial dances? That's what the sound re-minded me of. Damn if Ty Farraday wasn't praying for rain or something.

My bedroom window was open because the night was warm. I raised the screen and leaned out. "Do you have to make so much noise?"

"It's not me. We wired up a sound system so the chant will carry."

Since he was speaking and the chant was still going on, I realized he was playing a tape tonight. It made sense, unless the horses needed to hear him calling, in their heads from his head. "What about the maracas, or whatever you call that rattling sound?"

"It's oats in a coffee can. My horses recognize the sound and come running for a treat."

I took a deep breath. "These are not your horses. Most likely they have never been fed oats. Certainly not from a coffee can. What the devil are you thinking?"

"That if you couldn't sleep, sweet pea, you'd come down and keep me company."

"Besides being arrogant, you are rude, selfish, manipulative and—"

"Does that mean you won't share the cookies I brought?"

"What kind?"

"Oreos."

That was playing dirty. I could have resisted Fig Newtons. "Got milk?"

"I was hoping you'd be a sweetheart and bring some."

So I put on my sweats. No way was I going outside in a scrap of ribbon and lace. I filled two plastic glasses with milk, then picked up a couple of napkins to prove I knew how to entertain. I gave the big dogs biscuits so they would go back to sleep, and left Little Red inside. If the mares did come, I didn't want him barking at them or nipping at their heels.

Ty had spread a blanket over the wicker sofa's cushions, and had another to use as a lap rug. He also had the wicker coffee table, with his booted feet propped on it. He patted the space beside him, then raised the blanket for me to slide under. I set the milk and napkins on the table and sat down. The sofa was only a two-seater, and he took up more than his half, sprawled in loose-limbed comfort. We were closer than I would have liked, but not quite touching, so I leaned back. He held a cookie up to my mouth, and held it while I took a bite.

Who knew cookies and milk could be so sexy?

Who was I kidding? It was the cowboy who was sexy.

He could be feeding me lime Jell-O with canned fruit floating in it and I'd think that was sexy, too. Like now, when he used his thumb to brush a cookie crumb off my lower lip, and his touch was soft and tender and stayed way longer than there were crumbs. I licked my lip, and he inhaled deeply.

"You know, you were right," he said.

"About trying to find the colt first?"

"No, about the coffee can. I have no idea if these animals can eat our food. Maybe they live on moonbeams."

I thought back. "The troll was huge, but I don't think I ever saw him eat. And the little boy we were all looking for never thrived here, so he had to leave in order to live. And I dreamed the colt didn't like the food he was given. Maybe that's why he seemed so weak to me."

"But this"—he waved his arm at the whole yard, the piles of stuff I could see in my backyard—"was all I could think of to do."

Instead of putting his arm down, he put it around my shoulders and pulled me a little closer. I felt warmer that way, so made no protest. "You could have helped me dream."

"Darlin', if I were lying next to you, we wouldn't be dreaming. And if I did fall asleep, maybe out of satisfied exhaustion, I'd only dream about waking up next to you for another go-round."

I tried to pull away, but he tightened his grip. "I'm not being pushy, just honest. Besides, the only dreams I ever remember are more about fillies, the two-footed kind, than about horses. Much as I love them, they don't figure in my dreams." He finished his milk and another cookie. I shook my head. I was done eating.

"That's the problem, Willow. I do love the horses. It's in my blood, just like liking women, but different. I have to try to help if they're in trouble. That's what I do, who I am. It's part of being so close I know what they're thinking most times. Like the other side of the coin, or the small print on the contract. I have a gift; I have the responsibility to use it. So when I got the call to come and saw the situation for myself, I knew I had to find the mares and try to help them. I can't dream up the colt, but I can maybe work with the white ladies. I had to try."

I understood. It was kind of like going to doctors with a problem. You got a different opinion from every one. A surgeon tells you that you need an operation. An oncologist prescribes treatment. A shrink says it's in your mind. They had their specialties, their fields of expertise. I still didn't know what mine was, but it wasn't facing danger, not if the peril was in sitting next to a warm, muscular body, inhaling the scent of spices and horse and virility, staring at an empty lawn. "Is that a roundabout apology for not letting me try my way?"

"Hell, no. Real men don't admit they're wrong. They try to make you understand why they act dumb, is all."

I smiled. "No explanation needed."

He leaned over and brushed my forehead with his lips. Cookies and kisses, what a night! What a seduction, no matter what he said.

I pulled the blanket tighter under my chin, a physical barrier and a silent sign in body language any guy could understand. You didn't need to be a horse whisperer or a mind reader to interpret a wool wall. Lord knows I did not need the blanket on top of me, but I wasn't giving in to a rogue and a rambler, not even if the heat from his arm around my shoulders was raising my temperature a few degrees already. To say nothing of where our sides were pressed together. I could feel the warmth right through my sweatshirt and his denim shirt. The only thing is, the heat was coming from inside, not out. I was glad for the darkness and the blanket, so he couldn't see where my nipples were making little tents on the front of my shirt after that oh-so-brief touch of his mouth on my skin. I took a deep breath—which only made the evidence of my interest more prominent—and asked, "So what have you seen so far?"

He stroked my shoulder with his hand, but almost absently, as if he were used to petting Paloma Blanca as they rode, just for the contact. I had to pull the blanket away before I started to perspire.

"Fireflies," he said, now kneading the muscles of my

shoulder and neck. He must have taken the lowered covering as an invitation I couldn't rescind without acting like a prissy spinster.

"That's all?"

"A couple of little bats. I don't know what breeds you have here, and they moved too fast to tell."

I shuddered. "Bats."

He rubbed my neck. "Don't worry. They're just keeping the flies away."

"Anything else?"

"A doe leading her fawns toward the grains I spread around. Two raccoons fighting over the apples, and a rat carrying off a carrot."

What a guy! The man could talk and turn my insides to mush at the same time. And chant. But that was on tape, wasn't it? So the beat I heard this time really was my heart, or his. I tried to gather what wits I had left. "Wow, you managed to bring vermin to my back yard with your cockamamie plan. Lovely."

"They were always here. You just never saw them. Besides, you don't have plague-carrying city rats. Yours are wood rats."

"How can you tell?"

"These are the woods, aren't they?" He pointed toward the pine trees at the back of the property.

I wasn't sure about his reasoning, but I was certain the hand that did the pointing didn't belong under my sweatshirt. "Um . . ."

"And a couple of mosquitoes, but not as many as you'd find in Texas. I thought I heard an owl, so I hope the mice won't come. I'd hate to think I baited them out in the open to make a meal for someone else."

"But no white mares."

"Not yet."

I groaned when his fingers found those hardened nipples and the sensitive skin at the sides of my breasts. His fingers were warm and callused, but not rough. Just right. I groaned again. Wanting more? Needing to end it all right here? I couldn't think straight enough to decide.

He kissed me, which was no help at all. Lips, tongue,

teeth. Sparks, flames, fire. His hand at the elastic of my sweat pants, my hand reaching for his neck to bring him closer, except the brim of his hat got in the way and brought me back to reality. "Hey, Tex, do you go to bed with your boots on, too?"

"Only if I'm in a hurry." He took off the hat, but I had my hormones under control by now. "I better go in."

"Shh." He put his finger over my lips. "Look."

"The mares?"

It was a fox, trailed by three kits. You seldom saw foxes these days, except as roadkill. A mange had nearly wiped them out a few years ago, letting the rabbit population explode. Now the foxes were coming back to feed on the bounty. These were coming to check out the vegetables. "If they get a taste for Grandma's crops, you're in big trouble."

"The fences will keep them out of her gardens. Unless she has chickens, too."

"No. One of her friends supplies the eggs for the farm stand and Grandma's kitchen."

We stayed quiet to watch the young foxes tumble around, then wrestle over an apple two of them wanted.

"Thank you."

"For the kisses? That was nothing, darlin'."

"For giving me the night."

CHAPTER 22

"I'D GIVE YOU THE MOON AND THE STARS if I could," Ty said. "And I'd do anything to keep you from dreaming about that colt."

"Like seducing me?"

"Hell, pumpkin, that idea came way before I knew what was really going on. I was hard at the first sight of you in that sassy little sundress, all legs and eyes and attitude. No heft to you at all, but there you stood, ready to defend your lambs from the big bad wolf. I was a goner. I wanted you then. I want you now. I'll likely want you for a good long while."

I noticed he didn't say he'd want me for forever. I doubted the word was in his vocabulary, or in his genes. Not that I blamed him. How long had we known each other, anyway? It's not that I wanted happily ever after with him, either. I just wanted the happily ever after part. Didn't everyone?

Crickets joined his chant. Maybe tree frogs. I couldn't tell. It sounded good, a night chorus. So did his low, rumbling voice with its soft drawl: "But wanting you has nothing to do with wanting to keep you out of that young horse's head. Colts are skittish and easily spooked at the best of times. The idea of you sharing nightmares with another creature, an alien creature at that, terrifies me. People who go down that rabbit hole sometimes don't come back."

"I know."

"And your colt is already half out of his head with fear and despair."

"I know."

"But you want to do it anyway?"

"I have to do it. Like you said about helping the horses. Somehow I got connected. I dreamed him. I drew him. Now he's my problem."

Ty leaned back and slouched lower against the cushions. "You know, a person could lose an arm or a leg and still be himself. He could manage. But to lose your mind? That would be the worst thing I can imagine. Trapped in your head, drowning in bad dreams? That's too big a sacrifice, too big a chance to take."

Without his touch, I was feeling the cool night air again. Or maybe it was his words sending a chill down my back. Did he think I wasn't afraid of going bonkers? I spend half my life worrying that I'm already crazy. And that's without the colt's night terrors. "I won't get lost in the baby's thoughts," I told him, trying to sound confident enough to reassure both of us. "I didn't before. Now I know what to expect. I'll be stronger."

"Easy to say, and you are strong. Strong-willed, anyway. But you have no control over your own dreams, less over someone else's. Make that some*thing* else's. And you'd be on your own. I can't go there with you. You and I both know that. I couldn't get there if you needed help."

I reached over and took his hand. "But I am not yours to protect and defend."

He brought my hand to his cheek and kept it there, a comfort. He made a half-laugh. "I guess I am just hard-wired to look after people I care about."

He did care about me, not just sex. I knew that in my heart. Maybe happily for now was possible, and enough. "It seems to me that you're hard-wired for a lot."

"Sex and protecting my woman? Honey, that comes with the apparatus. It's called survival of the species."

"For a caveman."

"So I'll beat my chest. I'd toss you over my shoulder

and drag you back to my cave if I thought I could get away with it."

That could not be the cave my father warned me about. The cowboy might be larger than life, but he was not Batman. "You wouldn't get far or for long, not with me kicking and screaming the whole way. I hate caves."

He laughed. "I can't say I like them much myself. I like open spaces, big sky." He tilted his head back to look up. "Like this one."

More of the clouds had drifted away and you could pick out galaxies, if you knew what you were looking for. I found the Big Dipper, which was about the extent of my astronomy. We did have nice night skies here at the end of Long Island, far away from city lights.

In comfortable silence, we enjoyed the view and the feeling of being the only two people in the world, together. Then he said, "I gave up the macho crap years ago. Brawling and drinking and tomcatting. I'm still a man. My stepmother taught me to be responsible. My father taught me to never hit a girl. You have a problem with that?"

"No. I like knowing that chivalry isn't dead. And that you worry about me. What I don't like is you telling me what to do, or what I can't do. Or trying to keep me from what I know is the right thing to do."

"Yeah, I figured you didn't like anyone taking the reins. So why did you send for a rider if you thought you could mend your own fences?"

"Why do people take their cars to a mechanic? Because it's the right person for the right job. Sure they could learn to fix it themselves, but no one could learn to do what you do. I can draw and I can dream, but I'd never know how to communicate with the mares. I need you. I just don't need you interfering with my part of the job."

"What if I have a better idea of getting your job done?"

I was listening. It's not as if I was looking forward to those ragged emotions pouring from the young horse. "Let's hear it."

"Okay, what if we get Doc to hypnotize you? With me right there. He could wake you up at the first sign of trouble. Or help me connect with you to lend my strength and knowledge of horses. Then it doesn't have to be at night. You don't have to be tired. And much as I regret it, blondie, we don't have to be in bed together."

His plan was tempting and his disappointment was sweet. "But hypnosis isn't the same as sleep. Do you even dream in a trance?"

"I don't know. But it's worth a try, isn't it? We can do it first thing in the morning, before going out to that ranch."

I liked the idea of a safety net and Doc as spotter for my high-wire act. Besides, I wasn't getting a whole lot of dreaming done tonight anyway. If I fell asleep at all, I figured a tall, lean cowboy'd be riding the rem range.

I said I agreed if Doc agreed, and Ty sighed in relief. Then he kissed me. He really did care about me, I guess. A kiss so tender, so gentle, showed it. He deepened the kiss, showing he still wanted to get me naked. I responded to the caring, then I responded to the caveman. The kiss led to the edge of who gives a damn about tomorrow. Then I heard a rustle in the grass.

I jerked away, out of his arms. I pulled my sweatshirt down, without knowing how it almost got over my head in the first place.

"It's only a possum."

Only a possum? Only a heart attack in a fur coat. And a reminder of what we were doing besides communing with nature. I shifted an inch away on the sofa. "We're here to watch. Nothing else."

"Hmm."

"Nothing else," I insisted. We weren't teenagers making out on the front porch. When the time was right, when we were ready, when we knew each other better, when nothing was going to slither across my foot. Then. Maybe.

So we watched and waited and wrapped the blanket over us. I leaned my head on Ty's shoulder when my neck got stiff from being in the same position. He put his

hat back on and started to chant along with the recording. I could feel the vibrations through his chest. "What
are you saying?"

He let the recording go on without him. "Repetitive
sounds, mixed with an ancient incantation to the Great
Spirit. It's supposed to be beckoning, praising, welcoming. Soothing, restful, peaceful."

I didn't know about the mares, but it sure worked for
me. Soothing, restful, peaceful . . .

. . . I showed Hetty the sketches I'd made, and she
smiled. She knew she'd get out of the tiny prison soon,
and get her revenge, too. She touched the horseshoe
charm on her necklace and went back to sleep. Good
girl, I thought in my dream. She was a brave kid who'd
make a great superhero, Hetty and her horse.

The horse.

The colt was lying flat out in a thin layer of straw,
limp. Not dead—oh, God—not dead!

I could feel my panic rising and tamped it down. No.
His chest rose and fell. He was worn out, weary, waiting for the end, but he was alive. Maybe that's why I
couldn't feel his thoughts. I didn't want to wake the poor
baby. Hell, I didn't want to crawl into his head or have
him in mine, not after Ty's reminder. But I was here, and
I had to tell him to hang on. I had to find clues to his
whereabouts. I had to keep dreaming.

I drew a picture in my head, a willow tree, a weeping
willow. "Me."

The white head rose up, as if looking for someone.
My sleeping self clenched her fists against a coming rush
of emotion, but the horse was too weak or too forlorn to
project his desperation. His eyes shut against the glare
from the overhead light bulb. His drained condition
was bad, but maybe better for talking than the blinding
agony. Maybe we could talk.

We had no language in common. So we'd use images.
That was me, right? The Visualizer. I put up the willow
tree again in my head, like a slide show. "Willow. Me."

"H'tah," came a whisper in my head, with pictures
and emotions.

H'tah, not Hetty. Ah. I projected joy, that I knew my friend's name, that we could communicate. He blew air out his nose. Ty might have known what that meant. I didn't.

I tried to picture puzzlement, but had to settle on "What happened, H'tah? Where are you? Why can't you free yourself or call to your mother?"

He laid his head down again. I'd gone too fast, given him too much that he couldn't understand. Slow down, Willow. Slow down. I was in control. I was strong. I could do this.

I was dreaming.

I didn't know what I was doing.

Then I noticed one of H'tah's rear legs was swollen, red and bloodstained. I pictured that leg in my head, and tried to project caring and curiosity.

Now the flood of emotions and images came hurtling at me. A monster! Yellow eyes, noise, terrible smell, speed.

I quickly drew a vehicle. "Car."

Yes! More images, more terror mixed with pain this time. The metal monster flung H'tah into the trees. The mares disappeared in the sweeping light.

"I couldn't follow," I wailed.

"No," I shouted. "I am not you! I'll help, but I am not you." I tried to breathe deeply, calmly, peacefully. I concentrated on feeling that things would get better. "I promise. What next?"

Another monster, two-footed. In coveralls.

So Snake did have H'tah.

A sack over his head, a thunderous noise, speed, smells, roughness, then here. Alone. Abandoned.

"No, do not despair! Even if you do not know where you are, I do." Damn, I kept forgetting he could not understand English. I mentally drew the closet or stall or wherever H'tah was. Then I put grass outside, and a man in a cowboy hat and me, tearing down the walls, coming to get him. "Tomorrow. I promise."

He sighed. I hoped he understood my feelings, if not my words.

I played him some of Ty's chant, restful, peaceful, soothing . . . until it was drowned out by a scratchy humming, heavy footsteps, things being dragged aside, metal rasping.

H'tah started trembling. He lurched to his feet, holding the wounded leg out to the side. He pressed himself against the wood plank so hard I felt my own flesh bruise.

"No, no, baby. Be brave." In my head, I tried to draw a willow tree between me and a white horse. I couldn't fill in the drooping branches fast enough to hide the white coat.

Then there was Snake and the smell of alcohol and unwashed body.

"Monster!"

I couldn't tell if that was H'tah or me.

Snake came in, shined a flashlight in H'tah's poor eyes, and started shouting: "Cure me, damn it! That's what you're supposed to do! Cure the cancer, you bastard."

H'tah did not understand. I showed him a man with a tumor in his belly. He shook his head. I saw a huge white stallion pressing his forehead to an injured horse, who got up and trotted away.

H'tah couldn't cure anything. He was too young. The stallion was the only one who could. Pride. Sire.

Snake was furious. He grabbed H'tah's short mane and shook him.

"NO!" I screamed.

"Cure me!" he shouted.

H'tah fell down, moaning.

Snake reached behind him, to the bucket I hadn't noticed him bring into the stall. "Maybe this'll make you try harder!" He pulled out a snake as thick as his wrist, as long as the cell was wide, as black as Snake's heart. He uncoiled it from his arm and flung it at H'tah's head.

My head!

"Get up, get up!"

H'tah got his feet under him and backed as far as he could go. The snake hissed and writhed itself into a circle.

"Hetty," I started to call. But she couldn't walk. Couldn't get there. Wasn't in this part of the dream.

The snake was coming toward H'tah, its mouth open, tongue flicking back and forth, tiny eyes burning into mine. Coming. Toward me.

I knew I was sending my terror to H'tah. I couldn't help it. "Get up. Trample the evil thing. Use your front legs. Jump on it, H'tah. Jump. It's a snake!"

I had to help. I kicked my feet, flailed my fists, shrieked. "Snake!"

"Hush, Willow," Ty said, grabbing at both my hands. "There's no snake. It's only a tiny lizard coming out of the leaf mold."

CHAPTER 23

I WAS GASPING, PANTING, QUIVERING. Ty was
wiping blood off his cut lower lip.

"Did I do that?"

"And near broke my toes, stamping on them so hard."

"It was Snake. He has H'tah. He threw a snake. Snake
wants a cure. H'tah can't. Only his sire can. Snake—"

He put a hand over my mouth. I could taste the blood
from where he wiped his own lips. "Slow down, Willy.
It was a dream, that's all. A nightmare from the white
ladies."

"No. It was real, it was happening." I had to sit down
again, before my legs gave out. One of the blankets from
the sofa was already in a heap on the ground, so I sank
onto it, then pulled the other blanket around me against
the ice in my blood.

"It was real." I started to cry. I couldn't help that,
either. Poor H'tah, left with that maniac. And a dead
snake. I know it was dead, even if my last image was
of the horrid thing still moving, with its head flattened
under H'tah's hoof. I shook at the image, and cried
harder, great sobs that bent my spine.

Ty was kneeling beside me, rubbing my back.

Eventually the sobs ended on a hiccup. I straightened and he handed me a handkerchief. Not a tissue,
but a real cloth handkerchief. I thanked him and blew
my nose. Now I felt almost capable of coherent speech,

except I didn't know what to do with the sodden hand-kerchief. I kept it wadded in my hand. "Did you say the mares really came?"

"Yeah, just before you started screaming like a banshee."

I looked past him, to the empty yard. "Did you get to talk to them?"

"There was no time. They vanished when you started yelling about Snake."

"Not Snake, Fred Sinese. A snake. A big, black monster of a snake with tiny yellow eyes and a forked tongue and—"

He held me close, my head against his chest. "Yeah, sweet pea, I get the picture. Maybe the mares did, too. Horses don't like snakes much."

"H'tah didn't."

"H'tah?"

"That's his name, only it's got a click in it, and it's attached to images and emotions. There's a huge white stallion, filled with pride and confidence, but I know it's still our colt. I think he must be the heir of his herd, the prince. Every time I thought about his name, I felt like bowing to royalty or something, but he's still a baby."

"That doesn't make a whole lot of sense, Willy."

"But it's their language, that's how they talk, with pictures and feelings and sounds." I didn't say that was how Grant explained it. Not with another man's hands around me. "I think they learn some of our way with words if they are here long enough."

"Okay, let's go on. You saw H'tah, or whatever you call him?"

"Yes. His leg is injured. Maybe that's why he cannot vanish. Or he's too young. He couldn't cure Snake's cancer, either. Only his sire can."

Ty's hat was off, and he ran his hand through his hair. "Damn, Willy, this sounds like one of your stories. How can you know it's not your imagination speaking?"

"Because I didn't put the healing magic in my book. Letty, the Froeler girl, the one in the wheelchair, mentioned it for a story she's writing, but I didn't use it. And before you're thinking that somehow I tapped into Letty's dreams, she's not from Paumanok Harbor." Which is to say she's not skilled the way some of the natives were.

He sat back on his heels. "The curing business is from old myths. The unicorn's horn was supposed to heal any illness. That's why they got hunted out of existence, according to ancient legends. The myth still lives, with the unicorn's horn transposed into a rhino's horn."

"I thought that was for impotence."

"Needs curing, doesn't it? Ask any man who can't get his hands on Viagra. The poor rhino's almost extinct, so a lot of men think it works. Black marketers sell it for other maladies, too. All that information has to be tucked in your mind somewhere. That's what dreams do, bring up stuff you were thinking about, or things you've forgotten."

"It wasn't just a dream," I insisted. "The snake was real."

"Snakes are common enough in nightmares. A lot of women are terrified of them. Men, too, but without all the sexual connotations."

I pushed him so hard he nearly toppled over. "What, you think I am a silly old maid, afraid of a man's penis? And that's what I dream about at night?"

"Whoa, Willy. I didn't say any such thing. You might be a tad uptight about—"

"I am not uptight about sex, just because I have scruples. And that was a snake, not a black dick slithering around."

"And you don't think you might have been projecting your own fears into the nightmare?"

"It was real, the whole thing. Not Hetty, but the sad little prince losing his will to live, Snake's desperation, that black serpent. You'll see when we get to the ranch and find H'tah. There'll be a dead snake nearby."

"Then I'll be sorry I ever doubted you and your dreams. And I don't really doubt you. I've seen enough weird things in this world to believe just about anything. I just had to make sure. If you say it's real, then it's real."

"And I'm not crazy?"

"Darlin', you're as sane as any of us, and twice as strong in your mind. How many people could keep themselves apart from what they were dreaming, and not get swallowed up in the terrors? You defended yourself and the colt, and you came back."

I started shaking again, now that the adrenaline was gone from my blood. The cold remained. I felt sick at leaving poor H'tah behind. "Hold me?"

He did, and the shaking stopped. I let his warmth seep through me. I wasn't insane. I wasn't afraid of sex, only of getting used or getting my heart broken. It might be too late. I sniffed again and told him I was sorry about the mares. I knew how much he wanted to see them and talk to them. "Maybe tomorrow night."

He shook his head no. "I think you sent them to the ranch. Or to look for snakes, anyway. I don't know how good they are at directions or locations. They could be anywhere, back home maybe."

"Not without H'tah. If they heard me or saw my dream, they know he is alive and waiting for rescue. They'll find him now. I hope they get there soon. Maybe they'll kill that devil and his snakes and free H'tah themselves without waiting for us."

"Maybe they found the missing son already, thanks to you, and we can all sleep better."

"But we'll still go to the ranch in the morning?"

"We'll go have a talk with that bastard, that's for sure. If the mares didn't get him, I will."

"And we'll find the dead snake." And an empty stall.

And it'll be over. Then Ty'd be gone. We both knew it, knew our time was limited. We both also knew we had something drawing us together. Chemistry, pheromones, or maybe some witchcraft from Grandma Eve and the matchmakers at the Royce Institute. Whatever it was, you could almost reach out and touch the thread tying us together.

"You said something before, about protecting your woman. I'm not your woman, you know."

He pulled the thread tighter by smoothing my hair back off my face. "You are tonight, and for however long we both want. Not my woman to cook and clean and serve my needs and obey my orders. Not my woman to follow where I lead. But my woman to defend, yes, to cherish, to love." He pulled the top blanket closer, so we were both cocooned in it. "May I love you tonight? Now? Here?"

This was neither the time nor the place I would have chosen. This was the right man, right now, though. I needed to be wanted, to be held, to be warmed. I needed Ty's strength and understanding to fill the emptiness left by the dream. I wanted to be filled, by him. He was pure masculinity, and he did not lie. He did not promise tomorrow or forever. Just tonight.

I rubbed my hand on his shoulder, up to the long hair on the back of his neck. That was all the answer he needed. He kissed my eyelids, one after the other, then my ear, nipping at the lobe, breathing at the sensitive shell. Then he kissed my neck while I touched his cheek, his chin, his brow, like a blind person trying to feel the beauty of a sculpture.

He kissed my lips, then cursed. I tasted blood again from where I must have split his lip with my berserker punches. "I'm sorry," I whispered, and kissed his lip as gently as I knew how, then touched the cut with my tongue.

He groaned and rolled us both to the ground, side by side, bodies pressing everywhere for the whole length of us. And he muttered "To hell with the hurt," and kissed me again, with his tongue and mine exploring, learning, arousing almost past bearing.

I responded like a flower bud to the sun, turning into his kisses, then blossoming to his caresses. I could feel the dew between my thighs. I could feel his wanting me throbbing at my stomach. I needed to be closer, so I pawed at his shirt. It was gone, then my shirt and pants.

The man must have other magic besides horse; he could make clothes disappear with a kiss or two. Before I could feel the cold, he was covering me with his body, with his heat. We were skin to skin now, and I felt his hard flat nipples, his sculpted muscles, a faint line of downy hair that tickled.

There was magic in his words, too. Maybe he was casting a spell with my name, his name, endearments, compliments, encouragement, and sighs. The horse call still reverberated through the night, but his same low, deep voice was telling me how perfect I was, how much he wanted me, how beautiful my breasts were, just the right size for his hands. My skin was like rose petals, my waist the perfect width. I could understand how the horses adored him. I was mesmerized myself, lost in a fog of desire and arousal and expectation. I would have done anything right then, anything but make love to a man wearing boots.

That was cheap. That was for a quickie at a tawdry motel or behind a bar. If tonight was all I was going to have of Tyler Farraday, it was *not* going to be quick.

"No boots in my bed," I managed to grumble.

He laughed, and my belly did a flip-flop at the sound.

"This isn't your bed, darlin', but anything to oblige my lady."

My lady. How nice that sounded.

He sat up and tugged on his boots, cursing. I suppose he was used to one of those forked things that hold the heel while you pull your foot out. Or a valet, like the hero of those romance novels, to tug them off. I giggled at the thought.

He growled. "It's not funny. My hands don't want to work."

They worked perfectly on me. So did his mouth and his tongue, up and down my body, tasting, teasing. And I worked on his jeans. I got the snap, but the zipper was tight, straining to hold in a whole lot of wanting that wanted to be free, now. Ty growled again but rolled away. The jeans went flying.

All that was left between us was a pair of low-rise black briefs. I put my hand there and felt the hard length of him. He moaned, so I jerked my hand away.

"Don't be afraid."

"I was afraid of hurting you, that's all. I am not scared of sex. I am certainly not scared of this." I wasn't scared, just impressed. He was long, lean, smooth and very,

very hard. I put my hand back on his erection to prove my courage. Hey, I had some magic in my fingers too. I could make it buck and make him gasp at the same time.

"You should be afraid, Willow mine. That's a lethal weapon you've got in your hand."

"Still arrogant, I see."

"And you're still tense."

I knew I was, but not out of fear. I wanted to please him, but I worried about all the other women he must have known. Women who had to be better at this than I was, more sure of what a man wanted. I wrapped my hand tighter, but he pushed it away. "Not if you don't want to be disappointed, darlin'."

I knew I wouldn't be. The briefs were tossed.

"Protection?"

He cursed again, long and loud enough to still the crickets, but he got up, covered me with the blanket, and searched for his blue jeans.

"Aha!"

I heard the foil packet rip, and then he was back under the blanket. "Cowboys, cavemen, and boy scouts. Always prepared."

Condoms and cookies. What a guy.

What a lover.

He made an art of foreplay, but his lovemaking was a masterpiece. I must have pleased him, too, because he did it again, only slower and longer. Then he asked if I wanted to ride, and that was good, too.

Except for Susan trudging through the yard looking for us.

"Holy shit. Is that how you cure the nightmares?"

It works for me.

CHAPTER 24

I NEVER WANTED A ROOMMATE. Now I remembered why. They never picked up after themselves. Except now, of course, when Susan bounced around finding my clothes and Ty's all over the backyard, with the apples and carrots and whatever droppings the grateful wildlife had left. She had a flashlight, having been on duty at Grandma Eve's after work, keeping the basil and the oregano safe. She almost didn't need it, because the sky was starting to show pink in the east. I had no idea where the time had gone. Well, I did, of course, if I were honest.

I was honest enough to admit I'm a coward. I ran rather than face the sunrise, Susan, and the smiling seducer of innocent maidens. I know that last wasn't the whole truth—I wasn't blameless in my lapse of judgment—but I liked the sound of it. I gathered the top blanket, leaving Ty to fend for himself, and fled into the house. I could hear my cousin giggling all the way. Ty was chuckling, so I hated both of them. With a smile on my face, too.

The answering machine was flashing red, so I hit the message button. Then I yelled for them to get inside, quick.

They came running. Ty had on his hat and his jeans. The black briefs, denim shirt and alligator boots were in his hand. He looked like a rumpled god, with gold chest hair. I knew it felt soft, while the rest of him was hard.

"What did you want, besides to stare at the beef-cake?" Susan stepped in front of him, blocking most of my view. "I'd have thought you memorized every inch by now."

I hadn't seen him in the light. But with Susan in the way, I remembered why I'd shouted for them.

"I got a message from Snake. It must have come while I was outside."

I replayed it for them.

That gravelly voice of his didn't say hello, didn't give his name, just threatened to sell his information to an-other interested party unless I came up with a bid higher than the two hundred thousand dollars he was prom-ised, by noon tomorrow. Which was today. His words were slurred like a drunk's, but the meaning was clear. If I didn't come up with more money, I'd never see the ho— He corrected himself: the package I was looking for.

The message ended in a piercing yowl of pain or panic.

"I bet the ladies got there then."

Susan looked confused, so Ty explained about my dream and the mares while I played back the next message.

"This is Chief of Police Haversmith"—not Uncle Henry tonight—"and I don't know what you've been doing in the dark."

Susan snickered. Ty batted at her with his hat.

"But all hell broke loose here while you were sit-ting cozy in the backyard. The effing empath mares tore through town and sent a tsunami of really, really bad feelings in their wake. We're had two suicide tries, three attempted murders, six calls for domestic violence. Half the windows on Main Street are broken from rocks or bricks. The other half of them are pockmarked with shot-gun pellets. The effing police station got hit with a tear-gas canister. Two dozen cars had their tires slashed or the windows broken. George Maclay shot his brother's dog with a bb gun. The dog'll live, but George might not, after the brother got hold of him. Two nonaccidental car

crashes, four arson fires, six ambulance calls, one near
drowning. We had to double up patients, and still send
to Amagansett for backup. We've had everything but
the effing partridge in a pear tree. Come daybreak, we'll
have every news reporter from Manhattan to Montauk
out here, plus the county sheriff and the state cops, if not
the FBI. I want to know what the hell you and your effing cowboy are doing about it."

The third message was from Grandma Eve. The fields
were fine, not a blade of grass stepped on, but Doc wasn't
feeling well. She was taking him to the emergency room.

The next message was from her cell phone. Doc was
fine. They were on the way home.

"They got back a couple of hours ago," Susan reported. "Both of them tired but okay."

My father left a garbled, static-filled message. My
hands were shaking so hard I could barely find the replay button. He must be on a golf course or out of range
of a cell tower, because he kept cutting out, but I pieced
it together as something about a bad view. He must
mean Bayview, the ranch. I shouldn't cook at it? I had
no idea if he was scaring me away from Snake and the
ranch, or telling me not to have a barbeque at the beach.
No matter. I was damn well going to that ranch. Love
you, too, Dad.

I found my cell phone and dialed the chief on it, so I
could replay Snake's message from the land line.

"Hold on, play it again so I can record it."

I did, and he yelled, "Got him. Now we can pick him
up. Threats, extortion, obstruction of justice, possession
of stolen property. Hell, we'll get him on animal cruelty
if nothing else."

"What about a warrant?"

"We don't need one if we see a crime being committed. Or a citizen in danger. After last night, every person
in this town is in danger and I have the right—no, the
duty—to go check up on every one of them. We'll worry
about the technicalities later. Half an hour. At the ranch.
I'll bring Big Eddie and Ranger."

With the chief there, we wouldn't need Kelvin or K2,

thank goodness. Uncle Henry wasn't the best truth-seer, but he'd be good enough to deal with Snake's lies.

Ty was already calling Connor, telling him to meet us there. I flew up the stairs to get dressed, but I could hear his sharp intake of breath behind me. I guess I forgot I couldn't hold the cell phone, the land phone, and the blanket all at once. I winked at him and ran faster. I threw on some jeans and a T-shirt without bothering to check for ticks the way everyone out here knew to do. God knew I could be crawling with them after a night in the grass, on and off that blanket. Where we were going there'd only be more. I was not going to think about what else was in the grass at the ranch.

Susan said she'd make coffee and find some food for us to take. She had to stay behind to help Grandma Eve and get some rest before work tonight. Her parents were already in town, checking Aunt Jasmine's school for vandalism.

I shouted down a plea for Susan to put the dogs out and throw some kibble in their dishes.

Ty went out with the dogs to gather up that can of oats, just in case.

Poor Little Red was upset at being left again. I picked him up for a quick cuddle, telling him how much I loved him and he had to be brave and defend the house and the big dogs and I'd be back soon. He bit my ear.

We were off.

Ty drove. Fast. I called out the turns, hanging onto the door, hanging onto the coffee mugs, trying not to think about H'tah, ticks in sensitive places, bad cooking, or the grim look on Ty's face.

We saw flashing lights ahead and Ty sped up to follow the chief's car and the K-9 unit. Connor on the motor bike fell in behind the caravan. Uncle Henry did not use his sirens, I guess so Snake wouldn't have warning. According to Susan, the sirens had sounded all night, so no one would think anything of one more. Maybe Uncle Henry didn't want to add to the town's jittery nerves or wake up anyone who'd finally gone to sleep. I didn't know; we hadn't heard the fire whistle, the ambulances,

or the police sirens. Maybe they were on the other side
of town. Or the horse-calling chant was too loud. That
must be it.

As we drove, I did notice a car tilted into the ditch at
the side of a road, a tree with its bark half scraped off,
lawns with tire tracks cut into them, smashed mailboxes
everywhere. Hell had come to Paumanok Harbor all
right. I prayed it was over.

We all parked in the overgrown drive for what had
been the ranch's main house. Snake's rusted old Dodge
pickup wasn't in sight, not where it had been yesterday.
With him gone, our search would be easier, if not as
legal, maybe.

Uncle Henry dragged himself out of his seat and
leaned against the car door, looking at the burned-out
foundation, the brush and bramble where the lawns and
fields used to be, the falling down bunkhouse and stable.
"Damn shame about this. I used to come help exercise
the horses years back. Couldn't ask for a better job for
a kid." Then he looked out at the bay glittering in the
sunshine, Gardiner's Island in the distance. "But it's one
hell of a place to put a house. Prettiest view around."

He looked over at me and Ty. "Unlike the two of
you."

Ty's split lip was swollen and raw looking, and my
cheeks were chafed raw from his beard. My earlobe had
tooth marks on it. The chief held up a hand to stop whatever I was going to say, something like the dog ate my
homework.

"No, I don't want to hear. You'd only lie, and you
know that gives me indigestion." He took a roll of antacid tablets from his shirt pocket and put one in his
mouth. "Can't say hearing the truth would make me any
happier."

Big Eddie let Ranger out of the back of his police
car and told him to go find something. The shepherd lay
down in the shade of the car and closed his eyes.

"Hey, Fred, you here?" Big Eddie called out.

"His truck's gone, dickhead. What do you think, he
lent it to someone? Snake has no friends." That was from

Baitfish Barry, the cop who'd been driving the chief. We were all standing upwind from him. "He's not here, so let's find the horse before Snake gets back."

The chief sighed and started pointing. "Barry, you go over there and see where the power line goes. Willow says there's a single light in a wood cell. Eddie, you start sniffing at the bunkhouse. You"—meaning me—"use your head to think about the colt and where he might be."

Ty headed for the stable where we'd looked yesterday. Connor and the chief followed him.

I stayed by the cars a minute, trying to listen for H'tah. Then I tried talking to him in my mind. I used my sketch pad to draw a willow tree on a hill. "That's me. I'm here. Where are you?"

I didn't hear anything but the men calling to each other, so I headed in their direction. They were in the dark stable now, where I had no desire to go. I circled the outside, looking up to see if I spotted an extension cord. And tripped over Fred Sinese. And six mostly dead snakes.

I screamed loud enough to wake the dead, but not Fred Sinese.

My father warned me. Bad view. Don't look. Not Bayview, not don't cook. I'd never cook again. Never eat again. Not after rushing away and puking up the muffin Susan had given me, the coffee, last night's cookies, and half my stomach lining, it felt like.

Ty was at my side, holding me up while I retched until my gut ached and my throat was raw. Then he handed me a handkerchief—the guy really was prepared—and brushed my hair back from my sweaty cheeks.

Big Eddie brought over a bottle of water, his own complexion tinged with green. He went back to where the others were huddled around the body.

Ty turned me to face the other way. "You shouldn't have seen that."

"You think?" I knew this wasn't the place for sarcasm, so I apologized and changed the subject. "Did the snakes kill him? Or the mares? Or did his liver just give out?"

It was the chief who came over to me, patting my back, and said, "Looks like everyone had a go at him. He's all swelled up from the snakebites, even if they're not poisonous. The dead snakes have hoof marks on them, but no telling if Sinese was already gone by then. What got him first, I'd guess, is the bullet hole."

"He committed suicide?" Maybe that was better than dying of cirrhosis. Definitely better than dying of snakebites, to my way of thinking.

"He got shot in the back of his head. Execution style."

While I was trying to make sense of that, the chief started calling his office, sending for the coroner, a medical examiner, and the county homicide unit. Then Big Eddie yelled to the chief from inside the stable. "I smell a horse. Snake. And snow."

I shook my aching head. Snow was another of my father's wacky warnings. It was about seventy-five degrees out.

Baitfish Barry thought Big Eddie was just as crazy. "Give us a break, Pinocchio. It's July."

"Not that kind of snow. Cocaine. A lot of it."

"Holy shit. We'll have the Feds here, no matter what."

"Shut up and find it," the chief ordered.

"No, find if the horse is still here!"

Connor called out, "I see where Sinese kept something. I can't tell yet if it's the dope or the horse. It looks like he put a fake wall up in one of the loose boxes, then piled old crates in front of the new door so it looked like the rest of the stall was filled with garbage. The door's partly opened today, but I missed it entirely yesterday."

Because I hadn't gone into the stable to call to H'tah. I went in now, leaning on Ty. We waited while Connor finished pulling boxes away from stall number six. I thought about the scrap of paper Mrs. Merriwether had given me. A nine, damn it. Only it wasn't a nine. It was a six upside down. We could have had H'tah out of here yesterday. Damn, damn, damn.

Sure enough, when Connor pulled the door fully open, we saw a pile of straw, a rubber bucket with water, and a dead snake.

Ty pulled me closer. "The mares got him out. He's safe."

The chief and his men started yelling. Eddie's nose had led them back outside to an old abandoned well, so overgrown you could have tripped over its rotten wood cover and fallen in without ever knowing it was there. Uncle Henry was cursing, Big Eddie was yelling at Fishbait that if he hadn't been standing so close stinking like a sardine, they'd know about the snakes. Rattlers, by god.

Then they started shooting.

Ty pulled me away again. He couldn't do anything about the continued gunfire. "That's an old smuggler's trick, putting a rattler on top of the stash. Who's going to put their hand in there to see what the snake's sleeping on?"

I couldn't take any more. I went and sat next to Ranger in the good, clean sun. H'tah was safe, that was all that mattered. Unless the Paumanok Harbor police killed each other.

CHAPTER 25

THEY DIDN'T FIND THE DRUGS, THE COLT, the gun, or Snake's truck. Not even with the squads of detectives on the scene. Before the outsiders got there, we all decided not to mention the magic in the night mares, just talk about stray white horses, a stolen foal, Snake's extortion. We knew not to mention Big Eddie's nose. If they ever solved the drug case, old Ranger was in line for another commendation. As for the chaos in Paumanok Harbor, everyone knew the region was subject to odd sun spot emissions, weird fault lines, and mass hysteria. Uncle Henry swallowed the whole roll of antacid tablets and started on another.

The detective who interviewed me wanted to know if Snake had attacked me, I looked so battered. Then he wanted me to describe discovering Snake's body, which I couldn't do without gagging, so I just pointed. He could go look himself. I knew the image was burned into my memory forever, but maybe these homicide cops were tougher, having seen so much.

Nope. I could hear one of them retching, messing up the crime scene more. A couple of others hurried past me, rushing for the bathroom in the bunkhouse or into the bushes. "Beware of more snakes," I called out to them. "And ticks. And poison ivy." I knew I was sounding like my father, but they all thought I was crazy already, looking for a horse no one had seen, so what were a few cautionary warnings?

After Connor, Ty, and I gave our accounts of events, we were free to go but not to leave town. Which meant Ty'd be here a few more days at least. I was too drained to be happy about that, or sad he'd be gone soon afterward.

Connor rode the motorcycle back to Rosehill to wait for Ty to drop me off, leaving Ty and me alone. We didn't talk on the ride back to my place, though, having speculated endlessly while we waited for our turns to give our statements. The detectives wanted to separate us so our information wouldn't be contaminated, but the chief spoke to them, so I could keep leaning on Ty's shoulder until it was my time to talk about the phone calls and our visit here yesterday. I stayed leaning on the ride home.

We all needed showers, food, rest. I needed to check on my grandmother and Doc, so we all met at the big house in an hour. I brought Little Red, to appease the Pomeranian and to aggravate my grandmother. Grandma Eve fed us anyway and put something in our iced tea that settled my stomach, if not my nerves. Susan was baking brownies, which smelled wonderful.

Doc looked older than yesterday. Connor stayed far away from him, not shaking hands or sitting close around the kitchen table when we sat to tell our stories again, this time without leaving stuff out.

First they explained what happened to them last night.

After watching the fields for hours, my grandmother and her old friend went to bed. I didn't ask whose bed; they didn't tell. They were awakened by a scream—that might have been me—and a wave of emotion so overwhelming, so frightening, so enraging, that Grandma started throwing her pots and pans around, to drown out the sound in her head. When that didn't work, she found herself mixing up a potion that could have poisoned half the town if it got in the public water works.

She was still shaking her head. "Me, who's sworn never to do harm."

Doc couldn't project calm or reassurance, not to her, not to the source of the emotional turbulence. He tried and tried, but never found enough of his own inner peace to spread to Eve or the others. The failure, the desperation, the knowing his best all-out effort was never good enough, had him feeling weak, clammy-skinned. He and Grandma had a flaming battle about calling the ambulance, and settled on her driving him to the emergency clinic.

The mares' mental outpourings had a different effect on Susan; the deluge gave her a piercing headache and blurry vision. She instantly interpreted the symptoms as a return of the cancer with a tumor in her brain, her worst nightmare.

All three of them wanted to know how come Ty and I weren't affected by the mare's distress.

"Uh. . . We weren't sleeping."

Neither was Susan at the time, and she'd pulled out a tuft of her own hair, which was a shame, now that it was growing back after chemo.

The only reason I could think of why we were spared was that our emotions were as engaged as possible for two people to be. Together, maybe we were strong enough to fend off anything from outside. We hadn't heard the sirens, hadn't felt the flood of emotion. I shrugged. "The luck of the Irish, I guess."

Susan slammed the oven door on the brownie pan. Little Red jumped in my arms and growled. "You're not Irish."

Ty's explanation satisfied them more: the mares left us before sending out the mental shock waves.

Connor escaped most of the tumult because he wasn't in the mares' path to the ranch, but he did feel a sudden overwhelming thirst for a drink.

He looked at Ty. "But I didn't have one."

Ty tipped his head.

Connor knew something was desperately wrong when Paloma Blanca and Lady Sparrow raised a ruckus. Then he started hearing sirens. He was ready to ride to my house when he couldn't reach Ty on his cell—Ty had it turned off to keep the night quiet except for his chant— but Connor knew Ty'd kill him if he left the horses.

"Damn right."

Then we told them what happened at the ranch. Or what we thought happened. I wasn't sure about the chronology of the thing, and I doubted if the medical examiner was going to be any more definitive. But as far as I could figure, with Ty adding a point here and there, we laid it out for our attentive audience. Connor was too busy eating the leftover vegetarian lasagna Susan put in front of him. Ty sipped at his coffee, with a dash of brandy. I was waiting for the brownies, so I had time to talk.

I explained that Snake must have had at least one partner. The Snow Man. That was what my father had warned about.

"Your father's warnings have never been worth the breath he takes to blather about them."

Grandma Eve and Dad had never gotten along well. He was my father; I had to defend him. Wasn't he right about the bad view? I did not mention the alligator, the cave, or the banker. That was when it occurred to me that if Dad meant a drug dealer, he hadn't been seeing danger to Grant. Who I hadn't thought about in days, it seemed. I was happy he'd be safe on his snowy mountain. I had enough to worry about right here.

"The cocaine dealer is definitely dangerous, just as Dad said. Big Eddie smelled the drugs, and Snake had to know they were there."

Doc wanted to know how bad the coke trade was in Paumanok Harbor.

I didn't really know, but Susan said it was all over the bars and night spots, and a couple of kids had been expelled from the high school in June for snorting in the bathrooms. She'd been offered a boatload of pot when she was doing chemotherapy, from everyone from her old school friends to the postmaster. There was an open market. Someone had to be satisfying the habits of all the rich summer people in East Hampton, so why not Snake?

He wasn't rich enough, for one reason, passable in polite company for another, or smart enough. I thought his part in the illegal business was hiding the dope until someone else could transport it or deliver it. We all knew the stories about the Prohibition era and the smugglers off Montauk. There was even a chain of stores called Rumrunner. Men in small boats would meet larger ones off shore, bring the contraband back to dry land, stash it in people's homes, then truck it around under piles of fish. The job had to be easier these days, with radar and satellite trackers.

Grandma Eve added that the police knew all about the widespread use of the drug. They made arrests when they could, but no one saw any benefit to hauling in the recreational users, not when the dealers were still at large. The Coast Guard searched as many boats as they could, but there were too many boats, too many harbors, too few Coast Guard patrol boats. The county narcotics squad would be thrilled to shut down the operation at the ranch, if it was as large as Big Eddie's nose said it was.

First they had to find the missing dope, which meant finding Snake's truck and his partner.

According to my dream-conversation with H'tah, someone had hit the colt with a car, then scooped him up before the mares could return to help him vanish. I thought that might take two men. H'tah appeared to be as tall as a small pony, although not as wide.

Sure as hell neither Snake nor the Snow Man picked up the injured animal out of the goodness of his heart, or to take him for medical care. I assumed they knew the mares were powerful, if only from the rumors in town. For some reason, maybe the same myth that had the Froeler girl give her fictional horse healing powers, Snake thought the colt could cure his liver disease. H'tah couldn't.

Snake needed money, maybe for a liver transplant. That told me he wasn't making it big in the lucrative drug trade. He'd called me. I recounted his message, and how it ended on a shriek.

Ty gave his theory that the mares went berserk after my dream of their kin being threatened with snakes or death. Almost everyone in their vicinity was affected, including Snake when the mares reached the ranch.

Maybe Snake went crazy. Maybe his partner did. Maybe the snakes they kept around to guard the drugs did, too. The Snow Man shot Snake, either because of the double cross, or because he went homicidal at the brain waves. Or maybe he was shooting at the snakes.

I assumed he moved the cocaine to Snake's pickup because no one would think to search the rusty old wreck. The truck was described on every police bulletin in the county now.

Somewhere in there, between the emotional assault and the assassination, the mares stomped the snakes, found H'tah, and disappeared.

We arrived, found the colt's hidden cell door partly opened, and Fred Sinese thoroughly dead.

Susan took the brownies out of the oven to cool. "Talk about a snake in the grass."

Grandma Eve wanted to know if the whole affair was over.

Affair? We had a one-night stand. Oh, she meant the mares. "I think so. Except."

"Except?"

"Except how did the Snow Man get there if he left in Sinese's truck? There should have been another car. And what if he took the horse along with the coke?"

I heard groans from everyone. I rubbed Little Red's silky ears.

"I mean, we don't really know that the mares rescued the baby, do we? What if they got there and Snake was already dead, his partner and the drugs and the colt already moved? Remember, Snake said he had someone else interested in information about the horse. That person might have gone there first. He might have had the gun."

Susan put the brownies on a plate in front of me, but

she slapped my hand when I reached for one. "They're too hot."

Red snapped at her fingers, but I didn't know if he was defending me or claiming the brownies. I put him down while I went to pour glasses of milk for anyone who wanted one.

Grandma didn't. She frowned at Red searching for crumbs on her clean kitchen floor, and she frowned at the idea of adding a third villain to the mix.

I found a loose walnut, so I broke off a piece of it for Red. "Why not? What would a drug dealer want with an injured horse?"

"What would the other bidder want it for? Besides," she asked, "why don't you think the mares didn't take their baby with them?"

"Because my bracelet didn't dissolve in the shower. Margaret said it would last until I found the colt."

"Are you sure she didn't mean until the colt was found?"

"That's not what she said."

Everyone thought on that while I ate a brownie.

It was Doc who finally said what we were all thinking: "Then the mares wouldn't have gone."

I had a drink of milk rather than answer.

Ty broke his brownie in half. "They would have tried to follow. Until light came."

"Which means they'll be back tonight?"

"I have no idea. Someone could be driving the colt to Canada for all we know. If he's still nearby, though, so are the mares."

More silence.

"I know what we need," Grandma Eve said after I'd eaten another brownie and Red was back in my lap, looking needy.

I expected her to say a good walk to burn off the calories or a pot of coffee or a nap. I needed all of them. Instead she named Joe the Plumber.

Before I could wonder if Grandma Eve had finally gone round the bend or her dishwasher was leaking, she said Joe was a scryer.

Very helpful, a scryer.

Susan said it for me: "What the hell is that?"

"It's a person who can see things. Not in the future, like reading entrails and such, although I've never held much stock in that messy business. This is more like crystal ball reading, only in the present."

"Is such a thing possible?"

"Joe says so. He often sees things in the sinks he's fixing, sees people in the swirling water. They're not always who he's looking for or thinking about, but he sees them, sees what they're doing at the time. I suppose he could make a fortune in blackmail but he's honest, our Joe, and never talks about what he sees. Except for his ex-wife and that drunk she ran off with. He sees them nearly every time he's fixing that upstairs toilet of mine, the one that keeps running on no matter how I jiggle the handle. They're always yelling at each other. Joe enjoys it so much, he never gets the toilet working properly."

"So he can tell us where H'tah is?"

"Oh, I don't know if he can tell where. But if he is somewhere here, as opposed to There, Joe ought to spot him, especially if you give Joe one of your drawings of the horse to concentrate on. Maybe we can figure out the location from what Joe sees."

"Call him."

Grandma sighed. "I can't. He's in critical condition from one of the car accidents. Someone sideswiped him, and his van went into the bay. They'll fish it out later, when all the volunteer rescuers aren't so busy. I heard that Joe was yelling about all his tools sitting in the salt water overnight when they airlifted him to Stony Brook Hospital."

"Damn."

That about summed up everyone's feelings.

CHAPTER 26

W E HAD TO WARN EVERYONE. AGAIN. We couldn't be certain the mares were still here, or if they'd come back, but the town couldn't take another night like the last one. We started making phone calls.

The drugstore would be putting sleeping pills and ear plugs in every sack. Grandma mixed up a special batch of her soothing teas to give away at the farm stand. Doc was getting a ride to the village square, where he'd sit on a bench talking to everyone, shaking hands, offering encouragement or conversation to anyone who sought it. The chief was putting on extra patrols, with a lot of the policemen hired from out of the village, ergo not sensitives. Susan planned tonight's restaurant menu around some special ingredients and recipes. Most important of all was what Bill at the hardware store was doing: bringing up boxes of Christmas lights from his storage basement and sending trucks to pick up more from every other shop owner in the Hamptons.

The lights might keep the mares away even if they couldn't keep the vandalism or violence away. Main Street stores already kept their lights on all night, and that didn't keep their windows from getting broken yesterday. We still felt the extra brightness was worth a try; we spread the word to sleep with the lights on, too.

Pretty soon Paumanok Harbor looked like Christmas in summer, with everyone outside on ladders, everyone who knew what was going on, that was. The summer renters and tourists and even the locals who were outsiders, i.e., not of the old blood, not espers, weren't affected by nightmares or mental firestorms, so they thought we'd all gone crazy. Worse, their houses were bare and undecorated, so it looked like some version of the plagues on Egypt, with only Israelite households marked to save their firstborn sons. So the Chamber of Commerce declared it a publicity stunt for some magazine, handed out free lights, and sent for photographers.

People were still nervous. Understandably. Not just because of the night terrors and the mayhem, but because we'd had a murder in town, which was an extremely rare occurrence. No one was going to miss Snake, but no one wanted to be sitting next to a killer at the barbershop, or standing near him on line at the bank. Some residents went to visit relatives elsewhere. Some tourists shortened their vacations. Some just canceled their reservations.

I was nervous, too. Not so much about the murder, but that I could be wrong about the mares. All I had was a dream, an intuition, a braided bracelet. Then again, a warning was better than having everyone relax, only to be bashed in the head with another brainstorm. Besides, in this town, people relied on feelings and intuitions. They'd understand. They also knew I was my father's daughter.

Within hours, everyone who needed to be warned was on guard, as protected as we knew how to make them.

By then, we were all exhausted and cranky—well, Grandma was always cranky. Without Doc's presence her mood soured worse, but she refused to take a nap or stop mixing teas and other herbal extracts that did heaven knew what. Susan finally convinced her to take Doc's lunch into town and keep him company on the square. He might need sunscreen, too. And a ride home soon, because he'd had as little sleep as the rest of us last night.

Ty and Connor were on their way back to Rosehill and their own horses.

"Will you try chanting again tonight?" That wasn't what I wanted to know. I wanted to know if he'd be back, if he wanted my company. Yeah, I wanted a pat on the head, the same way the dogs begged for affection or biscuits. Pitiful. That's what came of sex with strangers: insecurity. Not that I cared if he stayed or went. Not much anyway. The mares were what mattered.

He sounded undecided about it all. "I can try. But I think they left."

Unfortunately, I didn't. Also unfortunately, I didn't get the idea that he cared about my feelings. I knew my insecurities were skewing my attitude, but I figured I had a right to need reassurance after last night, after this morning and Snake. I told myself that if he didn't care, then I wouldn't care either. I turned my head when he would have kissed me good-bye, so his lips brushed my cheek.

"Willow?" That was all he said.

I looked away. "I'll be busy the rest of the day. I've been ignoring the dogs and my emails and my writing. Most of all my writing. I have deadlines, you know. And I have to call my parents, let them know what's going on so they don't worry and—"

He tipped my chin up so I had to look at him, at his soft green eyes and his not-quite-straight nose and the blond hair that fell over his forehead and the furrowed line between his eyebrows that told me he was trying to figure out my message. I almost changed it, almost put my arms around him and plastered myself against him. But Connor was waiting at the door and Susan was watching and I wasn't falling into his trap. I did *not* need him. So I stepped back and picked up Little Red, a furry chastity belt.

He seemed confused by my actions and words, as if no woman had ever let him go without begging him to stay or take her with him. I couldn't let myself be some kind of cowboy groupie. I hardened my thumping heart and said, "Call me and let me know your plans."

He kept looking at me. "I thought you'd help me

talk to some people about the ranch property later this afternoon."

My heart melted, fickle organ that it was, and started doing somersaults. "You are actually considering buying Bayview?"

"I can't say until I hear the price, but it's a good place for horses. Too good to let it be turned into some luxury condos or whatever you folks build around here."

"Mansions. We build too-big houses for people with too much money. You'll need to talk to the bank and the town lawyers who've been negotiating with the owners and everyone else who'll help. Wait, I know just the man. Dante Rivera is my friend Louisa's husband. He's rich as sin, loves playing with real estate, but mostly he loves this town. He'll do anything to keep it from turning into just another Ick Hampton. He donated land and helped build the community and arts center building."

"Sounds good. What's his talent?"

"Just making money, as far as I know. And babies. Louisa is working on her third. He's a good man. I like him a lot."

"Don't be liking him too much, darlin', or I'll be jealous."

I laughed. "Of Louisa's husband? He'd never look at another woman. Not that I wish he would, of course. Should I call and see if he's available to meet with you? We could go right now."

"Whoa, lady. First I've got to spend time with the horses. Then I've got to talk to my accountant, my agent, and my family so they don't worry. Maybe answer some fan mail I've been putting off. I have a lot to do, too."

I knew he was making fun of me, but I didn't care. He was thinking of staying! "But you'll talk to Dante tomorrow?"

"Sure. Maybe he'll know the local laws about putting a live-in trailer on the property while everything there now is being torn down and rebuilt. Stables come first, but the hired hands would need a place to stay. I don't think you'll have enough horsemen in the area, so

I'll have to bring in some. I wouldn't put a dog in that bunkhouse."

I rubbed Red's ear the way he liked. "Not one of mine, for sure."

"And maybe your friend will know if I can put goats there. Some cities have ordinances about farm animals."

"Goats? I thought you rescued horses?"

"I do, and people. I'd start with goats to crop the fields, and set up a cottage industry making goat cheese. That's what we did in Texas and on the reservation, too. Goat cheese is a delicacy nowadays, perfect for your tony summer folk. And it makes jobs for people who need them."

"The town fathers will love that. And Grandma can sell it at the farm stand." I was so excited I hugged him, just what I intended not to do. Just what I wanted to do. He hugged me back.

"Don't go getting ahead of yourself, sweet pea. The cost might be too high, the laws too restrictive. And that land might be contaminated. Who knows what Sinese did to it?"

"It'll be fine, I know it! I can almost see horses galloping over smooth grassy hills already."

He smiled, that wonderful slow grin that I could watch forever, like a gorgeous sunset. "Clairvoyant, are you?"

I grinned back. "No, just hopeful that you'll stay."

The words wiped his smile away. "I can't exactly stay here, darlin'. You know that. An operation like Bayview needs more money than I have. I'll be out earning my bread every chance I get. And then there's the Texas place and the reservation. A lot of horses depend on me. A lot of people, too."

"I see." I guess I did, because sometimes I felt like I had the whole of Paumanok Harbor resting on my shoulders. I dropped my arms from around him.

Ty rubbed my cheek with the back of his hand. "But I'll be back as often as I can manage. Every chance I have."

"For what?"

"For the horses, for the people I am responsible for, and for you. I'll take whatever crumbs you give me, panting after you like that silly dog of yours."

Who bites sometimes.

I needed a nap. Then I needed a walk on the beach, a dish of ice cream, a little computer time, a little work time. What I didn't need was the roller coaster ride of Tyler Farraday.

He was everything a woman wanted in a man: supportive, caring, honorable, sweet and funny, and a great lover. I might be sore from unused muscles, but I knew I'd want him again as soon as he got back. But he'd be gone. Not today or tomorrow, but he'd be gone soon. I kept reminding myself of that before I got too involved, if I wasn't already in way over my head. Right now I had to concentrate on the town and H'tah, not some here-today, gone-tomorrow Texan.

I already missed him.

I called both my parents and tried not to feel disloyal for being glad neither one picked up. I didn't need more warnings or more nagging.

I made a tentative date to meet with Louisa and Dante tomorrow morning. Louisa wanted to know what the devil was going on with the Harbor and with the devilishly handsome cowboy, but all I could tell her was that I hoped to know more by the time I saw her.

"No, I don't think you should take the kids and go to your mother's." She got along with her mother about as well as I got on with mine. "You weren't bothered by anything last night, were you?"

"You mean other than heartburn and needing to pee every other hour and never finding a comfortable position for sleeping? Oh, and both kids wanting to sleep in the bed with us? No, nothing out of the ordinary."

"Then you'll be fine tonight."

Susan went off to work at the restaurant, and Grandma and Doc got back from town looking tired but satisfied with what they'd accomplished. They had a few extra strings of lights, so I hung them up for them.

Mine must be the only dark house for miles, but I left it that way, just in case.

When I got back from the herb farm, I had three messages.

My mother was bringing two greyhounds home with her, because no one wanted a pair and they loved each other. I should buy two more big dog beds from Agway, but I had at least a week or two before she got here.

Check.

Dad told me to get flea shampoo while I was getting the beds.

Check.

"Oh, and watch out for a mate, baby girl."

A mate? That was usually my mother's line, that I was getting old and she wanted grandchildren. I guess her nagging had finally worn off on my father. I erased the message.

Ty was coming over, but after dark. He was going to try to attract the night mares once more.

Check. Wash hair, shower, shave legs. Check.

I wasn't going to sit outside again.

I wasn't going to make love with him again. Forget about shaving my legs.

I couldn't do it. Not if I wanted to preserve my sanity. I wasn't like Susan.

Casual sex wasn't enough for me, no matter how many fireworks exploded. It was exciting while it lasted, but it caused too much regret later. Like taking home all the rest of Susan's brownies. I loved them and I could eat every last one of them for dinner, knowing damn well how bad they were for my health and my hips. I'd hate myself in the morning. That was how I felt about sex without affection.

I guess love wasn't for me either.

Check.

CHAPTER 27

TY DIDN'T COME UNTIL AFTER TEN. He'd fallen asleep, and Cousin Lily didn't want to wake him.

I had his sofa ready in the backyard with blankets, brownies, and a bottle of beer. Not an epicurean combination, but stuff to get him through the night. I couldn't get through the first hour, sitting next to him. Actually, sitting on his lap, with his shoulder as my pillow, the chant vibrating though the night, through my blood.

It was mesmerizing. If I were a magic mare, I'd stop by just to see who was making such entrancing music. I found it so soothing, I had a hard time keeping my eyes open. I kept yawning.

"Go to bed, Willow. You've had no rest. I doubt the mares will come, or that you'll have any bad dreams. I want to stay out a few hours more just to be sure."

So I didn't have to say no about sharing his bed or mine tonight. Willpower was a great thing, if you didn't have to call on it.

I made my way upstairs with the tiny flashlight I had, and put the dogs out in their pen in front of the house. I washed up and changed to a nightshirt in the closed bathroom so no light shone through, then fetched the dogs in, gave the big dogs their good night treats downstairs, and climbed into bed with Little Red and his biscuit.

I lay there, listening to the chant and the crickets, and firmly closing my mind to thoughts of Ty. I had a new drawing of H'tah taped to the headboard right over my pillow, the colt with a willow tree shading him from danger. He was standing, outdoors and free.

Tell me you're okay, baby, I begged silently. I hope you're with your mama, but if you can, let me know.

Like asking a kid to send postcards home from camp. On Mars.

Little Red ate his cookie, circled around, then settled down next to my feet. Half asleep, I wondered what he dreamed about . . . running free on four legs? Or a rare steak with ice cream on the side?

Did horses dream? Sweet dreams, H'tah. Don't think about the awful time at the ranch.

Then all I could think about was the ranch. Snake and snakes and— No, I'd never get to sleep that way. Much better to think about Ty buying it, cleaning it, putting his horses on it. And his goats.

There was something reassuring about goats. Silly creatures, eating everything, maa-ing, climbing, butting heads with each other. Could Ty talk to them? I listened to his voice through the open window. My breathing fell into the cadence. My mind fell into sweet downy cloud oblivion.

I dreamed, but not the way I wanted. H'tah wasn't in it at all, but Ty was. My sleeping self smiled. I wanted that, too.

So did the dream Ty. He undressed, climbed into my bed, and did the disappearing act with my nightshirt.

A person had no control over her dreams, right? So I didn't have to tell him to leave. Good.

He was running his strong hands over my bare skin. Better.

Then he parted my thighs, his hand reaching lower. He parted my folds. I felt that glow in my belly, the word that I, writer that I was, could not give a name. Just a feeling, a heat, a happy place inside ready to get happier. Sometimes it never got better than this, but Ty wasn't going to disappoint, not in my dream.

Then I was lost to the rhythm of his fingers, his chant, his heartbeat. This was the best dream I ever—

This was no dream. I felt the scratch of his new stubble on skin that was barely healed from yesterday.

"What the ...?"

"It's almost dawn. I came to kiss you good night and tell you I was leaving. You smiled at me."

"I was dreaming!"

"Are you complaining?"

With his hand still tangled in my curls, still moving over the most sensitive spot? "Uh, where is Little Red?"

"On the floor, with a marrow bone from Miss Lily."

That was okay, then. Until Ty leaned over to kiss me. I turned my head. "Don't. Morning breath."

"Then I guess I should kiss you here." His lips were on my neck, then my breast, bringing the peaks to attention, one and then the other.

"Or here." Now he licked a path down my ribs to my belly, tucking his tongue into my navel.

"Or here." His mouth replaced his fingers.

What came after best? I did, three times.

Ty left early, before Susan was up, thank goodness. I didn't need her snarky comments or her tattling to Grandma. I was a grown woman, but I hated people knowing my business. They'd snicker when he left, or pity me. That was worse.

I stayed in bed as long as I could before the dogs started whining. Little Red's stomach was gurgling, never a good sign.

Then the phone started ringing, both the land line and my cell, which I had to locate before I could answer.

The chief, Aunt Jasmine, and Kelvin all wanted me to know that they'd pulled Joe the Plumber's van out of the bay this morning. Joe was pulling through, too. He'd be home in a few days. But the real news was that the divers who swam down to hook the van to Kelvin's wrecker found another car in the water: Snake's pickup. Joe's skid marks had hidden the pickup's, so it might have stayed submerged for ages.

The divers kept searching, with reinforcements from the DEA, but they found no drugs, no passenger, no white horse. The labs were checking the truck for fingerprints, residue, anything that could identify the driver, who might or might not be Snake's killer. They hadn't had any luck so far, nor at the ranch. Speculation was he—or they—needed the truck to transport the drugs from Snake's well, then they ditched it before anyone noticed someone other than its owner at the wheel. That old rust bucket was too easily recognized in the area, or on a highway if the police started searching.

The dope was likely already giving yuppies something to do with their free time. Which reminded me of the group rental at Tern Street, the house with all the surfboards and beer bottles. Those guys looked as if they'd know who sold recreational drugs around town. Maybe the chief could trade information for ignorance about their own illegal possession. Or maybe he could beat it out of them, not that Uncle Henry was a violent type, but he'd been without sleep for days, too. At this point, I didn't care what happened to the surfer dudes or Snake's murderer.

If the man had hurt H'tah, had chucked him in the water along with the truck, then he deserved to spend the rest of his hopefully short life in jail. If he'd taken the colt out of range of the mares or my dreams, I hoped his life was long and miserable and his dick fell off.

With that thought in mind, I called the chief. Then I called Ty to give him the news about the truck—and to hear his voice—and to confirm our appointment with Dante and Louisa.

Before meeting with them, he wanted to get a copy of the ranch's land survey so that he knew what he was dealing with.

We had time to drive to the town hall in East Hampton. As an incorporated village within the township, Paumanok Harbor had its own government, police force, and taxes, but it was still part of the larger territory that included the whole East End, from Wainscott to Montauk. The wider township had a town board, planning department, zoning code—and another tax collector.

We stopped in Amagansett for muffins that weren't as good as Susan's. Cousin Lily had already fed Ty bacon and eggs, so he only ate two. I couldn't imagine how he stayed so slim, but I checked the rear view when we got to the municipal building on Montauk Highway. Yup, those jeans fit perfectly, and yup, not an ounce of fat or jiggle. I almost tripped over a crack in the pavement on our way in, watching. I wasn't alone. Two middle-aged women bumped into each other, and a teenager holding a traffic ticket swallowed her chewing gum. It wasn't every day a real cowboy in high boots and a Stetson hat—this one made of straw—ambled down the street. Not even in East Hampton.

I admired that amble again, then had to speed up when Ty opened the door to the offices and stood there, waiting.

Ty got the map, for a fee. I got a lecture about calling ahead. Without taking her eyes off Ty, the clerk, a woman older than my mother, asked me about the Harbor.

"You're Willow Tate, aren't you? Eve Garland's granddaughter? Is it true someone put something in your air that has everyone hallucinating and shooting each other? Or maybe a virus? I won't let my kid go bowling there this week."

"That's good 'cause the bowling alley is shut down. But everything is under control now. Mr. Farraday is helping."

"I bet he is. I bet he is."

Ty winked at her, said "Thank you, ma'am," and took my arm before I tossed a stack of clamming permits at her.

To get my mind off what I acknowledged as nothing more than jealousy, possessiveness, with a bit of hometown pride mixed in, I tried to explain to Ty about the scattering of unfinished antique farm cottages and barns out in front of the modern, institutional, utilitarian town building.

I had a hard time with that, since it made no sense to me or anyone who had to pay taxes to the town. I knew the historic buildings were donated to preserve them, but on the town hall lawn?

While we were in East Hampton Village, we stopped to get Ty an overpriced burger. I had a salad.

The women on the street all looked at Ty, but he looked in the shop windows, deluxe this and diamond that. "Toto, this sure ain't Kansas anymore."

Which about summed up the Hamptons.

Ty dropped me off home, so I could get my car to do errands. When I drove through town, Paumanok Harbor's shopping area looked good, especially with the shiny new glass windows in all the storefronts. We met up with Louisa and Dante at her office in the arts building. Her kids were next door at play group at the community center.

After an initial bit of gauging each other's worth, Ty and Dante settled into an easy relationship. They were both such alpha males, so sure of themselves and their place in the world that they didn't have to kick dirt behind them or try to piss higher on a hydrant to prove who was top dog.

Dante was thrilled Ty was interested in the ranch. He'd been working to finance a deal with the owners to let the village keep it as open space, but money was tight these days. Ty's idea was far better, especially if it was going to hire local builders, local stable workers, and even give local kids a chance to earn some money for college while learning the value of hard work. He'd already investigated Ty's nonprofit horse rescue foundation, right down to the price of hay, if I knew Dante. Knowing his expertise at the computer, and his geek friends across the Ethernet, I wouldn't be surprised if he knew Ty's personal value, too.

He loved the goat cheese idea. More jobs, maybe making the ranch self-sustainable. Dante was prepared to help in any way he could.

"In fact," he told Ty, "I think I can work out a deal where you can have the land in a long-term lease, say a hundred years, without having to buy it or take out a killer mortgage, if you take care of the structures you'll need to build and agree to keep it agricultural in nature."

"For how much a year?" Ty wanted to know. The property was worth millions. I had no idea how much he was worth.

Dante smiled, showing dimples. "How's a hundred dollars a year? And any income is tax-free."

Ty sat back. "You can swing that kind of deal?"

"I know Mr. Scowcroft, the former owner. He'd lower the price considerably just to have horses on the hill again. And he likes me."

"Don't tell me you used to date his daughter, too," Louisa said.

"He likes me because I *didn't* date his daughter."

Louisa and I laughed, then had to explain to Ty about Dante's bad-boy reputation. Before his marriage, of course.

Ty got serious again. "So no property taxes because the land is in public hands. No income tax because it's nonprofit."

"There'd be school tax on the housing, and taxes for the fire department and the library, but our rates are still manageable. And I can get you good numbers on a loan for the buildings."

"What about a trailer to start with?"

"It's not what the town fathers like, but I'll see what I can do if it's temporary and could help get the operation going sooner. Oh, and if you could manage to fit in a pony camp, my little girl would be grateful. And that would help pay the bills, too."

"How come you can pull the strings? I thought the village had a mayor and a town board?"

Louisa laughed again. "They do, but Dante has the money and the contacts and the expertise. They'll listen. Besides, what have they got to lose? They've wanted to buy the land for years. Now maybe they can afford to if Mr. Scowcroft likes the idea. They'll see the ranch as a benefit for the whole community, not just a few hikers or bird watchers on the hill."

"I'll have to think about it and look over the property again as soon as the police let me. I just got a map this morning, but I haven't had time to look it over, see what's there, what's not."

"There's a nice little pond where we kids used to go skinny-dipping. You get Willy to tell you about her last visit to the pond. On second thought, chances are you'll hear it twenty times before the week's out." He grinned at me. If he wasn't Louisa's husband, I'd kick him where it hurts. "It's part of the village history. The best entertainment anyone had in years."

Ty looked at me and smiled, real slow. "I bet I've had better."

CHAPTER 28

GOOD FRIEND THAT SHE WAS, Louisa changed the topic of conversation while I prayed they would all think I had a sudden sunburn instead of terminal embarrassment. Jeez, was I never going to live that night down?

By the look on Dante's face, I'd guess not.

Louisa cleared her throat. "I have an idea that might help raise funds. That is, if you are staying on in the Harbor for awhile, Ty."

"I was going to stay for a few more days at least, but putting this deal together will take longer than that. That's if I decide the deal is even possible."

"It's possible," Dante insisted. "You know it is, or you wouldn't have considered buying the property in the first place. Now you'll only have to finance the buildings. Not you, personally, of course, but your foundation. I know it's well endowed."

"Yeah, but mostly by me, and I don't like touching the capital. I need to figure if the ranch's expenses are going to be manageable in the long run. You can't count on charitable donations to feed horses or pay vet bills, not in these times. I'd have to think about making it a riding school or a boarding facility for show horses or another equine training center, besides a rescue ranch. Some way where Bayview can earn more money than goat cheese can supply. I've already got two ranches to support."

So he'd have to be on the road more and more, performing at rodeos, horse shows, and arenas between football halves, like on his website. I didn't think his heart was in that. Mine sure as hell wasn't. How did you build a relationship with a guy who was never nearby?

Louisa's voice took on a hint of impatience, as if she were telling her children not to interrupt the adults. "That's all the more reason to listen to my idea."

"What's the expression about getting a bit between her teeth?" Dante gave his wife a fond look, but told Ty he better listen or they'd never hear the end of it. Or else she'd go ahead without his input.

That would be hard to do in this instance, because what Louisa proposed was a show of exhibition horsemanship, an extravaganza of a fundraiser.

"We could hold it at the school football field, which already has bleachers and lights."

Obviously, she did not know that the athletic department's portable lights were at Grandma's farm.

"And we can borrow more stands from the county. We'd charge a good amount, but let kids in half-price, and give a discount for locals and seniors. But we can have a special section for patrons and donors, at luxury box seat prices. And a hospitality area to sell refreshments, souvenir T-shirts, that kind of thing." She looked at the hat in Ty's lap. "And cowboy hats. Definitely cowboy hats."

Dante jumped on the bandwagon. "The vineyards like to support big events. I bet we can get them to donate the wine in exchange for a sponsorship banner. Major corporations like to be sponsors, too. It's great publicity and generates a lot of goodwill, and makes a perfect tax write off."

"And the restaurants always give us platters of food for free or at cost. We sell advertising in the program, and appeal to the heavy hitters who summer out here. A great show for a great cause. Who wouldn't kick in a nice piece of change to support a worthy charity that saves land from development, creates jobs, and rescues horses from death row?"

No one who wants to do business in this town, I calculated, or with Dante.

He said he knew horse lovers, too, and a lot of people to call on for help. His own foundation had ten employees he could get working on the event in half an hour. "We could make a bundle in one night."

Ty ran his finger over the band on his hat, not looking at me. "But I can't stay here forever."

"Hey, you're talking about my wife and my staff. Given a month, they could plan a coronation." He waved one hand around to indicate the arts building and the community center. "She got this place built almost overnight, didn't she?"

I thought it took almost a year before the whole complex was finished, but I didn't say anything.

Dante was certain they could get the show going in a week or so.

Louisa laughed and said they better make it two or three weeks, to round up all the contributions and get the printing done.

I knew I'd love to see Ty and Connor perform, rhinestones and sequins and all. Watching them exercise the horses was impressive enough; seeing an actual exhibition of their skill ought to be mind-blowing. Especially knowing the star was my very own lover. Me, Willow Tate, with a real hotshot performer. Who would have thought it? Maybe then people would forget about the lake incident when I was a teenager. The problem was, I wasn't sure about filling the seats with the art gallery and charity ball crowd. Would they really pay to see a couple of horses do circus or rodeo tricks? What if no one came to see the show? How mortifying for all of us, but Ty especially.

"They'll come," Dante assured me. "Everyone with a kid, everyone interested in saving the land or horses. Think of the Hamptons Classic Horse Show and how huge their attendance is. The polo crowd. The environmentalists, the animal protection people. And you're forgetting how famous our man is. Besides advising the Olympic equestrian team and anyone else with high-strung horses, he's headlined in Las Vegas and filled Madison Square Garden."

He did? It never said that on his website. I slept with a guy who had his name in lights? I would have bought nicer sheets.

"No, we were part of an American Lipizzan show, that's all. And Paloma Blanca is the star, not me."

And he was modest besides. Then he turned and asked my opinion, which felt good near my heart, that he cared about my views. "What do you think, Willow?"

I thought I'd expire from pride, but what I said was, "I think the townspeople can use the event, even if the ranch thing never happens. They're losing tourism money and everyone's nerves are frayed. The only thing I worry about is what if. . ." I was reluctant to discuss the night mares in front of Dante and Louisa. The Riveras weren't part of that phenomenon, and I didn't want to try to explain the paranormal to, well, to normal people.

Ty understood. "That's what I was thinking about, too. What if."

Dante didn't quite understand, but he tried: "What if they don't catch Snake's killer by then? There's safety in numbers, and we'll have all kinds of security. But I have confidence the shooter was from out of town, just using the ranch as a transfer station for the drug trade. We need to show the world that Paumanok Harbor is safe. No gangsters, no serial murderers, no weird hauntings or bad air."

Ty and I both knew any of that was possible. He looked at me. "You live here, I don't."

I thought about it. We ought to know soon if the mares were truly gone. And the lights would help protect the crowds. Most of them wouldn't be affected by the emotional sendings anyway. "It would be nice for the locals to have something to smile about."

He nodded. "I'll talk to Connor."

Louisa said she'd get started on the publicity and donor lists.

Dante took on the town, the county, and the corporations.

Ty stood and took my hand. "Sounds like we're doing a show, sweet pea."

"We? I don't have anything to do with it."

Louisa said, "Sure you do. You can design the programs. And a banner. We definitely need a banner at the entrance to town." She pushed her pregnant body awkwardly from her seat. Dante smiled and came over to help her up, which made me happy for both of them, and a little jealous. Just a little, when I noticed how swollen her ankles were.

"Louisa, are you sure you're up such a big undertaking as this will be? I mean, you're *big*."

She tossed her head. "This is nothing. And I've got months to go, so you don't have to worry about my whelping at the horse show. I will need your help decorating the tent, though."

No one had mentioned a tent. "What tent?"

"For the VIPs. And the press. Maybe the Secret Service."

"The Secret Service?"

"We may as well invite the Obamas and their kids. And the Clintons come out here sometimes. Dante contributed enough to their campaigns. Our senators and congressmen ought to appear. The county legislators, for sure, and maybe the governor, since they promised to help finance the land purchase if we could come up with the rest. Anyone who's running for office in November will show. And officials from the Nature Conservancy."

Good grief. And here I thought I only had a missing horse to worry about. "What if it rains?"

Dante looked at me and raised one dark eyebrow. "This is Paumanok Harbor, isn't it? Have you ever known it to rain on a parade or a fireworks display or outdoor graduation?"

Well, no, but we didn't talk about it much.

"So we better get busy."

Ty said he'd think about the ranch, but if Connor was willing, the show was on. He'd call in some favors and get a couple of his friends to perform, get someone else to provide calves or sheep to highlight Lady Sparrow's abilities as a champion cutting horse.

The American Lipizzan show was booked for the summer, so they were out. He'd notify some of his East Coast patrons, too, and the breeders and owners he'd worked with in the past. A bunch of them summered in the Hamptons, so they'd come and contribute generously if they wanted to hire his services in the future. He'd get his agent working on that, and publicity around New York City.

"And Connor was going to contact the local Native Americans. I don't recall their name."

"The Shinnecocks, in Southampton," I supplied.

"That's them. He heard they put on a big powwow in the summer and wanted to offer to ride for them if our schedule permitted. Maybe they'll come perform native dances."

Now I worried that maybe the school ballfield would be too small. And where would everyone park?

Louisa was ahead of me. "We'll shuttle people from East Hampton High School and the airport, use the Lighthouse parking lots in Montauk, too. And if parts of it are clear by then, we can park cars right at Bayview, so people can see where their money is going."

Dante and Ty thought that was a great idea.

I didn't. "What about the snakes?"

"Maybe we'll serve some up in the VIP tent."

I hoped Dante was kidding. Ty thought the mowing would get rid of most of them, and Louisa didn't seem concerned at all. She was already onto the next problem of finding someone to sing the national anthem.

"I wonder if Billy Joel can sing it? He used to put on benefit shows in Montauk, him and Paul Simon. I think they're both around this summer. And I heard Jimmy Buffet rented a cottage near the beach in Montauk, so he could surf. Wouldn't that be a kick? Or maybe we want that kid from the high school that made the finals on American Idol."

My head was starting to ache. Louisa and Dante seemed to be enjoying themselves, already making lists and writing down phone numbers. And Ty was grinning. I guess he liked being a star, too.

All I knew was that the guy was way out of my league.

CHAPTER 29

OUT OF MY LEAGUE OR NOT, it was my hand Ty was holding when we got up to leave the Riveras to their planning.

Louisa called us back. "I forgot. Do you think you could start your YA creative writing course here next week instead of in August? I hate to ask, what with all the other stuff going on, but we've lost a bunch of our instructors this month. The poet was in a car accident. And the scriptwriter packed up and left town. Dante was going to substitute with his computer game workshop, but he'll be too busy raising money for the ranch deal and twisting arms for the event."

"I'm not sure I'll be ready." I had notes and lesson plans, but I'd never taught anybody anything before. I needed more time to prepare. Like a year or two. Teaching at the arts center sounded great when I volunteered. Not so great when I actually had to do it.

"Of course you will be ready. You're a writer and an illustrator. Show the kids what you do. I already have five of them signed up. I'll put the notice in the paper this week, and we'll get a bunch more when they see your name."

"Yeah. Just like Paul Simon's or Billy Joel's."

Louisa laughed. "The kids in the Brain Surfing summer program are too young to know those old-timers. They know you because Mrs. Terwilliger puts your books in the hands of every teenager who comes into the library. Even the younger ones see your books on the shelf under the 'local author' sign."

Ty nodded encouragement. "I think it's great that you're showing kids how to use their imaginations. I'd love to sit in on the course."

I thought about all he was doing for the town, all he did for Connor's people and, of course, for the rescued horses. How could I refuse to put in a few hours a day for two weeks, especially after I'd agreed to do it? Louisa would be disappointed. Five kids would be disappointed. Ty wouldn't like me. That mattered, but, hell, I wouldn't like me. That mattered more.

I fiddled around finding my sunglasses in my tote bag. "I guess I can get it together. It's not as if I know what I'm doing anyway."

Louisa clucked her tongue. "Show a little confidence, Willy. We all know you're an award winner. You'll be great. And look at it as a learning experience for you, too, as well as the kids. The next time you give the course you'll have it all down pat."

I dropped the sunglasses. "The next time?"

"Sure. If it's the success I expect, we can offer it again at its scheduled week next month. I'm hoping some of our other teachers come back, though. They did sign contracts."

"I didn't."

"You didn't need to. I know you'd never let me down."

Oh, boy. Guilt from a pregnant woman. I started for the door again. Ty and Dante shook hands, but then I remembered the Froeler girl and my promise to her. Damn, I seemed to be drowning in commitments.

"Do either of you know a family named Froeler? They have a daughter in a wheelchair."

"I know them," Louisa said, "but not well. We see them at fundraisers and at friends' parties. I've never felt the need or the desire to get to know them better. The mother's nice enough, I suppose. Skinny, pretty, and uptight. Younger than Willem. They say he married her for her dead husband's estate. I have no idea why *she* married *him*. I'd say he was authoritarian, but that might be typecasting from his German background. He's definitely patronizing."

Dante said he'd played in a benefit golf tournament with Froeler once and bumped into him regularly down at Rick's Marina where they both kept their boats. They seldom did more than speak of the day's weather or the fishing.

When Louisa asked why I was interested in that particular family, I explained about their daughter wanting to take the class. "The parents won't let her. I got the idea they were obsessively overprotective. Maybe it's understandable with a handicapped kid, but I think she hardly leaves the property. She's homeschooled, so I thought she'd like to meet the other kids. Make friends. Express her creativity. Get out of the house. I thought if you knew the parents, you could convince them she'd be safe enough. I know she'd benefit from the experience."

"I'm sorry," Louisa said. "I'm not on close enough terms. They're more the cocktail party circle than the spaghetti supper at the firehouse crowd, and with the kids and all, we don't get to many of those affairs any more. I know Alice Froeler plays tennis at a club in Amagansett, but she's not on any committees here or active in any volunteer groups."

I could hear the disapproval in Louisa's voice. She was an indefatigable do-gooder and firmly believed in putting back into your community. Now she volunteered to call Mrs. Froeler in her capacity as administrator of the summer program, but she doubted her call would have any effect.

"For that matter, I don't recall ever seeing the girl in town, just in the car with the live-in gorilla who drives the family around and does errands. They say he's the girl's physical therapist and Alice Froeler's personal trainer. He's certainly muscular enough and grim enough for a workout drill sergeant, but he still reminds me of a bodyguard. Or a prison guard. All I've ever heard him called is Lewis, so I don't know if that's his first or last name, but he takes Alice everywhere when Willem Froeler goes back to work during the week."

Dante agreed the man was big and tough looking. But Lewis knew his way around a yacht, as if that mattered more. It did to Dante, who used to live on one of his own boats. "Froeler takes him as first mate when he goes fishing or over to Block Island. The boat's too big for one man to handle, especially if he's trolling for blues or trying to dock in a high wind."

Somewhere between my dreams and my book, I'd started to feel protective about Letitia, Letty. "That man Lewis is not rough with the girl, is he?"

Louisa had no idea. "As I said, I never see the child to speak to. The parents attend the exhibit openings and the concerts here in the summer, so I bump into them occasionally, but they never bring her. I understand there's a live-in housekeeper, too, now that the girl doesn't need a nanny or a nurse, so it's not like she's left alone with him all the time. For that matter, you know this town. I would have heard if anyone suspected Lewis was abusing the child. Or bedding the wife. I haven't heard anything like that."

"Okay, thanks for the information. I'll see what I can do about getting Letty to the arts center." I had my sunglasses on and was ready to leave, again.

"You better let me call, Willy. You'll never succeed if Mr. Froeler is there. He and your mother had a run-in a while back."

"Because they killed the pony?"

"She already despised him for that"—Ty gave his similar opinion of that action with a grunt—"but they argued afterward."

It seemed my mother, with her usual attitude of letting no stone go unhammered, wanted information on the pharmaceutical company Froeler owned somewhere in Nassau County to find out whether they conducted experiments on animals there. He told her, in effect, that it was none of her business. So she told him, in the exact words, to go screw himself. At the funeral parlor, during the wake for Rick Stamfield's mother.

"Oh, no."

"At least it wasn't at the funeral," Louisa said, as if that would make me feel better about Mother and her missions.

Dante laughed and commented on the Tate women's history of dramatics.

But Ty said, "I am going to love your mother, darlin'."

I didn't like the look on Louisa's face, as if she were planning her matron of honor outfit. I took a step farther away from Ty. "Don't call me that!" Then I asked if Mom ever found out about the animal testing.

Louisa shook her head. "I have no idea."

"What does the company make?"

"Money, as far as I know, from the way they live. Or Alice's first husband was really loaded. Froeler's generous enough, likes his name on the letterhead and the donor list. The hospital left him off the roster by mistake one year and he never contributed again. He's not here a lot midweek, so maybe we'll get lucky and be able to work on the mother without him."

"The kid really wants to write. Someone should encourage her."

"That'd be you. Let me call and see what I can accomplish."

"With all you have to do? I'll try by myself, to start. And I think a personal visit is best, so they can see I'm not threatening. Letty will be there, and I know she is on my side."

"Well, good luck with that. I'm sure you'll have enough kids to work with either way."

I wanted that one.

Ty squeezed my hand when we were back outside. "I like your friends and I like your town. You've got good people here, people who care. But you're the best, Willow Tate."

So I kissed him, right there in the front of the arts center. Someone beeped their horn and a kid on a bicycle whistled. Ty laughed. Then he asked me to go to dinner with him.

"You mean like on a date? A real date?" We'd already had wild, passionate lovemaking, and now he wanted to play the singles bit? Talk about putting the cart before the horse.

"A real date, you and me."

"What about the mares?"

"We can't do anything until after dark, either way. So let's enjoy ourselves. Maybe go out of town where not everyone knows you. I'll be busy the rest of the day talking to my show manager and PR staff about the show. What does Louisa want to call it? The Ride for the Ranch. And then phoning the lawyers about the property. I don't want to go too far with this if the town won't approve it. By five o'clock, the suits'll all be done for the day, and I'll need a drink and dinner and a beautiful woman by my side."

"I don't think Dante will let Louisa go out with you."

Now he kissed me. "Luckily that's not who I want."

I could feel his want right through our clothes. It must be contagious, because I didn't want to wait till after dinner. "You don't have to wine and dine me just to get into my bed. Save your money. You'll need it to build your ranch."

"You really think the price of a dinner is going to make a difference? Willy, the price of a ticket to most of my shows is more than a little thing like you could eat. Even in New York."

I made a mental note to ask Dante what he'd found out about Ty's finances. Just how rich was he, anyway? Football player rich? Movie star rich? Not that it mattered, of course. "I just don't want you thinking you have to, uh, buy my affections."

"Didn't Grant take you out fancy?"

Grant who? I hadn't thought of the Department of Unexplained Events agent in days. Which was easily explained by the way earthshaking sex tended to affect a girl's memory.

"He did. But we didn't have a whole lot of time for plain entertainment before he left."

"Well, that's what people do when they enjoy each other's company. They make time. And if we don't go out, we'll spend the whole night in bed and I'll be too drained by morning to do half what I need to."

Did that mean he wasn't going to stay over? Maybe what I took as his interest was just my admittedly active imagination.

When I didn't say anything, Ty asked if I'd rather go to the movies or bowling.

I'd have to dig up the movie schedule, but the bowling alley was still closed, thank goodness.

"Of course, we could go skinny-dipping at that lake at the ranch and you could tell me what had you blushing fifteen years later."

"Dinner sounds great."

He laughed. "You pick the place, as long as your cousin isn't cooking, your family isn't sitting at the next table, and no one asks about the mares."

"How about Montauk? You haven't seen it yet."

We picked a time, then separated. I did my errands on the way back to where I'd left my car.

Walter at the drugstore added another batch of condoms to my bag when I bought mouthwash.

Joanne at the deli gave me a half a tuna wrap, warning I was going to have a big meal later.

And Bill at the hardware store set the metal blanks at the key-cutting machine to chiming out "We Need a Hero."

Emil the jeweler was having one of his tools sharpened. "Bring your young man around to look at rings. The stones will tell if he's the right one this time."

The mayor was buying a new flag for Town Hall. Mr. Applebaum worked part-time for free, and was overpaid at that. Mostly a figurehead, he missed meetings and lost papers, but no one seemed to remember that come election time. A board of councillors ran the local government anyway. And he was a nice man.

"Want me to make people forget you were engaged last month to that Englishman? Or how about forgetting they all saw you making out on the arts center steps?"

"No, thanks, but if you could make them forget about that old incident at the ranch, I'd be grateful."

"No chance, Willow. It's too good a story to slip anyone's memory."

Getting out of town for awhile would be lovely.

CHAPTER 30

BEFORE GOING HOME I DECIDED to get groceries at the bigger supermarket in Amagansett. With Ty and Connor around, we were going through supplies fast, and the cranky Findels did not deserve my business. Besides, there were a couple of little shops there where I might find something special to wear tonight.

On my way back I drove past Osprey Street.

I asked Mrs. Desmond if she could make another cup of alphabet soup for me, with an H, a T and an A.

"You're looking to see if your hat is alive or dead? Or do you mean if your love for the gentleman in the cowboy hat has a chance? I'm sorry, Willow. This doesn't work that way."

"It's a horse. That colt we've all been looking for. I need to know if he is alive or not."

"Oh, dear. I hoped we were done with that. Let's have a look."

All the letters floated. H'tah lived. Somewhere.

Margaret assured me the braided bracelets usually worked. A person's finding wish came true if it were a worthy one, and if the wearer wished hard enough. "You didn't wish for a man riding a white horse, did you?"

"No, just a white colt. His name is H'tah."

"I thought his mother found him at the ranch. That's

how come things have settled down around the Harbor. We all figured that you found him and sent them to get him home."

"We can't be sure."

She bit her lip, but studied the bracelet she'd made for me. It still looked brand-new, despite showers and hand washings. "I guess you're still looking and wishing to find him. And you will. I'm not sure how or when, or if the village can survive it, but you'll have that bracelet until you do."

Then she handed me a shawl made of some gossamer stuff, dyed in all the blues of the ocean. It weighed as much as a spiderweb.

"Until then, this will be perfect for dinner tonight."

"You're not . . .?"

"Telepathic? Clairvoyant?" She laughed. "Of course not. I'm a weaver. But I got a phone call from my sister's friend who was buying potato salad at the deli."

She wouldn't take money for the shawl, so I promised to drop off a signed book tomorrow.

"Just have a good time tonight, Willow. You deserve it."

I did. That is, I deserved it, and I did have a good time.

We almost didn't make it out the door.

Either Ty was getting more good-looking every time I saw him or I was looking at him through love-colored glasses. Not that I was that deep into this relationship to give it the L word. Not yet. He was gorgeous in a sport coat and trousers with an open-collar blue shirt. They all looked like they'd been made for him, and I guess they had. Money, looks, class, and a soft southern drawl. Oh, my.

His smile when he saw me was even more stunning. I didn't find a blue blouse to match my new shawl, but I did spot a spaghetti-strap dress in green silk that worked. At first I had to ask the saleslady if it was meant for a nightgown or under something else, but she laughed and told me to try it on. The amount of fabric when I slid it off the hanger looked too small for a coat for Little Red. No bra was possible, but the saleslady said some women used Band-Aids if they didn't want their nipples pointing. I decided the shawl was good enough cover. And since the shawl was free, I went to the shoe store next door and bought high-heeled sandals with blue and green glass solitaires on the straps.

My credit card slips were already daunting, so I went to the pet store and bought Little Red a new collar. That was only fair, wasn't it, since I was going out without him? I bought chews for all the dogs, and went to the bookstore to see if they'd reordered my new book. There it was on the shelf, three copies this time. I was rich again.

And well dressed. Ty stood rooted to the floor in the doorway of my house. "Maybe dinner's not such a good idea. We should go to a movie where no one else can see you in that . . . that . . ."

I twirled around so he could see the view from the back. His indrawn breath told me what I wanted to know. "That sex goddess outfit?"

"Yeah. That, too. I'm not hungry. Don't feel like driving. My back hurts."

"I have some chips and beer and a comfy sofa."

"That works for me."

I took his arm and pointed him out the door. "Not on your life, cowboy. You think I got all fancied up just for you?" Well, I did, but he didn't have to know that. "You promised me a night on the town, and we're going."

"How long counts as a night?"

He ran his hand down the smooth fabric of the skimpy dress.

Not long at that rate. I headed for the car.

I should have headed in the other direction. Not away from his car, but toward East Hampton instead of Montauk. I forgot what that place was like in the summer. All the fancy restaurants that took reservations were fully booked. The ones that didn't take reservations had lines out the doors. The ones with no lines were mostly ones I wouldn't eat at. The food was bad, the owners had bad reputations, the bars were too noisy or too rough; they were tourist traps.

What the hell, we were tourists tonight. We ate at Gosman's, a huge complex right on the inlet to Montauk Harbor. We didn't eat in the big restaurant itself, but waited ten minutes for a table at one of its satellites, Top Side, that was on the roof of the clam bar and overlooked the jetties, the fishing docks, the beach across the way, and the sunset. That's why all the tourists were here. That and the lobsters.

I wore a paper bib. Damned if I was going to ruin this dress at one wearing. Ty had managed to get through three decades of life without eating a lobster, so he ordered one, too. Then I had to show him how to eat it. You cannot be serious, or even filled with lust, when wearing a paper bib and dribbling butter down it or getting squirted in the eye when you used the nutcrackers. I suppose watching him suck on a leg could have been a turn-on, if I hadn't been busy trying to winkle the last bit of meat out of the claw. Mostly we laughed and swapped stories about bad meals and bad dates and social mishaps.

While we waited for coffee—we were both too full for dessert—Ty took my hand across the table with its flickering candle in a glass jar. "Thank you. That was a wonderful meal. I don't get to eat with friends that often, traveling as much as I do. This was special."

I smiled. "Me or your first lobster?"

"Both. I will always remember this night, and this time. And when I think about it, you know what I'll picture? You. You are Paumanok Harbor." He ran his fingers through my hair, that I'd spent an hour getting just right. "The gold of the sun." Then he stared at my eyes. "The blue of the sky. That gauzy thing you're wearing is the water, and that dress is the green of the fields and the woods." He leaned over and kissed me. "And your lips are a rare delicacy, dipped in butter."

I couldn't help it. Tears came to my eyes. Not that I'm a weeper. I know men hate that.

Ty jumped back. "What's wrong? Did I say something stupid?"

Not as stupid as me wanting more. "It's just that the night is so perfect. You are so perfect. And you'll be leaving soon."

His eyes lowered to study where he had his hand over mine. He nodded. "As soon as the show is over. I can have my lawyers handle the details of the land, but I have other commitments. My work, promises to horse breeders, shows scheduled."

"I know. I am just being silly."

He touched his thumb to my eye, wiping away the moisture. And the makeup I'd spent another half hour on. "Not silly. You're being loving, because that is the way you are. I'll be back when it's time to build, or to move horses onto the ranch."

"It won't be the same."

"Life goes on. But what we have doesn't have to end. We don't have to end. Come with me, Willow. Come see how you'd like life on the road. New places, new people." He crumpled his paper bib. "New tastes to savor. New memories."

Me, who hated to stay in hotels, to fly in airplanes? Who had bad dreams about taxi drivers with eye patches? "What would I do while you are training horses or performing?"

"You could write your books, or go sightseeing or shopping. You could do whatever you want."

Except walk the beach with the dogs, stay in one place until I'd seen everything, grow my own pot of tomatoes. And for how long? "Until you moved on."

I didn't mean to another city and Ty knew it. He rubbed his thumb over the palm of my hand. "I've never felt like this about a woman before. Like wanting to be with her, just be with her, after I've been in her bed. Like this. Friends. Companions. Lovers. For as long as we both want. I didn't know it could be this way, so fast, so sure. I know I don't want to leave you. At least think about coming with me."

"I will." We both knew I wouldn't.

There wasn't much else to say, so we sipped our coffees in silence. You could hear the lapping of the waves against the dock, and every once in a while the engine of a boat going by with its lights on. The seagulls were gone for the night to wherever seagulls slept. If not for the fifty or so other diners, we could be alone.

While we waited for the check, a woman about my age asked for Ty's autograph. She had to be a tourist. The locals knew better than to bother a celebrity like that. That's why the big names all came here.

The woman said she'd seen both of his shows in Las Vegas, and she'd bought his video of the master class in dressage. When she started to tell him about her half-Arabian gelding, without once looking at me, Ty cut her off with information about the upcoming show at Paumanok Harbor. I worried the female would fall over the railing she was so excited. She rushed back to her table to tell her friends, and you could see the buzz spreading through the crowd like wind through beach grass.

He really was famous. Maybe not a household name—not my household, anyway—but enough that two more people came over to ask for an autograph or if he was going to be training at any of the local stables and could they come watch. Even a guy I recognized from the polo club came to shake his hand. The jerk smiled at me, without recognition.

While Ty was talking to his fans, a woman came toward me with a paper napkin and a pen. I was proud, I was a star, I was somebody. Until she asked where I got my shawl.

Things went downhill after that. Literally. One of my brand-new sandals caught in a gap on the stairway planks down to the dock level. The heel broke off, and I lost my balance. The maitre d' was coming up the stairs with a bottle of champagne from the bar below.

Not good.

The maitre d' screamed. I screamed. The bottle and I both went flying. Then Ty caught my arm with one hand, the bottle with the other.

The people milling around the clam bar and the shops

all applauded. I heard someone say it was a miraculous save. Someone else said Paumanok Harbor and four people nodded. The maitre d' wouldn't take the bottle of champagne from Ty.

"Compliments of the house. If your lady'd broken her neck on the stairs, we'd have been liable for a lot more."

My mother always said I had disasters like this because I was so talented in other fields. If I were perfect, I'd get a swelled head.

Now I had a swollen ankle. And utter humiliation as fifteen people came to offer a hand.

Where was the mayor when I needed him?

Ty helped me over to a bench on the walkway and set the bottle down beside me. "Stay here."

What did he think I was going to do, hobble away like that nursery rhyme, one shoe off, one shoe on? I was going to go give that shoe store a piece of my mind, that's what, but tomorrow. Now I unstrapped both shoes. Someone handed me the heel of the broken one.

"Thanks. I'm fine. Thank you. Yes, I was lucky. Thank you."

I thought Ty had gone for a bag of ice, but he came back with that and an ice cream cone from the store across the walkway, coffee, with chocolate sprinkles.

He raised my leg to his lap and held the ice on my ankle while I ate. "That's what you give a kid who falls off a pony and gets back on. Happens all the time. No harm done," he said after feeling my foot for breaks.

No harm, except to my ankle, my shoes, and my pride. And I couldn't get back in the saddle to try again. But after the restorative powers of coffee ice cream and Ty's strong arm, I managed to stand and limp back to the car. He offered to carry me. I refused.

We got back some of the night's magic by driving out to the Point, to Montauk's famous lighthouse, the prime tourist destination on the east end. We got out of the car in the parking lot to see better. I leaned back against Ty, with his arms around me. I was glad for the support, glad for the warmth, glad for being here, with him.

Tonight the moon was shining above the tall lighthouse tower, leaving silver ribbons of diamond dust on the water below. With the ocean going on forever, the waves endlessly breaking against the beach, what did a broken shoe matter? We were all tiny grains of sand in the vast sea of the universe anyway.

"Now that is impressive."

"Almost as impressive as you saving me from a broken skull or something." I turned in his arms and pulled his head lower for a kiss. Now he tasted like pistachio mint. Not my favorite, but nice. Very nice.

We drove home a lot faster than when we left.

All the lights were off at the house again and the chant was playing from the backyard.

"Just in case," Ty said. "Connor's watching."

We went around back, me barefoot in the grass, hoping I'd picked up after the dogs carefully. Connor was on one end of the wicker rocker; Susan was on the other, with as much space between them as physically possible. They were talking quietly, so we left and went into the house.

Ty carried me upstairs. I carried the champagne and two glasses. I saw no reason to mention that my ankle didn't hurt anymore.

While he opened the bottle, I went into the bathroom. Then I did something evil. I went to Susan's room and rummaged through her drawers till I found a black lace camisole and matching tap pants. The top was too big, of course, but Ty already knew what I had, or didn't have, and he never seemed to mind. While I was in Susan's bedroom I used a dash of her perfume and lifted a bottle of body oil.

The lights were out in my bedroom when I got back, with a single candle lit. The champagne was poured into the glasses and Ty's clothes were in a neat pile on the floor, with Little Red curled up on top of them. Ty was lying across my bed naked, his skin glowing in the candlelight. Next week or next month did not matter. He was all mine for tonight.

Except he was fast asleep.

CHAPTER 31

THE DAY WAS CLOUDY; MY MOOD WASN'T. There'd been no dreams, just blissful sleep in a big bed with a big man. And a little dog on my other side.

We had sex in the shower, then champagne, orange juice, and Susan's scones. The breakfast of champions.

Susan and Connor were there waiting for us, still keeping distance between them, but on familiar terms. It was Susan's day off, and they were going to the beach.

Ty looked up from the stack of faxes and computer printouts Connor had brought over from Rosehill. He raised one eyebrow.

"The horses are all tended and turned out, the stalls cleaned. I hired Miss Lily's nephew to keep an eye on them while he helps her clean the guesthouse for the stage crew. Susan says he's a good kid. He has my cell phone number and yours."

Ty raised the other eyebrow.

"And I made the calls I said I would. The Shinnecock Nation dancers are confirmed for the show, and the sheep we had in Atlantic City are on their way. I'm waiting on a call about the herd dog act."

Ty nodded and went back to his breakfast and his papers. He was having scrambled eggs with his mimosa and muffin.

"Susan is going to teach me to surf."

Now both of Ty's eyebrows went up.

"I'll be careful."

"You break an arm, I'll break the other one."

"That's what you said when I flipped the motorbike last year."

"But this time I'll do it. Then I'll call your mother."

"That's really low."

"Have a good time."

"Why don't you come with us?" Susan was packing a cooler with beer and sandwiches and fruit. All my groceries from yesterday.

Ty straightened the papers: contracts, deeds, municipal codes, spreadsheets and about twenty more pages of official-looking documents. He gave her a four-letter-word look.

They left, in a hurry.

"What are you going to do today, Willow?" He put the papers back in the manila envelope. "I'll be busy with this stuff for the next week, it looks like. And making a million phone calls."

"I wish I could help you, but I wouldn't know where to start. As it is, I have a poster, a banner, and a program to design, a course to plan, a book to write, some problem parents to convince, a gambler to ask for the day's number, and a plumber to see about a stopped-up sink."

"I didn't know you were a gambler." He looked around the kitchen. "I didn't notice anything not working right either."

"Joe the plumber is a scryer. If he's back from the hospital, he'll show me where H'tah is. Mrs. Merriwether shares her lucky numbers. She might have another clue for me."

"You still can't let it go? No matter how long the mares stay away, you want to believe the colt is here?"

"I don't know about the here, or the wanting, but I have to believe he's alive and that I'll find him. Maybe the mares just gave up. Maybe they got called home. I don't know, but I have to keep trying."

"And you think a plumber and a numerologist are going to help?"

"I don't know what else to try."

*   *   *

Joe was home, but pretty banged up from jumping out
of his truck when it got pushed into the bay. He went
over the cliff onto the rocks, but at least he didn't drown.
His ex-wife was taking care of him, to her credit, but to
her annoyance and his additional misery. She kicked a
battered vacuum and said he was sleeping. Besides, she
thought the crystal water ball thing was a lot of crap, another way the lazy good-for-nothing avoided work.

Natalie wasn't from Paumanok Harbor, and she
didn't live here. Obviously.

"Hey, who's downstairs? I hear voices."

"Shut up, dickhead. You're supposed to be resting, so
you can get the hell out of bed and I can go home."

"I'd get better faster if I didn't have to listen to you
bitching every minute. When you're not tying up my
phone with that asshole you married."

"The only asshole I married drove his van into the
ocean."

"It was the bay, fleabrain, and I was pushed. You lived
here three years, and you still don't know the difference."

"I lived with you for three years, and I still don't
know why either."

Natalie hit the switch on the vacuum and drowned
out whatever Joe would have shouted back.

"I don't think the slob vacuumed since I left. You
may as well go on up. He's awake, not that you can tell
from his brilliant conversation."

Joe was glad to see me and the bag of scones I brought.
"If the bitch could cook, I might have stayed married."

I wondered why; there was always takeout. Then I remembered Natalie left Joe for another man. His huffing
was nothing more than male pride from a guy who was
black and blue from his broken nose to his swollen toes.

I explained why I'd come. I showed him a drawing of
H'tah and begged for his help.

He had reservations, besides a black eye. "It doesn't
always work. And less so the farther away you are from
who you're looking for. Sometimes it shows someone
you *don't* want to see real bad. Like my ex. It's the want-

ing that does it, I think. And it won't show location, only the person. I found a lost dog for your mother once, from the water in his bowl. That was easy; the black lab was sitting in front of the bowling alley. I recognized it right away. I ought to, bowling every Wednesday night. The doctors said I couldn't use my shoulder for a week or two. What do you think?"

"I think you should look for a landmark when you see H'tah. A street sign, a house, anything."

"I don't suppose you have his water bucket or anything?"

Damn, it was back at the ranch. No way was I going back there until the place was bulldozed. "Sorry."

"I'm a little woozy from the pain pills, so maybe we should wait a couple of days."

"Do you want the mares to come back?"

He jumped out of bed.

I was ready to try to catch him, but he sprinted toward the bathroom. "You're not hurt that bad?"

"Nah, I just want to aggravate the bitch."

"Joe, why don't you just find someone to cook and clean while you're recovering? Better yet, why don't you find a nice woman to marry?"

"You available?"

I took his arm in case he really was dizzy. "I can't cook."

"Damn."

Joe's house might be shabby, but his master bathroom was right out of H and G: all pickled wood and gleaming white porcelain, with a Jacuzzi and a double sink and a shower big enough for a ménage à trois. The towels and accessories and a thick rug were all seafoam green, with white starfish on them. None of the faucets dripped.

Joe put the stopper in the sink. Then he filled it with water. I waited, picturing H'tah as I'd last seen him, holding his foot at an angle, but standing. Without the snake. Oh, lord, don't let Joe conjure the snake!

Joe stared and stared. I thought maybe he'd gone off in a drugged haze or was overcome by the pain he'd denied. He was holding himself up by leaning on the sink.

"Do you see anything?" I looked over his shoulder and saw a sink full of water, nothing else.

"Yeah, I'm trying to figure what. It's blurry. Maybe because your friend's not a real horse."

I knew what he meant. "Try harder."

"It has to be him. White, small, swollen leg."

"You found him! He's alive?"

"That's hard to tell. Yes, his tail twitched. He's not moving around, though. His nose looks runny."

"That's not a good sign in a dog."

"Or a horse, I'd guess."

"Can you tell where he is so we can find him?"

He studied the water some more, pulling himself farther away from the sink. "It's dark, small, looks like rock. I'd guess he's in a cave."

A cave? That's what my father warned about. "But we don't have any caves! Find something else!"

"I can only see the horse, 'cause that's what we looked for, the horse and its immediate background. It's not like he's in some living room where someone could identify the furniture or the wallpaper. I can't see anything but the horse and bare dark walls." He breathed on the water, then swirled his finger around in it. "Nothing else. And it's fading anyway. So am I. Sorry, Willow, I've got to get back in bed before I fall over. The bitch would never let me live it down."

I helped him back to bed and pulled the sheet up for him.

"Do you think Janie at the beauty parlor might go out with me?"

"It can't hurt to ask."

"Okay, you can ask her." He rolled over and started snoring.

Now I had to find a cave. And a date for Joe the Plumber.

First, the Merriwethers.

Mr. and Mrs. Merriwether were packing their car, a Mercedes this time. They were leaving for Foxwoods, the casino in Connecticut.

"The roulette wheel is fairly reliable. Not reliable enough to draw attention, but quite profitable. We thought we'd do some fundraising for your young man." They got in the car, ready to go.

"He's not my anything," I lied. "But can you give me a number to help me find the colt like you did last time? It's more important than ever."

Mr. Merriwether started the engine. His wife put her head out the window and shouted, "Twenty. I've been seeing twenty horses all day."

"But I only need one of them!"

She shrugged, drew her head back into the car, and waved good-bye.

"Good luck!"

"You, too, dear."

A cave again, and twenty. And the Froelers. I needed all the luck I could get.

CHAPTER 32

THERE'S AN EXPRESSION THE LOCALS HAVE:
Summer people, some aren't. It's mean and nasty
and should never be on bumper stickers, but it is. I know
how offensive the saying is because I used to be a summer kid, helping on Grandma Eve's farm since I was old
enough to walk. My whole family was from here, but I
was still an outsider. They seemed to accept me now that
I was useful.

The year-rounders ought to know better than to be-
little the golden geese. The locals depend on the tourist trade, not vice versa. The full-timers deposited the
money, but still sighed in relief when Labor Day came
and the streets and beaches belonged to the home team.

Summer people, some aren't. That was the Froelers
in a nutshell. They owned a huge house that sat empty
most of the year, associated with the same people they
saw in the winter, shopped elsewhere, brought in their
own staffs. When they had to hire local workers for their
gardens and such, they treated the help like feudal peas-
ants, invisible, not worth speaking to.

The Froelers were rich, self-centered, and snobby. I
had to wait ten minutes after explaining who I was and
why I was there before they deigned to unlock the entry
gate. Then they left me and Little Red outside the front
door for another five minutes. Finally, a housekeeper in
a white uniform with a black apron came, took one look

at Little Red and told me I couldn't bring the dog in the house.

I'd brought the Pomeranian for a couple of reasons. First, I worried he'd destroy my shoes if I left him alone so long, so often, and second, because I wanted to appear nonthreatening. How could anyone not trust a woman carrying a six-pound furball? And yes, I thought Letty would enjoy seeing him, and seeing how a handicapped dog got to do almost anything one with four working legs could do.

"Perhaps I could speak with Mr. or Mrs. Froeler on the patio? I'd particularly like to see Letitia. She invited me to call."

The uniformed woman wrinkled her nose, told me to wait, and shut the door in my face.

And they wondered why they couldn't get good help.

After another five minutes of waiting in the sun, I heard heavy footsteps behind me on the porch. This had to be Louisa's gorilla, Lewis, the physical trainer and sometime driver. He was big and broad and had shoulder muscles where his neck should have been. He was wearing a muscle Tee and spandex shorts. I was not impressed. Too much of a good thing is not a good thing. He was dark and hairy and he had the puffed-up face of a steroid user. Not that I knew any athletes who cheated, but I'd seen that look on some of Susan's friends at the cancer center.

"This is Miss Letitia's therapy time. She is in the pool. You'll have to come back later."

He spoke too loudly, too gruffly, too sure of being obeyed. He looked more like a bouncer at a seedy social club than anyone who should be around a little girl. "You left her in the pool by herself?"

He flushed, then turned to walk around the house again. I followed him.

Letty was doing laps in the pool, but stopped when she saw me. She swam to the side, pulled herself out, and waited for Lewis to bring her wheelchair. I was happily surprised she was so strong. Maybe he was doing a good job, after all. No, he was scowling, and he didn't help her up. That might have been good therapy, but it was humiliating for the girl to have to drag herself over to the chair in front of company. I could tell, because she wouldn't look at me.

I hated him.

I waited for Lewis to leave, but when he didn't, I introduced her to Little Red, warning that he didn't always take to strangers, but he seemed to like her or the chlorine on her skin. Now she smiled, just as I planned. Then I told her I'd come to convince her parents to let her take my course next week.

The smile left her face. "So soon? I thought we had time to work on them."

"Sorry, but plans change. Have you heard about the riding exhibition we're working on bringing to Paumanok Harbor? It's going to be world-class. I thought I'd get the kids in the course to help me design the program."

"Oh." I could see the longing in her brown eyes. "I don't know if I'll get to go to the horse show. My parents don't like me out in crowds. Or near horses. They think I'll only feel bad that I can't ride. But I can enjoy looking at them, can't I?"

"I don't see why not. I look at expensive jewelry all the time. If your parents are home, why don't we try to talk them into it?

She told Lewis to ask her mother and stepfather to come out to the pool. I was disappointed that Mr. Froeler was around, figuring the mother was the easier one to convince, but I sat down where Letty showed me, at a grouping of tables and chairs and umbrellas set up at the far end of the pool.

She called after Lewis: "And bring refreshments, please."

"I don't think that's necessary. Miss Tate won't be staying long."

"My mother always offers *her* guests a drink. She says it's the polite thing to do. And the dog needs a bowl of water."

Lewis clenched his hands into huge fists that were bigger than my thighs. This was one scary dude I wouldn't want to meet on any dark corner, but he listened to Letty and went through a set of sliding doors to the house.

"He wouldn't do it if my mother wasn't home," Letty whispered. "But he doesn't like her to see how mean he can be."

"He never hurts you, does he?"

She laughed. "He wouldn't dare. Where else could he work and live and have the afternoons and nights to himself unless they need him to drive somewhere? Mostly he makes me do boring repetitions while he talks to his friends on the phone. I don't mind. It's something to do."

The parents came out. Mrs. Froeler hurried on her high heels, rushing to protect her baby from my evil influence. She was as pretty and polished as Louisa had said, and as twitchy. She took the tray from Lewis and put it on one table, then another, watching her husband all the time as if seeking his approval. Jeez, another marriage made in heaven.

Mr. Froeler himself wasn't what I expected, a storm trooper or something. He was slight of build, wore glasses and a comb over and was much older and several inches shorter than his wife. He should not be wearing khaki cargo shorts, not with those pale, thin legs. He sat down without shaking my hand or acknowledging my presence. He took the martini glass his wife handed him. The rest of us had lemonade.

He never looked at Letty or thanked Mrs. Froeler for the drink or the bowl of melon balls she placed in front of him. He did give me a brief, assessing look, sneered at the dog in my lap, and said with a slight German accent, "I hope you're not going to be as much of a pain in the ass as your mother."

Letty gasped, but I forced myself to laugh. "I doubt anyone could be. I just want to get Letty"—the mother frowned slightly, trying to avoid wrinkles, I supposed—"to come to a class for young people that I am teaching next week at the arts center."

"She already has tutors in every subject required by

the state and additional on-line courses for advanced credits. Taught by instructors with the highest credentials, I might add."

He might as well have said, "Instead of by a comic book hack." I hated him, too. I know I was making snap judgments, and I didn't intend to stick around long enough to change them. "But this is a session on creative writing and illustrating, not schoolwork. I already know your daughter has a great imagination, which should be encouraged and nurtured."

"What for? Will that get her into a better college? Find her a better job? My stepdaughter is handicapped. She needs to excel at her academics in order to compete with the other students who captain this foolish team or win that useless championship."

"Expanding one's thinking helps in every aspect of life and learning. Besides, she'll have fun. We're starting next week, and the class goes for two hours, for two weeks."

"She needs her therapy."

"She needs playtime, too, don't you think? She's a kid. I'll pick her up and drive her, if that's a problem."

Lewis was standing behind his boss' chair. He grunted.

"No, Lewis will drive. I do not trust anyone else with my stepdaughter's life."

For such a caring, devoted parent, Willem Froeler did a good job of ignoring his daughter's presence. Letty might have been another servant standing behind his chair like Lewis for all the notice he took of her. No "Do you want to go, Letty?" or "Do you have any interest in this course?" For that matter, I would have trusted Attila the Hun before letting Lewis near any kid of mine, but if that got her into town, I'd be content. "Then she can come?"

I looked at Mrs. Froeler, but she just looked at her husband and wrung her hands together. Great relationship these two had, and no business of mine why she accepted such treatment. His business was funded with her money, wasn't it?

"Please, Father. I can make up the training later in

the day. We can get one of the maids to watch me in the pool if Lewis is busy or out on the boat. I'd really like to go."

Froeler still ignored her. He emptied his martini glass and fished out the olive. "Tell me about the horses," he demanded of me. "Are they gone?"

"I don't know. No one has seen them in a couple of nights. I am still looking for the lost colt."

Now he smiled, showing teeth so white and perfect they had to be implants. "Are you? I doubt you'll have any luck. Is that cowboy looking, too?"

"No, Mr. Farraday is too busy planning the riding show and looking into establishing a horse ranch at Bayview."

Lewis grunted again. Froeler frowned at him. "I need another martini, Lewis."

"Yes, sir." I could tell Lewis hated being treated like a servant. Those clenched fists were held tightly to his sides.

"Farraday will never get it through the local planning board. They give preferential treatment only to locals, and no Texan is going to get by putting that much manure into the underground water supply. Times have changed since Scowcroft owned it. Rules and regulations are much stricter."

There was talk about a small composting facility on the grounds, so the manure could be turned into valuable fertilizer for people's gardens, or another income-producing business. I saw no reason to discuss that with Mr. Froeler.

He wanted to know what I did for a living, my credentials for teaching a course. I padded my bio a bit, lied a bit, and turned the table by asking what he did for a living, although I had a good idea, from Louisa. "You're not a banker, are you?"

His wife poured herself another glass of lemonade, the pitcher hitting the glass. "My husband is a medical researcher. He is going to find a cure for Letty. His company is looking into building another facility near here so he does not have to commute."

Ah, he mightn't be hoping to build on the Bayview Ranch property, by any chance? They'd never permit a medical facility there. My mother would be on it like an ant on a peony. So would Grandma Eve.

He took his martini from Lewis without commenting on his wife's burst of information and conversation. He asked again about the night mares, if I was affected, if I'd seen them, how I knew the colt was still nearby, where they went when they disappeared. He asked too many technical questions for someone supposed to have no paranormal sensitivity. I wondered if Vincent, the barber who saw auras, had ever cut his hair. I doubted it. Froeler would go to a city stylist—or a hair implant clinic—not a local barber where you waited on line for your turn. Luckily, I could be vague in my answers. I truly did not know enough about the mares myself to give out any details, and I knew better than to mention Margaret's weaving or Joe's scrying or Mrs. Desmond's alphabet soup. Or my dreams, for that matter.

He seemed angry that I had no answers for him. "You're Eve Garland's granddaughter, aren't you?"

I admitted I was.

"Did you inherit any of her talent with herbs and spices?"

"I can't cook."

His eyes narrowed. "I meant her supposedly healing potions and poppycock."

What, did he think I was going to steal his medical research? "No, I have no interest in what she grows or mixes."

"Is she a witch?"

Letty gasped again, and Mrs. Froeler paled beneath her bronzed skin. I set my lemonade down and sat up straighter in my seat. No one called my grandmother a witch besides me. "My grandmother is a world-renowned herbalist. And she thinks my course is perfect for young people who don't use their brains for much more than texting and video games." I smiled, showing my teeth, and I poked Little Red, so he showed his, too, only not in a smile. "She does not discuss the occasional frog who appears in her workshop."

"Frog, eh? I suppose it wouldn't hurt Letitia to attend your course."

It paid to have a grandmother with street cred.

I decided not to push my luck with mention of Ty's show. When they saw how happy Letty was with the arts center program, then maybe they'd relent about keeping her wrapped in a cocoon. She was grinning now, racing her wheelchair around the pool, laughing like a regular kid.

Her mother smiled. Froeler scowled at them both, and me. "I am sure we all have better things to do than make up fairy tales. Alice, the tennis pro says your backhand needs work. Letitia, if you are going to miss exercising next week, I'll insist on double time now. Lewis, I want to see if the mechanic fixed that throttle on the port engine. We'll take the boat out after lunch.

"And you, Miss Tate. Take your cur and leave. I am too busy for this nonsense about missing horses. Go write your little stories, but do not fill my daughter's head with such claptrap."

Little stories? At least I wasn't promising to cure a paralyzed kid.

"Janie, do you know Joe the Plumber?"

"Sure. How is he, anyway? I heard Natalie came back to take care of him. Or to see if he changed the life insurance policy."

"He's getting better, but he needs to get rid of her. He could use a little TLC, maybe some home cooking, a friendly face. You busy?"

"Can he fix the hose at the hair-washing station?"

"Maybe not today, but soon."

"I'll stop by after work with some fried chicken."

"That'd be great. Show Natalie he has woman friends of his own. Don't look at Joe—he's not at his best after the accident—but take a look at his bathroom if you get the chance. It's to die for. And he's kind of lonely."

Janie grinned. "I hear what you're not saying, sweetie. Thanks."

Two missions accomplished. Umpteen million to go.

CHAPTER 33

A NEW KIND OF CRAZY WHACKED Paumanok
Harbor over the head. Not that Paumanok Harbor
or the Hamptons needed another mania, especially in
the summer season, but there it was: Ty Farraday's Ride
for the Ranch. Suddenly the whole East End was turned
into a rock concert fairgrounds, almost overnight.

It wasn't magic, but it was close. Huge trucks, tents,
trailers, livestock, and mobile sound stages—and port-
a-potties—moved into town, tying up traffic for hours,
but few people were complaining. The merchants were
swamped and happy. Even the grouchy owners of the
little grocery store were pleased.

Everyone who could swing a hammer was put to
work. So was every caterer, every lawn mower, every
electrician and every computer geek to handle the new
website for ticket sales. I heard they emptied the jails to
fill the jobs that needed doing, commuting sentences to
community service.

Every hotel, B&B, spare room, or campsite was filled.
As soon as Bayview's front fields were cleared of brush
and weeds, with permission from the Scowcroft Corporation, production trucks and entertainers' campers
moved in. And sheep.

The Royce Institute agreed to let Ty's stage manager
and roadies bunk in the elegant Rosehill mansion with
its score of bedrooms. They were all filled and doubled-

up, as were the guesthouse, the pool house, and the apartment over the garage. Connor moved into Ty's master bedroom, because everyone knew Ty was sleeping at my house now. Cousin Lily imported all her in-laws, distant relatives, and old friends to help cook and clean and chauffeur.

I worried that the expenses would be so high the show couldn't make a profit, until Mr. Whitside from the bank and Dante Rivera, who was now the financial manager for the event, with his own staff, assured me half the services were being donated and the rest were at base scale wages. We'd make a profit, a very nice profit indeed.

So many tickets sold before they were printed, the crews needed to add extra bleachers on the football field. The baseball and soccer fields and running track became tent cities for hospitality and vendor areas, dressing rooms, pens for the animals, and more port-a-potties.

Trucks brought in bales of hay for ground-level seating, and left an open space near the shortened, narrowed performance area for blankets and beach chairs. Ty approved the new arrangement as long as a fence secured the perimeter, security forces ensured no one got onto the field, and no alcohol was served. He insisted on a dry venue despite protests that beer made a lot of money. He talked to Uncle Henry about trading passes to retired policemen in exchange for checking bags the audience carried in. No coolers were to be permitted. Ty was not exposing Paloma Blanca or his friends to a tossed bottle or drunken rowdiness, not at this family affair. They compromised on wine sales by the plastic glass in the tents.

Giant cranes hoisted scaffolding for the lights and amplifiers, and one of Ty's contacts donated the use of a camera crew and two huge screens to project the show from every angle, so people at the farthest points could still see everything, just like at a ball park. They even found a sign language volunteer and a Spanish translator.

Dante had the high school computer club making a PowerPoint presentation for the introductions and the intermissions. They were going to feature an airplane shot of Bayview this week, before the caravan arrived, and an archival picture of when Mr. Scowcroft had race-horses on it. They taped a spokesman from the Nature Conservancy talking about preserving open space and an address where people could send checks to help purchase the magnificent property. People from a horse-rescue organization made their pitch, too.

I worked up a logo for the event: Ty's profile in wood-cut style, with waves in front, horses on a distant hill behind. Louisa liked it so much, she ordered posters and T-shirts to sell, white ink on green shirts. As soon as they came back from the printer, and I signed the posters, she started the Boy and Girl Scouts hawking them and tickets at the post offices and supermarkets from Montauk to Bridgehampton. Meanwhile, Dante gathered so many corporate sponsors, he had to find new places to hang their banners and another tent with another wide screen for their reserved seating.

With no sign of the mares or sendings from H'tah, I stopped worrying about the money and started panicking about teaching at the arts center.

The twelve kids in my class were too excited to sit and think quietly about plots or characters. I chucked all my notes and lesson plans and decided we'd make a coloring alphabet book instead. They'd be for sale at the show with a tiny box of crayons, both a souvenir and a way to keep little children happy and quiet. If they made more money for the ranch, great. I promised to come back in August to teach the story session.

We divided up the alphabet letters and started to discuss what the kids wanted to draw to represent each letter. There were fights. Shouting, pushing, a few tears. And the kids behaved badly, too.

I never wanted to become a teacher. I didn't even like children.

I took a deep breath and told everyone to sit down and talk one at a time without raising their voices.

Letty spoke first. She claimed the P for Paloma Blanca. One of the local girls thought it should be a map of Paumanok Harbor. K2, the pudge with the runny nose, wanted to draw a pinto pony, like his hero, Connor's, horse. Letty was not used to being denied, especially by kids her own age, not as privileged, perhaps not as well-educated. They were careful of her wheelchair and friendly enough in greeting her, but they weren't about to sacrifice their own ideas for some uppity summer kid who got escorted into the building by her own muscle-bound bodyguard. This was their town, their arts center, their chance to help buy the ranch. I could see a lot of trouble coming, and Letty not coming back.

So I decided some alphabet letters got two facing pages, with as many drawings as we had finished in time to get printed. They just couldn't be too small for little hands to color in the lines.

One of the free, advertisement-supported newspapers offered to print up our pages tabloid size if their name went on the cover, so we worked on that, too. A bunch of my students had their own laptops to work on with intricate graphics programs, but the arts center had drawing pens and ink that made a wonderful mess. The kids loved them and produced wonderful drawings after their pencil sketches. I couldn't believe how talented some of them were, but Letty was the best.

She had good enough manners, thanks to her nannies and tutors, most likely, and quickly learned not to be arrogant about her skills. Some of the others went to her for her opinions when I was busy, which set her to glowing. K2 became her sidekick, except when his nose dripped.

"You've got to stop telling people their drawings are great when you know they suck."

She didn't understand his problem. She wouldn't tell K2 he was fat, would she? Why insult someone else's efforts? Especially when she wanted them to like her? But she stopped lying and made helpful suggestions.

The children learned to confer and cooperate, which was probably more important than what I'd intended to teach. Almost every letter of the alphabet warranted a debate.

A could be for Appaloosa or Airs above the ground—
they were all eager to see if Paloma Blanca could do
the classic Lipizzan leap. No one was saying. One little
girl wanted an angel on the A page, because her father
said that's what sponsors were called and his insurance
company was paying a bundle. We decided on America,
because members of the armed forces were forming a
color guard to carry the flag in for the national anthem.
Then we had to decide how to portray America, and
who was going to draw it.

B was easy, a sign on two posts saying Bayview, with
a horse peeking around the uprights.

C was going to be for a condor that K2 drew with
Letty's help.

They wanted dressage for the D, so I showed them
Ty's website to see what it looked like: a high-stepping
horse ought to be enough.

And so on.

"No, we are not drawing geldings. Think some more."

"Flowers in a field for F? That's a great idea, Mary
Jane."

H worked for the herding dogs. L definitely had to be
for Lady Sparrow since Paloma Blanca got a page of her
own. We brought up a picture of her on the computers
from the website.

Native Americans, Open space, Rodeo clown— Yes,
we were having two of them, friends of Ty's.

Sheep.

I claimed the T. I sketched Ty and his Stetson in car-
toon style, with running horses on the hatband ribbon.
We'd never get done in time if I didn't help, right?

X was tough, until someone yelled out, "An exit sign,
so people can find their way home."

We almost gave up on Z, but Mary Jane suggested a
zebra. It was almost a horse, wasn't it? No one liked the
idea.

Letty ran over K2's toes in her excitement. "How
about a horse sleeping, with z's coming out of its ear.
Then we could write Good Night. Thank you for
coming."

Brilliant.

Except it reminded me of H'tah, and how I wasn't looking for him.

Ty was so busy I seldom got to see him, and then it was with his friends or his business associates. There was no such thing as another private dinner for the two of us or a day at the beach. But we did get to spend the nights in each other's arms.

There was no frantic hurry now, no stolen moments between watching for the mares and searching for the colt. We had all night, and a few more days. By now we were comfortable with each other, although still learning what we liked in lovemaking. Ty was imaginative and innovative and always caring of my pleasure. And he brought treats and chew toys for Little Red. Who could ask for more? When I slept, it was with complete satiation and contentment and exhaustion. No dreams.

Then he left. Dante was flying Ty in his private jet to New York to meet with Mr. Scowcroft's lawyers, then to Albany to talk to the state comptroller and legislators about funds. If they had to, they'd fly on to Florida to urge Scowcroft himself into backing the plan and lowering the asking price.

My bed seemed awfully empty. So did my house. Susan spent all her free time at Rosehill, making friends with the mostly male show business people and helping Cousin Lily feed them. I didn't know if she was spending time with Connor, but I hoped so, rather than sleeping her way through Ty's friends and the crew.

I could understand how this was exciting for a small-town girl, having so many new men at her fingertips at once, but Connor needed her support. He'd been left as spokesman, the least talkative soul I'd ever met. I got the idea he disappeared whenever he could, because I saw him on the motorbike going through town when I went to and from the arts center. I wished Susan was with him; I prayed he wasn't surfing by himself. He was a big part of the show, according to the program I was sending to the printer.

I was the last person to offer to help with the interviews. I'd have been stuttering and stammering, even if there was only a high school kid behind the camera.

I couldn't help Connor, my jobs for the show were done, the class was going well, and I couldn't sleep. So I went driving.

It was me and Little Red, cruising around the Hamptons looking for a cave or a number twenty. I thought there was a long avenue in Springs with numbered side streets, but the street names stopped at Nineteenth.

I parked as close as I could get to Cavett's Cove in Montauk and walked along the beach by the lights from a nearby motel. When I got no vibes there, I drove back to Paumanok Harbor checking house numbers. Most people had taken down their protective Christmas lights, so it was too dark to read them. Other people never bothered to put up numbers, no matter how many times the police and firemen asked them to, for safety's sake.

At first there was more nighttime traffic than usual through the Harbor, but as the hours went by, I began to feel alone in the dark, spooked by every odd shape on the side of the unlit roads.

H'tah might be alone in the dark, too. I locked the car doors and kept going.

I parked at a dead end that overlooked the bay and stopped to admire the stars and the moon on the water, with a few boats bobbing at anchor. Any one of them could be a drug runner. Any one of them could have a frightened horse on board.

I must have fallen asleep while worrying, because I started to dream. There was no danger in my dream, no horse either. All I saw was a willow tree. A weeping willow, like the one I had drawn for H'tah. I knew it was me.

"H'tah? Are you there?"

I got another view of the same tree, not the way I'd drawn it, with my arms—the tree branches and leaves—around a little white horse, but just the willow tree. I woke with a start, not frightened, not in a panic, but knowing H'tah was calling me. I tried to project back "I haven't given up, baby! I'll find you. Keep calling!"

I knew he couldn't understand the words, and I didn't know how to tell him I was coming. I grabbed the pad I always carried, turned on the car's overhead light and drew the willow tree. Then I drew the horse, but at the farthest corner of my paper. I flipped the page and drew him closer. Another page, still closer to the tree. I closed my eyes and imprinted the pictures there. The next one was totally in my head, with horse and tree practically touching. "Visualize it, H'tah. See me coming for you."

Then I started driving. Speeding, I guess. The farther the car got from the water, the fainter the picture of the willow in my head. The closer to Bayview, the more vivid the tree, with leaves and grass. But was that my memory? Or H'tah's, a leftover remnant from his time there?

I had no way of knowing, except the tree I saw in my mind was not drawn in my style.

I knew at least twenty people were at Bayview, and I'd met most of them, so I drove up the hill to the ranch where clusters of campers and trailers were parked in the cleared area. A few lights were on, and I heard people talking softly, someone strumming a guitar. This could have been a cattle drive, except for the lack of cattle. And these were show business people, not cowboys. I spotted my cousin sitting at a picnic bench with the sound technician. Connor came toward me.

"Do you need something?"

"I thought I had a dream, maybe a vision, from the colt. I think he is still here."

"Here in Paumanok Harbor or here at Bayview?"

"Here. I can see the vision stronger from here."

Connor looked around. "There's no place to hide."

They'd bulldozed the buildings and filled in the old well before anyone was permitted to camp there. Uncle Henry declared the place a hazard, private property or not. Scowcroft's people agreed to pay for the work, rather than face a lawsuit or a court order. The mayor agreed to get the job done with town employees in exchange for permission to use the land temporarily.

"Nothing here but weeds," Connor told me.

And snakes. But only a few acres of the property were cleared so far.

I didn't even have a flashlight.

"I'll come back tomorrow."

"We'll be rehearsing. Setting up all the gear and testing the sound system. And three more damned interviews. I can't help you."

"That's okay. You're doing enough. Have you spoken to Doc lately?"

"Hell, no."

I forgot. Doc liked to touch.

"Maybe my grandmother's tea could help get you through those interviews."

"Who are you kidding?" He adjusted his jeans as if the witch could shrivel his privates from a distance. Lord knew what he was doing with her favorite granddaughter out here. He sure looked guilty of something.

"I still think you should call Doc. He's great for relieving stress."

So I called him in the morning. Then I went over to Grandma's house after my class was done. She was out in one of the fields, supervising a crew of pickers, thank goodness.

"I have to go to Bayview," I told Doc over a tuna fish sandwich.

"Sure. Lots to do over there."

"No, I have to search it. There are snakes."

"I heard they were mostly gone when the weeds were mown."

"No one mowed where I have to go."

He set his sandwich down and placed one of his hands over mine. "I'm sorry, Willow, I can't go with you. I couldn't walk over that rough ground, not with my cane."

"I know. I just need some of your courage." I felt better already, more sure of what I had to do.

"Why not wait for Ty to come back?"

"He'll be too busy."

"Then use your own courage, your own strength. You have it, Willy. More than enough."

Courage, strength, and a hug from a shrink with a healing, heartening touch. I was ready.

CHAPTER 34

I WASN'T READY. NOT TO GO to the scene of two of the worst events in my life. By myself.

So I called my parents. My mother wanted to know about the dog handler for the sheep herding section. Was he reputable, did he treat the dogs well, should I contact the SPCA?

"You know him. You both studied at the Royce Institute." I told her his name, and that his border collies were the happiest dogs I've ever seen, and they slept in his trailer with him at night. "He sends his regards, and asked if you were divorced or not."

I'd like to know, myself, whether my parents were getting back together.

She didn't answer. "I'll put your father on the phone. He's worried about you."

What else was new?

This time my father told me to beware of sand pebbles.

"Wasn't there a famous book by that name?"

"Just watch out for them, baby girl. I love you."

"Me, too, Dad. Feel good."

"I will, after your mother and those dogs leave. She's trying to get me thrown out of the condo, I swear it."

Maybe they'd be better off away from each other after all.

Then I thought about sand pebbles. What kind of

danger could lurk in them? A piece of glass, maybe. I added that to the snowman and the banker and the cave and the number twenty. So now I was warned.

I was still not ready.

I tried to get Uncle Henry at the police station to lend me Big Eddie or any other of his weapons-carrying lieutenants. Big Eddie was temporarily hors de combat from the smells of sheep and new-mown grass from a recent visit to sniff the campers at Bayview for drugs or weapons in case the killer had come back. He was resting today, because he'd be stationed at one of the show's entrances with Ranger to ensure no illegal substances got smuggled into the stadium. Everyone else was too busy planning traffic patterns, emergency procedures, and how to get free tickets. Uncle Henry told me to wait the three days till after the show. That's what he was doing about Snake's murder and the drug deal gone bad, although the Feds were snooping around. And wanting free tickets, too.

A falling out among thieves; that was the spin they were putting on Snake's death for now while the medical examiner collected evidence at the morgue. In three days, Uncle Henry said, he'd have all the manpower we needed to walk every inch of the Bayview hills, and charge it to the department as looking for crime scene evidence. Which, of course, had been trampled on and mowed over by now.

When I said I couldn't wait that long, the police chief asked if I saw spirits.

"No, just the colt. And the occasional troll."

"That's good. They used to say the cliff there was haunted. Some horse-wrangler died there, maybe forty, fifty years ago. No one ever proved if he jumped or got pushed over, but he's still hanging around. Maybe that's what got Snake so mean and crazy."

Oh, boy. I couldn't have a cop, but I'd have a ghost for company.

I tried to get K2 to come. He'd been there the first time and hadn't seemed frightened by much. In fact, I'd bet he'd be thrilled to go on a ghost hunt. I found him at his father's garage, eating a hot dog. He couldn't go with me. Didn't I remember? Letty had invited all the kids from the course out to her house for a pool party this afternoon. Wasn't that cool?

Odd was the word I'd have chosen first. The Froelers entertaining local kids, encouraging Letty's friendship with mechanics' sons and fishermen's daughters? Mr. Froeler and Lewis must be away on business. On her own, Alice Froeler would do anything to make her daughter happy.

Before I left, I told K2 why I was going to Bayview. "The colt is still there." Then I waited.

No sneeze, no nasal drip, no need for a tissue. K2 was confirming my dream, so I had to get going.

I still wasn't ready. I went home and changed my shorts for jeans, my sandals for thick winter knee-high boots I found in my mother's coat closet. I also found an ankle-length yellow slicker with big pockets for water, bug repellent, a drawing pad, and marking pen. I grabbed a pair of thick gloves and one of my father's old golf clubs.

Now I was ready for snakes or spooks, ticks and poison ivy, if I didn't expire from heat exhaustion first. I left a message on Susan's cell telling her where I was going, on the off chance I didn't get back. I figured she'd send out a rescue squad sooner or later, when she was done collecting phone numbers and Facebook friends. I kissed Little Red good-bye in case I met the ghost or a snake and died of heart failure. Susan would take care of him, I hoped.

As I drove toward the ranch road, I heard heavy equipment way before I saw five wide grass mowers from the highway department clearing the front hill for additional show parking. The equipment operators would never hear my calls for help if I was in trouble. The engines were so loud, most of the men wore ear plugs. I waved and drove on.

No one was at the temporary campgrounds at the top of the hill, which was no more than I expected. Everyone was working hard to get the show set up in time on

short notice. I parked and walked past the trailers and
the sheep pen to the edge of the cleared area. I looked
ahead of me and felt like Columbus, on my own, facing
the unknown, praying the world wasn't flat.

So far it wasn't. The damned ranch had more hills and
valleys than it had trees. My leg muscles started to ache
in ten minutes from all the ups and downs. Good thing
my ankle was all healed.

I passed highbush blueberries with some fruit the
birds hadn't picked clean, lots of blackberry brambles
wherever the sun got through, cat briar that made me
glad for the protective layers, no matter how I sweated
beneath them. Wild grape vines hung off the scrub oaks
and shad trees with their gnarly limbs. A scattering of
pines had their trunks permanently bent away from the
prevailing winds, but they made homes for the birds I
could glimpse in the branches.

Every once in a while I stopped to listen for slith-
ers or whispers in my head or a tortured soul bewailing
its fate. All I heard was a squirrel scolding me and the
wind picking up. I realized I wasn't so hot anymore and
looked up to see that dark clouds had filled the western sky. Now the place seemed more desolate than ever,
haunted or not. I could see where someone might lose
his mind. Snake sure had.

I followed deer tracks when I could, and avoided
where I knew the lake to be. I didn't care if phragmites
had filled the whole thing or if it had dried up. H'tah
couldn't be there; nests of snakes could.

I went deeper into the property to where the land
might never have been cleared, or not since Native
Americans had camped here. I stopped again to check
the line of the sun, but the clouds had obscured it. Great,
I should have brought a compass. At least I had my cell
phone. Which couldn't get a signal, so far from a tower.

I took a drink from my water bottle and spoke out
loud, just to hear my own voice: "Are you hiding, H'tah?
You needn't be afraid. It's me, Willow." That's when an
image popped into my brain. The willow tree. He was
here!

"Where, baby? Where?"

I had my drawings of the horse and the tree. I tore one in half and held them up, arm's length apart. "Show me how to find you."

Just the willow tree.

Could there be a weeping willow out here? I'd recognize one of them, for sure, but there were none in sight, nor had I passed any. I kept going, kept thinking of the colt, with the image of him as that proud young equine prince that defined his name. I wished I knew Ty's chant. Hell, I wished Ty were here.

I saw the tree in my head, but I could not hear any words or feel any emotions not my own shaky ones. Maybe he was too tired or too weak to send more than the equivalent of a boat's automatic distress call.

I listened hard enough to hear waves and seagulls over the wind sounds. At least I knew I was headed north, toward the bay. I kept on, not worried about any creatures but the one I wanted to find. I touched the bracelet on my wrist. I touched the pendant around my neck. You and I, H'tah. You and I.

That's when I heard a new sound: like gravel being thrown at a window. Or like sand pebbles falling down the cliff side. I stopped in my tracks and spotted the remnants of an ancient split-rail fence, with only a few uprights remaining, just feet from me. Whoops.

I had reached the end of the world. And mine, if I took five more steps. As it was, the wind was scouring the tip of the cliff, sending those small stones hurtling into space onto the beach beneath. Far beneath, from the sound of it. Stones might survive the drop. I wouldn't have.

"I have to go back, H'tah. I'm afraid the whole cliff top will crumble if I get too close to the edge. Don't worry. I'll come back from the beach side." If I couldn't get to him by land, I'd go by the sea.

Which was easier said than done. First I tripped over a small log hidden in the grass. But there were no trees this close to the edge, so exposed to the elements. I kicked the log aside, damning it for getting in my way,

and saw a small round hole, about ten inches across.
After what was in the old well, there was no way on
earth I was going to look down that hole. It was far
too small to get a horse through, anyway. I put the log
back in place so Uncle Henry and the detectives could
find it.

By the time I worked my way back to the car, a few
people were moving around the campground, but I
didn't recognize anyone. I knew better than to discuss
Paumanok Harbor peculiarities with strangers, but I
didn't get the chance. They all kept their distance from
the crazy woman in a long hooded yellow slicker and
winter boots who was brandishing a golf club.

I drove to Rick's marina, thinking. I wondered if Ty
knew that the ranch property extended as far as the
shore. It might have beach rights, too, which made it
more valuable for the luxury estates to sprout there if
Ty couldn't negotiate a deal. The cliff edge also made
Bayview more perfectly situated as a drop for offloading
smuggled cocaine. Maybe the hole I found was a way to
bring the bundles up to the ranch. A winch? A dumb-
waiter? Uncle Henry could find out.

Rick was too busy to ferry me over to the seaward
side of the ranch land, a deep-cut indentation in the
jagged shoreline. "Getting there won't help anyway,"
he told me. "You can't get ashore except at dead low
tide on a full moon, because normal tides go right up to
the cliff face, eroding it away piece by piece. You can't
get close enough on account of the rocks either, unless
you've got a dinghy or a canoe, which'll get all cut up if
you're not careful. An inflatable would never make it."

He went on to say that the full moon was in a couple
of days and he'd take me out for a look-see after the
fundraiser. He jerked his head toward his docks, which
had never been so crowded with boats.

"They've all come to see the show. Or be seen seeing
the show. I'm charging double for moorage and my wife
is running a taxi service to get them into town."

I couldn't give up. "Even if there's no landing on
the beach, maybe there's some kind of structure on

the shoreline we could see by binoculars from your runabout."

He shook his head in exasperation, wanting to get back to work. "Where would anyone put a structure? It's a sheer cliff, with no beach in front. If there was something like a cave dug in the cliff someone would have noticed it years ago."

A cave? Now I had to go, immediately. "Is Mr. Froeler around?" I had a half-formed idea of asking him or Lewis for a ride out of the harbor to look for Bayview on its hill. If Froeler was interested in the property—not that he had a chance of building a medical research lab there—he'd want to see the waterside approach.

Rick pointed to a sleek fiberglass yacht. "That's it. They usually go fishing at full moon when the bass bite better."

"Is there anyone else around I could hire to drive me? Maybe an outboard I can rent?"

"It's not safe, not with this storm coming up. Your father would murder me if I let you take a boat out in this chop, and it's getting worse by the minute. That's what has me so busy, making sure the weekend sailors have their boats tied properly."

I studied the blackening clouds. "Is it going to be a big storm?"

"A doozy. There were a series of fronts on the radar, all coming through for the next few days. Thunder and lightning and downpours, gale-force winds, possible tornadoes farther west. Our weather guys encouraged them to meet up and get it over with, so there's no worries the night of the show."

"Couldn't they just divert the storms around Paumanok Harbor like they do for the Fourth of July parade?"

"Not if they want to watch the show, too."

"But the colt is there, at Bayview!"

Rick was a Stamfield, a truth detector like Kelvin and K2. He didn't scratch his ear. The colt was there, all right.

He called the harbormaster, who had to make sure some damnfool kayakers made it back to shore soon. I could come along.

Great, I was getting to go out on a boat again. A small boat, in the middle of a hurricane. Good thing I missed lunch.

Elgin was one of the weather magi. He knew to the minute when the full brunt of the storm would hit. He also knew about the colt and wanted to help, but he told me again that there was no beach in front of Bayview. "That's Bunker Cove," he said when we were underway in the twenty-foot patrol boat, bouncing in the chop. It was a deep cut in the sand dunes, he explained, with rocks seaward. A person couldn't even walk there from either side, not unless the tide was full out. You couldn't climb it either, not without bringing half the cliff down on your head.

"Bunker Cove?"

He told an old story about how the settlers drove the mossbunkers into the cove, then strung nets across the opening to trap the fish. A valuable harvest that was, for oils and meal, right through the early nineteen hundreds when the mossbunkers disappeared. And then there was that tragedy at Bayview.

"I think the mayor's grandfather made it so no one remembered about the cove or the cliff, so no one was tempted to try to scale it from either direction. It's just not safe enough."

I could see why not when Elgin pointed toward shore. The cliff face had been carved out, leaving a deep overhang at the top. That's where I'd been standing, with nothing beneath my feet except a yard or so of dirt and my father's warning. And yet . . .

I felt H'tah's presence. He was here, somehow, despite there being no beach, no boathouse, nothing but water. I borrowed Elgin's binoculars and tried to plant my feet and focus, with the boat pounding up and down. My stomach, too.

There. A few feet above some rocks that looked climbable, the sand and dirt and clay of the dune appeared to be a different color: the color of structures I'd seen in Montauk when I drove around looking for Cavett's Cove.

I handed the binoculars back, so Elgin could sweep for the kayakers. "Did the Navy ever have fortifications here like they did in Montauk for World War Two?"

"Sure, they were scattered up and down the shore. Lookouts, ammunitions depots, communication posts. They weren't here to protect us, but to guard the entrance to Long Island Sound from German submarines before they could get down to Manhattan by the East River."

Bunker Cove had nothing to do with mossbunker fish, but a real concrete bunker. "I guess old man Applebaum was better than we thought."

So was my father. The sand pebbles saved my life. And it wasn't banker and cave, but bunker and cove! He was close, anyway.

"He's here, the colt is here! In that bunker. And he can't get out by himself."

"How the devil did he get in?"

"The snowman. And Snake. There must be a way to get up or down from Bayview. I just didn't see it."

"All they'd need is an airshaft. They drop the cargo here, someone winches it up. No one knows about it. Safe as houses."

I wanted to kick myself for not looking down that hole under the log. There must be a bigger opening somewhere else. "We've got to go in!"

Elgin was already turning back toward Rick's marina, figuring the kayakers must have headed in. "How, missy? All I've got is the life raft. It'd be capsized against those rocks at the next wave. Maybe the tide'll be low enough tomorrow when the storm surge passes."

But the storm came in force that afternoon, and stayed. Add three small squalls together, you get a near hurricane. Dante had to land his plane in Westhampton, which was spared most of the wind, and hire a car to bring them back, including Mr. Scowcroft. The old tycoon wanted to see the show and the property one more time before deciding its fate.

I flew into Ty's embrace as soon as he walked through my door. He was wet and cold and exhausted and I didn't care. I plastered myself against him, locked my lips to his. His hat fell off. I stepped back—on it—and started to babble.

"We have to go to Bunker Cove, only it's not about fish, it's an army bunker and H'tah is there! There's a hole on Bayview land, but the tide might rise in the storm and he's already weak and all he can do is whisper my name, only it's a picture of a willow that's dropping its leaves and I don't know how much longer he can hold on. We just have to save him."

"I missed you, too, darlin'."

CHAPTER 35

"TAKE YOUR HANDS OFF HER, you bloody bow-legged bastard!"

I looked up, over Ty's wet shoulder. "Grant?"

Grant grabbed Ty by the shoulder and spun him around, then brought back his fist, ready to flatten the slimmer man.

I jumped between them. "Don't hit him! He has three thousand people coming to see him in two days!"

"Five thousand, sweet pea," Ty drawled, putting his arm back around me. "Not that Lord Fauntleroy here could manage to hurt me. Dante found him wandering around the airport like a drowned rat, so he flew him back with us, but his bed's been taken at Rosehill, so I brought him here."

"And no one thought to warn me?"

"I wanted to surprise you, Willow. Some surprise." There was murder in Grant's black-rimmed blue eyes, but now the anger was directed at both of us. I quickly stepped away from Ty.

I felt disloyal, cheap, and mad at both of them. "You could have called." I kicked Ty's hat across the room. Little Red jumped on it and started wrestling it to death.

"My hat."

"The hell with your hat. My woman!"

"I am no one's woman, not either of yours. And

you're both dripping all over my mother's living room. You"—Ty—"can sleep in my room."

Grant made a noise I would have run from.

"You"—Grant—"obviously survived your adventure in one piece, so you can survive a night in my mother's room with the two big dogs. I'll sleep in Susan's bed. By myself. And if either of you start any trouble, I'll sic Little Red on you. And tomorrow we will go find that colt. Understand?"

Ty grinned. "Yes, ma'am."

Grant nodded. "That's what you asked me to do. I came as soon as I could. Your hired gunslinger obviously didn't get the job done."

Ty's smile slipped a bit. I took his hat from Little Red and handed it to him. I almost laughed at the expression on his face, like a kid whose ice cream cone fell into the gutter. This was too serious, though.

"Between a horse whisperer and an otherworld linguist, maybe one of you geniuses can talk to H'tah and find a way to get him out. If not, neither one of you is worth your weight in fertilizer." Which was a polite way of saying they were both full of it.

I stomped up the stairs, snatched a nightshirt from my room, and slammed the door to Susan's. I wasn't going to talk anymore to my previous lover or my current lover. In the same damned room.

Except I forgot to put the big dogs out for their last pee of the night.

By the time I put on shorts and a shirt and went downstairs, the two men were sitting in the living room, a bottle of Maker's Mark and two glasses between them. While the dogs were out in the fenced run, I explained about the deep-cut cove, the bunker, the possible airshaft, the undercut cliff top, the tides, and the storm. This time I was a bit more coherent, but still tried to make them understand the urgency.

"I know we can't do anything tonight, but we need a plan."

"That's what we're working on, darlin'. We want the outlander colt out as much as you do."

I wasn't sure about that, but it was the best I could hope for tonight. "Don't call me darling."

Both of them laughed. The bastards were friends. I tried not to think about being a chew toy between two puppies. Or that Ty Farraday might have wanted me just because DUE Agent Grant did.

I'd face that tomorrow, too. After we rescued H'tah.

Except the storm never let up. Thunder boomed all night, and high winds ripped at anything not nailed down. Ty came to kiss me good-bye about one o'clock. He had to go check on Paloma Blanca and Lady Sparrow.

Grant came to kiss me hello about two o'clock. I sent him away. I wasn't going to try to explain about Ty in the middle of the night. What could I say? Besides being a linguist, Grant was descended from another of the original Royce families. I couldn't lie to him and claim Ty and I were just friends. He must have seen Ty's shaving kit in the bathroom anyway.

I went back to sleep, as much as I was going to sleep this crazy, scary night. Two of the hottest guys in town—no, in the universe—kissed me, and here I was, quaking alone in a lightning storm, hugging a Pomeranian so tightly he growled.

Morning wasn't much better. The rain had let up some, but the wind was still howling, with forked lightning right overhead. I waited for a break in the boomers before putting the dogs out. I had to go out, too, because I was afraid to let Little Red off the leash in case he got swept away.

We weren't getting anywhere by boat today, not with that wind. A couple of phone calls told me the roads were bad, too. Ty was out helping re-anchor the tarps covering the riding field, so the surface wouldn't turn muddy or unsafe. Tomorrow's show was not in jeopardy.

H'tah was. I thought about waking up Grant, but I needed to find a way to get to H'tah, not end a relationship that should never have happened and had nowhere to go.

Uncle Henry made note of the bunker and the possible airshaft, but he couldn't send someone out to dig up the ranch. Half the streets were flooded—damn those imbecilic weather magi for messing with Mother Nature—and all his cops were out detouring traffic.

Kelvin from the garage could get through anything with his auto body tow trucks, the ones that dragged tourists' cars out of the sand, but both of them were already in use, with another three cars waiting to be pulled out of ditches or mud.

Connor would be with the horses if Ty was in town, so I couldn't count on his help. Everyone else at Rosehill was at the school, making contingency plans. The people at Bayview had been evacuated there, rather than have them sit in metal RVs waiting for the lightning to hit.

I called the harbormaster to find out when the storm would be gone. Not until tomorrow, he speculated, to guarantee good weather for the show. Elgin promised to try to get me out to the cove then, at low tide. If not tomorrow, the day after.

"I'm sorry, H'tah. You know I would if I could." I drew a picture of lightning and wind-driven rain battering a willow tree. I hoped he got my thoughts, I hoped he understood. Now I felt as if I'd broken my promise to him, as well as disappointing Grant. I got no response, not even when I tried to nap after the sleepless, stormy night. Tomorrow, I kept repeating.

When I went to look, Grant had already left. He called to say he was at the Riveras' house, finding out from Scowcroft what he knew about the bunker and access to it. He was also meeting with the Feds later to call in technical assistance. They'd have everything in place in twenty-four hours. Grant had influence everywhere. If he said he needed Air Force One, chances are it would fly over Paumanok Harbor. After that, he had an appointment with Martha at the real estate office to go over some plans for renovations at Rosehill.

He'd stay with Dante and Louisa tonight. His tone of voice was cool but hopeful. I couldn't encourage him with an invitation to come back. I said I'd see him tomorrow.

*   *   *

But tomorrow was the Ride for the Ranch.

The weather was bright and beautiful but still windy. The harbormaster said we still couldn't get close enough to the cut to launch a raft.

I thought about paddling into the cove on a canoe or a kayak or a rowboat. I suppose I could scuba dive from Rick's marina. If I knew how to scuba dive and wasn't terrified of sharks and jellyfish. But what could I do when I got there? Even if I wasn't drowned or dashed on the rocks, I couldn't get H'tah out, not by myself.

Not that any of them would be much help, but Susan was busy cooking for the meals the Breakaway was catering at the food tent. Grandma was in town with the Garden Club, spiffing up the flower boxes that got damaged in the storm and arranging displays for the show grounds. Doc was having brunch with his old friend Scowcroft. Susan's father was draining the farm's fields to save the early crops, and her mother was at the school, organizing the kids who would hand out the programs and sell the alphabet books.

I didn't bother calling the police. They'd be swamped today. So would everyone involved with the show. Ty couldn't have gotten much rest last night, and he needed to be refreshed and relaxed and ready to entertain five thousand people. No, I heard it was up to eight thousand tickets sold. That mightn't be a lot by Yankee Stadium standards, but it was almost three times the population of Paumanok Harbor.

I'd already missed the midmorning's low tide. I couldn't miss tonight's. But how could I miss the show? So I had to get to H'tah before then. Which meant putting on my mother's raingear and boots, slogging across the muddy ground of Bayview and lifting—shudder— that log over the airshaft. Maybe it could lead to H'tah, or maybe I could call down to him, keep him company for awhile until we could get to him.

I called Grant first.

He was already on his way to Bayview Ranch, so I met him there. The greetings were awkward, but we were mature adults. I only cried a little. Grant didn't, although his beautiful blue eyes did get cloudy. He wouldn't show emotion, not in front of a handful of tough narcotics agents with a real drug-sniffing dog, a heat sensor, metal detectors, and a brush-cutting machine. They also had orange mesh fencing and signs from the police office: "Danger. Fragile dunes. Stay back."

They'd already found the airshaft. I called down it, sent pictures down it, paper ones and mental images. Nothing.

They dug around in the muddy earth, but couldn't make the hole big enough for a man to be lowered on a rope, not without caving in the entire shaft.

"Not on top of the horse!"

They looked at me as if I were crazy. They didn't care about the colt, only the drugs the dog was barking about.

With the ground so soft and sodden, the Feds didn't dare bring the machinery any closer to the edge. They gingerly placed the signs, then hung the orange fencing between them and around the airshaft. They'd go by water at low tide tonight, but they weren't going to open the bunker, only watch from the Coast Guard boat on call. They figured that whoever stashed the coke in the bunker would come to retrieve it at the full moon, tomorrow night.

"No, you cannot wait that long!"

One agent in a blue windbreaker, obviously worn to cover his shoulder holster and weapon, told me the decision came from Washington. They didn't want the drugs. They wanted the smuggler, the supplier, the dealer. He ordered me to stay away.

But I was the one who found the airshaft. I was the one who led the police to Bayview Ranch in the first place. They wouldn't even know the drugs existed without me!

Grant pulled me away before the guy in the windbreaker put me in handcuffs. They'd handle it, he said. The situation was too dangerous for me anyway, what with murderers and drug runners. He gave one of my drawings to the Federal agent to show to the colt if they reached him.

"I'm supposed to show a horse a picture of a tree?"

When put like that, he might call for a straitjacket instead of handcuffs.

Even Grant doubted H'tah was still alive, so long out of his own world without the proper food or comfort. Joe the Plumber saw him as sickly, I knew he was injured and weak, so how many days could he last? Besides, water might have breached the bunker or flooded through the airshaft. He might have drowned or suffocated.

"No! He couldn't have!"

"Then where are his sendings? Why will he not reply to you, or to me? I've been trying to talk to him all morning."

I had no answers, only more tears. Now the windbreaker man thought we were both nuts.

Feeling helpless, I left.

And got home in time for a phone call from Mrs. Froeler.

Her husband and Lewis were taking the boat out overnight for striped bass fishing, and he'd ordered his family to stay in the house while they were gone. Yesterday, he'd agreed Letitia could go to the benefit show, but today he rescinded his permission. Now Letitia was near hysteria, with her breathing ragged and eyes all swollen from crying.

I couldn't figure out what Mrs. Froeler wanted me to do about it. "I guess I could speak to her, but she's still going to be disappointed. She's been working on the programs and the alphabet book for two weeks, and the horse show is all she ever talked about."

"I know. I want you to take her."

"Without you?"

"I cannot disobey my husband."

Now I was as angry at Mrs. Froeler as I was at her tyrant of a husband. "Of course you can. You're not his slave or his subordinate. Besides, his demands are unreasonable and cruel. No one has to follow orders like that."

"Do you really think so? I. . . I try to please him to make up for what he's missing. He wanted a son and I never . . . That is . . ."

I almost said he had her money; that should be enough. I just told her, "You can take Letty yourself and have a good time. If you need help with the wheelchair, I can lend a hand. But watch out for her all night? That is your job. You also need to encourage her artistic talents. You'll see, her drawings in the alphabet book are that wonderful. What Letty needs is to see the horses."

After a pause, Letty's mother murmured that her husband was not himself these days. He used to be different.

Oh, and Willem Froeler used to be a cuddly teddy bear of a sugar daddy? I didn't think so. He was a petty tyrant who wanted a clone of himself—after he got control of Alice's bank accounts. The pig. "You have to think of Letty and how happy she'll be. Tonight could be the best experience of her young lifetime. What else does she have of her own, for her own pleasure? Another lap in the pool?"

"You are right. I'll do it. I'll bring her tonight."

"Great. I'll be in the bandstand. We'll make room for you two, so you don't have to chance Letty being pushed or not getting seats close enough to see everything. There's handicapped parking at the base of Bayview's street and special buses will bring you right to the show grounds."

After we disconnected, I wondered if she really had enough courage to show up. Hey, I faced a field of possible snakes and I was the biggest coward in five counties. And maybe Froeler would never find out they left the house.

I didn't know if I was jumping to conclusions because I didn't like the guy, but I called Grant and told him about Froeler and his muscleman, Lewis, and how they were taking the boat out tonight. Sure, fish bit better by bright moonlight, but did they have to go tonight, when every other soul in Paumanok Harbor would be in town? That smelled more than fishy to me.

Grant said he'd call Washington for background

checks, notify the Coast Guard to monitor Froeler's yacht, post agents on the beach to either side of the cove and more in camouflage on the top of the cliff.

"Remind them not to get too close to the edge. Sand pebbles."

CHAPTER 36

O NLY ONE THING COULD HAVE DISTRACTED me from worries about the white horse.

Tonight wasn't about me or Grant or H'tah or sex. It was about Paumanok Harbor, the sheer magic of the place, the ordinary magic of a whole village getting together to make something wonderful happen.

Think Fourth of July and Christmas and Mardi Gras, all packed into a little town. Think goodwill and friendship and a common goal of saving something precious, and having a rousing good night at the same time.

Think lights and music and glitter and cotton candy and eight thousand people—maybe ten thousand with all the overflow crowd watching from another projector on the village commons.

Think pride and patriotism as the color guard marched in bearing the flag and circled the stadium, followed by the high school marching band in bright white uniforms playing "God Bless America." Everyone stood.

Think Ty Farraday, because it was his show. He walked in behind the band, leading the grand parade customary at circuses. I don't know why he was on foot, but he was as commanding a presence as if he'd ridden in on an elephant. He wore a black shirt with white embroidery and aurora crystals to sparkle in the light, tight-fitting black pants, high boots with cutwork, and a white Stetson. He held the hat up and waved it to the crowd as he followed the flag to the imported mobile bandstand.

The sound system was there; so was a professional announcer, the producer, director, and Ty's manager, various state, county, and a couple of Federal dignitaries, Mayor Applebaum, Doc and Grandma Eve with Mr. Scowcroft, the Rivera family, Letty and her mother, K2 because he begged to sit with Letty and fetch her junk food, Chief of Police Haversmith, Grant, and me.

Ty bowed as he reached the raised bandstand. Everyone applauded.

Next came Connor Redstone, looking magnificent in Indian regalia atop Lady Sparrow. Both had feathers in their hair. Members of the Shinnecock Nation danced in next, followed by Indian drummers. Then came two tumbling rodeo clowns, four cowboys in leather vests and chaps riding on cutting horses, the dog handler and his three border collies with red, white, and blue kerchiefs around their necks.

"Uh-oh," the PA blared. "Someone's missing. We can't start the show, folks. Sorry."

The audience looked stunned for a minute, then started stamping their feet and chanting, "Paloma Blanca, Paloma Blanca."

Ty pretended to look around as if he'd misplaced his mount. Then he shook his head and whistled. From the far end of the field, from the chute the entertainers used, the white horse entered the arena. She wore no saddle or bridle, nothing but red ribbons braided in her mane, flying loose behind her as she trotted toward Ty.

What a sight she was, enough to bring a lump to your throat. Like watching an eagle soar or hearing a bagpiper play "Amazing Grace." No one made a sound until the magnificent animal stopped inches from Ty and arched her neck to bow her head. Then the applause thundered through the crowd. They loved her already.

The mayor welcomed everyone, then the announcer cued the "Star Spangled Banner." The high school band played and a young woman I hadn't noticed on the field sang the difficult anthem. She should have won the talent contest.

Then everyone left the field except for Ty and his horse. He walked to the center of the arena and she followed, snatching the hat off his head. That was the sign this part of the show was all for fun.

Ty wore a mike, so everyone could hear him giving orders, which the prancing mare didn't obey. Instead she cavorted and spun in circles around him, keeping the hat out of his reach, to the amusement of the audience, especially the children.

He pulled a carrot out of a pocket. She shook her head, and his hat, no.

"An apple?"

No again.

"How about a kiss from my favorite girl?"

She dropped the hat, skipped closer and pressed her lips to his cheek with a smacking sound heard through Ty's microphone. The audience went wild. I wiped away a tear.

After that, Paloma Blanca pirouetted, rose on her back legs, counted by tapping her hoof, and performed a dozen other circus tricks.

While they were performing in the center of the field, the two clowns placed colored flags along the sidelines. Ty would tell Paloma Blanca to find the red one, and she picked it up and carried it back to him. Then he asked her for the hat. She grabbed his Stetson again, but dropped it when he shook his head. The mare trotted up the line, looking at the pictures on the flags. She brought him the one with the hat. Whatever he called for, she brought back to him, even when the clowns mixed up the placement.

"One more question, Pal. Who is the prettiest female in the place?"

She shook her mane, crow-hopped, and kissed him again.

"Yes, of course you are. But who is the second prettiest?"

This time she danced over to the row of flags still

left, all colors, all different pictures. She looked at each, shook her head, then picked up a green one and brought it back to Ty.

"A tree? The second prettiest female here is a tree?"

The Lipizzan nodded. Ty turned the flag to the audience. "What kind of tree do you suppose this is?"

The picture was projected onto the big screens so everyone could see. "A weeping willow tree," thousands of voices shouted. "Willow. Willow. Willow."

I'd kill him. If I didn't die of embarrassment first.

"Stand up and bow, you idiot," Grandma Eve said, giving me a shove.

So I did, trying not to notice Grant's scowl.

Everyone applauded, Ty and Paloma Blanca both bowed, then they walked off the field to cheers and whistles.

The clowns did some tumbling, then set up barrels for the cutting horses to race around in timed matches, then in a row. Not one barrel got tipped, not one clown got stepped on. The announcer told us that each of these horses had been a wild pony, considered excess by the US government but rescued by the Farraday Foundation and trained at his ranch in Texas.

More applause.

The Native Americans performed next: chants, drumming, and dances that impressed everyone with their stately beauty and reminded everyone there of their ancient heritage and culture.

Then it was Connor's turn. Still wearing buckskin with fringes and turquoise beads, he and Lady Sparrow flew around the barrels, then the flags put back in the field, with Conner leaning over to grab them, his fingers almost touching the ground.

He did flying dismounts, remounts, leaps from one side of the horse to the other, with only one hand on the pommel of Lady Sparrow's saddle. While she galloped, he stood on her back, turned to ride backward, did handstands, and finally stood in the saddle, arms up and open, like the condor he was named for. They completed an entire circuit of the field in that position, at that speed. Spectacular.

The dogs came next. The shepherd had the three border collies by his side until a flock of sheep, some black, some white, some gray, were sent down the entrance chute, scattering in every direction. The people on the ground got ready to jump away, but the fence protected them. And the dogs got to work. In about five seconds they had the flock herded into a tight circle in the center of the ring.

At a signal from the handler, the dogs separated the flock into three separate circles, by color. Then they moved them into rows of alternating colors. Finally they formed an odd, hard-to-recognize pattern, until I looked up at the screen. An overhead camera on the high scaffolding was projecting the view. The sheep formed a perfect bowlegged cowboy in gray pants, white shirt and head, and black hat and boots.

The crowd went wild. No one had ever seen such a thing or knew it was possible.

The dogs took the sheep off in an orderly run toward the exit, then came back for their bows.

The emcee announced an intermission, during which a crew cleaned the field and repaired any uneven spots in the grass from the flags or the racing horses. The officials spoke, showed the tape the students had made, and reminded people of the location of the food tents and the restrooms.

I handed K2 money and he brought back a tray filled with stuff I am sure Grandma Eve would never eat, nor would Mrs. Froeler let Letty, who couldn't seem to wipe the grin from her face. K2 reported that most of the T-shirts were sold, and all of the signed posters and the alphabet books. All that was left were a few Stetson hats and a couple of my books.

"My books? What are they doing here?"

"Mrs. Terwilliger thought the library ought to help raise money, so she got your publisher to donate a box of your books. Now that everyone knows who you are, they're buying them as fast as they can. You're famous, Willow."

Yeah, as Ty Farraday's girlfriend. Before I could mull

that over, Susan brought food from the VIP tent, and Grant took K2 to fetch drinks.

According to the program, which I knew by heart, only three acts remained, the clowns, then Connor and Ty again. Letty was already sad that the night would end. Her mother started to look nervous that they'd be caught out when they got home. They weren't the only ones to wish the show could last forever. Me, too, except I had to pee. No way in hell was I using a port-a-pottie, not after a thousand little boys. I set my water bottle aside.

The clowns did rope tricks. I swear they could make the ropes sit up and sway, like cobras in a basket. They lassoed each other, a chair, a girl from the audience, and one of the uniformed policemen stationed near the fence. The crowd loved that.

Then Connor rode out again, this time in pure cowboy duds, if a cowboy was headlining in Vegas. His shirt was red-and-white striped-and-sequined satin, and his britches were silver. His long braid was caught up under a silver Western hat. He and Lady Sparrow trotted to the center of the grass and waited. Soon the flock of sheep was sent down the chute, chased by the clowns waving red, white, and blue banners. The clowns set the banners in front of three wooden gates and pointed. One of the white sheep had a red stripe on its rump. A gray one wore a blue star, while a black sheep had a white stripe. It was Connor and Lady Sparrow's job to get the right color sheep behind the right colored gate.

Horse and rider spun around, dashed into the milling flock and singled out each of the marked sheep. Then the mare almost sat on her haunches to keep the chosen sheep from doubling back to its friends. Horse and rider dashed and darted to and fro, with Connor leaning to one side or the other, Lady Sparrow at a flat-out gallop or a careful trot until the right animal was in the right place. It took about two minutes and a lot of cheering.

After that, Connor herded the rest of the flock out the entry chute, then he herded the clowns out, too. For his finale, he leaned over the horse to pick up the flags, then leaped into a standing position on Lady Sparrow's back again. He held up the flags and twirled them as the pinto raced around the ringed area.

"Con-dor," the chant started. "Con-dor." Letty and K2 shouted the loudest.

When the shouting died down, so did the lights. For a minute the field was in blackness while the announcer introduced the crowd to the art of high dressage and described some of what they would see: tempe changes, extended trots, caprioles. He asked for quiet during the performance because of the concentration required. Then he reintroduced Ty Farraday and the Lipizzan mare, Paloma Blanca, the white dove. A single spotlight suddenly flared down from the high scaffolding. Horse and rider were framed in the circle of light.

I heard gasps from the audience, or was that from me? Ty was in formal dressage apparel, according to the whispered information from the PA system, skintight white breeches tucked into gleaming black, high boots, a short black jacket, yellow vest, and black silk top hat. He looked like the cover hero of a historical romance.

"Shite," Grant muttered beside me. "He's gorgeous."

He was. "But I hope you remember that I ended our nonengagement before I ever met him or heard about him."

Grant squeezed my shoulder. "I know, Willy. But this is easier on my pride."

I smiled, relieved. He'd forgiven me. Then I forgot about everything except Ty. The announcer whispered to the audience that Ty and Paloma Blanca were going to perform a musical kur. "That's k-u-r, a medley of songs, with a change in gait with every change in music."

Then he was silent. The audience was silent. Flamenco guitars thrummed through the speakers, and Paloma Blanca danced. She was gleaming, rippling muscle and the most graceful creature on earth. She swayed and she skipped and she pranced as the music changed, and never missed a beat.

Ty's mouth never moved, or his hands, or that absurdly elegant top hat. I'd always understood the rider guided the horse by subtle shifts in his weight, or pressure from his thighs. I knew the strength in those thigh muscles. They'd made me dance, too.

The pair waltzed from one end of the field to the other, then did figure eights across the grass and on diagonals, then sashayed sideways across the short side of the ring, always moving to the music, never repeating a classical gait.

Everyone held their breath as Paloma Blanca skipped to the center of the field, changing her lead at every step. They all knew what was coming for the finale, the signature movement of the Lipizzan stallions.

But no one knew what was coming first, not even Ty. I was watching him, so never looked at anything else until I heard the gasps and a shout or two, then footsteps on the wooden bleachers.

"Behind you," the announcer whispered in Ty's earpiece.

"I know. Key the chant tape. Get Doc to keep the crowd calm. No lights, no flashbulbs."

Ty put Paloma Blanca into an extended trot, her legs far forward, as he rode toward the bandstand.

And twenty gleaming white mares trotted behind her in a row across the field, their legs extended and pounding in unison with hers, to the beat of Ty chanting.

Of course there were twenty. Mrs. Merriwether had given me the number. And of course they'd come back for H'tah. Only this time with reinforcements. They were incredible, like the finest pearls, glowing with a light all their own.

"Friends, please stay seated," Doc's soothing voice came over the chant. "There is nothing to fear. Take your neighbors' hands." He reached out to Grandma Eve on one side, Mr. Scowcroft on the other, who each took another's hand. I found mine in Grant's and Letty's. "Now think about welcoming these beautiful creatures who come in peace and love."

I could feel the tension easing. Until Uncle Henry got on the microphone. "This is Chief Haversmith. Anyone who uses a flashbulb, your cell phone, camera, or video recorder will be shot."

So much for love and peace. But no one fled their seats or fainted. Or had night terrors.

When Ty and Paloma Blanca reached the bandstand, they turned to face the mares, still in a straight line across the width of the grass. The mares stopped. Paloma Blanca bowed to them. All twenty mares bowed back simultaneously.

Ty nodded, told the sound man to key the final music. He set his horse into a canter through the exact center of the mares, who turned and followed them, at a canter. With the spotlight on Ty, and the mares giving off their own translucent light, he had Paloma Blanca change gaits again, then gather herself, raise up on her hind legs, then kick those legs out behind her until she was suspended in air.

The mares followed suit in perfect precision.

Paloma Blanca hung there—I sensed Ty was surprised at how long she stayed above the ground—like the white dove she was named for while, one by one, the night mares blinked out of sight.

Ty and his horse bowed to every corner of the stadium, then rode out the exit to a thunderous, standing ovation. Only we could hear him say, "Clear the arena. They are coming back."

Chapter 37

"THEY WANT TO TALK," WAS ALL TY SAID on his private mike as he rode out the performers' exit.

The chief got on the PA system and started having his expanded police force herd everyone out in as orderly a fashion as the collies herded the sheep. All the lights were on now to guide the way to the extra buses hired from all the school districts and private companies to shuttle people back to the parking areas. Hundreds more cops kept the traffic moving.

During the fast-paced emptying, Mayor Applebaum took the microphone and thanked everyone for coming, then said how tonight provided one of the most amazing bits of magic most of us would ever see, so we should forget that it was totally, absolutely, irrevocably impossible. Of course, if they ever wanted to have such an event in town again, they should send in their donations.

Ty and Connor came back in fifteen minutes, changed into street clothes, which for them meant cowboy boots and jeans and denim shirts. The horses were safe in their trailer; the other acts were thanked or paid and were on their way home. Ty sent most of the stage crew away, back to Rosehill for the big celebration dinner planned there. They could come back in the morning to pack everything up.

Most of the audience had left, all of the dignitaries, and the Riveras with Mr. Scowcroft, who gave Ty a thumbs-up. Letty and Mrs. Froeler were still on the bandstand, waiting for more of the crowd to disperse. K2's father, Kelvin Senior, was going to drive across the grass from the performers' gate in his heavy SUV to pick up them and Doc and Grandma Eve. And Mayor Applebaum, who'd forgotten where he left his car.

Ty started the chant tape and turned off all but an emergency light on the bandstand. He told me to come down to the field with him.

"And the silver-tongued devil, too, I suppose," he said, looking at Grant. "We might need him. Everyone else, stay quiet and calm. No matter what."

Uncle Henry spoke to his men on walkie-talkies. A few of the chosen police started to filter back, along with some other locals who wanted to help, despite the dangers. Everyone who knew what havoc a few mares had caused understood that Paumanok Harbor could not survive the wrath of twenty.

Grant spoke on his cell phone to his DUE agents posted with the FBI, the DEA, and the Coast Guard, telling everyone to hold off. He understood, too, what would happen if the colt was caught in the crossfire. He was in command now, because this was his field of expertise. "The horse comes first, then the drugs and the murderer."

At last, people were on my side.

K2's father drove up, but Ty made him turn his lights off. He stayed parked at the side of the bandstand.

I heard Doc tell everyone to hold hands, but the three of us were out on the grass by ourselves. Connor was off to the side, tapping his thigh in time with the chant.

What the hell was I doing in the middle of a field dressed for the occasion like Annie Oakley, waiting to be trampled or have my sanity sucked out of my skull by creatures that did not exist in my world? I was ready to run back to Doc's comfort or to Kelvin's truck to hide under the seats.

Then Ty took one of my hands and Grant took the other. I was not alone. I'd be okay. I took a deep breath, listened to Ty intone the words to welcome the Great Horse Spirit. Grant was speaking, too: three words in a language that was half sound and half mental sending, that I could never comprehend.

"Brothers," he translated the word he'd learned from my troll and his half brother, Nicky. "Friends. Peace."

So I did my bit. I let go of their hands and held up my pendant with its ancient runes. I thought an image of the colt as prince of his people. "I and thou, H'tah. You and me."

And they came. All at once, all in that straight line facing us like the Rockettes. They bowed the way Paloma Blanca had, in precision. We bowed to them. Then one stepped forward. I knew she was H'tah's mother. Don't ask me how I knew, but I did.

She came within three car lengths of us. Up close, I could see she was shorter than Ty's horse, a bit stockier. But her coat was truly luminescent, her mane and tail long and silky. Her eyes were blue. Not albino pink, but pale blue, like a winter sky. And sad.

Ty's lips were moving, but I did not hear the words. The mares did not so much as twitch an ear, but they stayed placid, without projecting fear or fury. Grant was the most expert extra-linguist, son of the former best in our world. The Verbalizer could not seem to utter enough words to communicate. I was the Visualizer, so I pulled a sketch from my pocket, H'tah wrapped in the willow tree.

I got a picture back in my head, the willow tree by itself, losing leaves. I had only words in English and pictures in my head. "Yes, he was calling me. I think I know where he is, but I cannot get him out by myself. I guess you could not either. We are going tomorrow, at low tide." I tried to flash images of the cove, the bunker, the water, the precipice of Bayview above. Then I waved my hand at Ty and Grant and the people on and near the bandstand. "Friends, who want to help."

She shook her head no. I had a vision of the willow again, with no leaves at all. A tear fell from her eye.

"No! He is not dead!"

She quivered, then shook her head again. One leaf returned to the tree in my mind.

"We cannot wait!" I yelled to the others. "We have to go get him now!"

"But the tide's wrong," someone called back, Rick from the boatyard, I thought.

"And the G-men are on the cove like barnacles," Uncle Henry muttered.

The mares grew restless. Bad feelings started to seep into my soul, and everyone else's, I supposed. Distress, disappointment, depression, growing dislike. Uh-oh.

I turned to the others. "Do you want to let him die? Do you want his family to grieve and blame us?"

"Hell, no," came back from the raised stage.

"Then we go tonight. Now." I faced H'tah's dam. "We will help free your son." I flashed the picture of the regal young horse.

They flashed out of sight.

Grant was on the phone. "Froeler's boat is headed toward the cove," he yelled. "We've got to get there before he moves the drugs and the colt."

I heard Mrs. Froeler cry out, then sink to the bandstand floor. While Doc tended to her mother, Letty demanded to know what her stepfather had to do with the missing colt, so K2 told her. His father bopped him over the head for being so blunt.

"What did you want me to do, lie to her? I don't have any tissues."

Letty refused to get into Kelvin's truck unless it was taking her to Froeler, to convince him to let the baby horse go.

"He said he was finding a way so I could walk. He said it was a surprise, a magical surprise, like in my story. He took the missing foal, for me?" She was sobbing. "And now the baby is going to die? Lewis must have done it. He'd do anything."

The two Kelvins led mother and daughter away.

Uncle Henry had some of the townspeople pull out their cell phones to call every para-weatherman they knew.

"Tell them to get together and lasso the onshore sea breeze. We need it to blow backward, holding off the tide."

The chief next ordered every SUV squad car and the fire rescue vehicle and the beach patrol three-wheeler to meet him at the public launching ramp a mile down the beach from Bunker Cove. He told the dispatcher the men and women might have to trek in, if the four-wheel drive trucks couldn't navigate over the rocks. He directed another crew to head across the ranch for the hill overlooking the cove, to secure the area and the airshaft. "Stand as lookouts, but don't send the damned cliff down on top of us. And everybody waits for my signal before moving on the beach."

Ty wasn't waiting for anyone. He and Connor were racing back to the horse van, with me and Grant running behind them.

"That huge thing will never ride across the sand," Grant called out to Ty.

"No, but the horses will."

We raced to the launching ramp. Someone spoke into Grant's earphone that Froeler had anchored, then launched a life raft. Two men were in it. The FBI also reported that Lewis was Viktor Luwiscki, who had a long arrest record for everything from assault to possession to attempted murder for hire. He'd never been convicted, though.

Ty drove as fast as he dared, with the horses in the back squealing in fright. He tried chanting to them, but they were still frantic. Me, too.

Then we were at the launching dock, just a concrete slab between boulders where weekend boaters could back their trailers down to the water. Elgin, the harbor-master, was there, loading cops and locals into life vests, then onto kayaks and dinghies and inflatable rafts. The moon was bright enough to tell that the tide was fairly low, and that the rocks along the shore were indeed prohibitive. Some of the chief's forces took off on foot.

Froeler's boat had no lights on, but the moonlight bounced off all the chrome. I couldn't see the raft or the Coast Guard boat that was prepared to blow the yacht out of the water. Everyone was staying back, as ordered, until we were positioned and knew what was going on.

Ty and Connor had the horse gate down, the horses out. The pair was not happy. They'd performed; they wanted their comfortable stalls, their treats, their rest.

"Soon, my girls, soon," Ty crooned to them, steadying the mares. Connor leaped up on Lady Sparrow's bare back. Ty found a rock to stand on for a leg up to Paloma Blanca's taller back, with no saddle either. Then he held a hand down to me.

"Me?" On the back of an immense horse, with nothing to hold onto? "I'll run down the beach." Of course I was already out of breath and out of courage.

Grant didn't give me a chance to finish. "I forgot what a coward you are. I guess I'm better off without you." He hoisted me up and over, into Ty's lap. Ty wrapped one arm around me, and his other in Paloma Blanca's mane. "Go, girl. Go like the wind."

I tried not to scream. I really did, especially when the huge horse raced past the running policemen with their guns drawn, dodged boulders, and sometimes splashed through the water to avoid rocks that could trip her or break her leg, sending us to smash on the rocks. Then I couldn't scream because I had a mouthful of sand and salt water.

"Damn, riding to the rescue on a white horse. Who'd believe it?" Ty laughed, leaning lower. "We're almost there, darlin'."

I didn't know if he meant me or the horse.

We heard the argument before we turned into Bunker Cove. Ty pulled up. Connor wheeled Lady Sparrow to a halt behind us. The police were climbing boulders, the locals trying to run through the water. The light craft were coming around the bend, too. Grant, the best in shape, was right next to us, whispering on his cell to coordinate the men headed for the cliff summit. Ty held his hand up for silence, and we all ducked behind the large rocks that kept Bunker Hill enclosed. Ty held his palm over Paloma Blanca's nose so she wouldn't make a sound. Connor did the same with Lady Sparrow.

"I told you I want the horse alive." That was Froeler's voice, between gasps for air as they landed their raft.

"And I told you we couldn't move the merchandise unless they were at that stupid rodeo." Lewis, of course, wasn't winded at all after paddling in to shore and dragging the raft onto the sand. "They're suspicious enough already. And that horse is what set the whole thing off. We could have had a pretty little business going forever. But you had to get clever and offer Snake money."

"It wasn't my fault the bastard got greedy. And crazier. He thought about selling the beast to the oddball blonde and her head-case friends. No one double-crosses me."

"So you had me off him. You owe me big time now, old man."

"So go on. Open the bunker. Get me the horse, then we'll talk money. It's worth a fortune, way more than the drugs."

"Only if you can keep it alive and do your experiments."

"I told you, I had to wait until it was too weak to drive me as crazy as Snake with its sendings."

"I don't want to hear about your bullshit sendings. I'm getting the merchandise first, Froeler. Then I won't have to take orders from you ever again. You and that stick you married or the brat."

"I said get the horse."

"Go to hell."

We heard a gun cock.

"Kill me and who's going to carry the pony to the raft, huh? Who's going to lift it onto the boat? You?" Lewis laughed, a sick, harsh sound.

Then we heard keys and chains and a metal door creaking open. We crept closer, leaving the horses tied to rocks. The police were behind us now, and however many of the espers who managed to get there, including Susan and Rick from the marina and Bill from the hardware store and Bud from the gas station. Some of the boats were landing, too, including one with Doc and Grandma Eve. They came ashore behind us, away from Froeler's sight as he waited on the damp sand and seaweed exposed by the rare low tide.

Then the bunker door slammed shut. Froeler started shouting, "Get me the horse, damn you!"

"Get it yourself, you bastard. I'm getting out of here," echoed back.

Ty held his hand up again, to wait.

The police chief listened on his earpiece and whispered, "A truck's coming toward the edge. It's Kelvin's, but the kid is driving it."

"K2 would do anything for Letty. I bet he's bringing her to her stepfather, to save H'tah."

Three men whispered the F-word, one with a British accent. "Can't your men stop them?"

"Not without alerting Froeler and Lewis, whatever his name is. From down here they'll just think it's someone leaving the parking area after the show. Wait! Oh shit."

"What is it?" we all demanded.

Now Grant was listening to his cell phone, to whoever he had stationed at the top of the cliff. "A pile of rocks is moving. There must have been another hatch to the bunker, inside the cliff. It's about twenty yards east of us."

We couldn't see the top of the sheer wall from down here. Everyone cursed, but Grant gave orders and Uncle Henry repeated them to his men.

"Wait for Lewis to get out, away from the hatch. Then move in, unless he is bringing the horse up with him. Shoot if you have to, but not the horse. Repeat, not the horse. We have enough evidence to get him for the murder, so it's a justifiable shoot. And get those kids out of there."

We waited—me in agony—while Froeler cursed and tried to climb the boulders up to the bunker entrance. "Lewis, open the frigging door."

Lewis didn't. We knew he was freeing the upper escape hatch door. We also knew Froeler wasn't going anywhere, not with the Coast Guard already on board his yacht, according to Elgin's information.

Uncle Henry reported from his walkie-talkie: "He's thrown a suitcase out. Now he's out, with another satchel. No horse."

Grant and the chief and Elgin were all yelling into their phones. "Move! Move! Go now!"

We climbed the last rocks before the cove and poured onto the shoe-sucking wet sand and slippery seaweed and mud on the shore under the cliff. Froeler was standing on a rock beneath the bunker doors, staring up. A coil of rope and some blankets were at his feet.

Vincent the barber shouted from behind us: "He's got an aura. Be careful."

I'd already concluded Froeler had some talent, but no one had any idea what it was.

The chief wasn't waiting to find out: "Halt and put your hands up, Froeler. You are under arrest for attempted murder, accomplice to murder, drug running, obstruction of justice, and enough other crimes that'll see you in Sing Sing for the rest of your misbegotten life."

Letty's father turned, saw us coming toward him, some with guns drawn. Then he looked out to sea, ready to make a run for his raft. But coming ashore, dancing on the water in one of Paloma Blanca's skipping steps as if they were the corps de ballet, were twenty white mares, side by side by side, blocking his path.

Then someone shouted from above: "He's got the girl! The snow man's got the girl!"

"Hold your fire!"

"Froeler, drop the gun."

He was trembling. "I need the horse!"

We heard a bullhorn from above. "Lewis, let the girl go. You cannot escape."

Lewis must have dragged Letty to the edge of the cliff. We could see him, and the gun to her head.

"Get me a way out, or I throw the girl over."

I shouted "No!"

Froeler was shouting that the whole thing was Lewis' idea, that the snow man shot Snake. He organized the drug drop offshore. He sold it throughout the East End. "I have proof. I can tell you his supplier!"

"I'll kill your daughter," Lewis screamed again.

"What do I care about that cripple? She's not even

my daughter. The rich widow needed a father for her kid, is all. I got money for my lab. But not enough. It's the horse I need now. With the creature's mental power harnessed, I can create the mind drugs of the century. I can have everything I ever wanted. I can rule the world."

"Father, no! Let the colt go!"

"Shut up, you little twit. You're my ticket out of here," Lewis shouted, shaking Letty.

We heard gunfire. The walkie-talkies all blared. "He's shooting at us, so we can't get a bead on him without hitting the girl. He's headed toward Kelvin's truck."

Froeler fired upward, at where Lewis had been. "You bastard, leaving me here after all I've done for you. You were nothing but a two-bit felon."

The mares stamped.

"Wait, Kelvin's kid is moving the truck."

"He's eleven. Can he drive?"

More shots. I guessed so.

"Get down, K2."

Then Lewis screamed. Letty screamed. The cops and the agents screamed. "Snakes!"

I screamed, even if I was nowhere near.

Lewis came back to the edge. He had no way out, and he knew it. He shot down, at Froeler. The German fell off his rock and landed flat on his back, not moving.

The mares were on solid ground now. They pawed at the loose stones, sending vibrations I could feel through the soles of my shoes. I tried to tell them no, but it was too late.

The cliff started to cave in, beginning with the overhang. We all ran back, away. Lewis came hurtling over with the chunk of ground he'd been standing on, to land on the rocks below. He didn't move. More of the high dune started to crumble.

Letty!

I saw her at the top, trying to drag herself back from the new edge with her arms, but the earth beneath her was slippery from all the rain, and giving way. I heard shouts from the men above: "Stay back, it's going."

K2 was howling. Someone must have grabbed him,

most likely his father from the cursing, because his cry suddenly turned into a sob.

And Letty started to fall, shrieking.

Ty pulled my head to his shoulder, so I couldn't see.

Then his arms fell to his side and I looked up. A horse, a bigger, stronger, brighter white horse had appeared in the air, in the capriole that was airs above the ground. Only this one, who could only be the stallion, the ruler of the herd, truly was airs above the ground, yards above our heads and right beneath Letty. She landed across his back.

He winked out of existence, then reappeared on the beach near us, as sand and mud and rocks pummeled down onto the shore of Bunker Cove, burying Froeler and Lewis.

Connor rushed to take Letty from him, and hand the unconscious girl to Doc and Susan and Grandma Eve. "She'll be fine. No broken bones or internal injuries." Then Connor raced back to where Ty was already digging at the landslide that covered the bunker entrance.

H'tah!

CHAPTER 38

I JOINED THEM, PAWING AT THE HEAP until my nails were all broken and my fingers were bloody. Someone pushed me aside so stronger hands could do the work. Bill the telekinetic could move the smaller stuff out of their way, and Bud and Elgin worked to keep the breeze blowing the waves back so that the others could work on dry land.

Grant was on the walkie-talkie, trying to get his men down the hatch where Froeler had appeared.

"Shoot the fooking snakes! Get the horse."

My job? Picturing the rocks flying away, so the mares didn't trample the diggers. The stallion stood at the head of their line, watching. I kept my mind going like a camera on automatic, shot after shot of progress, rock by rock, inch by inch. "We're trying. We're going as fast as we can without causing another cave-in. H'tah, if you can hear me, if you can sense me, your mother is here. Your father, too, I think. We're coming. Hang on."

The prettiest picture I ever saw was right there in my mind, my tree, with leaves. "Yes!"

The mares must have seen the same picture, or one of their own. They pranced. The stallion snorted and pawed the ground. Ty started chanting to keep them from starting another landslide. He sang in time to the rocks he heaved. Now the men worked faster, in time to his beat, in concert.

As last I could see the rusted metal doors of the bunker, bent out of shape and not touching in the middle, so Ty and Connor had to put their backs to them to push.

"Wait!" Big Eddie yelled. "I smell explosives. Lewis must have booby-trapped the entrance to blow."

Oh, God.

Ty and the rest stepped back. "Do we have a bomb squad?"

What did Paumanok Harbor need with a bomb squad? And the Feds were all up at the top of the hill. Grant quickly called his agents back from the hatch.

I couldn't explain bomb to the night mares and their mate. I pictured fire, more things flying, with sound effects. I guess they didn't have WMDs where they lived.

The stallion didn't care. He charged ahead, bashing the doors with his front hooves.

Ty and Connor hit the ground.

Now the mares understood: fire, noise, metal and concrete and rocks flying. They shrilled their distress. Everyone on shore clapped their hands over their ears, but the sound of terror tore through us, through our minds.

Ty and Connor seemed oblivious to the mental pain. They rushed past the stallion, through the fire, into the bunker.

My heart in my throat, I pushed the other diggers aside, took a deep breath and followed them. "H'tah?"

I heard the two cowboys fumbling around in the smoke and the dark. The space was bigger than I would have expected, going deep into the hill. I bumped into a ladder that Lewis must have used, and some duffel bags and cartons that were smoldering from the explosion at the entrance. Then I heard him.

"Willow."

"This way! He's here. He's alive!"

The two men lifted the poor baby, all limp, ragged, and dirty. He struggled, but I put my hand on him. "Not monsters. Friends."

Then we were outside, in the fresh salty air, gulping. Someone ran forward with a blanket. They laid the colt down. Connor ran his hands over H'tah and shook his head. Too weak.

The mares keened in distress, pushing forward to circle us, but then the stallion stood over his son. He lowered his great head to H'tah's and he breathed into his face.

H'tah lay still.

I started crying. I could hear weeping behind me, and sorrowful whinnies. Someone patted my sleeve, and someone else put wet blankets over Ty and Connor, to smother the smoldering embers of their clothing.

The stallion kept blowing air onto his son, their foreheads touching. Ty nodded as if he heard and understood words no one else could hear. He sang part of the ancient song that welcomed the Great Horse Spirit, and proclaimed him brother.

And H'tah raised his head. The mares raised their heads and bugled their joy. H'tah stood, shook himself, and took a tottering step. Then another, firmer this time. His broken rear leg was suddenly straight and unmarred; his blue eyes were clear. He butted heads once more with his sire, then pranced proudly toward me, a bedraggled prince, but a prince for all that.

I held my arms out, and he came to me. I lowered my head until we were forehead to forehead, like he'd been with the stallion.

"I and thou, Willow. I and thou."

I only sensed his words, but I spoke back out loud. "You and me, kid, you and me." I kissed his satiny nose before he bounded off to greet his mother and his aunts. They disappeared into the night sky.

When I turned around, the stallion was forehead to forehead with Ty, then Connor. I hadn't noticed how bloody they were, gashed from the explosion or burned by the fire, but the cuts and raw skin disappeared and their rasping breaths eased. They bowed to the stallion. He bowed back.

He spoke, in our words, but in our heads. "Your kind has done great harm. And great good. My family should never have wandered where they were forbidden. Now they are returned to me. I pay my debts."

Ty held up his hands, unscarred, unburned. "You have, sire."

"That was nothing." He turned to look at the others, gathered a little distance away. He singled out Letty. We all heard his voice, in our minds. "You tried to stop this madness. I saved your life. I would make you walk, but I cannot. You are not of our common ancestry."

"The ride was enough."

"You will ride my kin here in your world. That I can see to. They will hold you safe and cherished above all others."

Then he fixed his blue eyes on Connor. "You are brave and true, son of my ancient friends, but troubled. You see illness and cannot cure it, which tears at the tender heart you try to hide. I cannot help you fix your people. But I can give you the power to cure mine. You will be the best healer ever known among my kin."

Connor slid to his knees, there in the muck, and bowed his head. To hide his tears, I thought.

The stallion—the king of his kind, I knew, even if Ty had not called him sire—searched for Grant. "This is not your home range." He shifted his gaze to me.

Grant shook his head. "I know."

"Yet you are brave and true also, dedicated to keeping peace between our worlds. I give you the words. Words so you may speak when the need arises. Words so we may speak."

I heard the sounds and saw the images that made up the language of the night mares' world. I heard the translations, and I saw Grant repeat them back to the stallion, in reverence and in perfect memory.

"I thank you, great H'ro."

H'ro—if that was the stallion's name and not a word for king or gift-giver or sire-of-many—took a step toward me. My knees turned to linguine.

He towered over me, but bowed until his head touched mine. "Bravest of females, you gave me back my son, the future of my people."

"No, I am not brave," I told him, my voice quavering with nerves. "Ask anyone. I just tried to help a lost baby."

Do horses smile? This one did, or maybe I felt the warm feeling in my soul. Ty and Grant both grinned.

"I cannot give you your heart's desire, because I do not know what that is. You do not know what that is. But I can give you my promise that your children will never be sick. Your sons will never be broken or lost. Your daughters will know no despair of losing a child."

He might be a king, but I kissed his nose, the way I did Little Red. "Thank you. You have given me a future to build my dreams on."

At last it was Ty's turn. He'd lost his hat, his hair was singed in places, and his shirt hung in tatters. He'd never looked better. Or happier.

"My brother."

"My friend."

"This is not your home range either, you know. Not your hills to roam and fill with sons and daughters of your blood."

Damn, they both looked at me again.

"I wish. But I know. I'll be leaving soon."

"Yes, you must. But not without my gift."

H'ro blinked out of existence before he said what his gift to Ty was. We were all bewildered, and drained, as a matter of fact. We'd have to face digging out bodies, dealing with the mess of Froeler's plots and unraveling Lewis's smuggling operation. The mayor was already helping Letty forget her father's last words, to remember only that he tried to cure her.

Then we heard a noise, a horse's high-pitched squeal. Not of pain, not of fear, but something else.

"That's Paloma Blanca." Ty started to run toward where he'd left her, but then he stopped and smiled. That slow grin started at his mouth and traveled to his eyes and caught my breath in my throat.

I felt it, too. A wave of desire so strong that I wanted to leap into his arms. I guess everyone else caught the stallion's emotional projection, too. Connor and Susan disappeared behind the rocks. Grandma Eve and Doc climbed into one of the boats and let it drift out of sight. Rick and Bud and a bunch of others decided they needed to get home. Their wives would be worried. Grant held his hand out to Martha from the real estate agency. "We need to talk about the renovations at Rosehill. Your ideas were wonderful."

So was the smile she gave him back as they hurried down the beach.

I wasn't jealous in the least. I was in the bunker, on a pile of blankets, not caring if the roof collapsed on us or the lingering smoke made my eyes tear. Or was that joy and love and Ty's lovemaking?

We might not have tomorrow, but tonight—that was another gift from the magic horses. Not just the lust of a rutting stallion or a mare in heat, not just the relief of living through a harrowing experience, not just repaying a debt, but love and fellowship and wanting to share one's heart and soul.

We did.

The next morning we drove the horse van through town and stopped to pick up breakfast at Joanne's. Susan was there, beaming at everyone. "I'm cured," she said, hugging me. "Free of cancer. Connor said so."

I rejoiced with her. Now maybe she could stop living as if she had to cram all her life into the next six months.

Mrs. Ralston was there, too, picking up bagels. "It's a boy."

I felt the damn blush cover my cheeks. "But it's too soon, I mean, I'm not—"

"Not you, dear." She pointed to the horse trailer. "The mare. It's a boy."

Ty grinned. "And here I thought last night was my gift." He kissed me, right in front of half the town, it seemed. "It would have been enough, but this . . ."

Meant more. I knew and didn't mind. Not really.

He appeared dazed by his good fortune. "I don't know how I'm going to explain it to the Lipizzan registry."

I laughed. "Or to anyone else when your new stallion takes to disappearing. You'll figure it out. You can do anything."

He kissed me again. "Almost anything. I can't uproot a willow tree, can I, darlin'?"

I might be pregnant, too, though it was far too soon to tell. The equine-inspired passion hadn't left time to fumble for protection. Or to think about the future or the healthy children H'ro had promised. I knew Ty would offer to do the right thing, but I couldn't marry a traveling horse whisperer on those terms, no matter how exciting and strong and brave and caring he was. He'd be leaving soon, and always.

I knew he'd be back when the ranch was ready to be filled with his rescued horses, just like Grant would be back when the Royce Institute was ready to open its doors in Paumanok Harbor. But I had my own life to lead, my own dreams to follow.

So I decided to go back to the city as soon as things settled down and start my next book. I already had the title: *Fire Works in the Hamptons*.

Damn, were those sirens I heard?

Coming in November 2011
The third novel in the *Willow Tate* series by
Celia Jerome

FIRE WORKS IN THE
HAMPTONS

Read on for a sneak preview

WHERE DO YOU GET YOUR IDEAS? That's the most common question people ask authors at book signings, writers' conventions and library talks. The stock answers are: the idea fairy, dreams, newspapers, in the shower, or the idea mall, where an author would shop all the time if she had better directions or a GPS.

But what if the writer's ideas, especially those fantastical, off-the-wall ideas, actually come from another universe where magic abounds? Where trolls and elves and night mares and mental telepathy really exist? What if an author's brilliant visions were nothing but presentiments of forbidden visitors from that unknown, alien universe trespassing on Earth?

Then the world as we know it is going to hell in a handcart, and the author is getting walloped by the wagon as it races past.

I needed a man.

Last time I had a girl, then a boy and a troll. Now I wanted a man, a strong, heroic type. For my new book, of course. I'd sworn off real men for life, or until I finished my next book, whichever came first. After all, I'd known and loved two of the most wonderful, talented, intelligent, adventurous, gorgeous and sexy men—who weren't right for me. What was left? A dull-as-dirt accountant? Been there, done that. And so what if I was thirty-five? If I ever decided to make my mother ecstatic by giving her a grandkid or two, I could always adopt. That's what she did, with dogs. I petted Mom's crippled Pomeranian, who now appeared to be mine. He sniffed my hand for a biscuit. Dogs were a lot easier than men.

Don't get me wrong; I like having a man in my life. What I didn't like was them taking over my life, or them leaving. Picking up the pieces was too painful, so now my career comes first.

I write books, illustrated graphic novels for the young fantasy reader, under the pen name of Willy Tate instead of my too girly-sounding Willow Tate. Kids love them, reviewers love them, my publisher loves them. How cool is that, getting paid to do what I like best?

I write better in my Manhattan apartment without the distractions of the beach and the relatives and the small-town calamities that seem to occur regularly in Paumanok Harbor at the edge of Long Island's posh Hamptons. I might—just might—be responsible for some of the recent chaos, so the sooner I get back to the big city, the better for all of us. I'll leave the week after Labor Day, when my houseguest goes back to teaching middle-level science at a private school in Greenwich, Connecticut. I am happy to have my old college roommate here for the week, but I can't write with Ellen in the house. I have to show her around, see that she's entertained and fed, keep her company on beach walks and bar hops. That's what old friends are for, isn't it?

A few more days and we'll both be back at our jobs in the real world. My cousin Susan can look after my mother's other rescued shelter dogs if Mom doesn't get back from saving a pack of greyhounds in the South, if she can't shut down the tracks altogether. Susan is already living at my mother's house, avoiding her own family's disapproval of her wild ways. I don't exactly approve of all the men she drags home either, but I am only ten years older than Susan, not my cousin's keeper.

So nothing is going to keep me in this tiny, ingrown, backwater town past the end of the tourist season.

I'll take Ellen to the last big fireworks display in East Hampton on Labor Day weekend, then start packing. I want to see the fireworks, too, for the new story I am working on, or would be working on soon.

The idea for the new book came from all the idiots setting off firecrackers on the beach near my mother's house all summer long. Some were pretty, but most were just loud enough to wake the neighbors and scare the dogs. Inevitably, some kid burned his hand or lost a finger or set the dune grasses on fire. Just as inevitably, the slobs left beer bottles and trash and still-burning coals on the bay-side beaches. Paumanok Harbor's small police force tried to stop them—the bigger, more dangerous ones at least—but the shore was long and dark, and no one wanted to ruin the Hamptons' summer economy by chasing down and arresting tourists. Or their own neighbors' kids.

Illegal firecrackers were easy to come by. I'd seen them sold on street corners in Pennsylvania and Florida. Fools bought them—and recklessly transported them in their own cars!—even though everyone knew only a licensed pyrotechnician, a Grucci-type, could safely set off the really spectacular displays.

That's what I wanted. Not some gunpowder geek, or once a summer sparkler-setter, but a fire wizard, a pyromage, a red-hot superhero. He'd shoot flames from his fingertips, encircle bad guys in blazes, fight evil with fire. He'd start backfires for forest rangers, and warm stranded mountain climbers until help arrived. A regular Lassie with a flare. Literally.

And there he was, right in my living room when Ellen and I got back from breakfast in Amagansett, the next town over. A man I'd never seen before was fast asleep on the sofa. Tall enough that his feet hung over the end, dark and handsome; he had an unshaved shadow on his strong jaw, a thick lock of sable hair fallen on his forehead, another sticking up in a boyish cowlick. He was nicely built from what I could see under Mom's patchwork quilt and the black T-shirt he wore. Yup, my hero, except his mouth hung open, an empty beer bottle sat on the coffee table, and one of Mom's old dogs whined next to the couch. The white-muzzled retriever wanted his quilt back.

Ellen took a seat near the sofa and sighed at the stranger. "Oh, my. That's better than the raspberry muffin I just ate. And not half as fattening."

The guy might be a good model for me to sketch, but he sure as hell wasn't an invited guest. I stayed standing up, ready to reach for the fireplace poker or the heavy dog-breed book on the coffee table.

"Quiet," I whispered to Ellen, not ready to defend us from a waking trespasser. "I bet he's one of Susan's strays." My mother brought home old, injured, or abandoned dogs. My cousin brought home men. With abandon.

"Can I keep him?" Ellen asked. "Please."

"He belongs to Susan."

"He's too old for Susan."

He did look more late thirties than mid-twenties, but age didn't count, according to Susan. If a man was breathing, he was fair game. Everyone figured that my cousin's collision with cancer changed her attitude. I never heard of chemo killing a person's scruples, but I made allowances for her, which was why she lived in my house. Besides, she was a great cook.

"He has dimples!"

"Come on, El, we don't even know if he's housebroken."

"Any man this gorgeous has to be."

"Okay. We'll get him a collar and you can take him back to Connecticut with you. Maybe you should buy a six-pack to win his loyalty away from Susan."

As if the name conjured her up, Susan shuffled into the room from the kitchen, a blue pottery mug—mine from one of the craft shows—in her hand. She was wearing an oversize Snoopy T-shirt—mine, too, dammit!—and her hair, pink this week, was in pigtails. She looked about sixteen instead of twenty-six. No one would guess she was head chef at our uncle's restaurant. She was definitely too young for the Romeo in repose.

At least she hadn't put in all the eyebrow hoops. And the nose stud must have been too uncomfortable because I hadn't seen it this week. Not that I missed it.

"He's not too old, and he's not mine," she said now, sitting on the edge of the coffee table sipping her tea. "But he does look cute sleeping like that."

"Yeah, as cuddly as a teddy bear. Get rid of him. You know I draw the line at finding your lovers in my living room."

"I told you, he's not my lover. He stopped by the Breakaway for a late meal last night on his way back to the city from Montauk, but his car died in the parking lot. No one answered at Kelvin's garage to come tow the car, and all the motels were booked with the Labor Day crowd. When the restaurant closed, I offered a ride and the couch. That's all. We stopped off to admire the sunrise."

I'm sorry to admit I snorted at the unlikely tale. The sound wasn't ladylike or mature, and showed a big lack of faith in my own cousin. Little Red, the three-legged Pomeranian, started barking at the sudden noise or when he finally realized yet another stranger had invaded his territory. The bark turned to a snarl when I tried to shush him. Red weighed six pounds but had a seven-pound mean streak. He'd been abused before he came to Paumanok Harbor, so we all made allowances for him, too.

The stranger jerked awake. His eyes, a nice soft brown with yellow flecks, focused on the angry dog, the other dogs, Ellen, me, then finally Susan. You could see his relief at recognizing someone in the room. He gave her a tentative smile.

"Barry, this is my cousin Willow, her friend Ellen. Ladies, this is Barry Jensen." Susan sipped her tea again while the man blinked and brushed his hair back from his eyes. He was definitely cute, but now that he was sitting up I could tell he was older than I thought. The lack of sleep didn't help, but the lines and wrinkles added character to his face, without taking away from the good looks. Clark Kent with a dash of maturity. I could go for that. For my book, of course.

He looked at me. Not at Susan whom every male found adorable, and not at Ellen, who was pretty in a wholesome, unfussy way, and whose lush figure still made heads swivel when we walked through the village. I made myself pet Little Red instead of trying to hide the coffee drips on my ancient T-shirt, or finger-combing my windblown blonde hair, trying to cover the darker roots, wishing I'd had it colored last week. Wishing I hadn't had a million-calorie muffin for breakfast, too.

"I am so glad to meet you," Barry said. "I've heard great things about you."

"Me?" Okay, I wasn't great at conversation, either.

"When Susan told me who lived here, I was floored."

"You must mean my mother. She's famous. Too bad she's still in Florida."

"Your mother's the dog-lady, isn't she?"

I nodded, gesturing toward the canine collection. "That's my mom, all right. She can do anything with a four-legged stray. Three legs if you count Little Red."

Barry ignored the animals. "But you, you're Willy Tate! I've admired your work for years. I was at that convention where you won the YA graphic novel award. I've followed your career ever since."

So maybe he was a hero, after all, instead of a marauder or a mooch. Darn few people outside of friends and family knew my name. "Thanks."

"I've met a bunch of authors in my day. I work freelance for a small-town news syndicate and website. I do the book page. And I've sold a couple of reviews and articles here and there. But to write and illustrate, both. Wow. And now here I am, on your couch. How's that for luck?"

Luckier than sleeping in your broken-down car, I supposed, or on the beach. "Would you like a cup of coffee? I could put some on. Or tea? I think we have orange juice."

"Nothing, thanks. I don't want to impose."

Ellen went to get the coffee anyway and came back with a bowl of cereal, a creamer of milk and a glass of OJ.

Barry smiled his appreciation, but kept looking at me. "Damn, I wish I'd met you last week when I didn't have to worry about getting back to Manhattan, or finding a place to stay until the car is repaired. I'd love to write an article about you. You know the kind of thing, how the author lives, a personal glimpse into the real world of a fantasy writer. I can see the picture now, you on the beach, dogs romping in the waves. It could be a winner."

Ellen leaned forward from her chair next to the sofa. "It would be great publicity, Willy."

"I bet Barry could sell an article like that to a bigger audience," Susan added. "Or get it all over the Web. I know you're a big fish now, but your pond is kind of small. With the right PR you could sell a lot more books. Maybe get a bigger advance next contract. At least you could get your expenses paid for the next ComicCon."

I refused to think of having to speak at another of those huge conventions. Instead, I admired Barry's dimples and nice white teeth.

The idea of free publicity won me over, not the dimples or the smile, I swear. "Why don't I give you a ride to the garage? We could talk along the way. Then, if Kelvin says your car needs a lot of time for parts or whatever, maybe I could ask around town for a place where you can stay."

"That would be great! Maybe some of your talent will rub off by proximity. Or maybe I'll learn enough just listening to you to start the novel I always wanted to write. You"—he politely gestured toward Susan and Ellen, after me—"can be my inspiration. Three beautiful women."

Red snapped at his moving hand. "And a ferocious watchdog." He tossed Cheerios at all three dogs.

Yeah, cute. And Mom always said you could judge a man by how he treats a dog. Besides, I needed to see more of him to develop a feel for my fire wizard, facial expressions, musculature, the way his body moved. Character development, you know, research. So I invited him to come watch the fireworks with us. . . .

Celia Jerome
The Willow Tate *Novels*

"Readers will love the first Willow Tate book. Willow is funny, brave and open to possibilities most people would not have even considered as she meets her perfect foil in Thaddeus Grant, a British agent assigned to look over the strange occurrences following Willow like a shadow. Together they make a wonderful pair and readers will love their unconventional courtship."

—*RT Book Review*

TROLLS IN THE HAMPTONS
978-0-7564-0630-1

NIGHT MARES IN THE HAMPTONS
978-0-7564-0663-9

To Order Call: 1-800-788-6262
www.dawbooks.com

DAW 170

Gini Koch
The Alien *Novels*

"This delightful romp has many interesting twists and
turns as it glances at racism, politics, and religion en route.
Darned amusing." —*Booklist* (starred review)

"Kitty's evolution from marketing manager to member of
a secret government unit is amusing and interesting
...a hilarious romp in the vein of 'Men in Black'
or 'Ghostbusters'."—*Voya*

TOUCHED BY AN ALIEN
978-0-7564-0600-4

ALIEN TANGO
978-0-7564-0632-5

ALIEN IN THE FAMILY
978-0-7564-0668-4

To Order Call: 1-800-788-6262
www.dawbooks.com

DAW 160

Seanan McGuire

The October Daye Novels

"...will surely appeal to readers who enjoy my books, or those of Patrica Briggs." —*Charlaine Harris*

"Well researched, sharply told, highly atmospheric and as brutal as any pulp detective tale, this promising start to a new urban fantasy series is sure to appeal to fans of Jim Butcher or Kim Harrison." —*Publishers Weekly*

ROSEMARY AND RUE
978-0-7564-0571-7

A LOCAL HABITATION
978-0-7564-0596-0

AN ARTIFICIAL NIGHT
978-0-7564-0626-4

LATE ECLIPSES
978-0-7564-0666-0

To Order Call: 1-800-788-6262
www.dawbooks.com